The Shifters

Taylor Landrum

First published by Dog Ear Publishing
4011 Vincennes Rd.
Indianapolis, IN 46268
www.dogearpublishing.net

ISBN: 978-1-4575-3322-8

Library of Congress Control Number: has been applied for

This book is printed on acid-free paper.

This book is a work of fiction. Places, events, and situations in this book are purely fictional and any resemblance to actual persons, living or dead, is coincidental.

Printed in the United States of America

Dedicated to:

Charles and Adrienne Landrum

Special Thanks To:

Belinda Landrum

Robert Wade Williams

Al-Sawab Sawab

Kylie Dino

Robert Langevin

Thomas Louie

Anthony Howard

Chapter 1

ROSLYN VALEZ

London, England - April 18, 1948

"This is your idea of fair?" Gordon exclaimed, looking around the room in disbelief.

Tension permeated through the six of us sitting in Martin's private meeting room as Gordon's eyes lasered across the long, oak dinner table. The ornate table was even older than the mammoth stone castle in which it was housed, and its roughly hewn sides were harsh underneath my hands. Pockmarks of age dotted the table's surface in a few spots, and I anxiously swirled my finger in one of the small pockets in front of me.

"Gordon, Gordon. You know all too well that I do not operate within the realm of fairness," Martin admonished him, looking straight back down the table.

His face was illuminated by a silver ensconced chandelier that threw a dim light around the room, but considering Martin's incredible wealth, the fixture was actually relatively modest. Although the chandelier's six electric lights gave good visibility around the table, it still left the corners of the room dark and shadowy.

As I looked to my left and right at the two opposing parties, I noted the contrast between the two men sitting at the ends of the table. Martin Evers, who sat directly to my left, was the scariest and most intimidating man I'd ever encountered; to the far right was the mild mannered Gordon Stevens, his most trusted advisor and only confidante in the universe. Currently however they sat in adversarial positions, and they stared at each other testily past Allard Clearwater, Elizabeth Rhodes, Chen Lake, and myself, who were all seated in the fine wooden chairs between them.

With his long, wizened face scrunched into an expression of deep consideration, Allard Clearwater sat to my right between me and Gordon, and his tall, lean frame and gray hair constantly reminded me of the fact that he was actually the eldest Shifthunter in Martin's army. Even seated it was easy to see that he was at least six inches taller than the rest of us, but his gangly stature and patronly nature were poor indicators of his surprising physical power and sharp military mind. Both Gordon and Martin often deferred to him on matters of tactical strategy, and I often wondered if there was anyone in the world that looked more mysterious and sage than he did.

Seated across from him was Elizabeth Rhodes, who was as young and vibrant as Allard was aged. She sported a cascade of lush, curly red hair, which billowed down her back and around her shoulders, and her sharp green eyes always sparkled brightly from above her round, freckled cheeks. She was undeniably attractive, and she had a soft, curious voice and a naturally kind demeanor to match her innocent, youthful features. Despite the favoritism she received because of her undeniable attractiveness, even I had to admit that her features were nearly perfect.

"Gordon, you're too noble," Martin said suddenly, shaking his head as he addressed him condescendingly from across the table.

"This is the most realistic situation for their skill set. As you know, our assassins must be able to strike in close quarters do so unfailingly," he said.

His eyes glowed as Gordon made to counter him, but Chen Lake spoke up first.

"If Elizabeth can ever develop into an effective assassin she will have to be operate in conditions like these," he reasoned, looking down the table at Elizabeth.

Chen was another one of Martin's Shifthunter Elite, and as a human he looked about thirty years old. His youthful, Asian face radiated an inner violence beneath its eerily calm expression, and Elizabeth immediately looked down and away.

"Chen is right. Our true mission is not to build a powerful army. Our mission is to eliminate shapeshifters," Allard acquiesced.

He was looking resigned, and I could tell that the hour-long discussion we'd been having was finally coming to a close. Even though Elizabeth and I were both only ten years old, we had experienced enough to know that Martin rarely ever changed his mind once he came to a conclusion. Now that Gordon's support was finally giving in, there wasn't much left to discuss.

"This is not a fair test of Elizabeth's abilities," Gordon continued to argue, but as he shot a betrayed glance at Allard his argument wore thin.

"I never thought Elizabeth should be used as an assassin. We need to diversify our army, and she will be extraordinarily useful as a scout. It's hard to hunt shapeshifters without being able to detect them," he contended.

As he looked earnestly down the table, his sharp golden eyes found no tread in Martin's cold, blue ones. Martin's prominent features and decidedly youthful glow contrasted sharply with his full head of frost-white hair, and he looked hard and unwavering.

"Are *your* scouting abilities not enough?" Martin asked Gordon seriously, looking intrigued.

Gordon matched Martin's stare with as much disagreement as he could afford to muster.

"My scouting skills are fine," he answered deliberately.

"But I can only be in one place at a time. Elizabeth would allow twice as much coverage, and she hasn't even developed a killer instinct or learned the nuances of hunting yet. If she dies today we will be wasting an invaluable Shifthunter," he argued vehemently.

Martin just shook his head.

"Be that as it may, we cannot afford to waste time and resources on potential. If Elizabeth earns her spot in my army today than you will have proven your point," he said decidedly.

The finality in Martin's tone brought a look of deep distress to Gordon's face, and he made his final plea with distinct desperation.

"What about the treaties?" he asked.

"The world is expanding, and shapeshifters are popping up more frequently then ever as the human population increases. We need to continue to be global, and the diversity of our army is what makes us so successful. If we are to keep our end of the deal, not a single shifter on the entire planet can escape us, and –"

Martin interrupted him with a swift pound on the table and words that were sharp and finishing.

"I do not have the slightest doubt that we will control the shifter population as specified in the treaties," Martin said.

"You know this as well, and you also know that the treaty does nothing more than protect our weak, human brethren. Although I would die for our cause, we ourselves are not endangered, and as long as I am alive I think that everyone in this room would wholeheartedly agree. There are no free shapeshifters, and the treaties are not endangered. We've delayed this process long enough already, and now we are going to determine which of these young ladies is worthy of officially becoming a Shifthunter."

With uncontested power, Martin scooted his throne-like chair away from the table with a loud screeching sound, and stood up to face Gordon across the long table. Gordon, who had already risen to his feet in his earnest plea, turned his expression to stone. With solemn defeat he took a step away from the table as well.

I held down the butterflies in my stomach and prepared myself, knowing that another moment of life and death was upon me. I was already becoming accustomed to death, because after being torn from my parents' home three years ago by Gordon Stevens, I had been given no choice but to become accustomed to the violent ways of shapeshifters.

I was already long removed from the innocent child I had once been, and although Elizabeth's story was similar to mine, unlike me she had been her parents' only child, and she had been pampered her whole life prior to being brought here. Whereas she had grown up in a wealthy English province and lived in luxury prior to accidentally shapeshifting, I had been living in the slums of Southern California as the eldest of three, born to a single mom who could barely keep us from starving.

I had already been growing up quickly just trying to help my mom keep my brothers alive, but now that I was three years deep into a conditioning of killing and hunting, the amount of raw, adult-life imagery that already filled my young mind was beyond anything any other ten year old could imagine. I could understand why Elizabeth, having seen much of it also, was still struggling to cope. Although she had definitely gotten tougher as time went on, it was probably because we had seen death many times over, and even killed men ourselves. We had also seen dozens of countries and met their leaders, and we had traveled the world in everything from airplanes to submarines. We were even being educated with a dedication and curriculum that outperformed the greatest of schools.

It was a lot for anyone, but in spite of the benefits of our unparalleled training, we were unknown and invisible to the real world and as good as dead to everyone who'd ever known us. We were being trained to use our elite knowledge and ability as an instrument of evil, and the cruel world of shapeshifters was one in which anything but the strongest of us were hunted down and murdered on the spot by our own kind.

The few of us who remained were nothing but Martin Evers' soldier-slaves, and especially in times like these it seemed to me that the most powerful of us suffered the most. If I didn't serve Martin Evers unfailingly my whole family would be instantly slaughtered, and the same went for every other Shifthunter on Earth.

"Everyone stand, please," Martin beckoned then, shaking me from my thoughts.

At his command we all stood up obediently, and in about two seconds all six of us were standing around the large table. As I stole a look at Elizabeth my surge of anxiety grew even larger, because this experience was unlike killing grown men who I'd never seen before. I *knew* Elizabeth, and no part of me wanted to kill her or see her die. Martin looked from me to her.

"Whichever of you kills the other will truly become a Shifthunter today," he said, not downplaying the tension of the moment one iota.

He looked us each in the eyes a final time, and then I forced myself to look across at Elizabeth in final, due respect. It pained me to see her bright green eyes meet mine with a moist look of apprehension and fear, and I was sure my mutual dismay showed in my expression. I was dreading this moment as much as she was, but there was nothing we could do to stop it.

"You may begin," Martin ordered then, slapping his hand gently on the table, and with a pulse of determination I quickly stole my eyes away from Elizabeth's.

I looked down for a heartbeat to gather a last bit of resolve and then I shifted, instantly twisting and morphing downwards until I came back to reality in the smaller frame of my cat shift. With a quick shiver I shook off the grossly uncomfortable feeling of shifting, and then I leapt out from underneath my jacket and hopped from the floor to the chair seat, and then on to the table-top, scattering a few of the spotless china as I landed. With the keen, pinpoint eyesight of an all-black domestic cat, I instantly spotted Elizabeth flying up near the ceiling, now shifted into the tiny gray and red body of a Northern Cardinal.

As I moved nimbly down the table I quickly looked into the faces of the others, who were still standing in position around the table, and the looks in every eye told me that everyone in the room knew that Elizabeth stood no chance. It was an unspoken truth that the only reason she had even been considered as a Shifthunter was because Gordon had always favored her, and it seemed that now his influence had run out.

A Northern Cardinal was nothing compared to Shifthunters such as myself, because although I shifted into the body of an average house cat, I was one of the even rarer shapeshifters who's alternate form was genetically mutated from its standard version. I had been imbued with a tail that ended in a tiny, curved scythe instead of a fuzzy tip, and the point of my tail-blade bore a poison that would end Elizabeth's life in seconds.

As I reached the center of the table I crouched down low and moved my tail into striking position, and with an internal clench I cinched my final remnants of hesitation. I couldn't afford to feel sorry for Elizabeth right now, and I focused my eyes on her. As I watched her, she twisted her fleet body in a high arc to the left, and then she circled around the ceiling. Like most shifters, she was rather large for a natural version of her shift, and she had a deeper red on her tail feathers and wingtips than most Northern Cardinal females. She was truly pretty even as a bird, but as she gathered as much speed as she could and came streaking in for the inevitable attack, I was in total control.

Sorry Elizabeth, I thought, gritting my fangs together.

I had to admit that she *was* fast as she screeched over top of the porcelain cups with her talons extended, but as soon as the she was within my range I leapt up from the table and whipped my tail forward for the killing blow.

Not a soul flinched.

Chapter 2

MARTIN EVERS

Antarctica - April 18, 2013

*A*s I stepped through heavy, deep troughs of snow, a particularly strong gust of wind whipped up over the endless white of the Arctic and rattled my black leather coat. I buttoned it closed, but only to keep it from whipping around, not for warmth. I liked the cold, and the snow was my element. The icy wind against my face soothed me more than any sunshine ever could, and the sensation was one that I could still remember. It reminded me that I was human... at least somewhat.

Behind me, the deafening, repetitive thud of our helicopters' rotors whirred. I had left the chopper running for Roslyn's sake, as she had complained profusely about the biting cold the entire way up here. It would be a much smoother flight back without more of that, and I knew if the cockpit was an icebox when we finished here, Roslyn would do a good bit more complaining.

As I watched her dark and slender figure waiting for me a few hundred yards away, I cursed her immeasurable value for the millionth time. There was a triumphant, impatient stance about her that told me she had caught our prey... as she always did. I could imagine her petulant gaze as she watched me casually walking towards her now.

The Arctic wind blew in another fierce blast then and I wondered again why our quarry had chosen such a frigid place for his escape. If he had thought we wouldn't chase him all the way out here, the poor fool was gravely mistaken. I was the great exterminator of atrocities like himself, and to think that I would allow him to escape so easily was a capital insult. I was far too dedicated to leave these matters to chance, especially when the prey was as evasive and reviled as the man we had just captured.

The boots I had donned for the excursion were thick, high-topped, and well-suited for this weather, so for me the walk through the thick fluff was easy. I knew Roslyn's feet were probably soaked through however, because she had refused to take off her stylish leather boots in favor of more practical ones.

Accordingly, when I finally strolled up to her and the man at her feet, her youthful face clearly displayed her displeasure with my slow pace. Her dark brown eyes were narrowed into a piercing glower of loathing, and she licked her lips before addressing me in a clear effort to watch her tongue.

"How nice of you to join us," she managed when I stopped a few feet away from her.

Her voice was razor sharp with discontent, but her face was as enigmatic as always. She was impossible for even *me* to read, and she controlled her expression with such exponentially rare skill that even though I had been reading faces since the times of her ancestors, I had never come across a face as unreadable as hers. From years of dealing with me directly, it even lacked the omnipresent looks of fear and subservience that I was accustomed to receiving.

"You would be better served to remember your place," I reminded her calmly, ignoring her defiant glare.

Roslyn and I both knew her place well enough, and she took a minute to curb her attitude before speaking.

"Well?" she asked, nodding towards the man at her feet.

I looked contemptuously down at the man lying in the snow and reveled in the terror he radiated when he looked back up into my eyes. As mutual recognition passed between us, I hoped he could see the merciless black pit that lied beneath them. For shapeshifters such as himself I was the harbinger of death.

"Percival Smalling.... I remember you," I greeted him, ruminating.

It had been many years since I'd last seen Percival, and as I stood over him now I kept my death-stare trained on him.

"You chose a wonderful place to run to," I taunted him, motioning towards the snowy landscape that stretched in every direction.

As the three of us looked out at the white snowscape, there wasn't a single sign of life between us and the gargantuan frosted mountains in the distance. Percival's final hope for escape had evaporated with the last fume of gas in his snowmobile, which had conked out a few miles ago.

"Many years ago you benefitted from my employment of Gordon Stevens, but he is no longer here to convince me that weak shifters like you deserve to live. Although you've done a remarkable job of surviving this long it seems your day has finally come," I said.

I examined the man's smallish, aging body and thought back to the early nineteen-hundreds, when Percival had served me as the most durable and reusable lab rat of all-time. Back then he had actually been more useful than I would readily admit, but he had also been one of the twelve shapeshifters who had escaped my authority when Gordon betrayed me and freed all of the shifters in my original dungeons in London.

Besides Percival only two of those escaped shifters still lived, but Percival Smalling was the eldest of them; he was actually one of only three shifters on Earth older than I was. It was odd seeing a shapeshifter with Percival's long, unshaven beard and disheveled hair in this day and age, and when I thought about it I realized he had to be over three hundred and fifty years old by now. The fact that he had so far outlived me did not please me.

"Well Percival, you know why we've come," Roslyn said then, looking down at him with scornful impatience.

"Have you seen enough?" she asked, looking over at me.

"I have seen enough," I said, looking Percival dead in the eye.

With eyes full of fear he looked from me to Roslyn as she leveled her revolver at him, and then without hesitation she squeezed the trigger. With three loud pops Percival Smalling slumped lifelessly into the snow, and then Roslyn tucked her gun back into her beltline with practiced efficiency. As a crimson tinge began to die the snow around Percival's body, Roslyn took a last satisfied look at him and then wordlessly headed back towards our chopper.

Three Hundred Years of life, gone in a flash.

I followed her a minute later, and as I watched her sleek, curved body hustle towards the warmth of the cockpit I allowed myself a moment to remember why I kept her around. Even though it amused me that the cold was having such a great effect on her, she was somehow still graceful even plunking through the thick snow. She was also both beautiful and mysterious, both ruthless and tempered, and perhaps most importantly, reliable. She was undoubtedly my most prized Shifthunter, and easily the most dangerous woman to ever live. Although it seemed her extraordinary resilience had wavered a little here in the frozen tundra, her purposeful, confident stride was apparently unflappable.

As another gust of wind whipped over us she pulled her expensive designer coat tightly around her, and I considered the fact that if I had still been capable of physical attraction I would have found Roslyn incomparable. Her green eyes and dark features contrasted with a rare symmetry that would captivate any man besides myself, and it was only because I had buried almost all of my human emotions that I rarely recognized her beauty.

For all of her outward attractiveness however, Roslyn had actually developed a relentless stoicism and determination over the years, and a few minutes later when I climbed back into our chopper she was already in the pilot's seat with her seatbelt fastened and her aviators on. She had already donned her helicopter headset as well, and as I settled into my seat next to her, her gloved hands gripped the yoke readily.

"Thank you for leaving the heat on," she muttered, a slight begrudging in her voice.

"I didn't need any more of your complaining," I explained simply, nodding for her to lift off.

Roslyn gave a slight nod of appreciation and then made to pull back on the yoke, but before pulling us into the air she stopped short.

"Will we really hunt shapeshifters forever?" she asked suddenly, turning towards me.

Although her eyes were invisible behind her aviator frames, to my complete surprise there was the tiniest bit of softness in her voice. It was a softness I hadn't heard from her since she was a child, and it was also a softness that I wasn't keen on hearing.

Although her question was one that every Shifthunter undoubtedly pondered, the answer would always remain the same.

"We will hunt shapeshifters until the last shapeshifting scum is dead," I replied unapologetically.

Despite my appreciation for Roslyn my voice was ice cold and unwavering, and there was a long pause before she responded.

"And that they will be," she said finally.

With those words all traces of softness disappeared from her face again, and I settled into my seat with satisfaction. Although we were both shapeshifters ourselves, Roslyn knew that I would kill her without hesitation if she ever wavered in her dedication to our mission.

Chapter 3

ZADE DAVIDSON

Castille, New York - September 9, 2013

As I looked out of the windshield at the ugly, familiar woodland around me, I was so enveloped in this rare moment that I couldn't be depressed by it. Although the sparse groves of pine trees and sprawling grass fields created the same, plain landscape that they always did, all it took was one look down at the wood grain in the dashboard or one fierce purr of the engine for me to remember that my Uncle Spencer had actually let me drive his Mercedes this year.

It was like a dream come true, and considering that his Mercedes was a brand new SL550, being allowed to take it for a solo test drive was more than enough to take my mind off of the ugliness of Castille. I took a moment to indulge in the new-leather smell of the interior, and then I pushed the gas pedal a little harder. As the car acquiesced instantly and picked up speed, I couldn't help feeling like a king, or at least someone of a lot more importance than Zade Davidson.

Even though I'd only passed a few drivers on this secluded road, every driver I'd passed had given me a look of awe and jealousy, which I returned with a smirk of satisfaction. I was only seventeen, but I was driving nothing short of a space-car; I was surrounded by a marvelous myriad of buttons and advanced technology that arranged itself on the doors, steering wheel, and dash. I moved my right hand down to the smooth wood and supple leather of the stick shift, and even though it was an Automatic, I felt like Michael Schumacher. The sensation of my hand wrapped around the silver steel at the top of the shift knob was literally glorious.

BEEP! ... BEEP! ... BEEP!

As I whipped the car around another turn, a slow cadence of beeping began to suddenly emanate from the inside of the Mercedes. It wasn't alarmingly loud, but I couldn't figure out where it was coming from even after a quick survey of the GPS navigation system and the odometers. I pushed a few buttons on the touchscreen GPS system, but none of the screens showed any explanation for why the car was beeping.

BEEP! BEEP! BEEP! BEEP!

While keeping my eyes on the road I checked the center console, but after my quick glance down I only saw a pen and a pad of paper inside, which were apparently thieved from the Marriott Marquis in the city.

What in the world is that sound? I thought.

In about the span of a minute the beeping became so much louder and quicker that I finally decided to pull off to the side of the road and put an end to it. With a graceful hum, I parked the Mercedes on the wooded shoulder of a straight patch of road and yanked my cell phone out of my pocket, suddenly realizing that the sound was probably coming from my phone, not the car.

But, as sure as I'd been that my phone was the cause, when I turned the phone over in my hand I saw that the grayscale outer screen wasn't flashing or beeping. I opened it in confusion, because the sound had elevated to a near-blaring that seemed to be coming from inside the car itself.

What the heck?! I wondered, looking around the car with an increased sense of urgency.

I was almost as afraid of wrecking my Uncle's car as I was happy to be driving it, and there was no denying that the beeping sound was not passive. Although I wasn't seriously worried yet, as I searched for the source of the beeping I slowly realized that the sound was an utterly familiar and annoying one that I'd heard a thousand times before. As I stopped for a moment to try and pinpoint where I remembered it from, understanding hit me at the same time as the world around me began to fade.

This can't be a dream, I thought, almost sick to my stomach.

I didn't want to accept it, but both the landscape outside and the details of the Mercedes began deforming before my eyes into shapeless, hazy masses.

This can't be a dream, I thought again, but as I fought against the beeping and the encroaching haze I felt heavy and immobile.

It *was* a dream, and I knew that there was nothing I could do to make it stay. The massaging purr of the idle Mercedes engine seemed far away, and everything in the world was fading except for the incessant beeping, which pulled me into a blackness that soon engulfed me.

When the last visage of dreamscape vanished, it was quickly replaced by a dark and cold reality.

BEEP!! BEEP!!

The relentless beeping of my alarm clock continued right into this reality, escalating until it reached a fever-pitch next to my face. Combined with the unceremonious end to my wonderful dream, the sound angered me to me the point that I reached one hand out of the covers and slammed the OFF button with the express intent of destroying my clock.

Ha! Back to your pathetic life, my mind taunted me.

As I pulled my arm hastily back under the covers I silently cursed the cold air of real life. As my mind whirred to life beneath my closed eyelids I remembered that it was Monday... and therefore one of the fifty-two worst days of the year. For a waste-of-life seventeen year old like me, Monday morning meant the end of lazy weekend nights and the beginning of a week of hell.

No, no, no, I lamented, but I knew my silent pleading was futile.

After laying in the cocoon of my comforters for a moment, I forced my eyes open and saw that my alarm clock was not broken, and that the little digital red numbers on the display read 6:03 AM. Underneath of the time, similarly styled letters read September 9th in a slightly smaller font. It was the second Monday of the school year, which meant that in addition to my internal clock being unadjusted to six o'clock wake-ups, my teachers were going to start laying on the curriculum hard and heavy today.

Eventually I forced myself to swing my feet over the edge of the bed, and when they touched the ground, even the carpet was ice cold. I wasn't surprised, just disappointed. My parents never strayed from their frugal ways, and they neglected to turn on the heat every year until it was absolutely freezing. When I crossed unhappily to my window and took a look at the thermometer stuck to it, it was clear that my parents were either unaware or didn't care that it was a cold and windy 45° outside.

So much for global warming, I thought sourly.

I shook my head and shuffled down the hallway to the bathroom, and when I got there, the scruffy sight greeting me in the mirror confirmed what I could have guessed last night: I should have gone to bed at a reasonable hour instead of wasting time trying to download a movie on my computer. The fact that I was only trying to download one *single* movie at a time was embarrassing in this digital age, but because of the quality of our internet connection, it had taken until well past midnight for the single movie to download.

As a result there were now bags under my eyes that I knew would be there all day, and they didn't help my looks in the least. I was the '*epitome of average,*' as my best friend Chace so kindly put it, which meant that today I had the pleasure of adding dark, sleepy circles to my plain brown eyes, plain brown hair, and bushy eyebrows.

I splashed my face with water in hopes that it would lessen the sleepy look, and then examined by nonexistent biceps, which further disheartened me. My lack of self discipline had forced me to give up on lifting weights a long time ago, and it was only thanks to my voracious appetite that my arms had enough mass to keep them from looking scrawny.

I sighed, and then I went robotically through the rest of my morning routine. A ten minute shower followed a 30-second dressing session, and then 30 minutes later I was full of cereal and orange juice and lugging my backpack towards the bus stop.

So far my brain was still in shut-off mode, which counted as a relative success, but the bus ride that followed my cold walk to the bus stop was the first truly mortifying part of the day. Not only did the crisp morning air shock me awake, but the bus was manned by Mr. Thompson, who was the fattest and smelliest bus driver on Earth. It was also full of overly energetic and excessively talkative underclassmen.

Mr. Thompson himself was literally a human obstacle, and he smelled like sweat and cigarettes even at 6:50 in the morning. Moving past his large jiggly leg, which always spilled into the aisle, was like a passenger rite of passage, and since I was a Senior, I stuck out amongst the underclassmen like a sore thumb. I always rubbed against Mr. Thompson on the way to my seat, and I looked like Loser McGee climbing off of the bus with the freshman a lonely fifteen minutes before the first bell. While even some of the Juniors drove to school and parked their cars in the student lot, I absorbed the humiliation of being one of the few Seniors still without a car.

Today, as was my custom, when our big yellow school bus pulled into line precisely fifteen minutes before the first bell, I hurried off of it and into the brick school building as fast as possible so as not to be seen by anyone. Even though it was only the first day of the second week of school, I had already honed my dipped-head, prayerfully-inconspicuous dash.

Once inside, my goals of getting by as subtly as possible remained the same. For as long as I could remember I had paid about as much attention to what my teachers were saying as I did to the ballerina championships, and therefore I had been persecuted by almost every teacher I had ever had for my inattentiveness and obvious lack of interest.

I didn't care about a single school subject, and besides a major interest in girls and a slight interest in sports, movies, and video games, I wasn't sure that I cared about anything else in life. I went through each school day becoming gradually numbed until the final bell rang; so much so that through the first five periods of the day, I had totally forgotten that there was actually a small, rare hope for excitement today.

Despite the endless lectures and boatloads of homework my first five teachers had dumped on me, my sixth period Biology II teacher, who had been absent during the first week of school, was finally expected to show up. Through the grapevine we had learned that we were his first and only class here at Castille High, and in a school where 90% of the faculty had been here longer than any student could remember, the arrival of a mysterious new teacher was interesting fodder.

I had even heard Mrs. Davis, my ancient English teacher from my previous period, mention to our class to welcome our new adjunct Biology teacher if anyone happened to see him around the school. It wasn't much, but the tiny pep in my step that came with the walk to last period today was a rare sight that I carried all the way until I walked through our classroom door. Our new biology teacher was dressed in a plain, collared shirt, a plain brown tie, and even plainer khakis, and as I got closer I saw that his hair was gray-ish-brown and his face was serious. He looked only slightly younger than the average Castille High teacher, and besides his unnaturally sharp golden eyes, he looked decidedly unspectacular.

After four years you should know better, I chided myself. With a hung head I made my way to my customary seat in the back row of the classroom, silently making a pact to never hope for anything positive from this place again.

"Davidson!"

Just as I settled solemnly into my seat, someone called my name for only the second or third time today. I looked up and saw my best friend Chace Redman sauntering in, greeting me with his hands in the air and his familiar, cereal box smile plastered across his face. I was still getting used to actually having class with him – this class was the first time it'd happened in our entire four years of high school – and a surprised smile crossed my face.

"Redmannnnn!" I called back, trying to match his enthusiasm.

His permanent good mood instantly radiated through the room, as Chace was both the most well-liked person I'd ever met and by far the most popular student in our school. He was also a star athlete and a straight-A student. He had been that way ever since we had crashed bikes on the Path ten years ago and become instant best friends, and it was highly regrettable that none of his charm, intelligence, or popularity had rubbed off on me during all of that time.

On cue, as Chace made his way to the seat next to mine, he had to maneuver his way through a sea of smiles and hi-fives to get there. When he eventually made it through the groupie mob, he sat down and propped his feet up against the legs of the desk and reclined against the lab tables behind us, scanning the classroom idly for a moment before turning towards me.

"The new teacher's got some intense eyes," he whispered observationally.

"Yeah," I agreed, but my tone was obviously unimpressed.

I looked towards the front of the class at our biology teacher, whose golden eyes were the first thing I locked onto. For some reason he looked right back at me as soon as I looked his way, and I quickly looked elsewhere.

"From what I can see that's the only cool thing about him, and his eyes are actually kinda creepy. Hopefully he's OK with this class being my nap period," I replied.

Chace chuckled and let his reclined seat come forward.

"He won't bother you, you blend in well," he poked.

I knew he meant it good-naturedly, but I still had to fight to keep the disappointment I felt from showing on my face.

"I'm invisible to everyone but the teachers. *They* always notice me staring off into space," I said.

Chace chuckled again and gave me an unapologetic look.

"Well, you're luckier than me. I don't have a choice. Everybody thinks I know everything so I never get a break. I'm hoping that since this guy is new he won't expect me to answer every question," he said with a sigh of exasperation.

"I don't know who you think you're fooling," I responded, snorting.

"You *choose* to answer every question."

"Yeah right," Chace snapped defensively, but we both knew that he intentionally and actively participated in every class.

He discreetly pointed over to the teacher's desk, trying to change the subject.

"Check out his briefcase too... it looks like a Suitcase Bomb."

I snorted louder than I had intended to when I followed his finger and saw a large, silver briefcase lying on top of the teacher's desk at the front. There was no doubt that it looked exactly like the type of briefcase that housed time bombs in James Bond movies.

"It looks pretty sketchy," I agreed, shaking my head.

I stared at it for another second before the teacher cleared his throat loudly, garnering the attention of the murmuring classroom. As I looked ahead at him, his piercing eyes were staring straight back into mine. For a second my breath caught in my throat as he glared at me, but then he snapped his eyes away and surveyed the classroom with calm evaluation.

"My name is Gordon Stevens. I'll be your Biology II teacher this year," he said, introducing himself and pointing to his last name written behind him on the blackboard.

"As I understand it, this is the advanced level Biology II course?"

I quickly made to raise my hand in contradiction, but someone else had already beaten me to it.

"We're mixed. Some of us are on the regular track," a girl's voice corrected him.

Mr. Stevens looked momentarily surprised, but he shrugged.

"Ah, I didn't know that. But, be that as it may, we might as well all learn the advanced material. The more you know, the more powerful you'll all be. The textbooks for both levels are exactly the same, and the only difference between the two tracks is the speed at which we cover material. However, considering that all humans are ninety-nine-point-nine percent genetically the same, I don't see any reason why we can't all learn together," he countered, nodding at her.

There was smug affirmation leaking from his pores, and from the far back row I groaned in disbelief, along with a few of the other students who were on the regular track. There was a reason we were on the regular track, and if it wasn't for Castille High's poor staffing, we wouldn't be in the same classroom as the geniuses. Thankfully, the other people like myself were also upset by this sudden revelation.

"That's not fair. I don't learn as fast as the advanced track people," a kid named Blake protested.

He was a chubby kid who could beat anyone but Chace in a video game, but he was admittedly slow at picking up all manner of school concepts.

"A little bit of extra study time and you'll all be able to keep up," Mr. Stevens answered him sharply, and he turned his decisive look out at the rest of us.

I shot a quick sideways glance at Chace, who shrugged and smirked. I could already feel the weight of 'extra study time' bearing down on me.

"This can't be legal," I hissed angrily.

The girl in front of me gave a little giggle, and I looked up and saw that it was Valerie, a cute blonde girl who read obscure books, drew fancy pictures, and denied every male advance to date. The fact that she had laughed at my joke was nothing short of a victory.

"It's obviously legal," Chace whispered back.

He was unaffected by this change, but I *needed* to pass this class this year.

"I'm not kidding. I didn't sign up for advanced Biology," I continued I said, directing my complaint at Valerie.

She was also on the regular track, and she started to turn around to agree with me, but just then Mr. Stevens interrupted us.

"Excuse me you two, but every day is a great day to challenge yourself," he said smartly, looking straight at me.

His bright golden irises were alive as he stared me down from the front of the classroom.

"I understand that you weren't expecting such a challenge, but that just means I'll be watching you especially to make sure you're keeping up," he said succinctly.

His face showed no hint of anger, but his eyes were so intense that I felt like they were burning holes right through me. Chace gave me a quick kick, followed by a 'shut-up-and-pay-attention' look.

I nodded sheepishly as Mr. Stevens thankfully turned his attention back towards the rest of the class, but as he began to speak now, he was already getting into the thick of our first biology lecture.

"Since we are a week behind we will unfortunately have to skip any more formalities. We're going to just jump straight into the beginning of the material, and I'll have the syllabi printed for you all by next week. Since you all have some background knowledge from Biology I, the first unit we will be covering this year is Cell Biology. Which of you all knows anything about Cell Biology?"

Although Chace had instinctively made a move to raise his hand, Mr. Stevens called on a kid in the front row, who began explaining his very limited knowledge of atoms and molecules. I lost interest in him and the whole class in general at that moment, but when he was finished Mr. Stevens ordered us to take out our textbooks and turn to some page in it. Once we got there Mr. Stevens proceeded to draw all kinds of symbols on the chalkboard that I couldn't even begin to understand. To me it seemed like by the time I even could correlate his drawings to what I saw in the book, he was four more pages ahead.

In my head I colorfully cursed Castille High for throwing me into this mixed-level class with this overachieving teacher, and then I tried my best to remain out of sight. Keeping up with Mr. Stevens' teaching pace was already impossible, and I decided that instead of wasting my efforts on passing honestly, I would mentally condemn the people eagerly tuned in to his lesson. That included Chace, the consummate student, who was obediently deep into his textbook, probably many pages ahead of everyone else already.

As I watched him and the others I couldn't help but wonder how they could focus on something as boring as a biology lecture when I felt like I had been sentenced to an hour-long term of utter boredom. Every effort at tuning in to the lecture turned my mind to mush, and even with my best friend sitting next to me I felt caged by the pale, unpainted walls of Castille High. The gloom was intensified by the bareness of *these* particular walls, because Mr. Stevens hadn't even put up any posters or anything to decorate them.

Considering he had grabbed the piece of chalk he was using straight off of the ledge, I realized the only thing in the classroom that I could even attribute to him was his briefcase, and it appeared that even that bulky piece of hardware was useless in his teachings. He hadn't so much as looked at it since the moment I walked in, and its two silver sides were still clasped tightly shut with what appeared to be a combination lock and a few metal buckles.

Does he even have a textbook of his own? I wondered.

Although his lecture was flowing as smooth as a river, I looked around and didn't see one. It struck me as odd that he had come to class without anything to prepare himself for teaching, but with the way he rambled on knowledgeably about molecular components, it would be fair to assume that he didn't need the textbook. Although he gestured and pointed with animated youthfulness as he explained things, his confidence in his knowledge made me think he was even older than he looked.

As my mind and eyes began to wander, I alternately followed Mr. Stevens' movements without any idea what he was saying and stared outside into the gray bleakness of the Castille fall. The lone window, whose lame view was of a small tree and a plain field, was my only other muse besides the clock, which I trained myself to only look up at after long intervals. I was navigating the waters of idleness with learned expertise, and I remained in my revolving state of inattentiveness until the sharp clearing of a throat snapped me to attention.

"At least your lack of focus is consistent," Mr. Stevens' voice said coldly, interrupting my daydream.

Startled, I jerked my focus away from the window and tried to pretend like I was paying attention.

"Sorry sir," I quipped, straightening and trying to sound genuinely remorseful.

Mr. Stevens narrowed his hawk-eyes scornfully.

"I doubt you're sorry at all. You haven't been paying attention the entire period," he said, looking up at the clock and looking genuinely annoyed.

I followed his eyes and saw that only 45 minutes had passed, which meant that thirty more minutes remained in our hour-and-a-half class period. I opened my mouth to defend myself, but Mr. Stevens turned back towards me and cut me off.

"You'll be responsible for the homework due tomorrow anyway, whether you heard what it was or not," he said, and with a disdainful glare he dove right back into his lesson.

I caught another full load of harsh looks from the rest of my class and heard a disapproving sigh from Chace, and when I nudged him even he refused to mouth me the homework assignment.

I felt scathed on all sides, so much so that I suddenly had the mind to just walk out of class, but I calmed myself and tried not to stew. Any thoughts of me graduating with the rest of the class of 2014 rested on me at least *passing* this class. With the entire year left and an inevitable number of failed tests as well, getting further onto the teacher's bad side was not going to help my cause. Since I was apparently the only person not paying attention to his lectures, now I could only hope that hawk-eye Mr. Stevens wouldn't hold that grudge against me all year.

If only I could ACTUALLY turn into a hawk, I thought wishfully, taking one last glance out of the window.

I'd fly straight out of that window and leave Castille forever.

With great effort I sighed and forced my attention away from the window and back onto Mr. Stevens' lecture.

Chapter 4

ZADE DAVIDSON

Castille, New York - September 23, 2013

Despite my most desperate wishes there was no such luck for me turning into a hawk. But, after that first day of Biology, the rest of the week thankfully passed by without major incident. All of my classes were difficult, boring, or some combination of both, and by the following Monday Mr. Stevens' antagonism seemed to have plateaud. By the Monday after that he seemed to have grown used to my inattentiveness as well, at least enough to let me sit quietly in the back, and today as always, school and Biology had been inundating and uneventful.

As was also typical for my daily routine, I had successfully spent the time between the final bell and dinnertime napping in my room. Even though it was an abnormally sunny day, the effort of surviving the entire school day had been more than enough to give in to my faithful midday slump. After waking up two and a half hours later, I now sat at the kitchen table across from my parents, pushing around a bland medley of grilled chicken and rice.

"How was your day?" my dad asked, swallowing his food.

"It was good… same as always," I lied.

Although I'd hated school since my very first day, my parents never failed to find that idea absurd. Although they'd never admit it, I knew by now that both of them had either been outcasts or nerds during their younger years, and any amount of coolness they might have had was now absolutely long gone.

"School's always good? Well that's nice to hear," my mom said, looking up as well.

I stared at her for a second, dumbfounded by her seriousness. She was smart, but at moments like these I couldn't help but wonder if she was a droid.

"It was *OK*," I amended.

You know I hate school, I thought.

The repetitive series of questions I got at dinner time made the food taste even worse.

"Senior year is supposed to be the most fun, I'm glad you're starting to like it. How was your nap?" she asked.

"It was necessary. I had a long day," I answered truthfully.

It was silent for a second as both of my parents took time to fork more food into their mouths.

"Do you have any homework? What are your plans for tonight?" my mom continued when she finished chewing.

"A little homework, no plans. Not much happening since it's a school night," I said.

My mom nodded, not catching my 'no-duh' tone.

"Well, you know the rules. Homework before plans," she said.

She looked back down at her food, apparently satisfied with the status of my life, and I looked over at my dad. He wasn't paying attention; he had already gone back to reading an article in one of his science magazines. I shook my head and returned to my plate hopelessly, and after sticking my fork in a piece of chicken I let my mind drift elsewhere.

As usual, my mind first wandered into dismal reflection. When I looked around at my parents and my kitchen and my house, I knew it started there. Love was more of a forced sentiment than a real presence in my family, and even though it was still there in that awkward, forced way, it completely lacked the passion I'd seen in Chace's family. For me, family time was an experience that had peaked when I was seven years old during the one vacation we'd ever taken, and even then we'd only gone two hours away to New York City.

My dad was a bookworm, but his waffling interests ranged from mechanical engineering to chemical science, and he never seemed to find solid footing or good money. His inconsistency had caused him to change jobs frequently, and fail in the pursuit of turning his wealth of book-smarts into a wealth of profit. For the last four years or so he had spent his days working a dead-end office job and waiting anxiously for his plethora of magazine subscriptions.

My mom on the other hand was not quite the bookworm that my father was, but instead she suffered from workaholicism. She worked 55 hour weeks at the power plant, where she sat at a desk and did endless paperwork the entire time. I had only been there once, but one of the lasting images from my childhood was the 'Bring Your Child to Work Day' trip I had taken with her.

I remembered that she worked out of a small, dingy trailer, which was dwarfed by the huge steel beams of the power plant behind it. The empty office inside had been dimly lit by a single standing lamp in the corner, and hard carpet had covered the floor. The only other piece of furniture I remembered was my mom's desk, which had been barely visible beneath the mountains of papers on top of it.

I had always felt like it had been even worse than school sitting in that office for eight hours, and every time I even thought about that day I could feel the stuffy air of her trailer squeezing the life out of me. I had no idea how my mom spent 50 hours a week in that place, but I knew that *I* would never go back.

"I think it's great you're going to community college next year, too."

My mom's sudden statement cut off my thoughts, and I looked up from my plate in a bit of surprise after I registered what she'd said. For monetary reasons my parents had actually been ecstatic when my academic advisor told them that I would not likely get into any major universities last year, and that had of course devastated any hope of me leaving Castille. I knew the academic portion of it was my own fault, but I felt hamstrung by the fact that even if I *had* done well in school, my parents couldn't afford to send me beyond Castille Community anyway.

"Yeah," I said, looking back down unenthusiastically.

Although I appreciated her effort to continue our conversation for once, her choice of subject brought out my barbs.

"Even besides the money we will save, you'll be able to get acclimated to college classes right at home," she said.

I took a slow, deep breath.

"Greeeaaaat," I said, mustering up as much sarcasm as possible.

I rolled my eyes and turned away from her, but for some reason she kept talking.

"Well, Uncle Spencer called today," she said, switching tracks.

Before she even could continue my heart sank even lower. My Uncle Spencer was a rich, gloating monstrosity of an uncle. I couldn't comprehend how he'd been born from the same two people as my subtle mom, but our mutual hatred for him was the one thing my dad and I shared.

"He said he'll be coming up for Thanksgiving this year. It's the first time he's ever come on Thanksgiving!"

My mom sounded suddenly gleeful, but my dad didn't try to hide his groan.

"With his new car I assume?" I asked, sighing.

My mom finally caught on to my total lack of excitement and huffed.

"Don't be rude. He's visited at least once *every* year, and it costs him thousands of dollars to stay away from his business," she chided.

The smart way that she reprimanded me made me think that the spirit of my Uncle Spencer had come inside of her and spoken the words for her – she sounded exactly like him. I snorted in response.

"Thousands of dollars is nothing to Uncle Spencer. I mean, what kind of car does he drive now anyhow? A Batmobile?" I asked sarcastically.

My mom gave me a hard stare but didn't answer. There was truly not much she could say, because the truth was that my Uncle Spencer owned a highly profitable lumber company in North Dakota. He came once a year on varying holidays, undeniably with a keen intent to gloat in front of my father, and it was a painful experience for both us. One of his chief jabs was the fact that he always showed up driving some new and extremely expensive foreign automobile, and he didn't allow anyone but my mom near it.

"We should all be proud of Uncle Spencer's success," my mom concluded a long time later, trying to still remain positive.

Despite her efforts, even *she* knew that he was brutal. News that he was coming was never well received, and since I had finished my food, I took the opportunity to excuse myself from the table.

"Well, that's cool, Mom. I'll be in my room if you need me," I said.

I was careful to keep my tone tolerant, and I made a short chore of my dishes. When I was finally able to lie down in my room again though, I sighed with the satisfaction that I was successfully fed and away from my parents. My life was sad enough without their antagonizing, and accordingly my room was only a moderate refuge from them. Once boredom quickly settled in, I looked around at the small area of my room in an effort to determine if there was anything worth doing in here besides sleeping.

I first looked to my desk, which was a small brown wooden one with an old computer monitor on top of it, and saw nothing of interest. It sat next to the door, muddled with unused books and papers, and with all of the mess currently on top of it, it looked eerily similar to the one I had vowed never to work behind.

I looked to the far end of the room next, where my similarly disorganized closet stood, and I only saw the multitude of shoes, shirts, and jeans spilling outwards from its mouth in a way that made it look like it was puking out dirty clothes. It was an ugly sight and I finally settled on my TV, but even that was only a little twenty-two inch box that sat on the floor across from by bed.

I was too lazy to walk over and manually turn it on, so I flopped over and looked back up at the ceiling. Like most days, I felt restless and useless, and I knew it was because of my total lack of productivity. I had no money, no car, and no job, and laziness had infected me like a plague. I felt stuck in a vicious cycle, because the fact that I had no money kept me from getting a car, which kept me from getting a job, which kept me from getting money, and so on.

In a nutshell I felt worthless, but before I could let my depression sink too deep I decided to get off of my bed and move to my window. As I lifted it up a gust of cool air came through the screen, and as I looked out at the bright fall evening, I arbitrarily ran my eyes over my fitting address – 1212 Unseen Road.

It was an ominous name I always thought, and as I looked around I saw nothing but motionless driveways and the first signs of orange on the leaves of the trees. After a few minutes I turned away from the window again and glanced over at the only poster in my room, which was an old one that my dad had given me a long time ago. To this day I couldn't fully understand its meaning, but pasted above my TV in big white letters it read:

"He that is down needs fear no fall"

It had never meant anything to me, and as usual I pondered it for only a second before I moved my eyes down to my carpet and sat on my bed again, noting the repulsive grayish-brown it had turned after so many vacuum-less years.

Gross, I thought.

I turned my nose up and started to lean back onto my bed again, but then my phone buzzed next to me. I picked up the clamshell-style cell phone, and flipped it open; it now displayed a message from Chace on its cheap tri-color screen:

"Hot dogs at my house. They'll be off the grill in 30 so hurry"

The message was a gift from above. I was at Chace's house in a swift 25 minutes following the mile-long walk down the Path to his house, just as the sun was beginning to set. By the time Chace turned the first crispy, juicy dog over on the grill, I was sitting at a little round Plexiglas table on his deck next to two very attractive girls.

"Carrie," a girl with dark red hair and green eyes introduced herself first.

"Selen."

The exotic-looking girl with curly brown hair and tan skin next to her smiled and shook my hand as well.

"Zade," I said, introducing myself in response.

As strange as this sudden setup would seem to most, it was one I was well used to. I could tell by the way they looked at me and suppressed dismissal that they had already been enchanted by Chace's persona, and now were subtly disappointed that mine paled in comparison. As many times as Chace had set me up so beautifully, I still scrambled to seem even remotely competent.

"Where do you all go to school?" I asked, trying to seem friendly.

The one named Carrie spoke for both of them and answered, "Herndon."

I quickly hid my expression of disgust... Herndon was Castille's bitter rival. Prior to Chace's athletic dominance the last three years, they had made a habit of annihilating Castille High in all of the major sports.

"Do you go to Castille too?" the girl named Carrie asked, seeming not to have noticed my expression.

"Unfortunately," I answered, smirking and rolling my eyes.

They both laughed.

Well, that's one victory, I thought.

"Hey! We beat Herndon in football now," Chace piped in.

He turned towards the two girls from his position tending the grill a few feet away and flashed one of his pearly white smiles. They laughed again with him, more heartily this time, showing off pristinely white teeth of their own.

"Maybe I'll push you off this balcony. We'll beat Castille then," Carrie joked.

"Yeah," Selen agreed.

Chace raised his arms out wide, challenging.

"You can try," he taunted.

Carrie laughed again.

"Our math teacher is the football coach and he absolutely hates you," she said.

Chace shrugged and flipped a hot dog.

"Wait 'til the 30th. He'll really hate me then," he said.

As he began to shovel the half dozen grilled hot dogs onto a paper plate I looked from him to the girls curiously. They watched him with unmistakable admiration, as nearly every girl did. Ever since the fateful day that we collided bikes on the woodland path that wound between our houses, we had been inseparable. And, ever since that day, the theory that opposites attract had proven to be supremely prevalent in our relationship.

I was the average suburban white kid whose whole life could be summed up by the word regular. Chace was the tall, light-skinned black guy, who was as intelligent as he was athletic. In even his most ordinary movements, he moved with the confidence of someone who succeeded in everything that they did. He was confident but not quite arrogant, which made him as lovable as he was successful.

He served the hot dogs deftly – two for him and I, and one for each of the girls. His Smartphone buzzed loudly against the table as he sat down, but he took one look at the screen and silenced it.

"Mr. Popular?" Carrie poked.

"Actually no," Chace denied, shaking his head.

"It's the head coach of this Division II School. He's been blowing me up."

His face showed that he was genuinely annoyed. For all of his successes, he seemed to permanently lack awareness of his appeal. He seemed to take no notice of the interested look that passed between Carrie and Selen.

"Who *do* you answer the phone for then?" Carrie asked.

The smile on her face was seemingly permanent, and she leaned forward with genuine interest.

"The Division I teams," Chace answered honestly.

Both girls' eyes widened. To me it seemed like they fawned over him like he was a jewel, and even after all these years it was still sickening in a way. I was tempted to ask Chace and the girls how they knew each other, but I knew better. Chace met girls by osmosis it seemed. His mere existence was a chick magnet.

"I heard you could be the top recruit on the East Coast by the end of the season," Selen said, puffing a little at her knowledge.

I could see the start of subtle competitiveness between her and Carrie. After hanging with Chace so often it was a display I was familiar with, but despite my envy I enjoyed watching this part of it play out.

"I'm not *that* good. There's some players in Florida who'd make me look like a fool," Chace lied modestly.

I couldn't control my snort. That was an exaggeration if I'd ever heard one. Scouts from basically every football powerhouse in the nation had spent time in our hallways soliciting Chace's services. He was 6'3, athletic, and posted a 4.0 GPA. He was a bonafide prospect.

"What a lie," I said.

The girls nodded knowingly, agreeing.

"I know he's lying. I read the papers," Selen said.

Chace just took another bite of his hot dog and looked humble, but after he finished chewing he deftly changed the topic, chatting idly with the girls as we munched our hot dogs. The hot dogs themselves were nothing short of delicious, and we all complimented Chace's cooking skills... Carrie and Selen slightly excessively. I chimed in during the conversation where I could, but Chace held their attention without really trying to.

"Wait, Zade, you're going to CCC too right?"

At the sound of my name I tuned in to the conversation and saw that Chace was throwing me a bone to get into the discussion like the consummate friend he always seemed to be.

"Yep, Castille Community all the way. My parents can't afford to send me anywhere else," I said.

I shook my head sadly.

"I also don't have the grades to go anywhere else," I admitted.

Chace gave me a disappointed, disapproving look.

"If I force myself to do some school work I might get good enough grades to move away from here in two years or so," I said optimistically, but inside I wondered if even that were possible.

I hoped that the fact that two more years of Castille life felt like be an unbearable eternity would be enough motivation to make me do well, especially once Chace left for a four year university somewhere else. College and our subsequent best-friendship separation was something neither of us wanted to dwell on.

"We're going to CCC too," Selen told me.

She turned towards Chace.

"I'm studying to be a massage therapist," she said silkily.

She seemed to be losing the Chace sweepstakes, because despite the unhidden intent in her eyes, Chace took it in coolly.

"That's pretty cool," he said, smiling.

In a smooth movement, he glanced down at his watch and then turned towards the girls.

"Thanks for joining us for hot dogs ladies, but it's getting late. I think Zade and I are going to head in," he said.

Immediate looks of disappointment appeared on the faces of both girls.

"We'll do this again soon," Chace reassured them, flashing another smile.

I watched in awe of Chace's deft command as he ushered the girls out of his cushioned lawn chairs and towards the steps of his deck. He hugged them both, but managed to slip a quick kiss on Carrie's cheek.

"Thanks for having us over," Carrie called as they headed down the steps.

"Bye!"

They both waved to Chace and I as they reached the lawn and made their way out of the gate in his wooden fence. When they went around the corner of his house and disappeared, I smiled at Chace in bewilderment.

"Where do you find these girls?" I asked.

Chace smiled.

"I'm a lion. If I don't catch the gazelle we'll both starve," he said.

He punched me jovially as I started to help him clean off his deck. I laughed and dumped our empty plates into his trash can, unable to argue with his analogy. Even though it was dark out now it wasn't *too* late, so after we were finished cleaning I walked home and made it to my bed at a reasonable hour.

However, I laid in my bed awake that night for hours. Thoughts raced through my head like sports cars, mainly centered on my own accumulating failures. In a world of competition it was hard not to envy Chace's all around greatness, even though he was my best friend. I couldn't think of one thing I did *nearly* as well as him, and that depressing truth denied me my favorite reprieve - sleep - until the wee hours of the morning.

Chapter 5

ZADE DAVIDSON

Castille, New York - October 11, 2013

By the second Friday in October, two distinct things had become apparent. First and foremost, instead of being the glorious end of mandatory school, Senior year was going to be the torturous finale. Secondly, this was true although school itself had not gotten any worse. What made senior year the worst of them all was the fact that I couldn't help but be inundated by a singular question that even I wanted to know the answer to:

Once Senior year was over, what was I going to do?

"Go to community college," was my tentative, truthful answer, but everyone over the age of 18 who heard that response demanded a better one. This ranged from both of my parents, whose partial fault it was that I was going to community college, to adults everywhere. Cashiers at the grocery store, cashiers at the department store, and essentially every older person I had come into contact with had been determined to figure out what I was going to do once I graduated high school. The question had become so standard that I soon couldn't help but hate it.

It was only one month into school, and I was more stressed and uncomfortable than I'd ever been. Today, after a normal morning, the school day had gone by as drearily as always despite it being Friday. Our sixth period class however was in its classic pre-class Friday uproar, and things brightened for a tiny bit. Chace and I talked freely along with the rest of the class, and he was telling me and a few other onlookers about a particularly vicious run he had at the game last weekend, which I had watched in full detail myself.

Mr. Stevens was even later than usual, so after Chace's rendition he still had time to get in a few moments of weekend plotting.

"So what's the plan for tonight after the game?" he asked over the mild mayhem.

I looked at him reproachfully as he sat down next to me.

"As if I'd know," I said sarcastically.

He laughed and rubbed his upper lip in thought.

"I know of a few parties we can attend," he said, smiling excitedly.

I shrugged.

"I tag along. Whatever you're doing I'm down to do," I said.

"I'll see you at ten then," Chace directed.

He fixed his face into an unflinching glare and *I* laughed this time. Anyone else would have seen it as extremely ironic that *I* was giving *him* a hard time about hanging out, considering everyone else at our school would have died to have the offer.

"Senior year won't last forever. I'm not going to let you waste it all sitting in your house," he said, popping me lightly in the shoulder.

"Thank God Senior year won't last forever," I muttered.

A second later there was a small bang and a loud creak and the old wooden door to our classroom opened. Despite the initial roar of the classroom we all quieted when Mr. Stevens entered. His peculiar but amiable personality had a propensity to give way to ruthlessness if he was not given the full attention of the classroom, but no one was prepared for the sight before us now.

Since I had spent most of the last two weeks studying Mr. Stevens himself rather than his biology lectures, I had determined that he operated as a paradox of controlled chaos. Normally, the chaotic part of his brain showed itself in his ability to passionately ramble on for hours about complex biological concepts... without even considering the aid of a textbook. The controlled, neat half of Mr. Stevens' brain demanded that his mysteriously useless briefcase always be within a few feet of him, and that he wear the same perfectly pressed outfit every day.

As of now, this latter pursuit seemed to have been recklessly abandoned, because today he looked as if he had been tossed into our school building by an F5 tornado. His slightly graying hair was not just scruffy and uncombed but was in complete disarray, as were his clothes. A stained white t-shirt was visible beneath his soiled and also-stained dress shirt, and a taped bandage bound one of his wrists. How he had gotten past administration unnoticed was a true mystery.

Jaws dropped and eyes widened as he attempted to hide a limp and moved across the front of the room to his desk, his head low. Everyone waited for him to speak; watching as he carefully put his briefcase down on top of his desk and buttoned his shirt.

I glanced over at the briefcase; it too looked like it had taken a beating on the way to Castille High. It's well polished casing was now splattered in light brown mud.

"Hello class," he said at last, finishing his attempt to straighten himself.

"As you may be able to tell, I am in no condition to do much teaching today. I would have stayed home, but I used all of my sick days for the semester during the first week of school."

His voice was somber but resolute.

"Obviously unforeseen circumstances have arisen, but I am here, and therefore you all will learn. If you have all brought your textbooks – as you should have – then you can open up to Chapter Seven and begin reading."

No one moved as Mr. Stevens sat down for the first time this year. He readjusted his briefcase for a moment, but when he looked up from his desk, he looked very displeased that everyone was still watching him intently.

"Do that right *now*, if you don't mind."

His voice cut through our ranks, sharp and threatening. At once we all reached into our backpacks and took out our textbooks, and besides the sound of textbooks thudding onto desks and being opened, it was silent. Tension hung over the classroom like an anvil, but no one dared look anywhere but into the pages of their text.

I hefted my own heavy volume onto the desk and opened it, but I only pretended to read. Even though I wasn't nearly brave enough to cross Mr. Stevens, especially in his current state, I also wasn't going to give up my anti-education sentiments that easily.

After the first quarter-hour I carefully peered up from my book, curious to see if everyone else was really reading. Much to my surprise, the walls that had always dripped with subservience had brought forth a dramatic change. From my vantage point, the faked reading was blatant. Even the brown-nosers were sneaking glances at Mr. Stevens every half minute.

When I saw that one of them was Finnegan Montpelier, the only student who could even come close to challenging Chace for valedictorian, I followed suit shamelessly. For once I was caught up in the moment with everyone else, and I didn't even feel ashamed that we all were shirking our reading and staring at our battered teacher. Mr. Stevens was just lucky that his desk was in the corner of the classroom, making it hard to get a good look at him.

Everyone had their own tactics for staring at him, and I found myself so caught up in the curiosity that I almost jumped at the sound of a sudden whisper coming from my left.

"What's up with Mr. Stevens? He looks like he got attacked," Chace whispered earnestly.

I turned my head slightly and pursed my lips, silently trying to hush him. Mr. Stevens had already proven his supersonic hearing; there was no need to test it further. I mouthed the words "I know" and nodded in agreement as Chace, realizing his mistake, quickly and rather slickly slid back down into his textbook. I did the same, making sure not to make eye-contact with Mr. Stevens as I returned to pretending to read, even turning the pages for effect. Today did not seem like the most opportune day to get on Mr. Stevens' bad side.

However, as I perused the pages absently, a cock-brained idea popped into my head. I realized that my notoriety as the anti-student could finally make itself useful. Mr. Stevens' distraught appearance had sparked my interest, and I figured if I wasn't going to get a good grade anyway, I might as well take my chances on getting a better a look at him on his worst day. I called it revenge for calling *me* out when I was staring out the window on the first day.

As the idea solidified in my head, my curiosity abounded.

Mr. Stevens doesn't seem like a person who would throw away his dignity lightly, but who would have beaten him up in the middle of the afternoon? He's got to be almost 60 years old!

I checked the time on the clock and shook my head in silent bewilderment. Looking back down at my textbook, I scanned it for a word that I didn't know the meaning of, which was unfortunately easy to discover. They popped up all over the page, so I chose the one that seemed the most obscure: 'Demystify.' I'd never even seen the word before, so I hoped it would qualify as a legitimate word not to know.

Now that I was anticipating it even more the end of class took even longer to get here, but when the bell eventually rang everyone looked up, but no one moved. Once the bell had rung through its three tolls, Mr. Stevens waited a second and then flatly announced:

"You are dismissed."

His eyes were like razors as he spoke, and it was three or four seconds before the first students actually accepted his dismissal and stood up out of their chairs. The usual hubbub and jubilation of the weekend was entirely muted in our classroom, and it could only be heard coming in from the hallway as students exited. With a sneaky look I told Chace I'd meet him later on, and then I intentionally waited until most of the class had filed out to get up.

When I did get up I headed straight towards Mr. Stevens with my finger slid carefully between two pages in my textbook to mark the page. He stopped passively grilling the last few exiting students and looked up at me in genuine irritation as I approached him. His golden eyes scorched me remorselessly, melting the little bit of courage I had somehow scavenged.

It was too late to turn back now though, and I walked right up to the edge of his desk as bravely as I could and opened to the page I had marked in my textbook. As I put it down my nostrils were assaulted by a noxious smell, which I could only describe as a combination of dirt and sweat masked by heavy amounts of cologne.

As I searched the page for the word 'demystify,' I detected a third, somewhat familiar smell as well. It was a strange, subtly foul smell that I couldn't quite remember yet, but it was nothing like you would find in a laboratory or anywhere else I would imagine Mr. Stevens could have come from.

"I was reading the chapter and I don't know what this word means," I said, pointing to the word on the page.

I tried to make my question seem as authentic as possible, but as I asked it I realized how insignificant one word in an entire chapter was, and therefore how obvious my plot was to Mr. Stevens. He eyed me for a second, nearly fuming, before he turned his attention to where my finger pointed. He cited the definition, probably verbatim from the dictionary, but as he did so I snuck an up-close look at him.

In that brief glance I saw that there were quite a few buttons missing on his shirt, and that his face was scratched in a few places near his hairline. I also saw that his right hand wasn't so much as bandaged as poorly taped, and it looked like he had just taken wads of athletic tape and quickly wrapped it, leaving it looking like a dirty club.

From this distance it was nothing short of amazing that he had even made it to class. What had at first been a childish curiosity exploded into a world of curiosity, but I kept my expression tight-lipped and unrevealing.

"Thanks," I said as Mr. Stevens finished reciting the definition.

He looked up from the book and into my eyes for a moment and I again regretted my decision to get this close. For a painstaking moment under the glare of his fierce golden eyes I felt as see-through as a piece of transparency paper. I forced my eyes away then, nodded again in thanks, and then grabbed my book and darted out of the room at once, feeling his eyes bore into my back as I left.

Chace greeted me on the other side of the door, his expression curious.

"What was that about?" he asked.

I shrugged, still a little disconcerted by Mr. Stevens' glare.

"You know me. I was curious. I was trying to get a better look at him," I explained plainly.

Chace gave me a skeptical look.

"Well?"

I shrugged again, remembering the smell.

"He just looked beat up, like he got into a fight or something. He had a few scratches on his face and his shirt was missing some buttons. The weirdest part was just the way he smelled. He smelled terrible. He was wearing a bucket of cologne to cover it, but it kind of smelled like he just came out of a bird cage or something."

Chace raised his eyebrows, but now that I thought about it, I realized that the other smell emanating from Mr. Stevens was most like the way my mom's old parakeet smelled. It had died when I was still in elementary school, but underneath Mr. Stevens' heartily applied cologne, I had smelled that same feathery scent.

"He's a weird guy," Chace said, shaking his head.

We took a few steps down the hallway and then an odd look crossed his face.

"Where's your backpack?"

I recognized the unfamiliar lightness at once and realized that in my haste I'd left it on my desk. I cursed aloud and started back towards Mr. Stevens' room.

"You're a fool. I'll catch you after the game," Chace said, laughing.

"Yeah," I agreed.

I re-entered the classroom in a nervous rush, not only hoping to minimize contact with Mr. Stevens but also needing to hurry to catch the bus. But, as I pulled the door open, I saw two very surprising things at once. At first I just saw the backside of Mr. Stevens' open briefcase, which marked the first time I had seen it open. A split-second later I caught a glimpse of the silver gleam of a pistol, which Mr. Stevens hurriedly dropped into the open briefcase and shut away.

I did my very best to act like I'd seen absolutely nothing, but his fiery gaze sucked me in like a magnet. The way it pierced through me it could only be saying one thing: *We both knew that I'd seen the gun.* I ripped my eyes away and turned them towards my backpack sitting on my desk and kept them there. The door to the classroom shut behind me, and an almost crippling surge of adrenaline flooded my brain at the realization that we were alone.

I wove through the desks to mine at the back as discreetly as possible, nonsensical fear gripping me. I was sure that he wouldn't shoot me here in the school building, but there was no doubt in my mind that he didn't have the authority to carry that gun in here. With every step I prayed harder and harder that he wouldn't say anything about it.

It seemed to take forever to get to my backpack and back towards the door, but eventually I made it there. The whole time the awkwardly tense silence was thick, but fortunately Mr. Stevens didn't say a word. The sigh of relief that passed through my lips when I finally closed the door behind me was long and heavy from my held breath.

I took a look down the hallway and saw that only a slight trickle of students remained, and most of them were athletes milling around. That meant that the buses were leaving, and I would be taking the hour-long walk home if I didn't hurry. I had no intentions of doing that, and I literally sprinted through the hallways, ignoring the frowns of the few students I blazed past.

Our school was shaped like a big rectangle, and after zig-zagging down a few short hallways the glass doors to the front office appeared on my left. Standing in front of them was one of the administrators, my least favorite in fact, and she stepped out into the center of the hallway to block my passage and force me to slow down.

"No running!" she screeched.

Her name was Mrs. Pepper, and she was a short fat lady who was known for her strict adherence to the rules and merciless punishments. Nonetheless, I had a mission to accomplish, and I ignored her and ran right around her.

"Seniors should know the rules! You should be setting a good example –" her voice was cut off by the sound of the doors slamming behind me as I burst outside.

I knew that despite her prickliness she was too lazy to chase me, and when the sun of afternoon hit my eyes I saw the line of school buses pulling off. With an anxious head-swivel searched the line of busses to see whether Bus 57 had already left, and to my relief I found it near the front of the line and I made it on with a few seconds to spare.

I ducked into my seat in the back of the bus as quickly as possible, but as soon as I sat down and caught my breath, the door to curiosity flung back open. My mind was instantly flooded with a plethora of unanswerable questions.

Why did Mr. Stevens have a gun in school? What is he going to do now that I've seen it? Does it have anything to do with why he looked so rough today? What else is in his briefcase?

I was thinking so many things at once that I had to check myself.

Calm down. So what your teacher came to school looking like he fought a mountain lion? Everyone else has forgotten about it by now. Just think about the weekend.

I tried to do that, but unlike everyone else I had seen Mr. Stevens with a gun. Even though I doubted he carried it with any hostility towards people at the school, I couldn't help but be curious about why he had it. Unfortunately, I also knew I would never know.

Back to YOUR boring life, I thought, looking out the window at a cold, dreary day.

The light fog and gray sky bore down on happy thoughts like the dark clouds that they were, sucking up the rays of both hope and sunlight. Up front the clamor of the students seemed like a distant roar – a crowd that I had no part of – until I heard my name called from somewhere at the front of the bus.

"Zade!"

As I tried to identify who in the mass of voices was calling me, a kid named Seth leaned over the back of his seat and waved his arm.

"Yo!"

My eyebrows rose slightly in surprise.

"Hey," I answered unenthusiastically.

Seth lived a few houses down from me, but we rarely spoke. He was a rowdy, mischievous kid whose villainous ways had been his trademark for as long as I'd known him. He wore long cargo pants to school every single day, and his hair was gelled and spiked like some punk from the 90's. Unsurprisingly, he was packing a fresh pack of cigarettes against the palm of his hand as he talked to me.

"What you doin' after school today?" he asked in his gravely drawl.

He was a year younger than me but his voice sounded like that of a 40 year old chain smoker.

"Nothing. I'm probably just going home," I answered honestly.

"You down to do somethin' fun?" he asked.

His voice was slick and there was a disconcerting gleam in his eye that quickly determined my answer.

"I'm OK, thanks," I declined.

"We're not doing anything illegal," he tried, trying to sound reassuring.

"We're just gonna go hang out downtown."

I thought about it for a moment. Seth, who lived with his ancient grandfather, had probably never even heard of the word supervision. He had therefore developed into a prototype trouble maker, and I guessed that his idea of 'hanging out downtown' probably meant wreaking previously unfathomed levels of havoc.

"Who is we?" I asked.

"You ask too many questions," he said, chuckling.

He noticed my wary expression and added,

"No pressure, man."

He gave me a crooked smile and then turned back around and rejoined the fray. I slumped back down into my seat and tried to decide whether or not I should go. 'Downtown' meant Historic Castille, which was never exceptionally fun, but at the same time I had no other plans. Part of me felt like hanging out with Seth in Historic Castille wouldn't be worth the walk, yet another part of me knew that if Seth was known for having fun.. For what it was worth, *his* face was usually contorted into a shady grin, whereas mine seemed fixed in a dull frown.

The more I thought about that dull frown, the more I hated it, and by the time the bus came to a rest at the top of our cul-de-sac, I had convinced myself that there was nothing to lose. It *was* Friday after all, and compared to sulking in my room, hanging in Historic Castille couldn't be that bad.

As I climbed off of the bus I shifted all of my depressing thoughts to the backburner and tried to focus on having fun for once. Seth and his friends had already gathered in a small circle at the bus stop, and were jeering at a little trumpet-toting fresh-man who lived farther up the street. She looked innocent, frail, and afraid, but she somehow managed to ignore them as she trudged towards her house. I felt a stab of guilt as I approached them.

"Hey Zade! You comin' or not?" Seth beckoned.

"I'm coming," I said, accidentally forgetting to hide my lack of enthusiasm.

Seth smiled broadly and pointed towards his two cohorts next to him, ignoring my bleak attitude.

"Good, you'll be glad you came. That's Slippy, and that's Ace," he introduced.

Normal names, I thought sarcastically.

I hesitantly shook hands with Slippy, a tall dark-haired boy wearing a plaid button up shirt, and then Ace, a stocky red haired boy with freckles. They both looked like the potheads in anti-drug commercials, and Ace was pulling out a pack of cigarettes as we spoke. They all smelled strongly of cigarette smoke already.

"Cancer stick?" Ace asked, extending the pack towards me.

I shook my head, trying not to seem as repulsed as I felt.

"No thanks."

I was appalled that he was going to offer someone a 'cancer stick,' let alone put one into his own mouth. I was desperate for change and excitement in my life, but not *that* desperate. Ace shrugged and pointed the open end of the pack towards Slippy, who pulled out two of them and handed one to Seth. They passed around a lighter and immediately began to condemn Castille High in a variety of foul words.

I was obviously out of place as I stood and watched and listened, but I took a little comfort in the fact that we at least shared a hatred for school. I also took comfort in the fact that Seth, who was short and olive skinned, was the leader of the trio. Since we had lived on the same street since elementary school I doubted he would just leave me to the vices of the other two. As they tossed their cigarettes the one named Slippy turned towards me as if he had just realized that I was still there.

"Who's he?" he asked reproachfully.

He had a nasally voice that I immediately disliked, and he carelessly exhaled his last puff of smoke in my face.

"Zade Davidson," Seth answered.

"He lives on my street."

Seth pointed down the hill towards my house.

"He's coming?" Slippy asked.

Both his voice and face looked insultingly unconvinced.

"Yeah."

Seth's voice was equally final, but Slippy and Ace didn't look persuaded. As a strong gust of chilly wind blew, neither was I.

"What exactly *is* the plan?" I asked, trying not to seem annoying.

Seth stepped forward as his two friends rolled their eyes, clearly annoyed nonetheless.

"We're going to hang out in Historic Castille. Nothing dangerous," Seth said.

Who said anything about danger? I thought.

"What do you mean by that?" I asked.

Seth grinned mischievously.

"You ever been to Fordham Street?"

Chapter 6

ZADE DAVIDSON

Castille, New York – October 11, 2013

"We're going to Fordham Street?!" I exclaimed, and at the same time my heart sank.

At hearing my outburst Slippy face-palmed, and then he nudged Ace, who just shook his head.

"Don't be a yuppie. We're just going shopping," Slippy said, trying to sound reassuring.

"You see? Nothing dangerous," Seth agreed encouragingly.

I looked at them both suspiciously, but didn't say anything. Seth apparently took that as acceptance, because he nodded to his two cohorts and gently pushed me a couple dozen yards down the street until we broke off onto a paved pathway and into the woods. It was a known route amongst anyone who lived in central Castille, nicknamed the Path. It was the lone grand feature of our town because it ran right through the center of it, spidering out in multiple directions and connecting you to almost anywhere important.

Fordham Street, where we were headed, was in Historic Castille, which was a fitting name for the historic, downtown section of town. It was a miniature city of old preserved buildings and shops, and it almost reminded me of a city stuck in the late 1800s. Its Main Street was a pleasant and bright promenade through the middle of it, but near the bottom was Fordham

Street, a secluded side street that had long served as the unpatrolled hub for illegal activity in our town.

Most of the Path ran through the woods, and at this time of year the tall trees of the forest around it were leafless. Their bare branches stretched over top of it like skeletal fingers, slicing through the sparse sunlight. It was a scary scene at night, but luckily it was at least still afternoon and enough of the gray sky filtered through the branches that visibility wasn't an issue.

Although I was as familiar with the Path as anyone, I felt weird traveling it with my current posse. I walked a few feet behind them, trailing along disconnectedly while they gossiped and continued to light cigarettes. I felt left out already, but my pride wasn't going to let me to give up this quickly.

I resented the fact that if I was going to pass my classes in school I had to carry all of these two-ton textbooks, and I noted that the other three backpacks looked exceedingly light. As the air filled with smoke I started to stew, until I remembered the leftover fruit snacks from lunch that were still in my backpack.

I reached into the front zipper pocket and pulled out the unopened bag of fruit snacks, which sagged with the weight of fruity goodness. There was a loud squeak as I pulled apart the pouch and popped the first strawberry dinosaur gummy into my mouth. It was delicious.

The only one with a backpack is the only one with some fruit snacks, I gloated, rhyming in my mind.

"Fruit snacks!?"

Ace's voice cut through my joy as he turned towards me before I could eat a second gummy, his eyes gleaming. I paused for a moment, unsure of what to do. Slowly and grudgingly, I then extended the open bag towards him, offering him one.

I realized my mistake a moment too late. With a quickness that his weight would not have seemed to allow him to possess, he snatched the whole bag. Tilting his red-haired head back in a quick, triumphant pose, he dumped the entire bag into his mouth, chewed twice, and swallowed. I froze, shocked as he tossed the now-empty bag to the ground.

"SUCKERRRRRRRRR!!!" he garbled victoriously.

He wiped the back of his hand across his mouth and smiled sadistically. Anger and humiliation blazed through me at light speed as Seth and Slippy turned towards us and began laughing uncontrollably.

"Gotta be fast on your feet," Seth said, shaking his head.

"I can't believe he let Ace's fat self get them from him," Slippy agreed.

My face flushed with even more anger and my fist clenched on its own. I wanted nothing more than to punch Ace in the face.

"Calm down, buddy," Ace said, eyeing my fist.

I was somewhat insulted by the fact that his voice was so calm and unafraid, but both Seth and Slippy watched me interestedly as well. There was nothing I could do; I was outnumbered and overmatched. I convinced myself that they were just fruit snacks, and pooled every ounce of my determination to suppress the rising fury in my chest.

"Are we going to keep going or what?" Seth asked impatiently.

I nodded, and I instead channeled that anger into a determination to keep my guard up. I gritted my teeth and continued after them, and even though it was cold, when we finally reached the familiar break in the Path that cut towards Historic Castille my newfound determination was still going strong. I had almost reached the point where I was unafraid of whatever danger we might be facing on Fordham Street.

Still, I was a little anxious as we emerged from the woods down a slight hill and into the back of Parking Lot D, one of the four designated parking lots scattered around the old-fashioned town. We were graced by slightly warmer sunlight now that it wasn't all blocked by trees, and my three knucklehead guides began to whisper excitedly as we crossed the lot. I had to pick up my pace to keep up with them now, and I couldn't help but wonder what was exciting them so much. I was under the impression that today was going to be nothing shy of routine activity, and I hoped their excitement was merely a factor of the sunlight.

"It's kind of quiet up here today," I commented, looking around the unpopulated parking lot.

Only Slippy turned back towards me. His pale face and abnormally long and crooked nose made him look like a big bird.

"Yeah?" he asked, snorting sarcastically.

"Wait 'til we get to Fordham Street."

He brushed back his slick, greasy black hair with one hand and rejoined the conversation with his friends. I took that as an invitation to keep quiet, and I put my head back down and retreated into my own thoughts once again. I wondered where Slippy's parents had taught him to treat a guest, but decided they probably hadn't.

A minute later we came out onto the wider, broader, and brighter sidewalk of Main Street, and I began to become more nervous about going down to Fordham Street again. Its reputation was undoubtedly tainted by conservative parents trying to steer children clear of its vices, but even *police* didn't visit Fordham Street unless there was a shootout or a murder. All other crimes seemed to go unpoliced, and even though murders and shootouts probably only happened at night, the fact that they happened almost every month made me wary.

It was hard to believe such a place was attached to Main Street, which was otherwise lined with antique shops and expensive restaurants; all located in similar, early nineteenth century buildings. Somehow the drama never seemed to spill outwards from Fordham Street, and Historic Castille remained a quaint place, and one of the few in Castille that I normally enjoyed visiting.

When we got to the bottom of the sloping Main Street hill, the white letters against the brown street sign labeled 'Fordham St.' gave no outward appearance of being any different from those of the other streets. The big stone buildings towering around the street sign were basically identical to all of the ones before them, and to anyone not familiar with Historic Castille, Fordham Street looked like just another quaint side street.

However, when we turned down the narrow, unpresuming entranceway and cut around behind the first building on our left, we came out into what looked more like a big, hidden flea market than anything else. For all I'd heard about it I had never seen it before now, and even though it was far different than I had imagined, I felt a sudden spark of adventure.

There were few traces of the blissful nostalgia of Historic Castille here besides the buildings themselves and the cobblestone street, but a plethora of carts, stalls and booths were sprawled out into the street and tucked down in the dozens of alleys lining it.

These kiosks carried all types of goods and were manned by all types of people, and between the merchants and the shoppers there were probably four to five times as many people here as in the rest of Historic Castille.

Scattered frequently amongst them were numerous suspicious looking men and women, most of whom were so blatantly sketchy that in normal places they were probably profiled and followed by security. As we passed the first building the door opened to allow two very well-dressed men to step out, quickly shake hands, and then move briskly off in separate directions.

As questionable as their exchange had looked, there was a routine air about their interaction that made me wonder about the dynamics of a place like this. The sounds of Fordham Street were a subtle roar, despite the volume of traffic, and no one seemed too concerned with anyone else. As a first impression I didn't mind that part of it at all.

I imagined that it was able to exist because it seemed to maintain a delicate balance between freedom and total lawlessness. Even though we passed an abundance of dark, menacing figures and junkies curled in the shadows, they had all kept to themselves…. at least so far.

"I guess everyone decided to come here," I said observationally, breaking a long silence.

"It's always like this," Slippy said, and he gave me another 'shut up' look.

I complied and returned to taking in Fordham Street. I noticed that many of the mobile stalls had raw meat or vegetables on the counter, yet right next to them would be a cart with brand name sneakers displayed. From hardcore skaters to a professional-looking lady in a striped business suit, the population of people trafficking through was widely diverse as well, and it was hard not to lose focus and let my eyes wander around. In doing so however, I almost ran smack into Seth's back when he stopped.

"Watch out," he said, giving me a reproachful look.

He and the rest of the gang took a quick left down the alleyway we had stopped at and huddled up about halfway down, deliberately positioning themselves into a little triangle that left me out of the discussion. I stood awkwardly a few feet away, but instead of focusing on their rudeness I leaned in to catch snippets of their conversation.

"…Mr. Lake isn't an idiot," Seth was saying.

"…we'll be long gone before he notices anything," Slippy countered in a nasal whisper.

There was some soft whispering and then Ace said loud enough for even me to hear:

"I did not do all of this walking just to sit around second guessing ourselves."

I tried to pretend I wasn't listening while they huddled in silence, but the words I'd already heard were quite enough to alarm me. I was even more alarmed when they quickly broke the huddle and headed down the alley again, apparently forgetting I was even with them.

"Do I need to do anything in particular?" I piped up.

"Oh, yeah. Zade."

Seth turned around, and his thoughtful expression confirmed my suspicion that they had forgotten about me.

"How good are you at stealing?" he asked plainly.

His eyes were inspecting, but I met them.

"I don't know. I mean, I've stolen before," I said cautiously.

Seth raised his eyebrow, but I was telling the truth. Every trip had scared the daylights out of me, but Chace and I had spent a few months of sophomore year raiding a particular shopping center in North for petty things like cheap watches and CD's. I certainly didn't feel like doing anything like that today, but I also hadn't come out here to be left in some mysterious alleyway.

As I contemplated my answer Seth looked over at Slippy and Ace, who both looked unconvinced. When he turned back towards me he looked me up and down, eyeing my backpack and shoes in an inspecting manner.

"Come with us," he said decidedly, waving me ahead.

I paused for a second, mildly surprised, and then hustled forward with a twang of satisfaction as Ace and Slippy frowned. As we continued ahead I took a quick look down at my standard issue jeans and sneakers and inwardly laughed at how they had passed inspection.

None of the others seemed overly anxious, so I managed to stay relatively calm as Seth led the way down a small stone staircase about twenty yards into the alley. He then pulled open a heavy black metal door on the right, ushering us inside.

Into the underworld we go, I thought as the rusty door creaked open. There was no mistaking the aura of questionable activity that drifted out from the inside.

We entered into an empty basement full of a half dozen long wooden tables, arranged in rows in the middle of the floor and against the walls. The room smelled strongly of rotting wood, although the tables themselves seemed to be precisely sanded and in good condition. Big black cases were centered on top of each of the tables, and green rubber bins were centered underneath. The black cases were closed, but a few of the green bins were topless, revealing hordes of shiny ammunition.

Ammunition?

I perked up instantly and re-examined the angular shapes of the black cases in front of the bins. I now understood them to be guns of various make and model.

Now this is more like the Fordham Street I'd heard about, I thought.

I followed Seth and company between the well-sanded tables towards another black door on the opposite side of the basement, but approximately halfway there a huge, tattooed man suddenly emerged from a side room.

I did my best not to jump out of my shoes; he looked like a giant. He reminded me of Paul Bunyan, because he was at least 6'5 and he probably weighed close to 270lbs. He also had a fittingly huge crocodile tattoo covering his left arm, and as I looked at it I realized his bicep was probably bigger than my head. A long ponytail swished behind him as he advanced on us.

"Who are *you*?" he asked, looking directly at me.

"Zade," I blurted out, caught off guard.

The giant man furrowed his eyebrows at my awkward response, but Seth stepped forward and took over.

"He's with us, Roman," Seth said, placing a hand on my shoulder.

The man's expression didn't change as he looked down at Seth, and for a second it looked as if he didn't know them either, but after a tense moment he nodded in recognition.

"Ah... the runners for Chen. I remember you," he said finally.

He looked me up and down and then nodded towards the black door.

"Go ahead," he said.

Without another word he headed back into the little side room he had come out of and disappeared behind the wall. I turned to see that Seth and the others were already heading through the door at the back, and I hurried to catch up. As I followed behind them, I wondered what kind of market there was for military guns in peaceful Castille.

"Don't mind him," Seth whispered once the door closed behind us.

"He's pretty chill. He would only kill you if you tried to steal something," he assured me.

Comforting information, I thought sarcastically as Ace and Slippy both snickered.

The door we had gone through led into a dark and musty stairwell, and both the walls and the stairs were stone and uninviting. They spiraled up a couple dozen steps before ending at another nondescript door, which Seth opened into a dim, spacious flat.

As I swept the room with my eyes it reminded me of a penthouse common room, except that it was set in a stone, nineteenth century foundation. The walls were stone and bare, and with no lights on and the drapes pulled over the only visible window, the room was only illuminated by the bluish, flickering light that came from a wall-mounted flat-screen TV.

From what I could see the furniture was sparse but luxurious, and besides a small table against the back wall, the furnishing merely consisted of a plush red couch and a long glass end table that sat across from the TV. The whole room smelled heavily of cigarette smoke and incense; the combination of which was overpowering and unpleasant. I stifled a cough as I filed onto the soft and expensive-feeling carpet behind the others. We stood in the doorway for a second before Seth cleared his throat gently.

"We're here Mr. Lake," Seth called, his voice unmistakably reverent.

There was no audible response, but after a few seconds a door opened on the far side of the room and three figures entered into the room. Even in the lowlight I could see that they all wore suits, and even without any real fashion sense I could immediately tell that the form-fitting business suits were of the expensive variety. As they crossed towards us the tallest one in the middle came quickly to the front and turned on a light, gesturing towards the couch when he recognized Seth and the others.

"Welcome boys," he said cordially.

The brilliant jewelry that dangled off of his wrist glittered in the light of the lamp he had just switched on.

"I see you've brought a guest," he said, eyeing me.

The man was deeply Asian, and the way he looked at me reminded me of the way a cat looks at a new face: both curious and fearless. He seemed to assess me favorably enough, because he then extended a handshake.

"Zade," I said, reaching out and shaking his hand.

"Chen Lake," he introduced.

His handshake was hard and business-like, and now that he was right in front of me he looked even taller than he had at first appeared. His hair was neatly gelled, and he smelled strongly of cologne, which he had applied so thickly that it reminded me of the way Mr. Stevens had smelled earlier today.

"Have a seat," he invited, disengaging my hand.

As he did so he waved the other two suited men back into the room they had come from, inadvertently flashing his sparkling watch once again. They had still been lingering near the back of the room, watching, but at Chen's dismissal the two dark-skinned men nodded and disappeared back through the wooden door and shut it behind them.

"I guess we should get down to business then," Chen said as the other men exited.

At his direction we converged on the two long couches sitting across from his TV, and as we sat he reached onto the glass end table and lit an incense stick sitting on it. He pocketed his silver lighter as the first wisp of cinnamon smoke lifted into the air, and he took a moment to bathe in the fragrance before beginning.

"Just business as usual," he started, looking at Seth, Slippy, and Ace in turn.

"Fifteen standard VS diamonds for my client Tom Schwartz. You remember him?"

They each nodded.

"Tall guy with the blond hair? Lives in Pennsylvania?" Seth confirmed.

"Yes, but he's in Portland, Maine now. A thousand dollars each if you can get these there by Sunday," Chen said.

He put down a rectangular wooden box, which he opened facing us. Inside the box was a row of distended velvet pouches.

"Those on the far left are the VS ones that Tom will be buying, but I've actually got a few VVS and flawless sets too."

Although the least pure diamonds were the ones Seth and his friends would apparently be running, Chen picked up the rightmost pouch and jingled it fondly. All of our eyes followed the velvet pouch as he held it in his hand and then opened it, pulling out a single, tiny diamond.

"Beautiful, huh?" he said, holding the little gem up in the light.

His eyes glittered like the jewels he spoke of, as we watched the light play off of the clear diamond in ways I would have never thought possible. I had never seen anything so perfect in my life, and I had to consciously keep myself from gaping.

However, when Chen finally put the diamond back in the pouch and put the pouch back in the box, his eyes turned towards me with a wary expression.

"Your friend here, who is he?" Chen asked pointedly.

His eyes were on mine, but he had posed the question to Seth.

"We live on the same street, but he's never been down Fordham Street before. He's cool," Seth vouched.

At hearing that this was my first time on Fordham Street, Chen's expression changed to surprise.

"You've never been to Fordham Street?" he asked.

"No, sir. First time," I answered, shaking my head.

"Well, how do you like it?" he pressed.

Something about his tone suggested that there was an agenda behind his question but I shrugged instinctively. I wasn't exactly sure how I felt about it so far.

"It's interesting. It's not like anywhere I've ever been before," I said honestly.

"It is unique," Chen agreed, nodding.

"I've found it to be the perfect place to run my enterprise. There's no interference and a good supply of young talent to run my diamonds for me. Are you going to be helping in this venture? If so you'd be entitled to a part of the share," he said,.

A smile played at his lips but I quickly shook my head.

"No, sir. I'm just coming along for the sights."

Chen smiled fully and nodded again, thankfully turning his attention towards a snippet of news on the television. Chen had an aura of power that was intimidating. I wiped my sweaty palms on my pants.

This man is no fool, I thought to myself, and at the same time I remembered the fragments I had heard of the little conference between Seth and his cohorts.

I really hope they're not going to try to steal these diamonds, I prayed silently.

As that potential dawned on me, my level of unease increased again. The look of unabridged confidence on Chen's face told me that if thievery was their plan, they had no chance of success.

"How do you even get these?" Ace asked incredulously, staring at the row of pouches and distracting Chen from the TV.

Chen smiled slightly and patted Ace on the shoulder.

"I've lived a long time...I have my ways. The people I answer to are more powerful than you can imagine, and to them acquiring diamonds like these is little more than a profitable habit."

Curiosity coursed through all four of us, but before Ace could ask Chen another question I heard the vibration of a cell phone. Chen pulled his smartphone out of his pocket, which was flashing, and answered the call.

"Hello?" he said.

It was quiet for a few seconds as the person on the other end spoke, and then Chen responded in a tone far more deferent than the one he used with us.

"One moment, Martin... Yes, sir."

With a look of concentrated interest on his face Chen stood up and flashed one finger in our direction. We watched him walk towards the other side of the room, presumably to get better reception, but then he disappeared back into the room that his two partners were in.

As soon as the door closed behind him Seth, Slippy, and Ace exchanged wide eyed looks, and then with surprising speed Seth switched the positions of the most and least expensive pouches in the wooden box.

No! I screamed internally, gulping.

Although the deed was done and the pouches looked the same size from the outside, I was sure Chen would be coming out of his room to unleash his rage upon us any second.

He's going to kill us, I thought. My mind flashed back to the boxes of guns and ammo below us and I suddenly wished more than anything that I'd just stayed home. Fear and anticipation descended over me like a veil during the five long minutes that Chen was gone, and through my escalating dread I inwardly kicked myself for telling Chen my name. Despite racking my brain for some sort of counter-plan, I knew there was no way out now.

"Sorry about that," Chen apologized when he re-emerged from the room in the back.

"I've actually got some business to handle, but when I get word from the man in Portland that these are in his possession you three can return to collect your compensation."

I averted my eyes from Chen's at all costs as Seth picked up the pouch on the far left, which was now switched with the expensive one. Chen simultaneously reached into one of his jacket pockets and pulled out a folded piece of paper, which he handed to Slippy.

"The address," Chen said.

Slippy nodded and put the piece of paper in his own pocket as Seth did the same with the diamond-filled pouch. I focused on keeping my breathing even and unsuspicious.

"I'll call you as soon as these are delivered," Seth said with assurance, doing a good job of sounding trustworthy.

Chen shook hands with each of us as we stood up and headed towards the door, but in my mind I expected him to stop us at any moment. That didn't happen though, and it was actually Seth who then did something unexpected. Just as he opened the door to the stairwell he stopped and turned towards me with an expectant expression.

"You know, you might actually be of some use to us, Zade. Hold these in your backpack until we get off of Fordham Street and I'll give you some of my cut. They're valuable and you're the only one with a backpack."

His eyes were as hard as the diamonds in the pouch and silently commanding.

Me?

I opened my mouth to protest, but realized that that would be a mistake. Seth had timed it perfectly, making a scene or refusing would only draw Chen's attention and potentially blow the cover. As much as everything in me compelled me not to take part in this, I took the surprisingly heavy velvet pouch and zipped them into the middle pocket of my backpack, returning Seth's death-stare. Whether or not he understood what my look meant, to me it meant that he was taking these diamonds as soon as we were out of Chen's sight.

The musky stone stairwell just outside of the door to Chen's suite was not the right place to make the switch though, and we went down with a bubbling quickness about us now.

"Calm," Seth whispered when we got to the bottom, pausing with his hand on the door.

He waited for nods of understanding from all three of us before he opened it. In the back of my mind I was stabbing myself for even being here, but then the door was open and we were moving through the little basement-room again. The giant tattooed man he had called Roman was closing the top of one of the black bins as we exited the basement, and he waved a calloused, careless hand as we passed.

"See ya," he said in his husky voice.

"See ya," Seth answered for all of us.

He didn't sound nervous or tense in the least, and I had to at least commend his composure as we exited back out into the alleyway. A fragment of my nervousness dissipated as I took a breath of fresh air and sunlight, but I stopped Seth short when he got back to the intersection of Chen's alley and the main thoroughfare.

"Hey, take these diamonds back," I said, grabbing him by the arm.

The three friends all spun and looked at me with identical looks of agitated anger.

"Just keep them until we get off of Fordham Street," Seth hissed.

"No," I refused flatly, stopping.

Fire ignited in Seth's eyes as I started to take my backpack off.

"I already told you I'd give you part of my cut. *We* don't have anywhere to put it. *You* have a backpack. We can't just walk down Fordham Street with a million dollars in diamonds dangling around in our pockets," Seth said impatiently.

His voice was thick with urgency, but I was stuck on the amount of money these diamonds appeared to be worth. A new anvil of fear came crashing down on me, but Seth grabbed me now and started to pull me forward.

"We're all in danger of getting killed if you don't hurry up. If you just hold them until we get to Main Street I'll give you one," Seth pleaded.

Ace started to pull me ahead also, but as I fought them I met the curious eyes of a passerby and pulled my arms free.

"Fine," I said through gritted teeth.

With focused urgency we struck out again, but I knew I was in way over my head. This was as far from what I had imagined doing today as humanly possible, and I wanted nothing more than to get home alive. I barely allowed myself to think about the fact that I could end up going home with exponentially more money than I'd started the day off with, especially because Chen knew my name.

It would only be a matter of time until Chen found out what had happened, and all I could do was keep my eyes fixed on the building that marked the junction between Fordham and Main Street and pray that nothing would come raining down on me.

Then I heard the shouts.

Seth, Slippy, Ace, and I turned towards each other, all four of our faces frozen into the same look of pure panic. Together we turned around and looked in the direction of the voices, which were coming from behind us… fast.

We were caught.

"Run."

The words were a grave whisper as Seth spoke them, and I took off towards Main Street at an instant sprint. The mild crowd was parting at the commotion, but with Main Street still over a hundred yards away, that was unfortunately helpful to our pursuers. It was all but impossible to disappear into the crowd now.

I looked behind me and saw that the head of the charge was the tattooed man from the basement, Roman. In addition to being absurdly large, he also appeared to be unexpectedly fast. His long, pony-tailed hair whipped behind him as he gained on us.

"The one with the backpack!" a deep voice bellowed. I turned again to see him pointing directly at me.

I didn't know where Seth, Slippy, or Ace had gone, but there was no time to worry about that. Our pursuers knew who had the diamonds, which meant that they were converging on *me*. Making matters worse was the fact that this was Fordham Street; I knew there would be no cops arriving until long after they had already killed me and gone back inside with their diamonds.

My backpack bounced against my back as I skidded down the nearest alley, shouts of "Stop him!" and "Your dead!" following me. I was far from a fast runner, but I was also now very suddenly faced with a life-or-death situation. Getting out of sight extremely quickly was my only hope.

I blazed by smaller cutaways and passages in the alley, which flew by me in dark blurs. It was just my luck that I had chosen an abnormally dark and long alley, but fortunately I could see a dim grey light and stairs at the other end.

With the added weight of my backpack my lungs were already burning halfway to the end, but I willed my legs to run faster.

Get to the stairs, I bargained with my body.

Get to the stairs and this won't be your last day of movement.

A new rash of dark threats and obscenities flew at me from behind as the men turned down the alley after me. I turned behind me, seeing Roman still at the head and two more men behind him. He seemed to be gaining speed as he got closer, and I could feel his burly frame bearing down on me. I realized then that even if I made it to the end of the alley, whatever was beyond was unlikely to be a safe haven.

I had only one choice left. I took one last look behind me and then dropped my backpack in stride. It hit the ground behind me with a loud thud while I kept running, instantly feeling the rewards of lightening my load. In addition to the diamonds my cell phone and keys were both in there, but they were casualties I had to accept at this point.

Just as I reached the skinny staircase I heard the men behind me coming to a halt at my backpack. I prayed that they would open it, find the diamonds, and give up the chase. As I prayed, I hurtled up the crumbling stone steps three at a time, tripping and stumbling as I did so. Past the broken landing at the top there was nothing but thick woodland underbrush, and beyond that there was nothing but the woods themselves, but I didn't care. I mindlessly raced through it all, totally focused on putting as much distance between me and Chen Lake's men as possible.

Chapter 7

ZADE DAVIDSON

Castille, New York - October 11, 2013

When I first disappeared into the trees I thought I was safe. I had plunged into the woods at top speed, ignoring my burning lungs, but about 50 yards into the forest the sound of barking dogs shattered my hopes that I was in the clear. As soon as the sound hit me I willed my legs even faster, but my heart was gripped with deathly fear.

How in the hell did they get on the trail so fast?

In addition to being very winded, I was also baffled and terrified, which made the answer to that question quickly irrelevant. Behind me, the anxious barking was growing louder and closer by the second.

My mind's gears churned in renewed desperation, but I truly was out of options now. Outrunning dogs was impossible. Hiding was impossible. If I turned and tried to fight them I would die, but at least my death would be valiant. It was a catch-22, which meant that for now all I could do was keep running and hope my unconditioned lungs didn't burst.

Adrenaline surged through me, and my mind focused like a laser on doing everything possible to survive. With the ragged breathing of the dogs also now reaching my ears, I chanced a quick glance behind me. Through the trees I saw the streaking grey and white shapes of Alaskan Malamutes.

I couldn't even believe it was real, but already there was less than 20 yards between us; they would catch me in a matter of seconds.

Run faster!

It was a singular and hopeless plea, but it was the only one I knew to make. Fueled by bloody anticipation, the dogs dodged through the trees after me at twice my speed, yelping in excitement as they closed in. My heart pounded in my chest as fast as a marching band drum roll when I felt the nearest one coming close, and I anticipated the sharp pain of dog teeth biting into the backs of my legs and bringing me down.

But, at the moment I expected the dogs to launch themselves and latch onto the backs of my legs, my body went rigid. Simultaneously, whether from fear or something else, I blacked out. Or at least at first it felt like I blacked out. In that frozen moment, my mind seemed to physically disconnect from my body so that all of my senses were suddenly dulled. It rendered me only vaguely aware of anything around me besides a sudden, unbearable sensation erupting within me.

Although it wasn't painful exactly, it felt like I was being ripped apart, and the feeling spread through every inch of my entire body at light speed. It literally felt like I had swallowed a live grenade, which had then proceeded to explode inside of me. I had to assume I was somehow dying.

What made me sure that I wasn't being overcome by the dogs however, was the fact that during this whole millisecond of discomfort, the feeling was coming from inside of me. There was no ripping or shredding or even barking, but my spine, arms, legs, and chest all seemed to be bursting apart simultaneously, contorting and wrenching in what should have been crippling ways.

Before I could even try to form rational thoughts though, or even before I could try to analyze the situation and return to my body, I actually *was* hurtled back into a body. In an instant my senses came back to me in a staggering rush, and right away I realized that whatever had happened to my physical body in my absence was very, very wrong.

The first thing I noticed was that my senses of smell and hearing had both increased exponentially, and I could both smell *and* hear Chen's dogs behind me in the trees. My vision was incredibly focused as well, like God had pulled an HD lens over my eyes.

As I struggled to understand what had happened I saw that I was not lying on the ground, as I had assumed I would be after passing out. Oddly enough I felt raised instead, and decidedly humongous. I wondered if I was under the influence of some kind of drug, because fear had fled my body entirely, and it had been replaced by an almost unnerving calm and tranquility.

I tried to think if someone could have slipped me some hallucinogen, because it was extremely alarming that all of a sudden I felt so perfectly acute; it was as if passing out had somehow made me stronger rather than weaker. I couldn't begin to put the pieces together, because life was continuing nonetheless. The three Malamutes were all around me, jaws wide and snapping.

I told my body to run, but a new and insanely powerful instinct had taken over, and seemingly of its own accord my body crouched into a battle stance. It was literally as if my own body was no longer under my control, and before the dogs could react I was upon them.

I leapt from my crouch and landed on top of the closest one, sinking my teeth deep into its flesh. It yelped in surprise as I was rewarded by the taste of blood, which was oddly sweet and stimulating, and then with a shake of my head I ripped through its throat and tossed it aside. The next dog approached from my flank a second later, but I whirled to face it with incredible speed, and the resounding thud of my paw against its jaw sent the animal flying across the ground and into the base of a tree.

The third dog now faced me alone, its pack-mates laid out around us. It was bigger than the others but somehow still considerably smaller than I was. It looked out at me from black eyes with a disconcertingly *human* recognition. He smelled different from the others too, pungent and unfamiliar.

Odd, I thought.

It was all I had time to think, because I didn't currently have control over my body, and my new body was fully engaged in battle mode. The large Malamute and I circled for a few steps before I felt myself growl, a deep and terrifying sound, and as if on natural instinct, I made an aggressive charge forward. The dog bolted, racing off with its tail tucked and then disappearing in the direction it came.

As it high-tailed into the forest, the smell of fresh blood replaced the odd smell of the last Malamute and flooded my nose. I looked past the second dog, who laid unmoving against the tree where I'd thrown him, and towards the first dog. It too lay motionless on the leaves, but blood gurgled freely from a huge bite wound in its neck.

A clean kill.

Somewhere in my mind I knew that that thought and everything else that had just happened was terribly wrong, but for some reason I didn't focus on it. Despite the fact that I had barely escaped with my life, I felt no sense of danger. I almost felt like I was in a dream, and time was flowing as smoothly as a stream in the summertime.

You have to run! There are still men with guns chasing you, I told myself.

I focused my mind and fought against the strange instincts controlling me, and with what felt like an immense deal of effort I managed to turn away from the dead Malamute and walk deeper into the woods.

You have to get home, Zade. Head home.

I felt like I had to talk to my body like it was a separate person, pleading with it to follow my commands. My limbs felt unnatural and heavy as I padded along, and I was sure my brain had all of a sudden been placed inside a huge machine that was too powerful to control.

It was then that the obvious issues at hand hit me like a tidal wave. I looked down, and where there should have been my hands and feet, there were now massive, white and black striped paws. I ran my tongue over what should have been human lips, and instead felt deadly canines that explained my vicious bite on the dog.

I suddenly realized that I had a tail, which I felt swishing back and forth behind me as if it had a mind of its own. It was so unbelievable that I was suddenly sure that I was dreaming, but it seemed I had literally transformed into a Siberian tiger.

I knew I was going insane, but somewhere behind me there was a shout, and I could hear the sound of feet crunching to a stop. Chen's men had probably come upon their dogs.

Run, I commanded my new body.

To my surprise, this time it listened beautifully, gliding swiftly and silently further ahead. For all my size I moved with agility when running, and as I ran I saw the trees passing me in a colorful fall blur. The release was mesmerizing, and before I knew it I was gaining speed. Even without full control over myself the feeling of speed and power was intoxicating, and every sight and sound and smell had been magnified to the point of glorious specificity, like I was literally one with nature itself.

I didn't know how exactly to describe it, but I sensed every bird and every creeping or crawling rodent without even seeing them, or really even caring that they were there. All I wanted to do was to keep running; the feeling of the air rushing through my fur was better than anything I had ever experienced. It no longer mattered that Zade Davidson the human being was hardly in control and nowhere to be found, because this was the best thing that had ever happened to me.

Sadly, the glory was short-lived. A few minutes into the woods an unexpected, soft whizzing sound came from my left, slicing through my euphoria. It was followed by a sharp, pinching pain in my side, which caused me to pull up to a cat-quick, graceful halt. I turned my head in bewilderment to see what was causing the pain and saw a small, feathered dart protruding from my striped left hip.

What the – ?

I scanned the forest for the culprit, but I didn't have to look far. Emerging from around a tree was a man wearing a full length brown robe. It was hooded, and his head was bent down so that his face was hidden beneath the hood of his robe, but I could see that he was holding a fairly large tranquilizer gun and it looked like he was reloading it. In my mind that meant that whoever he was, he had just shot me.

My lips curled back to expose my deadly teeth all on their own, and rage boiled up inside of me unabated. The Siberian tiger instincts flared up and took over, and I was relegated to the role of co-pilot inside my mind.

Kill him.

The tiger instincts made the decision and immediately acted, and even though the man was thirty yards away, it still only took me two quick bounds to get within distance to launch myself at him, claws exposed. To my surprise he nimbly moved out of the way, significantly faster than I thought a normal person would have been able to, and my wild swipe drew air. I landed in the same spot where he had been, empty-handed.

Where was he?

I could smell him; he had that same pungent smell I had scented from that last Malamute. I whirled an instant after I landed, but whatever drugs were in that tranquilizer were already taking an effect on me. The quick twirl of my body was dizzying, and the world around me was blurry, seemingly moving much faster than I was able to.

I started forward but the lethargy of the tranquilizer had begun to grip me, and it suddenly became hard to even stand. As much as I tried to hang onto my consciousness I could already feel it leaking away. I stumbled a little, but fought against the urge to lie down.

Stay awake! You have to stay awake!

The cloaked man was nowhere to be found in all of this, but after a few seconds of searching for him I could barely even turn my head. My eyelids felt like weights had been attached to them, and I couldn't help but crumble ungracefully to the ground in an extremely heavy heap. My sedated limbs felt as heavy as lead, and the world around me was no longer moving fast but fading away... further and further until I passed into unconsciousness.

———

I woke up in pitch blackness, groggy and highly uncomfortable. I could tell that a good bit of time had passed, because I could barely make out the figure of the moon through the thick overhanging branches of the trees above. I stared up at its reflective glow from my back, my head roughly cushioned by the leaves of the woodland floor.

Woodland floor?!?

I snapped out of my groggy wake up as soon as I realized where I was. I was hit by an instant cold and I instinctively reached into my pocket for my cell phone, but there was no pocket there. Instead I slapped my hand against my thigh where my pocket should have been and felt skin. Panicked, I patted myself frantically and found that I also had no pants, no shirt, no underclothes, no nothing. I was completely naked and freezing cold.

I sat bolt up and rapidly pieced together my jumbled memory, first remembering running from some giant man named Roman, and then running from his dogs. I remembered that grotesque instant where my body felt like it was being torn apart and reconstructed, and the stunning image of two giant tiger paws in the place of my feet.

When I looked at them now however, they were exposed and very human. If it wasn't for the inexplicable absence of all of my clothes, I would have written off the euphoric tiger experience as some kind of hallucination. My survival of the dogs' attack would also be unexplained if I had indeed been dreaming, but whatever had happened earlier had left me ice cold and naked in the middle of the woods, and my naked human body was miserably unprepared for my current situation.

While attempting not to panic I climbed to my feet, my eyes slowly adjusting to the darkness. I had no idea how to get back towards civilization, and after a few moments of futilely scanning the forest I realized that there was nothing out here to give me a clue. It dawned on me that I had no choice but to pick a direction and rely on a combination of blind faith and pure luck, but I currently had little of both.

I couldn't help but feel like after all I'd survived I was now going to die, and I shivered and stood in place fearfully for a long time until a gust of icy wind stirred up and whipped harshly past. My teeth were already chattering from the cold, but that bite of wind sent some curse words flying through them. It occurred to me that I could have been lying out here unconscious for a long time, and since everything was already numb I knew I had to get moving soon or else suffer and freeze to death.

As I galvanized into action I shook my arms and legs vigorously, trying to rejuvenate them and get some blood flowing back through them. I made a funnel with my hands and blew some warm air into it, but my breath was hardly warmer than the wind and my hands remained numb.

As I started to move forward I did so gingerly, because even though my bare feet were mostly unfeeling, the dead leaves covering the forest floor were still harsh. I kept my eyes focused on the ground ahead, knowing that a single false step could end up being an excruciatingly painful one.

I was clueless as to where I was, which direction I was moving in, and which direction I *should* be moving in, but by at least going somewhere I was doing the best I could. I was still utterly bewildered by my situation, but I clung to the fact that by some miracle I had survived Chen's men and his dogs, which hopefully meant that God favored me enough to lead me home and see me through alive.

Within ten minutes my faith already started to waver however, because the walk I was currently undertaking had by then gained the crown as the worst experience of my life. Between the cold and the wind and the hopelessness of picking through the pitch-black woods it was taking every last ounce of my grit to continue ahead. There was an increasing urge to crumble to the ground in defeat and hope to see the morning, and after another ten minutes into the walk my mind was going as numb as my body.

A moment later I made my first misstep and gouged the sole of my foot on a sharp rock, which sent me flying into a fetal position with my hands curled around my excruciatingly pained foot. I couldn't tell if it was bleeding, but after a long time I got back up. I couldn't step on it properly, but I managed to press on at a much slower pace.

I felt like I might truly die; I couldn't feel anything besides the sharp pain in my foot and the throbbing pain my hands, which were cut and bruised from pushing past giant oak after giant oak. If I collapsed again I doubted I would get back up, and it was only some deep-rooted desire to stay alive that kept me going... until my feet literally gave out beneath me.

I went head-over-heels when my foot felt empty space where the ground should have been, and I descended an unexpected, leaf-covered hill, tumbling all the way down to the bottom before I came sprawling to a stop at level ground. It was another minor miracle that I didn't slam into any trees on the way down, but I didn't feel very thankful lying sprawled out naked in the middle of the pavement and hurting worse than I ever had in my life.

I knew I was covered in cuts and scrapes, and every joint on my body felt like it had been hit with a hammer. The cold-induced numbness of my body seemed to only block out pleasurable feelings, because I laid on my back with my eyes closed for at least ten more minutes, half-dead and hurting everywhere. I was almost sad that I wasn't all the way dead, because after a couple more icy gusts I knew I couldn't lay here all night.

I forced my eyes open, and with mountainous effort I spent the better part of five minutes trying to get to my feet. Every movement invoked pain, but the pain of the cold and the wind was worse. I had to get home if it killed me, but when I finally triumphed and managed to stand upright I saw a truly merciful sight. The paved trail I had come upon was the Path, and the section I'd come out on was right next to a tiny wooden bridge only fifteen minutes from my house.

The realization was a tiny beacon of hope, and now as battered as I was naked, I walked straight down the middle of the path in the direction of my house. I knew it had to be obscenely late, but I couldn't have cared less if anyone saw; my humility was complete. I was all but frozen into a bent and shivering stance, and my numb feet were nothing more than shuffling appendages. I honestly expected half of my toes to snap off by the time I got home, but losing a couple of toes was nothing compared to my desire to make it there.

With each step I drew my mind further and further away from reality, focusing on the mental image of my house and the warm bed that was waiting for me there. Even though the real life image of my house was dark and lifeless when I finally saw it, to me it was a talisman of safety. Despite the frostbite and whatever other ailments I knew would follow me into tomorrow, when I shuffled past the bus stop at the top of the hill I felt a great sense of relief in knowing I would at least survive.

When I made it to my backyard, I was barely able to lift the grill mat to find the spare key underneath. It was even harder to get the key into the keyhole at my back door, but eventually I made it happen and finally crept inside.

The warmth that engulfed me when my cold feet hit my warm carpet was glorious. Even though the heat was off, as always, it was ten times warmer inside then it was outside. I couldn't make it any further than my family room couch before I collapsed down, shivering violently while my body temperature adjusted to the relative heat of my house.

I was so thankful to be home and alive that I didn't care what time it was, or if anyone woke up. I only had enough strength to cover myself with the blanket draped over the back of the couch and continue to let the blood flow painfully back into my limbs. A long while later I woke from a half-sleep and managed to drag myself upstairs and into my bed, but it was all I could do to instantly pass out once again when my head hit the pillow.

Chapter 8

ZADE DAVIDSON

Castille, New York - October 12, 2013

The first rays of afternoon sunlight that burst through my window and onto my face the next day woke me up instantly. I snapped my eyes open like I'd woken from a bad dream, and even before they could adjust to the sunlight the choppy images from yesterday soared in, yanking me to attention.

Seth and his friends, flawless diamonds, men chasing me, vicious dogs and even more vicious cold; they flooded my brain to the point of chaos. I could hardly make sense of any of them, and that was before the most important memory dislodged itself from the pack: I had survived the whole ordeal because I had transformed into a Siberian tiger.

The idea was so bizarre and ridiculous that I truly wondered if I was going insane. Even the euphoric memories of being inside that tiger body couldn't stop my mind from clouding with doubt that it had happened. Besides the fact that it was both physically and biologically impossible, it was hard to believe that I had transformed into a tiger yesterday now that I was back in my human body and in my own bed.

The conflict made my head hurt, and I put it aside due to the roaring hunger swirling in my stomach. I tried to rise up out of bed, but an immediate, aching pain scolded me for the small effort it took to throw off my comforter and swing my feet down to the floor. I tried to get up from my bed and leave my room, but by the first couple of movements it became apparent that all movement was going to be painful.

It took a ridiculous amount of time for me to move from the edge of my bed, down the hallway, and into the bathroom, and when I got there I had to lean on the sink for support. Every muscle and bone fiber in my body felt like it had been worked out to the max. I looked in the mirror unsure of what to expect, but plus a few scratches, staring back at me was the same Zade Davidson I had seen yesterday morning.

I breathed a sigh of relief and splashed my face with cold water, somewhat surprised that I looked as good as I did. I looked over the rest of my body and noticed that strangely enough even the scratches on my arms and legs were healing up incredibly well.

At the urging of my stomach I made my way downstairs into the kitchen, bent over in a hunchback position in an effort to ease the pain of moving. The exertion was draining, and once I made it to the kitchen I collapsed into one of the wooden chairs at the dinner table. To my right, more bright sunlight shone through the big double window over the sink. It was uncharacteristically nice for a November day in Castille.

As my eyes adjusted to the brightness I surveyed our small kitchen, which my mom kept spotless at all times. I saw a note sticking to the refrigerator next to the sink, and my mom's handwriting on it was easily recognizable. I gritted my teeth and turned around in my chair to see the time on the wall clock behind me, which read 12:25, and then read the note.

'Dad and I are out running errands. There are some frozen burritos in the fridge. Hope you had fun last night but I'm surprised you came home. Dad and I will be home later.'

I couldn't focus on anything but the words 'Frozen burritos in the fridge.' A few minutes and a good deal of pain later there were three microwaved burritos sitting in front of me. I ate them silently and alone, but I was used to it and I was so happy to be eating that it wouldn't have mattered anyway. When I was finished a short few minutes later, I dropped my empty dishes into the sink and collapsed onto the family room couch.

I laid there for a few seconds in exhaustion, and as I did I decided that going down to Fordham Street was the worst decision of my life. As I started to grasp the consequences of losing all of my schoolwork, my cell phone, and my wallet, it was clear that the move had single-handedly screwed my life. Tiger fantasies notwithstanding, my *real* life had just taken a dramatic turn for the worse.

You thought your life sucked before, I taunted myself.

For a second I wondered what had happened to Seth, Slippy, or Ace, but besides the fact that they had set me up as the goat, compared to my own issues they were completely irrelevant. I actually figured that they had probably escaped, because our pursuers knew I had the diamonds and had focused all of their attention on me.

Whether it had been intentional or not, Seth had announced that I was holding the diamonds right in front of Chen Lake, which had tipped them off on whom to chase. To Chen it might have seemed like an innocent enough request, and I felt a sudden wave of nausea when I realized that for all Chen knew, the whole attempted thievery could have been my own personal plot.

It was too scary to consider, and I pushed the idea of him seeking further revenge to the back of my mind in favor of more immediate needs, such as the need to think of a legitimate excuse for the loss of my cell phone, keys, and wallet. I thought back to yesterday and remembered that my cell phone had been in my pocket, and my keys and wallet had been in my backpack. The backpack I had dropped in the Historic Castille alleyway… the loss of my pants was only explained by the seemingly impossible.

Every part of me wanted to accept that I had somehow evoked a hidden power cooler than anything I could have imagined, but I was *Zade Davidson*. That name meant nothing. Even though my memories were frighteningly clear, the razor sharp senses, the killer instinct, the pure power and speed of movement, there was a zero percent chance it was real. The idea that I had miraculously transformed into a Siberian tiger just in time to save my life was clearly some sort of hallucination.

With that belief at the forefront of my mind I took a moment to give an honest effort to wake myself up from this impossible dream. I literally pinched myself as hard as I could, and the pain from my self-inflicted pinch was genuine. Still unsatisfied, I got off of the couch and shuffled into the kitchen, where I picked up our house phone and dialed Chace's number.

"Hello?"

After a few rings Chace answered his cell phone warily, and I remembered that we hadn't talked since biology class. We were supposed to be going to some kind of party last night, and I obviously hadn't answered the phone at all.

"It's Zade, I'm just calling you from my house phone," I said.

"Oh," was all Chace said in reply, and he still sounded cagey.

"I know you're mad that I was M.I.A. yesterday, but I'll explain what happened yesterday later. First I need you to verify that I'm not dreaming," I said.

"You're not... unless I've been dragged into it with you," Chace confirmed.

I nodded on my end, satisfied that I could at least still discern reality. Everything seemed real enough, but after my ridiculous hallucinations yesterday I had to make sure.

"What are you doing?" I asked.

"I just finished a workout. I'm about to shower," Chace replied.

"I'm coming over then. I'm super sore, but if I can get my body to work I'll see you in a half-hour," I said decisively.

I purposely didn't wait for his approval before I hung up the phone. Between the parental firestorm that was sure to come later and the potential for retaliation from Chen Lake, my stomach was tied in a tight, nervous knot. I needed a reprieve from the looming suspense.

I took a moment to stretch out my exhaustingly sore limbs, and then after a slightly refreshing shower I got dressed and started to walk towards Chace's house. It was relatively sunny outside today, but the warmth was marred by the typically persistent Castille wind. I moved as fast as I could with the soreness in my limbs, but nonetheless I was exceedingly glad to be walking The Path alone and clothed this time.

About a mile into the woods The Path branched off into two different directions, and I headed down the leftward split towards Chace's neighborhood. This path forked off again a little while later, and I continued to follow the left-forking pavement through the trees and up a long and steep hill.

My body cried as I heaved myself up it, but a few yards after this branch of the Path crested the top of the hill, it led into the back end of a cul-de-sac between two houses. Here the dirty gray pavement and looming trees of The Path gave way to black tarmac, white concrete sidewalks, and the manicured streets of the richest neighborhood in town. The houses were all essentially mansions, and minus a gated entry and some famous people, I always felt like Chace's neighborhood was the Castille version of Beverly Hills.

In line with my general fortune, Chace's house was on the opposite end of the neighborhood, a decent trek that I had grown to both love and hate. Besides the naturally torturous physical walk, I was torn between jealousy and awe as I found myself ogling at the flowing fountains, five-man lawn crews, and covered pools present on more than half of the homes.

As usual, the foreign landscapers paid me no mind as I made my way through the streets to Chace's house, which was at the bottom of another cul-de-sac deftly named Palace Road. His lawn was even more perfectly tended and green than many of his neighbors', and not only was it clear of fallen leaves, but it was also cut into those perfectly even, football field-like strips.

On top of the landscape, his house itself was palatial. It had expansive bay windows along the front of its red brick construction, and two painted black columns on either side of the big, wooden front door. I had to step past Chace's mom's Land Rover parked in the driveway on my way up to it, and when I rang the doorbell and stepped back, the sunlight reflected brilliantly off of its stained glass insets.

A few seconds later Chace opened the heavy door, and as usual, he smiled.

"What's up dreamer-boy?" he welcomed, playfully antagonizing.

I couldn't suppress a little smile.

"I walked all the way here... I know that I'm awake *now*," I responded, snorting.

As I stepped inside I looked up at the elegant split-staircase in the middle of his foyer and the sparkling chandelier that hung from the ceiling in front of it. They were both majestic and the subject of ooh's and ahh's from unfamiliar guests, but I had seen them hundreds of times by now.

Chace's smile diminished as he noticed the worried look on my face and the lack of excitement in my tone.

"You don't sound happy about that," he prodded.

"I had a wild day yesterday," I said, not yet sure how to explain what had happened.

Chace gave me a strange look as I took my shoes off, and then I followed him across hardwood floors so pristinely polished that I could see my reflection in them. A door on the right took us down a flight of luxurious free-floating stairs and into his finished, MTV-cribs basement. When I hit the bottom step I made my traditional beeline for his downstairs kitchen, where his family stockpiled food as if they expected the second Ice Age.

"No respect," Chace commented, laughing.

I ignored him and grabbed a bag of name-brand sour cream and onion potato chips from his pantry, which was literally bursting with food, and then made a swift move towards his couch and TV.

At the start of high school Chace had been given free reign over this giant basement, which was segmented into four rooms. The main common room was home to a sprawling leather couch and a seventy-two inch HDTV, and spread out around that room were Chace's bedroom, a bathroom, and a storage room.

Chace's common room. in addition to its movie theater TV, also had space for a convertible ping pong/pool table and an extensive home gym system. The carpet was soft and pearly white, despite the fact that an ungodly number of hidden parties had taken place on top of it. It was one of the great mysteries in my mind as to how the carpet always returned to perfection, but I imagined the Redman family maid had quite the task cleaning up down here.

The walls were covered with artwork and awards, won by both him and his parents, so much so that I couldn't help but think of him as being the prodigal son of royalty. The plethora of accomplishments ranged from certificates of learning, to medals, to charitable recognitions and plaques, to even a shining State Championship ring, which Chace had won himself last year in basketball.

As I sat down on the couch I saw that one of the many plaques was sitting on the seat next to me, and I picked it up idly. When I turned it over I saw that the glass covering the front was slightly cracked, but through the fissures I could see that it was a picture of Chace's muscular father holding a State Championship wrestling trophy of his own.

"Your dad was beastly," I said as I put the picture down on the end table between us and the TV.

Chace sat down on the other end of the couch with a Gatorade in hand and snickered mockingly in response.

"*I'm* beastly. *I* am destined to be head of the pride," he boasted.

He grinned and flexed, daring me to challenge him.

"Funny choice of words," I said, suddenly reminded of yesterday's events.

Chace narrowed his eyes questioningly.

"What do you mean?"

I paused as I tried to find a way to explain what had happened without sounding delusional.

"Well unless I suffered from some extremely realistic hallucinations, I am *literally* a beast. I think I actually transformed into a Siberian tiger yesterday."

Chace's frown turned into a look of utter confusion.

"What?"

He guffawed and looked at me like I was crazy, but then he noticed my seriousness and broke into a laugh. I wanted to laugh too, but for some reason I didn't find it appropriate at the moment. For all I knew there was no other explanation for my being alive, but with no evidence to support my claim it was embarrassing trying to tell someone that I had physically transformed like some sort of mutant.

"So you're what, like a shapeshifter?" Chace asked when he gathered himself a moment later.

Despite his efforts to sound like he was seriously entertaining the idea, I could sense the sarcasm in his tone. Truthfully, I couldn't blame him.

"I don't know," I answered honestly, shrugging.

"What do you mean you don't *know*? You've gotta tell me how this happened," he pressed instantly.

"I will if you give me a chance," I shot back, trying to gather my thoughts.

Chace's face turned a little more serious and looked at me expectantly.

"I believe you man, but prior to now I was pretty sure that was impossible," he said.

I could tell that he was trying to cooperate, but now that I was putting the pieces of yesterday together so that I could tell Chace the story, I was gaining confidence that even the tiger-transformation part was real.

"Until yesterday I thought it was impossible too," I admitted.

I popped open my bag of sour cream and onion chips, and beginning with seeing Mr. Stevens' gun in school at the end of the day, I related everything that had happened from yesterday until the moment I called Chace this morning. When I was finished with both the chips and the story he looked uncommonly speechless, and it was almost a full minute before he responded.

"That's one the craziest things I've ever heard. You hung out with Slippy and Ace? They seem like the two most unlikely friends you'd ever make! Not to mention the whole diamond plot and transformation disaster," he added.

I could see that he was struggling to accept that I'd told him an entirely true story, and he rubbed his eyes as if to make sure that *he* was really awake.

"How do you think you returned to your real body?" Chace asked after a second.

I shrugged again, having fruitlessly tried to determine that myself.

"Maybe the tranquilizer," I thought aloud, remembering.

—"I could hardly control the tiger's body, and I had no control over turning into one in the first place. I definitely didn't have the slightest clue about how to turn back into myself. To be honest, I didn't even think about it."

Chace scratched his chin in his trademark thinking pose.

"I want to know more about the man who tranquilized you. He's more worrying to me than Chen Lake," he said after a minute of thought.

I narrowed my eyes in disagreement.

"Why? *He* didn't try to kill me," I pointed out.

"Exactly... but why not? It doesn't make a lot of sense for someone to be hanging out in the woods ready to tranquilize a rampant Siberian tiger. What kind of man hangs out in the woods with a tranquilizer gun? Even if he was a hunter or something I think he'd bring your body in or call a park ranger after he shot you."

Chace scratched his chin some more, and his eyes had a deep, thoughtful look in them. I couldn't tell if he was still trying to take my story seriously or trying to come up with an action plan, but it was clear that I had definitely dropped a bomb on him. It made me feel only slightly better knowing that someone else felt that this was as crazy as I did. Even personally, with the memories of my transformation fresh in my mind, I wasn't totally sure what had happened.

"I just hope Chen Lake doesn't want to kill me," I said.

Chace shook his head reassuringly.

"I highly doubt that, and even if he did, how would he kill you? Was it even bright enough in his den that Chen and his guys know what you look like?"

I frowned regrettably.

"Probably, but I know they saw my face when I was running through Fordham Street," I admitted.

Chace frowned as well, looking considering the information.

"You said Chen already knew Seth and his friends too, right? They've delivered diamonds for him before?"

"Yep, and if Chen found them or questioned them I doubt they would think twice before blaming everything on me," I said despondently.

"I wouldn't put it past Seth to have planned it that way," Chace agreed.

Chace knew everyone at Castille High anyway, but Seth's notoriety as a trouble maker was widespread. Chace gave me another reprimanding look.

"So, Chen knows your name and your cohorts, *and* might think you stole the diamonds on your own?"

Yes to all, I thought hopelessly.

I confirmed Chace's assessment with a slow, sad nod.

"Have *you* begun formulating of any kind of a plan?" he asked.

I gave him a self-protective look and threw up my hands.

"Do I look like I've had time to come up with a plan?" I burst defensively.

Chace looked a little taken aback, but I could feel my nerves wearing thinner as I felt the potential pitfalls in this situation starting to add up. I felt largely innocent in this whole affair, and the fact that I could face painful consequences for something I didn't feel responsible for was suddenly angering.

"I didn't even do anything!" I exclaimed abruptly, venting.

"I got *stuck* with Chen's diamonds, and I didn't kill his dogs on *purpose*! He's probably happy to have his diamonds back, but there's nothing he can do now about his dogs except get revenge. If he decides to come after me I'm doomed! I mean, Chen Lake is clearly a dangerous man, so as far as I know he could be coming to kill me any –"

"Relax!"

Chace cut me off with a vehement interjection before I could continue. His hand on my shoulder was forceful yet calm, and I fell silent for a second. As I caught my breath I felt foolish for having lost my composure.

"Listen," Chace began, his tone rational and reassuring.

"Chen Lake has his diamonds back. The two of his dogs that you killed are already dead, so there's nothing you or Chen can do for them. One of them even escaped. Unless he's seriously hell-bent on revenge, you'll probably never hear from him again."

As Chace and I's eyes met, I could that he truly believed I had nothing to worry about. Unfortunately, even though I was appreciative of his efforts I was still unconvinced.

"I still killed his dogs, and a half-million dollars is a lot of money," I argued solemnly.

"I don't think that's how this guy operates," Chace countered again.

"From what you've told me, this Chen Lake guy runs an illegal diamond business, not a murder cartel or a dog shelter. He's probably got a lot of dogs, and he's got to be satisfied that his diamonds didn't get away from him. He'll probably just take his diamonds and leave you and your poor choice of friends alone."

I tried to believe that Chace was right, despite the opposing feeling in my gut.

"They *aren't* my friends," I corrected, salty.

"Whatever," Chace quipped back.

I could sense some saltiness in his voice as well, and I remembered that I had effectively ditched him last night for Seth and company. I thought to apologize, but before I could do so he was moving on.

"Regardless of Chen Lake, we can still solve one of your problems right now," he suggested readily.

I looked at him questioningly as a peculiar smirk crept onto his face.

"Well, since I really *am* your friend, I'd like to see you transform into a Siberian tiger," he said.

His voice surprisingly showed no signs of disbelief that this was possible, but I didn't answer him right away because of my own extreme doubt that it was at all real.

"Honestly, I have no idea how I did it. If it's even real, I don't think I can control it," I admitted after a second.

"Exactly," Chace insisted, still eager.

"We've got to find out if it's real... and if it is, it would be nice to know if you could control it," he said.

He instantly stood up from the couch and started to walk towards the sliding-glass door along the back wall of his basement, waving for me to follow him. I wasn't sure why his extremely scrutinizing and analytical brain was so readily accepting that my shapeshifting powers were real, but I could tell he had already set his mind on getting to the bottom of it. That meant that I had essentially no choice in the matter.

"More than likely my transformation was just a delusion," I reminded him as I reluctantly peeled myself off of his couch.

Chace shrugged uncaringly.

"It *does* sound unbelievable, but let's test it anyway. If by some chance you actually *are* some kind of mutant, then that could go a long way towards helping you survive if Chen Lake decides to come after you," he reasoned.

I couldn't argue that point, and even though I was highly doubtful that someone as pathetic as I was had some kind of hidden power, my transformation yesterday had indeed seemed very real at the time. There was also no other explanation for how I overcame Chen's dogs. Nonetheless, if I could never make it happen again there would be no evidence it had ever happened in the first place, and I would have to instead accept that I was delusional. Anybody could claim they could transform into an animal; the moment of verification was everything.

"It *would* be an awesome," I admitted, allowing myself to consider it for a second.

Chace nodded in anticipatory agreement.

"Dude, it would be more than awesome. If you can really transform into a tiger that would be the greatest thing ever, especially if you can control when you do it. We'll be rich!"

Chace ushered me outside as he continued to inquire about my potential powers.

"You literally had *no* control over it yesterday?" he asked again.

I explained the sudden internal explosion that was burned into my memory.

"I honestly thought I was being ripped apart at first, except it wasn't painful. It all happened so quick that I can only describe it as being very *uncomfortable*. One second I was running, the next every bone and muscle in my body was twisting and morphing. It felt like I was being turned inside out," I recounted.

As we stood in the grass and squinted out at his expansive backyard, I thought of another complication.

"Don't forget about the fact that I couldn't exactly control my tiger body either. You'll probably need to find a safe place to be if I somehow manage to do this," I advised.

"I'll watch from the deck," he assured me, chuckling.

I looked out at his eight-foot wooden fence and wondered if it would be able to contain me if I lost control and tried to get free. I doubted it.

"I can't imagine what that would be like. I mean I've read fantasy books and imagined morphing into an animal, but for it to be actually possible is crazy. I'm jealous," Chace admitted dreamily.

I remembered the feeling of exploding into that enormously powerful body, complete with overwhelming urges that were impossible to resist. There had been so many senses… smells and sights and sounds had reached my brain with a previously unfathomed clarity.

"It was wild," I said, unable to put any of that into words.

Chace just nodded, but I could see his curiosity boiling. The curious mind of a genius is a hard thing to quell, and along that vein he immediately began executing his simple plan for testing my ability to morph.

Per Chace's instructions I stood in the grass in the center of his backyard a few minutes later, ready to use the fenced-in area as a testing ground. The cool afternoon sun beamed down on me like a spotlight as Chace stood fifteen feet above me on his deck, leaning over the edge expectantly.

We had both agreed that he was as safe as possible high and out of sight behind me, because even if I thought to attack him and cleared the gate at the bottom of the deck stairs, he would still have time to make it inside. If I cleared his eight foot fence instead, I would be running rampant through his neighborhood, but in the end I honestly doubted any precautions were necessary.

Now that the moment was upon me I had absolutely no faith that I would be able to spontaneously combust into a Siberian tiger. I couldn't help but feel extremely silly as I stood there staring at Chace's tall wooden fence, motionless and awkward. I didn't have the slightest idea how to induce a transformation.

I fought back the urge to give up before I even tried, and instead attempted to focus on a mental image of a Siberian tiger. Using a poster I had seen once on the internet as a template, I pictured every little detail, from the piercing yellow eyes and orange and black striped fur down to the giant paws and sharp claws. I closed my eyes and tried to feel every fiber of my body and imagine it twisting into a tiger's frame, just as it had yesterday.

Become the tiger, I told myself.

I repeated the phrase over and over in my head, and as my thoughts focused, my heart began to thump in my chest in anticipation. The more I remembered the feeling of the change and the animalistic power I had acquired afterwards, the more real it became. Soon it was no longer even a matter of believing; the cage of doubt inside me had been shattered. The memories were too crisp, and the desire to experience them again was too powerful for it to have just been a dream.

My brain knew it like it knew my name was Zade Davidson, yet after long moments of focus no change came. I tried with all of my might to will myself into the tiger I had effortlessly become yesterday, but nothing happened. I strained, muscles totally taut, but after a minute or so I was out of energy. I opened my eyes again and turned towards Chace in defeat.

Chapter 9

ZADE DAVIDSON

Castille, New York - October 12, 2013

"Zade that's ridiculous!" my mom screeched.

A few hours later at dinner I sat facing my parents, and after hearing that I had lost my cell phone, keys, AND wallet, my mom was expectedly livid. The real truth was both too wild and too unverifiable to tell them, so I had decided on a highly modified version of it. More specifically, I told my mom that someone had stolen my backpack while I was playing basketball after school. It seemed like a pretty legitimate excuse to me, but the fire and brimstone was now raining.

"I'm sorry," I said, trying weakly to deflect.

I looked down into my plate of chicken and potatoes and forced a forkful down my throat. They were as bland as always, but eating was a good way to buy time and think of good defenses in my interrogation.

Good lies, my conscience reminded me harshly. I looked up and saw that my mom was wavering back and forth between shock and anger, her face was twisted into a scowl.

"How did you lose all of your important things, Zade? You weren't watching your backpack at all? You know we can't afford to replace those things!" she exclaimed.

I kept my eyes down, thinking of how I had intentionally failed to mention that I had lost my clothes too.

"I know," I muttered.

"I don't even know what to say to you," my mom continued, wiping her face in distress.

—"It'll be at least a week before we can even get you some new keys made, and how are we going to communicate with you without a cell phone? Your irresponsibility knows no bounds," she berated.

I kept my face grave, waiting for the punishment I knew would be coming shortly.

"I don't know if you'll be getting a new cell phone until you graduate," my mom said, not intending to disappoint.

She looked over at my dad for support, and he shook his head in mutual disappointment.

"Maybe you'll be more careful with your next one," he said, tight-lipped.

Their words were dripping with parental scorning, and they knew full well that they were flushing my small social life down the drain with that decree.

"It wasn't my fault. I was just enjoying the game and someone stole my bag," I complained valiantly.

"It doesn't matter," my mom answered stoically.

—"You have to show more responsibility. Like your father said, maybe next time you'll take keep a better eye on your belongings. Hopefully not having a cell phone will be a good reminder to do that until we decide on your punishment," she huffed.

She made to get up from the table but then paused halfway.

"And you wanted a car? You can forget about that!" she said decisively.

The words stung like a colony of wasps, and I blinked back the tremendous knot of disappointment in my throat as she got up from the table and stalked off into the family room. My dad gave me a scathing look and followed her, leaving me to sigh and rub my temples alone at the table, feeling distinctly defeated.

It was a long time before I finally got up and mindlessly did the dishes, and I felt no satisfaction when I flopped down in my room afterwards. Some truly dismal realizations were beginning to settle in as I laid there, and I couldn't find anything positive to offset them. My failure to show any signs of shapeshifting earlier increased the likelihood that my tiger transformation was some sort of psychotic wave, and my residence in the furthest corner of my parents' doghouse meant that real life wasn't looking up either. One move of adventurousness had immediately brought a firestorm of repercussions.

Pull yourself together. At least you're still alive, I told myself.

I looked around my room, wondering how many more endlessly boring nights I would spend in here now that my social life was officially dead.

"Zade!?!?"

I cringed at the piercing sound of my mom's voice calling me from downstairs.

"What?!?" I yelled back.

This was generally against the rules, but I was already in a heap of trouble anyway.

"Get down here!" she barked.

There was an unexpected, renewed wrath in her tone, forcing me to peel myself off of my bed. I took my sweet time going down the stairs, but I started to feel less annoyed and more nervous the closer I got. When I met her in the family room my fears of a new infraction were confirmed by the savagely angry look on her face, and I braced myself accordingly.

"Look what I just found on our doorstep," she said, pointing.

I followed her finger and saw that sitting next to my dad's recliner, looking slightly more ruffled than it had been before I'd ditched it, was my backpack.

"I... where... how did that get here?" I spluttered.

I stared at the familiarly frayed straps of my backpack in total disbelief, terrified of what its arrival here meant.

"I don't know, but it's here," my mom said, hands on her hips.

"You'd better look and see if your stuff is still in there," she commanded.

I nodded and walked submissively over to my backpack, knowing that none of my belongings would be in there. Nonetheless I pretended to look anyway, unzipping the main pockets and digging past unused text and note books that had naturally been left untouched. For effect I checked the front pockets as well, and to my surprise I felt a familiar, hard object in one of them. Knowing that it would be confiscated if I revealed it, I held back any outward signs that I'd found anything and re-zipped my backpack in mock futility.

"It looks like they took my stuff," I said, trying to sound freshly disappointed.

I hung my head, purposely avoiding all eye contact.

"I don't know why they would bother to return your backpack, but since they know where you live whoever stole your stuff obviously knew who they were stealing from," my mom reasoned.

She gave me a harsh look of disappointment for a long time, and then she shook her head and disappeared into the kitchen. My dad had already returned to his newspaper, and I subsequently grabbed my backpack and lugged it upstairs to my room, wasting no time in unzipping the front pouch again and pulling out my phone when I got there. I turned it over in my hand thankfully for a second and then put it on the charger, switching outlets so that it was hidden underneath my bed.

My wallet and keys were still as lost as I'd expected, but those losses had little to do with the crippling panic that soon overwhelmed me when my phone came back to life. My notes application had been left open, and the threatening message I found typed there could have only been meant for me.

We know.

I looked at it, turned it away, and then looked at it again to make sure it was real. When I couldn't bear to look at it any longer I deleted the note, but combined with the return of my backpack it meant only one thing – that Chen Lake had found me.

How much time do I have? What are they going to do to me? Where can I go?

Panicked thoughts poured into my brain, and in an instant I abandoned all hope that I would be able to sweep yesterday's events under the rug. Chace had managed to convince me that since my attempt to steal $500,000 worth of diamonds was failed and unintentional that it could possibly go unpunished. I now realized how foolish that was.

Think, Zade. Don't panic.

I tried talking to myself to calm myself down, but even still my first inclination was to pack up and make a run for it. The only thing that kept me from doing that was my fear that if Chen Lake was out there waiting for me, dashing hastily into the street was a sure fire way to get myself caught. At the same time, sitting in my house unaware was just as bad of an idea.

At the moment it seemed like the lesser of the two evils, but then I remembered that I had a science kit stowed under my bed. I slid onto the floor and reached blindly into the rarely disturbed recesses of my under-bed, but despite the spider webs that instantly latched onto my hands I fought against the urge to pull out until I felt the rough plastic handle of the science kit.

Inside of it was an assortment of elementary science tools: X-Acto knives, vials, scissors, test tubes. I moved them aside until I found what I was looking for, which was the set of high-quality binoculars I found buried beneath the other items. I had no idea how these expensive binoculars had ended up in my flea market science kit, but they were finally coming in handy.

I turned off the light to room for a second, and after slinging the binocular neckpiece over my head I climbed onto my bed and looked out my little window James Bond style. Through the enhanced, Venn-diagram sights of the binoculars I scanned both sides of my street, looking intensely into the windows of every single car to make sure that they were empty.

Through the sights of the binoculars the insides of the vehicles were easily visible, and after a few minutes I had scoured every car on the street and not seen anyone. I climbed down from my bed then and turned my light back on, feeling slightly better about my immediate safety.

When I sat down again, I began to consider preparations other than running. In my mind only one thing was set in stone: Chen Lake and his cohorts knew exactly where to find me. The hiding portion of the game was up. Fortunately they hadn't decided to kill me immediately upon discovering where I lived, but I now had to seriously consider the possibility that my life was in danger.

The fact that I didn't know exactly why they had returned my backpack made me uncomfortable as well, because to me the only logical explanation for that was some sort of threat. Although the note they had left on my phone didn't imply anything specific, it did absolutely nothing to appease my discomfort, and I shuddered when I thought about the storehouse of weapons in Chen's basement.

As my imagination ran wild with nightmares of being abducted or killed I tried to focus on figuring out what to do next, but I was striking options off of my list much faster than I came up with them.

I knew I could never tell my parents, because they would go straight to the police. I could only imagine trying to explain to the cops how I stole diamonds from Fordham Street, then dreamt that I transformed into a tiger in order to escape the people I stole from, and then woke up hours later naked in the woods.

I knew Chace would loan me money if I asked him for it, but what then? Running around the U.S. with a couple hundred dollars as the only assets to my name sounded like a mission doomed before it could begin. All I could do at this point was feel trapped and sorry for myself, and out of a combination of laziness and exhaustion it seemed to me that my best hope was to wait until I was sure a drastic move was necessary before making one. The soft cushion of my pillow behind my head was begging me to leave the real world behind and get some sleep, and before I knew it I was waking up to a damp Sunday morning.

From the time I opened my eyes that morning until I closed them again that night, I felt like a caged animal. Fear, angst, and driving rain kept me cooped up in my room for the entire day, which consisted of a hellish cycle of eating, restlessly pacing, and wondering if my life was soon going to get even worse.

For the first time since my first day of kindergarten, Monday couldn't come fast enough. I went to bed far sooner than I was tired, and after a restless night I was turning off my alarm the next morning before it even rang. I was never so glad to go to school in my life, because school had a safety net of a thousand or so witnesses which actually made it seem like a refuge for once.

When I got there however, I quickly found that my efforts to lose myself in the school day were totally in vain. History, English, and even lunch all passed by in a blur. My brief flashes of preoccupation with them were overshadowed by the looming knowledge that I would eventually have to go back home, which was a place I now dreaded. Knowing that Chen Lake knew where I lived made every moment I spent at 1212 Unseen Road a nervous one.

Biology class came unfortunately quickly for the first time ever, and when I got there a small pre-class uproar was in effect. On my way to my seat I heard at least three groups of people gossiping about Mr. Stevens, and I suddenly remembered his bizarre antics on Friday. At the back of the classroom and waiting for me expectantly was Chace, who was in his seat uncharacteristically early.

As I sat down next to him he watched me put my backpack down, and then a second later his eyes widened and he punched me in the arm in shock.

"I thought you said you lost that?" he asked in a quick, hissing whisper.

I realized that it was the first time I had seen him all day, and that I hadn't yet told him about my backpack's mysterious return.

"I *did* lose it, but somehow it showed up at my house on Saturday night. My mom found it on our front steps."

Chace's expression mirrored how I'd felt the moment my mom had showed it to me.

"They know where you live?" he exclaimed.

"They found you *that* fast?"

I nodded solemnly as Chace's eyebrows narrowed in concern and disbelief.

"Dude, it didn't even take them 24 hours to find you! You're lucky they didn't just run up in your house," he said hurriedly.

His sudden worry did little to placate my own fears, and the exclamatory volume of his expressions made me paranoid. Chace's popularity often brought unwanted eavesdroppers anyway, and I presently motioned for him to lower his voice before answering him in a whisper of my own.

"That's the issue," I said.

"Why *wouldn't* they just run in my house? If they wanted to kidnap me or kill me I couldn't do anything to stop them."

Chace sat pensively for a brief second.

"Chen doesn't know that," he said.

"In his mind you killed his dogs and escaped him. That's pretty impressive for a teenager with no weapons."

I thought about that truth for a moment and realized that although Chace was as right as always, that left two major questions still unanswered.

"*I* don't even know how I did that," I reminded him, exasperated.

"And that still doesn't explain why they left my backpack. If they were worried that I was dangerous they wouldn't want to give me a heads up about attacking me," I complained.

Chace rubbed his chin thoughtfully again, and I could tell that the gears in his mind were churning furiously.

"Maybe it's not a warning," he whispered as his mind continued to work.

It wasn't something I'd considered, and I turned that possibility over for a minute, but then Mr. Stevens entered the classroom. It was almost as if he'd timed his entrance perfectly to synchronize with the bell, which rang an instant later, but besides being on time he looked relatively normal today. His dress shirt was tucked in and his tie was flat, and there was no sign of any of the injuries from Friday as he walked across the front of the room to his desk.

"Quiet down please," he requested as he put down his briefcase.

The class gradually quieted, and I could tell by the way Mr. Stevens turned to face us that he was actually going to address his appearance on Friday. Considering that, Chace and I put talk of Chen Lake on hold and listened along with the rest of the class.

"What happened on Friday is inexcusable on my part," Mr. Stevens began, clasping his hands in front of him.

"But it was also unavoidable. As you could probably tell, I was going through a little bit of a crisis. In hindsight I probably should've just called out for a substitute, but I thank you all for your cooperation and understanding."

"What happened to you?!"

A knucklehead near the front of the class named Lyle Roten shot a question at Mr. Stevens, who turned towards him.

"A personal emergency," Mr. Stevens answered succinctly.

His voice was forcefully stable, so much so that it bordered on eerie, and he looked out at us with his golden eyes flaming, almost daring another person to question him. When he was satisfied that the issue was dead he turned around to face the chalkboard behind him and wrote two words on the board: Cell Division.

"As you might expect, we are going to be having Friday's lecture on Cell Division today instead," he said, pointing towards the words on the board.

I slapped a palm to my forehead in frustration and looked down at my desk at the same time, knowing that I would now spend the next 50 minutes wallowing in despair.

"I feel you," Chace whispered discreetly as he whipped out his notebook.

I gave him a quick look of impending agony.

"If I could have your attention before you get too deep into the twilight zone, Mr. Davidson?"

Davidson?

I vaguely heard my name, and when I looked up I saw a sea of scandalous looks and Mr. Stevens' eyes now trained on me. I gulped.

"Yes?" I called timidly.

"I would like you to stay after class for a moment if you wouldn't mind," Mr. Stevens said.

His eyes were full of meaning, and both blood and alarm flushed my face.

"Ok," I croaked.

Mr. Stevens nodded in acknowledgment, but the instant he returned to his lecture I gave Chace a swift kick under the desk and a panic-stricken look. Chace gave me a shrug of encouragement, but I didn't feel very encouraged. Mr. Stevens knew I had seen him put a gun in his briefcase last Friday.

Please God. Don't let there be two people trying to kill me, I prayed fervently.

Even though Mr. Stevens was once again drawing pictures of cells on the blackboard, I was nervous. I couldn't imagine any other reason why he would want to see me after class. When he finished drawing some large, basketball-like shape on the board, he turned around and surveyed the students. I willed myself to be invisible and stared at my desk.

"Can anyone tell me what that is?" I heard Mr. Stevens ask.

"Prophase," Chace answered confidently when Mr. Stevens called on him.

I flicked my eyes upwards and saw a couple girls turn around and bat their eyes at him admiringly. I inwardly gagged.

Like moths around a light bulb, I thought.

"Correct as usual, Mr. Redman," Mr. Stevens affirmed, also appreciative.

He then continued back into his lecture, and I took to staring down at my desk and trying to block out the rest of the classroom. Cell division did little to distract me from my anxiety, and sadly now that I was even less excited to see the end of this class, it came swiftly. I was caught off guard and still staring at my desk when the bell rang, but the usual relief that accompanied it was missing.

"Good luck!" Chace said cheerily as he and everyone else hustled into the hallway.

He had a way of seeming like he overcame all of life's obstacles with the greatest of ease. I had none of that charisma however, and as I thanked him for the good luck wishes, I felt none of the calmness or collectivity he had tried to impart.

As soon as I was left alone with Mr. Stevens, I packed up my own stuff and walked towards the front of the classroom with as much fearlessness and quickness as possible.

"How was your weekend?" Mr. Stevens asked me cordially when I approached his desk.

He smelled like a heavy dose of cologne like he always did – a different brand today maybe – but the same effect. Mr. Stevens' voice was casual however, except that his unnervingly sharp eyes never left mine as I stood opposite him.

"Good," I answered stiffly.

Mr. Stevens raised his eyebrows.

"Good?" he asked.

I was caught off guard by the knowing disbelief in his voice.

"Well... you know. Since there was no school it was relaxing," I stuttered.

For some reason Mr. Stevens still looked like he didn't believe a word I was telling him, and I was sure that he could hear my heart thumping rapidly against my ribcage.

"I won't profess to know *exactly* what you did this weekend, but I doubt that you found it relaxing," he said.

His voice was suddenly and unexpectedly accusing.

"What I *can* tell you is that you are fortunate to be alive, and that is more than a lot of people in your position can say for themselves. The best way for you to *stay* alive would be for you to disappear entirely, but in lieu of that you should keep your mouth shut and stay away from Castille. Some secrets should remain secrets."

He narrowed his bright eyes in mortal implication and scrutinized my face.

"Of course," I said, nodding in fearful affirmation.

Stay away from Castille? Surely he meant Historic Castille, I thought, but I wasn't really sure.

I couldn't fathom how Mr. Stevens would know about my adventures in Historic Castille, but without saying it I tried to convey in my voice that I would never tell anyone about him carrying a gun in school.

"Is that it?" I asked tentatively.

"I also wanted to tell you to get rid of your backpack," Mr. Stevens answered flatly, his eyes never leaving mine.

"What?" I blurted before I could stop myself.

Mr. Stevens looked stern.

"You'll want to do that as soon as possible if you're smart," he said sharply.

I stood there, as confused as imaginable, but with Mr. Stevens' eyes slicing through me it was very difficult to think.

"OK," I answered slowly after a long, baffled pause.

"Good," Mr. Stevens quickly answered.

He looked at me for another long moment and then nodded towards the door with such brisk dismissal that I found myself walking towards the door before I actually realized what I was doing. But, as I reached the door, Mr. Stevens called my name again. I turned around with my hand on the handle.

"Remember what I told you," he said, his eyes flashing.

I nodded wordlessly as I pulled the door open, as disturbed as I was perplexed. I wasn't sure if Mr. Stevens was threatening me or warning me, but I was sure I never wanted to be alone with him again.

Chapter 10

ZADE DAVIDSON

Castille, New York - October 14, 2013

G et rid of my backpack?!?

My anxiety about the whole situation made it even harder to come up with rational solutions, but I was still in deep thought over how Mr. Stevens knew about my activities on Friday when I walked out of the front doors of Castille High. I knew the buses were already gone, but by the time my brain came to reality and processed that there was no point in heading out this way, I was face to face with Chen Lake. If the strong smell of cologne coming from where he now stood hadn't caused me to look up, I would have actually walked directly into him.

"Zade Davidson."

Pure panic hit me as Chen Lake's familiar, accented voice addressed me. He took a step towards me, his hand outstretched. He was clearly not surprised to see me. Not sure what to do, I hesitantly shook his hand. His shake was like a vicegrip, and I couldn't withdraw my hand until a few seconds later when he allowed me too.

"Yes?" I answered carefully.

I tried not to sound intimidated, but I was both terrified and nervous.

"Where were you last Friday?" Chen asked calmly.

He looked as tall and imposing as he had in that dark lair, and the dark-tinted sunglasses that now covered his eyes made him look even more enigmatic. The same Bluetooth earpiece stuck out from behind his left ear, and he was wearing another well-pressed and expensive-looking business suit. There was no question that this was the man I had seen on Fordham Street Friday afternoon.

"At school," I answered, attempting to look innocent and confused.

Chen took a quick half-step towards me.

"Don't play with me," he reprimanded sharply.

In an instant his expression darkened, and he licked his razor-thin lips threateningly.

"I'm sorry," I stuttered, looking away from the dark glasses covering his eyes.

"It wasn't my idea to steal your diamonds, I promise!" I sputtered.

As soon I said the words I wished I hadn't. Chen Lake's eyebrows narrowed disapprovingly.

"Your attempt was pathetic," he spat, curling his nose up in distaste.

I quickly glanced around to see if anyone was watching me – if there was anyone even close enough to help me – but there were only three or four students standing outside, and they were way down the sidewalk on their way home.

"Seth forced me to do it, I swear. I had no idea they were going to try and make that switch," I pleaded.

Chen Lake's expression didn't change as he surveyed the empty front lot as well. He seemed unnervingly casual, similar to the lethal assassins in the movies. I fervently prayed that he wasn't.

"I have my diamonds back. That's not why I'm here," he said.

"What I would like to know is how you escaped us. I know for a fact that my dogs should have caught and killed you."

I felt my eyes being drawn back to the black lenses of his glasses as I cooked up a desperate lie. I realized that I was at a significant disadvantage not being able to see his eyes; between his stone-faced expression and the shroud of his glasses there was no way I could tell what he was thinking. I tried to match his pompous attitude and shrugged as innocently as I could muster.

"I was scared out of my mind. I just ran as fast as I could," I answered.

It was a stupid lie, and for a long time Chen didn't respond. As he stared down at me I did my best to seem both innocent and defiant, but internally I was just as scared now as I had been then.

"Of course you ran," Chen said after a few seconds.

"But I am not inclined to believe that you can run faster than dogs. My dogs not only failed to catch you, but two of them were also mauled to death. The report one of them –" Chen stopped, as if he was stopping himself from saying something he didn't mean to tell me.

"One of my men reported something very *interesting*," he said, amending.

He shook his head, clearly unconvinced by my story.

"The injuries to my dogs seemed inconsistent with the damage that could be inflicted by human hands. Are you saying that you have no knowledge of how this occurred?"

I gulped and shook my head, not trusting my mouth enough to lie again. My heart was now pounding in my chest so powerfully that I was positive Chen Lake could hear it. Despite his outward placidity, he now seemed to be subtly bristling. He took another step closer to me so that we were no more than a foot apart and his cologne swamped my nostrils; it was staggeringly strong.

"This is not a game, Mr. Davidson. Your life may very well depend on whether or not you tell me the absolute truth."

His voice was gravely serious, yet there was something in it that suggested he already *knew* the truth. If he was baiting me, I wasn't going to tell him anything... especially not that I transformed into a tiger and ripped his pets to shreds. Whether he believed me or not, I saw no positive in admitting to that.

"I don't know what happened to your dogs," I said again.

"I honestly just ran as fast as I could. I never wanted to be a part of anything that happened on Friday. All I wanted was to get home and get back to my normal life."

I forced the words out as confidently as I could, but even through Chen's black sunglasses I could feel his eyes poring over me, trying to read my mind. I took a step ever so slightly back towards the school.

"I'm afraid going back to your normal life is no longer possible," Chen said then, his voice tightly controlled.

There was a frightening assurance in his tone that compelled me to take another step away from him, but in an incredibly swift motion he closed the distance between us again. With his mouth twisted into a scowl of disgust he leaned forward, bringing his cologne-soaked face within a foot of mine. Fear rooted me to the spot as I searched the impenetrable tint of his shades for his eyes.

"Martin Evers does not have mercy on groveling, *rogue* scum," he spat, his voice drenched in absolute repulsion.

He loomed less than a foot away from me for another torturous second and then turned swiftly on his heel. Without another word he strode off into the parking lot towards a black Mercedes parked at the far end. Dumbfounded, I stood there in fear and shock for a moment with my mind frozen on one thought.

Who was Martin Evers?

I was beyond confused, but there wasn't any time to worry about that right now. It seemed very likely that Chen believed I had killed his dogs, and even though *I* wasn't even sure what had happened, I was sure that Chen didn't seem like he was going to let it go.

Propelled by dread I dashed back into the school building as soon as Chen reached his car, and as the front doors shut behind me I tried not to panic. I was internally terrified, but as I paused in the foyer outside of the main office to gather myself, Mr. Stevens' warning suddenly rang in my head.

Ditch the backpack.

The light bulb in my brain came on at the same moment.

It's a tracking device!

In a flash of understanding I walked straight into the nearest bathroom, and without bothering to go into a stall, I immediately turned my backpack upside down and dumped out everything onto the tile floor. Pens, papers, books, they all splattered onto the ground in a cacophony of noise, and as soon as my backpack was empty I dropped to the floor and rapidly searched for anything suspect in the mess.

Unfortunately I only saw my normal school supplies scattered out around me. Baffled, I reached into the empty main compartment of my backpack to see if something had managed to stay lodged inside, but as I felt around my hand grasped nothing but air. It wasn't until I pushed my hand into the very bottom that I felt a jagged piece of stitching ad something surprisingly hard underneath the fabric.

Of course!

I grabbed hold of the rectangular object and pulled hard, using my other hand to pull the zipper in the opposite direction so that my backpack was inside out. As I looked at my upturned backpack I was surprised to see fine stitching work along the bottom and a solid object about the size of a nineties cell phone protruding from underneath it.

I looked around the bathroom for a tool to cut open the stitches with, but saw nothing. Paper towels and toilet paper weren't going to help. With no other choice and my stuff still scattered on the floor, I set to pulling out the stitches one by one. The first strand was the hardest to get, but even then the work was tedious. It was a solid five minutes before I eventually ripped the bulky device out of the bottom lining, and I turned it over in my hand as I examined it.

The first side I viewed was solid black plastic, but when I turned it over to the other side I couldn't believe what I saw. What had initially appeared to be a boxy tracking device was not that at all. It took me only a second of staring at the yellow diagram of an exploding circle to understand that this was not a tracking device but an explosive... I was holding a tiny bomb.

I suppressed the urge to panic and chuck the thing away from me, and instead I held the explosive gently, careful not to dislocate any of the few exposed wires. I tried not to focus on the fact that at any second I was subject to being blown off of the face of the earth and I slowly stood up with the bomb in my hand, my mind racing.

As morally wrong as it seemed, I forced myself to believe that the bomb was no longer my responsibility, and focused on what my dad had once told me: heroics were only rewarded in the movies. Now was the time to be solely concerned with my own survival.

After a long, deep breath, I then gently dropped the bomb into the toilet bowl of the nearest stall and flushed, not waiting to see if the blocky object would fit down the hole. Instead, I fervently prayed that the water would miraculously diffuse the bomb and I sped out of the bathroom at full speed. Guilt and terror coursed through me as I dashed down the emptied hallways of Castille High, and I focused on the fact that I needed to get as far away from those explosives as possible.

Everyone needs to get away from those explosives, my conscience screamed at me, but I blocked my conscience out in the name of survival and kept moving.

It took about two minutes for me to snake my way to the back doors of the school, and when I burst out of them I ran into the back lot and immediately spotted Chace's silver Nissan Maxima parked in the far row. Through his windshield I could see him texting in the front seat, reclined way back in his usual afternoon position. Even though Chace was always late for football practice anyhow, today I figured he might need to miss it altogether.

Unsurprisingly, Chace didn't even notice me darting across the parking lot at breakneck speed, and I slid into the passenger seat of his car so fast that I was punching him in the arm and commanding him to drive before he could even look up from his phone.

"Drive," I barked.

Chace looked up from his iPhone and blinked a couple times, startled.

"Drive!" I said again.

Chace slowly brought his seat up and started the car.

"What's going on?" he asked, looking annoyed.

"Chen Lake showed up at the school," I said quickly, half out of breath.

I knew I sounded panicked, but I couldn't help it. Chace's eyes shot wide.

"Seriously? Did he talk to you? What'd he do?" he asked in a barrage.

"Drive first," I ordered, pointing ahead.

Chace slowly put the car in drive and started forward.

"What happened?" he demanded.

I shook my head and tried to convey the dire urgency in my voice.

"I literally almost ran into him when I was trying to catch the bus! I wasn't paying attention and when I opened the front door he was right there," I said.

Chace looked at me curiously.

"He didn't do anything to me, but you need to drive faster," I said very seriously.

Chace accelerated, but not fast enough for my liking. I decided to give him some incentive.

"I figured out why they gave me back my backpack. They sowed a bomb into the bottom of it," I blurted.

"What!? They sowed a bomb into your backpack!?"

Chace instinctively slammed on the brakes, jerking me forward.

"What did you do with it?" he demanded abruptly.

His eyes darted around the car, searching.

"It's not here," I assured him quickly, but I was nervous about being anywhere near the school right now.

"It might've doubled as a tracking device, I don't know, but I flushed it down the toilet in the front bathrooms so you should probably keep driving," I advised.

Chace processed my words and instantly slammed on the gas, throwing me back into my seat again. He was finally speeding around the school actively, though.

"You left the bomb inside *Castille*?" he asked incredulously as he decelerated into line behind a car at the exit.

"Would you be happier if I told you it was in the car? It was a bomb, what other choice did I have?" I retorted.

Chace snorted and threw his hands up, but he was clearly as concerned about things as I was.

"This is serious business. I'm going to have to figure out a way to get you out of this," he said quietly, rubbing his chin.

Chace turned out onto the main road; I shook my head in staunch disagreement.

"This is actually the last of your involvement," I said.

"Once you take me home, please, I don't want you to be involved in this anymore. I know it sounds crazy, but I think my life is at stake. You can't risk yours too," I said seriously.

Chace matched my hard look with a sarcastic one.

"Don't be an idiot. You're not going to die," he responded confidently.

I shook my head again, now wondering if Chace *did* see how serious this was.

"I'm not kidding, man. Chen Lake made it perfectly clear that my normal life is over," I explained.

I could still see Chen's vicious look, and I rolled down my window for a blast of fresh air. The frosty tinge told me that the cold of winter was swiftly approaching.

"So this is the end then?" Chace asked, glancing in his rearview mirror.

I pulled my head back inside of the car and rolled the window back up.

"Of our friendship? No."

Chace shook his head this time.

"Of me helping you get away from Chen Lake I mean."

"Oh, well then yes," I answered assertively.

"Well then I guess I'll be going out with a bang," Chace proclaimed, tapping his rearview mirror.

"That car has been following us since we left the school."

Without thinking I whipped around in my seat and looked through the back window. Driving dangerously close to the bumper of Chace's Maxima was a black Mercedes. More concerning however, was that Chen Lake's unmistakable face was in the drivers' seat.

"That's Chen," I said, slinking down fearfully into Chace's leather seat.

Chace looked into the rearview mirror again.

"I figured. That's why I've been taking all these random turns. He's definitely following me."

I cursed loudly, now realizing that we had indeed taken an inordinate amount of turns, and that we were also currently nowhere near my house. I chanced another look behind us through my rearview mirror and saw that Chen was still right on our tail.

"What are we going to do? Can you shake him?" I asked.

"I can try," Chace said, accelerating a little.

"But even if I do, what then? Who *is* this guy?"

Chace's eyes were locked on the rearview.

"Clearly a psychopath," I said, looking down hopelessly.

Chace took a deep breath as we both tried to stay calm and formulate a plan.

"You're a fool, Zade," Chace said a second later, shaking his head and sighing.

"And you owe me," he added begrudgingly.

Before I could respond he gripped the steering wheel tightly and slammed on the gas, and simultaneously his engine roared into gear and we lurched forward. With my back pinned to the seat Chace sent us blazing forward, but after only a brief moment of separation Chen concurrently accelerated and closed the gap between us once again.

I watched the speedometer rise from fifty miles per hour to sixty and then to seventy, and we careened around a bend in the road at what could only be described as an insane speed for the suburban road we were on. We barely avoided flying off of the road and into the forestry to our right, and with Chen moving just as quickly behind us I honestly thought I was going to die.

"What did you do to this man?" Chace asked plaintively, continuing to pick up speed.

I would have responded, but just then Chace blazed through the Stop sign at the upcoming intersection.

"*You're* going to kill us if he doesn't!" I exclaimed, but Chace ignored me as Chen followed suit behind us and paced through the intersection as well.

I looked over at Chace, and saw his eyes on the road and his jaw set squarely and tightly. I knew this was probably not a good thing for our safety, and accordingly Chace cut a sudden left turn that sent my head and shoulder flying against the passenger door. Our tires squealed wildly as we spun out and across both lanes of the residential neighborhood entrance, but the unexpected maneuver was expertly executed. Through the smell of burnt rubber and the dizzying vision of a complete 360, I saw Chen's car whiz by the street completely, disappearing from view a millisecond later.

Chace punched the gas again and drove us deeper into the neighborhood while I tried to catch my breath and reorient myself.

"Did we lose him?" I asked tentatively, trying not to jinx us.

"I don't know," Chace answered, looking around at the large homes and expensive cars around us.

We were undoubtedly in a nice neighborhood, but Chace sped to the end of the street and took another sharp left turn. He then sped down this street too, trying to distance us from Chen.

"Where are we?" I asked.

"Montgomery Hills... you've never been here before?" Chace asked back.

I shook my head.

"It's pretty quiet except for when people have parties," Chace informed me.

"It's a huge neighborhood though, and all the streets look pretty much the same. Unless Chen comes out here often he should hopefully be a little lost right now."

Chace took a right turn this time and pulled up behind a tan SUV on an nondescript cul de sac. His Nissan was well hidden behind the bigger car and he cut off the engine and took a deep breath.

"We should hopefully be OK here. I saw the design in the newspaper once, and there's like fifty different streets in Montgomery Hills. Simple probability says we should be safe," he explained.

I noted how he continued to check his rear view mirror and pursed my lips.

"Right," I said doubtfully.

Chace looked salty, but just then the sound of a car behind us sent us ducking down. We both looked into the rearview expectantly, but the white Toyota SUV pulled straight into the neighboring driveway and released its middle-aged female driver. We both breathed sighs of relief and rose back up as inconspicuously as possible, but my heart was pounding.

"The only problem with Montgomery Hills is that there's only one exit. I'd bet Chen will play his odds and sit there once he figures that out. We might just have to wait him out," Chace said pensively, frowning.

I nodded and cursed my luck aloud. Chace shook his head.

"At least I'm missing football practice," he said, ever-positive.

I was surprised at the lack of sarcasm in his voice and the little smile that creased the corners of his mouth.

"You're happy about that?" I asked.

He snorted.

"You've never really played a sport like this. Practice is important, but it's horrible. I'm on the ground half of the time, and the other half I'm running wind sprints! I'd rather play Dario Franchetti any day," he chuckled.

We both laughed, but after being startled by the sound of the Toyota-mom coming out of her front door to get the mail, we shut up again.

"I'm pretty sure The Path goes through here," Chace said when she went back inside, unlocking the doors.

"Let's check it out. We're just sitting ducks right here, and I doubt Chen is going anywhere for at least another half-hour."

I didn't like the idea of sitting here either, so I followed after Chace and stepped out into the afternoon, frowning at the gray skies. It was chilly, but a few yards down the sidewalk the concrete turned towards the woods, and we hustled down the cutaway until we were out of sight of the road. Sure enough, a few seconds later the cement sidewalk transformed into the dirty, signature tarmac of The Path.

"What do you know," Chace laughed.

"You were right," I admitted, letting out one laugh of my own.

I was still tense, but I had to admit that his infinite knowledge was useful on a daily basis. Even though a part of me hated having to defer to him in all instances, I would be even more of a loser than I already was without him.

We took to our own thoughts until the Path wound over a low, wooden bridge, and on one side of the bridge there was a wooden bench. It overlooked the slow-moving small stream below, and we decided to sit there for a minute in the relative safety of the woods. Although I had never been particularly fond of nature, in the last few days the woods had grown on me.

"So, what's your plan?" Chace asked after ten or so minutes.

He picked a pebble off of the bench and skipped it adeptly over the stream; I didn't have the first inklings of a plan for dealing with Chen Lake past getting out of Montgomery Hills alive.

"No idea," I grumbled defeatedly.

It was silent for a minute as Chace skipped another rock across the stream.

"Well you definitely didn't get rid of me as fast as you'd hoped," he said, smiling again.

I snorted.

"I don't just want to get rid of you, I *have* to get rid of you," I corrected him.

I tried to skip a rock of my own but it plunked skiplessly into the water. Chace looked hurt.

"Clearly Chen Lake is a criminal and he's hostile," I explained, trying to clarify in my most reasonable tone.

"If you get involved in with this it would make things a million times worse. You've got something to lose. Imagine the headlines: 'Star athlete and brilliant student disappears.' There would be riots!"

We both knew I was right, and although I was totally serious Chace laughed again. When he recovered he looked unfazed.

"We're not going to get in trouble," he said with total confidence.

He skipped another rock across the stream below, and this one bounced five or six times and onto the bank where the stream bent off into the woods. He let out a loud, victorious guffaw, which was almost too loud despite our location deep in the woods. I laughed too this time, and Chace grinned as he thought back to our narrow escape from Chen.

"Maybe I should take up NASCAR driving.. or maybe just professional getaway driving. I could do it," he said.

When I thought about the type of driving it took to get us this far, I knew it was not the time to deny that.

"Yeah, you really might," I agreed.

"Getaway driving wouldn't be so much fun if you got caught though," I reneged a second later.

Chace snickered dismissively.

"Yeah right! We wouldn't get caught," he boasted.

I could see in his eyes that he truly believed that, and even if it was just because he hadn't yet realized the reality of our danger, I was envious of his boundless confidence.

"You worry too much," he said after a few silent minutes, punching me in the arm.

"This guy Chen Lake won't waste much more time with you. He's already got his diamonds back so he's probably just trying to scare you straight."

I nodded, but to me, bombs, tracking devices, and car chases were more than just scare tactics. We waited for another thirty minutes just to be sure before we even considered heading back to the car.

"What time is it?" I asked when I noticed the sky darkening.

Chace pulled out his iPhone and looked down at it.

"Five-thirty on the dot," he said.

"Wow. Practice is basically over by now right?" I asked.

Chace just nodded and smiled.

"Safe to head back?" he asked.

I shrugged in decision, but Chace took this as an acceptance. By now it'd been at least two hours since we'd lost Chen.

"If Chen hasn't given up by now we're just going to have to lose him again," Chace reasoned as we started back down The Path.

As we walked I felt a little safer knowing that Chen at least hadn't found us here in the woods. I was still walking on eggshells however, and I was struck by terse surprise when Chace stopped me short with a quick arm bar to my chest. His blow almost knocked me backwards, but he pointed ahead and I saw a large, brown owl standing in the middle of the path. Chace and I looked at each other, confused both by the fact that it was standing in the middle of the walkway and the fact that it wasn't nearly dark enough for owls to be out.

"Is that an owl?" I whispered, baffled.

It looked like an awfully big owl to me, but Chace seemed unworried.

"I think it's an Eurasian Eagle-Owl," Chace said, cautiously taking a step forward.

"I've read about them and I don't think they are typically dangerous to humans, but I have no idea why one would be in our woods," he added after another step.

Despite his beliefs that the bird was harmless, it eyed him more menacingly with every step as he approached.

"You see it's eyes? I remember the golden hue from our textbook," he said.

I looked at the big owl and felt like the eyes looked vaguely familiar. I wondered if I had perused them in the textbook as well.

"Maybe it's injured... or deranged," Chace added then in a whisper, lowering his voice as he got closer to the owl.

"You never know with animals. It might be vicious," I cautioned in agreement.

Chace paused a dozen yards from the bird, apparently acquiescing that it indeed looked decidedly unfriendly. The way its beady golden eyes followed our every move was like it had some-how been waiting for us.

With me standing a couple yards behind Chace, we faced off against owl for an undecided moment, and the owl remained sta-tionary and unrelenting. It was sitting directly in the middle of the path, and it was big enough that it would have to move in order for us to get back to Chace's car. Unfortunately, it currently looked like it had no intentions of doing so.

"I'm going to throw something at it," Chace said finally.

Without taking his eyes off of the owl he retreated a couple of steps and picked up a sizeable stick and balanced it in his hand.

"Are you sure that's a good idea?" I asked.

Chace shrugged.

"It's either that or charge at him... Unless you have any other suggestions?"

I shook my head, figuring his plan was as good as any. Chace turned back towards the owl without wasting time, and after tak-ing aim he decisively hurled the stick straight at it's feet. It was a perfect throw, and the stick would have landed right in front of the bird and forced it to fly away, except at the last instant the owl merely shuffled nimbly to the side just before the stick would've hit him and the stick clanked harmlessly onto the pavement behind it.

Our mouths opened in disbelief as the owl moved back to its original position in the middle of the path, hooted loudly in out-rage, and spread its wings threateningly. There was no denying that the bird was challenging us.

"Is that normal?" I asked, taking a step back.

"Not at all," Chace answered, shaking his head.

He retreated back to a position next to me as well, and I shook my head as I watched the disgruntled owl.

When it rains it pours, I thought.

Now we've got deranged animals after us.

'I'm charging it," Chace said resolutely.

I didn't have time to stop him, and in an instant he had picked up an even larger stick from the woods and charged the owl, wielding the smooth stick like a sword. For a second I thought he was going to smash it dead on the spot, but as he swung the bird lifted off the ground and nimbly dodged the blow, rising past

Chace's face. With an incredibly quick movement Chace was able to recover and swipe at the bird again, but this time it just barely missed the owl's tail feathers as it streaked into the tree above. It hooted angrily down at us when it landed on a branch out of our reach.

"Come on," Chace called, beckoning me ahead.

He tossed the stick to the side and wiped his hands as I warily hustled passed where the owl and been and caught up to him. The owl hooted down at us with a ferocity, but we ignored the spooky creature and sped out of the cover of the Path and back onto the cement sidewalk.

"Dude that owl was crazy, –" Chace began when we slowed, but halfway through his sentence he stopped short.

I looked up where his eyes were pointed and saw a black Mercedes parked at the edge of the road less than fifteen feet away. Before we could even turn to go the other direction the driver side door swiftly opened and Chen Lake stepped out, as calm as ever.

Without even bothering to check who was looking, he withdrew and aimed a black handgun at my chest with one hand and closed the door behind him with the other. He advanced towards us with the barrel extended threateningly, and at point blank range we both instinctively put up our hands in surrender.

"Walk back towards the woods," Chen commanded.

We both backtracked towards the woods in sudden silence, our hands in the air. Like an ominously advancing tidal wave, the magnitude of being held at gunpoint crept further into my consciousness with every step.

This man wants to kill you... one false move and you're dead, I thought, trying not to panic.

As my pulse quickened to a paralyzing pace, I suddenly couldn't stop thinking about how much I wasn't ready to die. As inconsequential as my life had felt up to this point, I realized then that even the worst times I'd experienced were better than being dead.

"Stop right here," Chen Lake ordered, shaking me back to the present.

We had gone a few yards into the cover of the woods, and Chace and I stopped obediently. I swallowed hard as I looked at the barrel of Chen's handgun and then up into the dark lenses of his glasses.

"What do you want from us?" I demanded, but my voice cracked with nervousness.

Chen ignored me entirely.

"You! Hands behind your head and on your knees," he ordered gruffly.

Like lightning Chen Lake moved the gun towards Chace, aiming it specifically at him and motioning towards the ground. Chace looked at me and then got to his knees, but his face had been nearly as pale as mine. I watched him eye Chen cautiously as he put his hands slowly behind his head.

Chen stared him down for a minute, but then turned his attention back towards me.

"Well, Zade, obviously I am going to have to kill your accomplice, but I have been specifically ordered by Martin Evers not to kill *you*. I have been commanded to capture you and bring you before Martin Evers alive, and I would highly advise you allow this to happen the peaceful way."

His words sent a flood of dread over me worse than when the gun had been aimed at my body. Regardless of what happened to me, Chace was truly innocent and I had gotten him involved in all of this.

"I'll do whatever you say if you don't kill my friend," I pleaded instantly.

Chen gave me a comical 'Yeah, right,' look.

"For your sake I hope you prove to be more competent than you appear," he said in response, ignoring my plea.

I looked quickly over at Chace, but he was looking straight at Chen Lake.

"Please," I begged again, but there was a stone-faced coldness in Chen's expression that told me my appeal wasn't affecting him in the slightest.

It wasn't until after a few gut-wrenching seconds of him staring at us did his face twist up with a sudden curiosity, as if an intriguing fact had just dawned on him. He then looked back and forth between Chace and I and posed a question towards me.

"Your friend doesn't know that you're a shapeshifter, does he?" Chen asked, his voice conveying true surprise.

"A shapeshifter? What are you talking about?" I objected.

Chen ignored me and looked at Chace with what I perceived as a look of disbelief.

"*You* should choose better friends," he said pointedly, shaking his head at Chace.

He laughed with a quick, evil chuckle and then moved the trajectory of his pistol up towards Chace's head.

"Although I guess it's a little too late for that, huh?"

I watched Chace and Chen lock eyes, and then a mortal look passed between them. It was the merciless exchange between a killer and his next victim. Then Chen fired.

Chapter 11

ZADE DAVIDSON

Castille, New York - October 14, 2013

At the same instant that Chen squeezed the trigger and the clap of his gunshot pierced the afternoon, a dark brown shape streaked in from nowhere, slamming into Chen's outstretched hand. Although the sound sent the worst chill humanly possible jolting through my spine, Chen's arm swung wildly to the side and his bullet zipped a few feet wide of Chace's flesh.

The force of the impact against his arm sent Chen's gun spinning out of his grasp and splashing into the leaves a few feet away, but before any of us could react the brown shape was streaking in once more. With an attacking screech it slammed into Chen's cheek this time, knocking his sunglasses off of his face and sending him spinning.

I was utterly stunned, and I stood there and watched the same brown owl that had been blocking our path a few minutes earlier rise into the sky, circling around for another plunge. At the sight of movement in front of me I looked hastily back down at Chen and saw that he had recovered from the owl's blow, and with an athletic two steps he got within range and dove for his gun. Before he could land on it however he was beaten by the owl again, as it swooped in front of him and grabbed the pistol in its talons. As it elevated back up overhead it shrieked wildly and tossed the pistol so far into the woods that it was absolutely unretrievable.

"Now's our chance!" I bellowed suddenly, grabbing Chace by the arm.

I tried to pull him with me as I turned to take off down The Path, but he was rooted to the spot like an anchor.

"Come on!" I shouted again, jerking him, but then I looked from his gaping, horrific expression to where his eyes were fixated.

I looked behind me to see Chen Lake's body give one violent shiver, and then literally explode. In an instantaneous and mortifying eruption of flesh and bone, Chen's body burst through his suit jacket and dress pants, and in less than one second it expanded and contorted into that of an enormous grizzly bear.

There was literally no time for my brain to even begin to process what kind of insane sorcery had just happened; The Chen-grizzly immediately reared onto its hind legs and let loose a bloodcurdling roar that shook me to the soul. It shook its massive head in rage and then thundered back down to the ground, eyeing Chace and I with deadly intent.

It was a fact that we could never outrun Chen now, but we both turned to run anyway, and just as we did so the owl came to our rescue a final time, suddenly flashing in with its talons outstretched. There was another terrifying roar from the grizzly as the owl's talons gouged its eyes, and the last thing I saw before Chace and I bolted was the grizzly missing the owl with an enraged swipe.

Without even considering looking back we took off at a full sprint into the woods, and our feet pounded the pavement with the sole focus of creating as much separation between Chen and ourselves as possible.

"Through here!"

With a burst of determination I pulled Chace off of the Path about a hundred yards in, cutting sharply off into the woods and hopefully off of an easy trail for Chen. The shrubs and branches were thick away from the pavement, but we scrambled through the concealing foliage as fast as we could.

We did our best not to let the sharp sting of branches and leaves slicing at us slow our pace, because we both knew that they were nothing compared to the injuries that a raging grizzly bear would inflict. Even though we had no idea where we were going, where we were going and where we ended up were unimportant items compared to the need to escape.

Adrenaline pushed my lungs far past what I thought they would have been capable of, but eventually I caved to the burn when we burst out of a dense copse of trees and into a tiny clearing. We both bent over double, winded and lost, and after more than two minutes when I finally caught my breath, I straightened to see a ten meter clearing populated by brown knee-high grass. It had the feeling of a little haven, but I knew we couldn't stay stationary too long.

"Which way do we go?" I asked.

Chace returned to the upright position and looked around himself.

"I don't know," he said honestly, shrugging.

"We're in the middle of the woods."

He looked around and shook his head.

"Dude, this is crazy. What have you gotten us into? Do you realize that we just watched a human being transform into a grizzly bear?" he asked in disbelief.

I nodded in response, unable to dispute what we'd seen.

"That was the craziest thing I've ever seen," I agreed wholeheartedly.

Chace looked thoughtful for a moment, but then his expression slowly changed into a accusing smirk.

"Chen said that you're a shapeshifter.,. you really *can* turn into a Siberian tiger? How is that possible?" he demanded.

His tone was a mixture of incredulity and amazement, but I could only shrug. I'd already told him everything I knew in his basement on Saturday.

"I don't know how it's possible... you tell me!" I answered him.

"*You're* the biology genius!".

Chace snorted.

"Yeah, but *you* almost got me killed back there! You didn't tell me Chen Lake was after you because you were a shapeshifter," Chace exclaimed.

I threw up my hands helplessly.

"I didn't know that was why he was after me either, but I'm sorry," I said sincerely. .

I had absolutely no explanation for anything that had happened in the last few days, but the danger I'd put Chace in weighed me down with guilt nonetheless.

"I really am sorry. Now you see why I demanded that you stop helping me," I reiterated a second later.

I shook my head in both confusion and heartfelt apology. Chace sighed and shook his head as well, but I could tell by his manner that he had already forgiven me.

"I'm here now," he said simply, and then he grabbed my arm curiously.

"Do you realize that I would be dead if it wasn't for that psychotic owl?" he asked in disbelief.

His voice was thick with the impact of realization, but we had about one second to ponder that outrageous truth.

"Psychotic?!"

Chace and I both jumped back in horror as a voice materialized from behind us, but when I saw who it was my horror evolved into shock and confusion. Looking at us from beneath a brown, hooded robe was not Chen Lake or some other hostile, but rather our biology teacher Mr. Stevens. His unmistakable golden irises were almost glowing from underneath the shadow of his hood, and he approached us as if he expected to see us.

"What in the world is Mr. Stevens doing here?" Chace whispered to me, taking a step back.

Although I wasn't afraid of him, I took a step back as well. Mr. Stevens however strode directly past us without slowing, and in the glimpse I got of his face I saw his jaw set and his eyes fixated on the other side of the clearing.

"Well don't just stand there," he said gruffly as he passed us.

Chace and I did just that however, too stunned to move.

"If you want to see the sun tomorrow you'll get in gear," he barked, and then he disappeared into the trees on the other side of the clearing.

Considering the fact that Chace and I were absolutely lost – and the fact that Mr. Stevens had offered us a chance to see the sun tomorrow – we immediately struck out after him. We had to run to catch up with his slicing pace, but his purposeful movements at least made it appear that he knew where was going.

"We have a better chance against him than a grizzly bear," I whispered to Chace as we hustled through the woods after him.

From ahead I could almost swear I heard a tiny chuckle, but Mr. Stevens hadn't slowed and there was no way he could have heard me.

"He could be just as dangerous. Who knew that Chen Lake was a grizzly bear?" Chace countered in an even quieter whisper.

I shook my head, unable to answer but also unable to provide an alternative. Mr. Stevens' presence in the middle of the woods was nearly as disconcerting as Chen's transformation, but at least Mr. Stevens hadn't tried to kill us yet.

After a few minutes of speed-walking through thick forestry I began to wonder where he taking us, because if anything the greenery was getting thicker and more difficult to navigate as we went. However, with Mr. Stevens still fifteen yards ahead of us, I could do nothing but hope that he was leading us back towards civilization.

With adrenaline still powering me ahead I found that my limbs weren't quite as tired as I would have thought, but they were still in bad shape. After almost an hour of plunging through undisturbed thickets they had been pillaged by branches, thorns, and tree bark. Although it was mostly obscured by the green and orange leaves of early fall, the sky was darkening overhead as well, and I began to worry if following Mr. Stevens had been the right choice.

He led us onward like a man possessed, and Chace and I grunted and grimaced and tried to keep up with him until we were both bleeding. I was exhausted and in a pretty good deal of pain by the time my wish for civilization was *somewhat* granted. Mr. Stevens finally led us out of the woods only to come upon a deep ditch leading up to the side of a thin, winding road.

He was already a few yards down the road when Chace and emerged behind him, and there was no time to catch our breath as he struck out towards an old-looking Toyota Camry parked to our left. As we followed him towards it we could see that the car had clearly seen better days. It sported chipped red paint and a number of dents, and its hubcap-less tires straddled the slope of the woods and the road roughly.

"Off by a few yards," I heard Mr. Stevens mutter to himself as he unlocked the car doors.

The pungent odor of cigarette smoke billowed out from the inside of the car as soon as I opened the passenger door, and it surrounded me as I closed myself in. I heard Chace cough as he sat down behind me.

"Are we being followed?" I asked, unable to contain my fearful curiosity.

"Of course we're being followed," Mr. Stevens answered plainly, starting the car.

It came to life after a few rickety coughs.

"Chen's following our scent right now. I'd guess we've got about 35 seconds until he catches up to us here."

I shot a horrified look back at Chace, who gave me a similar look in return. Mr. Stevens, despite his earlier revelation, casually tilted a pack of Marlboro Red's in my direction.

"Cigarette?"

"No thanks," I said quickly, shaking my head.

"You?" Mr. Stevens asked, tilting the cigarettes towards the back.

"No," Chace declined from behind us just as quickly.

Time was ticking, but Mr. Stevens shrugged and popped a cigarette between his lips. He peered into his foggy rearview mirror and waited a final instant, and then he finally pulled speedily onto the road.

"Smoking won't do *us* any harm," he said, looking at me specifically.

He blew a gust of smoke into the growing cloud that began to fill the inside of the car. His emphasis on the word *us* was blatant, but I didn't know what he meant.

"Yes it will," I assured him.

He laughed aloud and turned his attention back towards the road, taking a long drag from his cigarette as he did so.

He's a biology teacher... he knows better than all of us that cigarette smoke is harmful, I thought suspiciously as he exhaled into the car.

"Do you mind if *I* roll down *my* window?" Chace asked emphatically after a few minutes of the smoke thickening.

Mr. Stevens nodded, and I took the opportunity to roll down my own window as well, which was unfortunately a difficult, cranking manual. I was still however thankful that some of the suffocating smoke wafted out once I had successfully done so. Chace was not so lucky. His window crank was stuck, and when he shifted to the seat behind mine he found that the crank was gone completely.

He opened his mouth to say something, but Mr. Stevens met him with a knowing flash of his eye. He had sucked his first cigarette to the filter by then, but he quickly lit another one. Chace sat up behind me and shook his head, while Mr. Stevens whipped us through the woods at the maximum speed of our jalopy.

The Castille woods were notoriously deep and secluded, and it soon felt like we had zoomed around an endless number of turns without passing another car. We passed only one other turn, yet the further we went, the louder the cacophony of squeals and clunks our car emitted.

"Where are we going?" I asked finally.

"To my house," Mr. Stevens answered directly.

He had finally finished his fourth cigarette and appeared to be satisfied.

"Is it safe there?" I continued.

Mr. Stevens shook his head but took a second to phrase his answer.

"Well... not anymore. Now that Chen knows I've helped you there *is* no place safe."

His tone was darkly smug and highly discomforting.

"Wonderful," Chace muttered sarcastically from the backseat.

His voice was accompanied by a frustrated sigh, and neither of us bothered to ask how he'd known Chen Lake.

"I don't see why you'd take us from one unsafe place to another but that's just me," Chace muttered darkly.

For all of Chace's positives, he had a tendency to become quite edgy when he felt dethroned, and Mr. Stevens quipped back at him instantly and icily.

"My house is the safest place for any of us to go right now, but if you would like to go someplace else then you are welcome to do that," Mr. Stevens said.

His voice was totally calm and he was in complete control, which was rare for Chace. I knew Chace to be quite antagonistic in this situation, but before I could turn to keep Chace from challenging Mr. Stevens, he was doing just that.

"How do we know that you aren't leading us into a trap?" he questioned.

Mr. Stevens met Chace's eyes fiercely in the rearview mirror. I watched helplessly from the passenger seat as they stared each other down.

"You think like a survivor Mr. Redman, but if I intended to kill you I could have done so ten times by now," Mr. Stevens said.

His voice was still as calm as if they were discussing homework.

"Against my better judgment I have actually decided to help you, but you are both welcome to be Martin's next victims if you'd like. I'm sure a Shifthunter like Chen Lake will be quite giddy if I leave you to your own devices."

There was a few seconds of silence as we considered Mr. Stevens' words, and then Chace and I questioned him at the same time.

"What's a *Shifthunter*? Who is *Martin*?" we asked respectively.

Mr. Stevens' eyes never left the road, but his voice turned grave as he answered.

"I will explain more about this later, but in short, Martin Evers is the enemy of every shapeshifter on Earth. Shifthunters are his personal army of shapeshifter assassins, and Chen Lake is one of Martin Evers' Shifthunter Elite – his favorite Shifthunter's and by far the most physically dangerous people on Planet Earth. Chen Lake is probably more evil and viperous than any man either of you have ever seen."

Mr. Stevens looked at me with a surprisingly pitiful look.

"Sadly, Chen Lake is only a minion to a far greater evil. Martin Evers is the embodiment of evil, and his power sometimes seems truly infinite."

Chace and I looked at each other and fell silent for good this time. It sounded crazy, but we were struck by what we had just heard. Mr. Stevens' little exposition on 'shapeshifters' had been as serious and passionate as his lectures on biology, except far more dire. As he continued driving through the woods, my mind kept returning to the incomprehensible memory of Chen Lake exploding into a giant grizzly bear.

My imagination ran wild with the terrifying possibilities of more people like him, but even then I couldn't shake *that* specific vision. It kept replaying and replaying until a long time later when the sound of tires switching from pavement to gravel finally caught my attention.

We had abruptly veered down a barely visible cutaway, which was just barely wide enough for our car to drive down. I hadn't seen a sign or anything demarking its entrance, and the narrow road was so inconspicuous that even someone who was specifically looking for it would most likely miss it completely. As we went down it, both car mirrors were no more than a foot from brushing against the low wall of bushes that grew at the edge of the surrounding trees.

After a few moments the tight road cut to the left, and we came into a gravel clearing dominated by an odd-looking house. It was nestled into the woods like an egg in a bird's nest, and it instantly reminded me of a medieval cottage. The house's low wooden roof sat atop gray stone walls, over which crawled a multitude of vines and shrubbery. They were only trimmed around three large, drape-less windows and a single wooden door in the middle of the house.

"This place looks like something out of a fantasy novel," Chace commented with a slight air of amazement as we pulled up to it.

"I feel like no one would even know this place existed," I said, agreeing.

"No one else *does* know it exists," Mr. Stevens confirmed eerily.

Chace and I exchanged looks as he put the car in park, but Mr. Stevens then turned to face us instead of getting out.

"Hopefully the fact that no one knows about this place will be enough to keep you two from walking into Chen Lake's hands again. Last Friday I watched you, Zade, shift right under Chen's nose and kill his attack dogs. You shifted right in front of another shifter! You essentially signed your own death warrant, and then today when I tried to warn you two not to walk out of the woods, Chace threw a stick at me and walked right up to him!"

Mr. Stevens' voice held back no consternation as Chace and I confirmed that the owl who had saved us in the woods was actually our biology teacher.

"I... I don't know what's going on," I admitted.

"Clearly!" Mr. Stevens erupted, looking exasperated.

"That morphing thing you do, it's called being a shapeshifter. Obviously you've been hiding this ability for a while, but you should know that although your ability is infinitely rare, it means that you are more cursed than the blackest treasures of the ocean.

Every other shapeshifter you meet, and even some normal people, will be actively trying to kill you. You can't even fathom how lucky you are that *I* was the first one to find you, because otherwise you two would be long dead. From here on out you would do best to trust no one."

Mr. Stevens' voice was harsh and deathly serious, and I looked back at Chace, whose return look confirmed that no matter, we at least trusted each other. I swallowed hard, trying to understand the fact that Mr. Stevens and I were 'shapeshifters.'

"I can't even control this morphing thing I do. I don't know -"

"We'll talk about that later," Mr. Stevens interrupted.

"But you can trust me for now. However, a shapeshifter's life is the only thing he has. There may be a time that not only will I leave you to die, but if necessary kill you myself."

Chapter 12

MARTIN EVERS

Belize Rainforest - October 14, 2013

As I plunged through the thickness of deep mud, one thought seemed as stuck in the forefront of my mind as the mud was to my shoes: I hated the Central American Rainforest. I hated that the sun here was bright, and that the woods here were alive with noise. I hated the hot weather and the sticky humidity to the point that I was sure that this was my least favorite place on Earth. Totally unlike the wonderfully freezing and lifeless Arctic that I had visited in April, or even the dead, dry heat of a place like the African plains, lush greenery and watery muck were the common themes here.

My clean-pressed business suit was covered in muddy water from the waist down, and my inconvenience was compounded by the fact that the insect-laden air was one of the chief nuisances I could imagine. Mud was caked to my Omega timepiece, but it mattered little as I plunged determinedly forward. I was far more concerned by the onset of the incessant buzzing of an endless supply of flies and mosquitoes. The thick cloud of bugs around my head was so irritating that it almost forced me to shift into the Wendigo.

Despite these ungodly conditions however, suffrage such as this was miniscule compared to my need to succeed in my ultimate mission. In one way or another it could be said that I had spent every waking minute of the last 220 years exterminating shapeshifters, and although many of my subordinates described my determination as madness and obsession, in reality those were probably fitting terms. Not a soul on Earth knew the true danger of failure as well as I did, and I would stop at nothing to keep the abominable shapeshifter mutation from festering.

Earlier today, after a boring few months of meetings, coordination, and managing the political aspects of the Shifthunter operation, I had been dropped by helicopter into this boiling tropic to investigate a highly intriguing issue. Sebastian Niles, who was my best tracker and one of the most dangerous creatures on planet Earth, had discovered something that even *he* was in awe of.

He had described what he'd encountered as an anaconda or a python… except that he had estimated it to be seventy feet long and thick enough to eat a full-grown bear. No natural anaconda could ever grow *that* large, and although ignorant, normal humans would write those dimensions off as pure fantasy, I knew better. Extraordinary measurements such as those were the tell-tale signs of a shapeshifter.

By my count it was now the sixth hour that we'd spent following this particular snake through the swamp, and along with Sebastian and a grunt named Ferris, we had fanned out into a triangle and patiently herded the beast towards a roiling riverbank. Sebastian and Ferris had actually been tracking the thing by helicopter for four days now waiting for rainfall, and after yesterday's downpour I had arrived at the perfect time. The river would be too full and turbulent for a beast of his size to cross it, leaving the behemoth with no choice but to face us once we trapped it at the river.

Currently we were all chasing it on the ground, and in my position at the forward point of our triangle I was the closest to the snake. For the last hour or so I had gotten close enough to hear it slithering just out of sight ahead of me. As I followed its trail, the broken tree trunks and wide divots that marked its passage told me that Sebastian's estimates were not far off.

This excited me, especially because the layout of the trees ahead of me was finally thinning. The river was near at hand, and as I raced tirelessly through the mud, the low rumbling of the tumultuous water soon joined the sound of the snake's slither and signaled the climax of our chase.

The louder the rumbling grew, the more vigor I poured into hounding after our prey, and I burst out of the trees and onto the slick, muddy riverbank almost before I was expecting to. My ears were instantly filled with the subtle roar of the angry water, and as I came to an abrupt halt at the edge of the trees I surveyed its depths, satisfied that the hardest part was over.

As I looked down the long, muddy embankment to my right, I saw a large black dog, which was really more like a mangy mutt to be truthful, emerging from the woods about thirty yards away. It was Ferris, and I nodded in grudging approval as I saw him. He was a pet of Sebastian's, and although he had good tracking skills and a hunger for killing, he was weak and gluttonous as a human.

I turned to the left then and saw Sebastian appear another thirty yards away, lumbering like the powerful man he was. He crashed out of the underbrush shirtless and grinning broadly, and like all of my Shifthunter Elite, he was in literally inhumanly good shape. His chest was high and protruding, and his arms were like steel pipes. Standing 6'6 and with speed like a deer, chasing after a snake on foot was even less of a workout for him than it was for me.

"Wait 'til you see it!" he shouted excitedly over the sound of the river, trudging through the mud towards me.

He pointed towards the roiling water at the edge of the river near where I was standing. The fast-moving water left the surface cloudy and opaque; I could see nothing. I wondered how long it would take the basilisk to realize that it couldn't cross, because not only was the river two hundred feet wide at this juncture, it was also moving at a speed that would drown anything but fish.

Fortunately, I didn't wonder long. What started as a brief ripple in the water quickly became a dark, streamlined shape, and as soon as the shape took form it multiplied exponentially in size and came slowly out of the water. As it rose up in front of me I felt the first jolts of genuine surprise that I had felt in half a century.

The snake before me was a monstrosity, and its scaly black-green body was every inch of sixty feet long. It was as thick as a tree trunk, and as it raised its massive serpentine head to its full height, I took a step back and cinched all remnants of surprise in favor of readiness.

Without backing down an inch I looked up at the towering anaconda and matched its beady yellow stare, while further down the river I could hear Sebastian laughing aloud as the snake hovered over me. On the other side of me I heard a low, aggressive growl from Ferris.

Before the tension built any further I calmly held out my hand for Ferris to stay back, and with my other hand I calmly motioned for peace from the snake as well. As dangerous as my predicament was, I knew that I could shift into the Wendigo and kill this creature in less than fifteen seconds. I had not a droplet of fear in my blood as I stood there. Instead, I allowed myself a tiny chuckle of disbelief.

I had documents on every Rogue shifter and Shifthunter alive and dead, and after thoroughly scouring those records last night I confirmed with my own eyes that this beast didn't match the profile of anyone in my files. Judging from the beast's easy recognition of my human signals, it wasn't a natural anaconda either. Before me was a true gem of the Earth: a moldable young creature of such fantastical proportions that even *I* was impressed.

From its enormous yet sleek body to its triangular head, it stood large enough to kill a man no matter what type of armament he carried. Beneath his reptilian smile, two sharp fangs peeked out and glistened like razors, and as I took a second to admire him, I knew that with the proper training a creature like this had the dimensions to challenge even Sebastian.

"So can I shoot it?!"

On cue, Sebastian's gruff, eager voice ruptured my thoughts. He had inched closer to where the snake and I were facing off and was now in point-blank range. His tranquilizer pistol was aimed at our prey with keen intent, but I raised my hand for him to wait also.

"Not yet," I said, keeping my eyes on the snake.

With my hand still outstretched I held Sebastian at bay and focused my total attention on the anaconda, trying to see the shapeshifter human that lied beneath this leviathan exterior.

"You're trapped," I said aloud, addressing it plainly.

I motioned towards my two companions, showing it that it was outnumbered. This was the final opportunity to surrender.

"Get ready," I instructed Sebastian.

From the corner of my eye I saw him itching at the trigger; loaded in the chamber of his gun was a tranquilizer dart filled with Shifter Serum, which would cause this creature to return to its human form if it refused to do so willingly. The snake didn't budge however, and it continued matching my gaze while neither attacking nor downshifting.

"Last chance," I coaxed, holding up three fingers.

As if to mock me, the serpent flicked out its long forked tongue and remained motionless, and I put down one of my fingers. A second passed and I put another finger down and I prepared to let Sebastian shoot. As much as I wanted to see this shifter bow to me, I would force coercion if it didn't want to do so willingly.

Unsurprisingly, just as I prepared to relinquish Sebastian's anxious trigger finger, it happened. In an instantaneous blend of scales and flesh, the giant snake convulsed and shrunk, and at the same time limbs exploded from its sides such that it was replaced by a dark, tan-skinned boy of no more than four feet tall or eight years old. His eyes burned bright green above his brown, rounded cheeks, and the soft fingers of innocence had yet to let go of his face. For the second time today I was genuinely impressed.

This shapeshifter here was a mere child, and from the looks of it he had stumbled upon his wretched powers as unexpectedly as we all do. For him to be showing such exquisite control over his shift with me and my men right here... well that told me that he could indeed be one of the finer pieces of organic clay I'd ever mold.

However the boy was still currently just that, and in response to his return to human form he looked genuinely horrified. I was a strange, white-haired white man who had just coaxed him out of some giant snake body he could have been stuck inside of for weeks, and the activities of such a beast during that time period would have undoubtedly been carnal. The poor boy could do nothing but eye me up for a minute and stand in place completely naked before weakly sinking to his knees and sobbing.

"Well, what do ya know?" Sebastian asked curiously, lowering his pistol.

He scratched a patch of his long beard and stood there looking at the sobbing boy with an almost dumbfounded expression on his face.

"Very surprising indeed," a silky voice agreed from my other side.

I turned and saw that the voice came from Ferris, who had downshifted and now stood next to me in his gangly, tattooed human body. He gave me a deferential nod.

"We're bringing him straight to the Warehouse then, boss?" Ferris asked.

His voice belied the reverence and apprehensiveness of a Shifthunter not used to dealing with me directly. It was a welcome reprieve from the pompous attitudes of the likes of Roslyn and Sebastian.

"Yes, get ready to signal in the helicopter," I answered him, turning back towards Sebastian.

He was still looking at the sobbing boy in the mud with the same befuddled expression.

"Ferris needs the receiver," I said, and Sebastian tossed the backpack that he was carrying to Ferris without taking his eyes off of the boy.

"Are you sure we shouldn't just kill him? He's a lil' young don't ya think?" Sebastian inquired as Ferris struggled to catch the backpack.

Sebastian shook his long blonde hair as he did habitually and scratched his head again. For all of his wonderful physical gifts, he wasn't the brightest bulb in the box.

"*All* of the shapeshifters we catch are this young, you idiot. We judge them on the power of their shift and their potential usefulness to our mission, not their age. If you would use that cooked lump of flesh inside of your skull, you might remember that this is just how I found *you*," I reminded him.

Sebastian looked hurt, yet even when he took a second to think my words over he didn't seem to understand the connection.

"This boy is no Sebastian," he boasted, laughing.

"I was only crying when you captured me because you'd gashed a hole across my chest. I had that scar for twenty years! He's sobbing for no reason. I had already killed four men by the time I was his age."

A proudly evil gleam flashed across Sebastian's eye, and I couldn't help but smirk a tiny bit at knowing that this boast was at least true. I had found Sebastian before the invention of Shifter Serum, and although he had only been eight years old at the time, he was so feral that I'd fought him myself to subdue him.

"We will find out whether or not he is the next Sebastian soon enough," I countered in concluding, and I advanced towards the boy to size him up better myself.

The kid stifled his crying slightly and lifted his head at the sound of my boots squishing through the mud towards him. As he looked up at me, his youthful green eyes were surrounded by eyelids that were red and puffy from despair.

"Tell me your name," I ordered, staring down at him coldly.

Despite his pitiful state there was an admirable bit of defiance in his eyes, and he said nothing.

"Tell me your name," I ordered again.

I inflected my voice with the command and threat that I posed, because from now on this boy's life was in my hands. Accordingly, the boy only paused for a last renegade moment before begrudgingly forcing the words out of his mouth.

"Brian Sann… Yo soy Brian Sann," he answered, exposing a thick Latin accent.

His voice was light and childish, and I made a mental note to have Roslyn teach him English immediately. Although almost all of my Shifthunter Elite were multilingual, and Roslyn knew Spanish better than any of us.

"Nice to meet you, Brian Sann. My name is Martin Evers," I said in a less intimidating tone, introducing myself in Spanish.

He looked up at me with an expression of surprise, but I didn't reach out to shake his hand or help him up. Instead I beckoned for him to rise, because it was already time to begin tempering him for his new life as a Shifthunter in training.

"Tell Manuel to drop the lines," I said, turning quickly towards Ferris.

He already had donned his set of clothes from the backpack, and he held the receiver ready in his head.

"Right away," he said.

His voice oozed with the urgency of someone whose life depended on it, and another tingle of satisfaction passed over me.

Chapter 13

ZADE DAVIDSON

Castille, New York - October 14, 2013

he kitchen area of Mr. Stevens' house was lit by a single bare light bulb hanging over the table. Once Mr. Stevens had unlocked the doors to his car, Chace and I had been ushered back into this room with rushed informality, and we now sat waiting for Mr. Stevens. He had dashed out of the house 'to scout the area,' and had not given us an idea of when he would return. There was no doubt he had seemed frazzled by the idea of having guests, and I could tell that our presence was interrupting a well-developed routine.

Chace and I were still stricken, but Mr. Stevens' sudden disappearance had at least left us ample to time to examine the kitchen he had left us in, which besides the crude light bulb and unpainted walls was actually rather modernized. In one corner there was a pricey Viking refrigerator, and on top of the counters there was a stack of clean silverware and a matching stack of expensive cutlery. Even the sink was overlarge and of some name-brand variety.

Besides the expensive accoutrements however the room was largely empty, and Mr. Stevens had hurriedly produced a chair for Chace from another room before he left while I had taken the only seat that had been at the small end table. Still somewhat numb from our escape , Chace and I sat next to each other at that end table in silence for over an hour until Mr. Stevens came back into the house. He drew back the hood of his strange brown robe and greeted us with a look of mild relief, but his demeanor quickly shifted into curiosity once he settled against the counter across from us.

"The good news is that Chen Lake's hunt is off of our trail for now," he reported breathily, almost secondhand.

"But the real question is for you, Zade. When exactly was your first shift?"

His urgency caught me off guard, and I repeated the question subconsciously.

"My first shift?" I asked.

"Yes," Mr. Stevens affirmed with an impatient air.

"When was the first time you transformed into a Siberian tiger?"

"Friday," I answered plainly.

Mr. Stevens blinked and paused for a second. There was an extended, awkward silence, and I realized that he was stunned by my answer.

"And you're really seventeen in normal, human years?" he asked eventually.

I nodded slowly, unsure of Mr. Stevens' point. His expression of disbelief confused me and he paused again to think.

What in the world is he getting at? I thought to myself.

"Is there something wrong?" I asked finally.

"I'm baffled," he began after another delay.

"This is the first time I've ever heard of a shapeshifter having their first shift at age seventeen. Assuming you know nothing about what you have become, you should know that you have already outlived 95 percent of your species because of how late your shifting abilities manifested themselves."

I stared at Mr. Stevens with what I felt was an appropriately incredulous expression.

"Most shapeshifters die by age thirteen or fourteen at the absolute oldest," Mr. Stevens continued, expounding.

"If they haven't been killed or captured by Martin Evers by that time, they would have to be one of the most resourceful people on the planet."

Mr. Stevens narrowed his eyes, examining me like a specimen. Against his fiery, golden-eyed glare I felt as flimsy and see-through as transparency paper.

"The first time you shifted was really less than a week ago?" he asked again, his voice serious but his face doubtful.

"The first time I did it was Friday. Honestly," I answered.

I was glad I was telling the truth, because for a good second Mr. Stevens' eyes probed mine with such ferocity that it would have been impossible to lie.

"You're a totally novice shifter," Mr. Stevens said slowly, half to himself.

"At least that adds up with your prior foolishness. I couldn't understand how you were so reckless, and then with the size of your shift I didn't understand how you weren't working for Martin. There was no way someone your age could've survived this long with your habits, Shifting right under the nose of Chen Lake was as dangerous a move as I have ever seen."

"I couldn't control that," I said in self-defense, wondering just *how* I had escaped with my life.

"Of course you couldn't control it!" Mr. Stevens retorted, snorting.

"No one can control their first shift. The problem with you is that your first shift is supposed to occur at a much younger age - ten or eleven years old at the latest. Shifting significantly slows down aging, so by the time your human body looks like it does now you would be 30 to 35 years old."

He looked me up and down.

"I'm not sure if this is a good thing or a bad thing," he said pensively.

"Although your human body is weak compared to any other shifter with your body-age, you're in the prime of your youth and therefore highly improvable."

Mr. Stevens frowned a little and I thought for a second that he was complimenting me, but then he quickly denied that.

"The issue here is that you're dreadfully behind in your development as a shifter. Time is not on our side in terms of training you to avoid our predators, and right now you're nothing more than prey," he said.

Mr. Stevens looked from me to Chace uncertainly.

"It was truly only for my own burning curiosity that I decided to help you, but now that I've done that I think there's a decent chance you'll at least survive another week," he said with a voice that *almost* sounded optimistic.

To me, his projection was ludicrous.

Survive longer than a WEEK? I had always hoped to live for at least 50 more YEARS.

"What do you mean survive another week? How long exactly do you think I have to live ?" I asked both seriously and indignantly.

Mr. Stevens responded with an ambiguous shrug.

"It depends on how long it takes Chen Lake to find us here. I'll spare you an exact estimate, but I will not deceive you into believing that there is an escape. There is nowhere to run and nowhere else to hide, and they *are* coming for you."

His tone was so resigning that the truth in his words was undeniable. Mr. Stevens' grave look made my heart feel like a giant cannonball in my chest, and with great difficulty I blinked back sudden tears of anger and disbelief.

"They're just going to kill me? Are they just going to shoot me or are they going to capture me first?" I questioned thickly.

Through my clouding vision I saw Mr. Stevens give me a slightly apologetic look.

"Shapeshifting is an offense punishable by a variety of means, but the most common of those is unfortunately death. If you *are* going to survive for any length of time you are first going to have to accept that your normal life is over. It cannot and will not ever be what it was before you shifted."

I let Mr. Stevens' words soak in for a harsh moment. There was truth written all over his face, and his words sounded eerily similar to Chen Lake's. I didn't want to accept it, but the majestic power of transforming into a Siberian tiger – the coolest experience of my life – was really the signature of a death sentence.

"Three hours ago you were my biology teacher! How do you know I'm a shapeshifter? How do you know about all of this?" I asked in desperation.

"One question at a time," Mr. Stevens answered, fielding my attack calmly.

"How do you know even know that I'm a shapeshifter? Chen Lake was the one I shifted in front of, not you," I said.

Mr. Stevens smirked.

"I was there... in owl form, of course. I was doing my daily surveillance of Mr. Lake's outpost, and I saw every moment of your harrowing escape. If I hadn't shifted back into human form and tranquillized you, I guess you would've run on in tiger form for quite a while and gotten killed by morning. At first I thought you might've been trying to come after me, but since you obviously didn't work for Martin I didn't kill you. It turns out I did you quite the favor."

I knew I should thank him, but I was so surprised by his revelation that I stared at him for a second, open-mouthed. Chace looked between us as understanding dawned on him.

"I guess I owe you another thanks," I said sheepishly after a moment.

Mr. Stevens merely shook his head and said nothing. I silently marveled at the rare wonders of chance and fate, and for a few moments we sat in our own thoughts. Today had now had quickly stolen the record from last Friday as the craziest day of my life, and everything that had happened between now and then was replaying over and over in my mind.

"It's already 10 o'clock," Chace said at some point, and I looked up to see Chace looking down at his cell phone.

When Mr. Stevens did the same, he nearly exploded.

"What in the world do you think you're doing?" he burst.

"Give me that! Do you want to get use all killed?"

Mr. Stevens looked enraged and reached for the phone, but Chace held it away from him.

"Whoa, whoa. They have the GPS technology and intuition to track us? I don't even see how they would know who I am but I'll just take the SIM card out," he said.

Chace quickly removed the SIM card with a paper clip from his pocket, and although Mr. Stevens gave him a scathing look, he stepped back.

"If either of you want to make it to the end of this week then you'll need to be fast learners," he lectured.

"The first rule you'll need to live by is that you should never underestimate Martin Evers. Phones, laptops, tablets... anything with internet capability can be used to track you. Always be aware, because every single one of his men literally *live* to track shapeshifters," Mr. Stevens said.

Chace and I both nodded in understanding, but after such an inexplicable day we were both overwhelmed and exhausted. It added an even more daunting element against our chances of survival, but surprisingly Mr. Stevens' demeanor quickly switched from blunt to hospitable.

"We've got an early morning tomorrow," he said, stretching swiftly.

"Survival and a sharp mind go hand in hand, and a sharp mind and rest go hand in hand as well. Therefore survival and rest go hand in hand, and we've got a lot of work to do tomorrow to keep you idiots alive," he said.

He immediately started moving towards the doorway from the kitchen back out into the hallway.

"I've never had guests before, but I'll see what I can do for a place to lay. Follow me," he ordered.

Chace and I robotically followed him into the dark hallway. I was starting to feel more tired by the moment, drained from the emotional and physical toll today had taken on my body.

"Do you have lights?" Chace asked as we followed Mr. Stevens past the small cone of light thrown from the kitchen bulb.

He chuckled and headed through a doorway to the right without turning on a light, and Chace and I followed his dark shape into one of the two rooms I had seen on the way in. I was ahead, and I almost fell down the small step into the room when Mr. Stevens finally clicked on a small lamp.

"I forget that normal people need light. I can't remember the last time I turned on the lights in here," he said.

I didn't doubt him. The dim light spilled onto a room that looked more like a storehouse than anything else. Besides a small, cleared rectangle of hardwood floor in the center, the room was clogged with an assortment of artifacts. A gigantic book shelf along the back wall overflowed with an absurd number of books. Glass cases full of gems, gold pieces, and textiles were everywhere. A big, expensive grandfather clock that was clearly long out of service collected dust in one corner of the room; shelves lined with curious vials and scientific instruments did so in the other.

I was quite sure we had walked into an unorganized museum, and everything just spilled relentlessly inwards from the walls. Even the walking space in the middle was encroached by a few stray books, the legs of a telescope, and some more similarly odd-looking objects. Chace, who was suddenly in total awe, whispered a few choice words as he stepped into the room behind me. With his eyes wide he made his way towards the small, cluttered table near the doorway, apparently unable to contain himself.

"This is Egyptian gold," he said, picking up a huge gold coin off of the top of a small stack of papers.

Mr. Stevens snorted and nodded, watching Chace as curiously as I was. Chace put down the coin and reached quickly to his left to pick up a peculiar, flat object.

"A Black Mayan Jade Celt?" he asked in bewilderment.

A *what?* I thought, but Mr. Stevens nodded again as Chace weighed it in his hand with something close to glee.

"This is unbelievable," Chace said, giving me a joyful look.

He proceeded around the room like a kid in a candy store, and Mr. Stevens and I watched him pick up various objects and shake his head again and again in repeated amazement. It was probably three or four minutes before he looked up towards Mr. Stevens.

"Where did you get all of this stuff?" he asked finally.

He was holding what looked like a medieval weapon, shaped like some sort of hatchet.

"To be honest those are just things I've collected over the years. It's amazing how much stuff you collect in a couple hundred years of life," Mr. Stevens answered casually.

He didn't seem to register the looks of confusion on our faces.

"I'm not sure if I heard you right, but did you say you've been alive for a hundred years?" Chace questioned, looking very confused.

"A *couple* hundred years, actually. 307 years, 4 months, and 3 days to be exact," Mr. Stevens corrected.

Even though what he had just told us was clearly impossible, I tried to calculate the math in my head.

"You were born in 1803?" Chace asked incredulously.

He had calculated the date almost instantly, and I piggybacked.

"Wait, you couldn't believe I was seventeen and you're telling me that you were born in 1803?" I accused.

Mr. Stevens nodded in his simple, signature way.

"Yes. Shapeshifters age quite slower than humans, and according to my research they can live for up to 500 years naturally. I'm only halfway there," he said.

He gave Chace an affirmative look, and Chace scoffed in response.

"You can't possibly expect us to believe that," he said, looking over at me.

Mr. Stevens' demeanor immediately turned chafing.

"Actually, no, because thanks to Martin Evers no shifter has ever lived that long. But regardless of what you two believe, you would both do well to remember that what you believe does not change the truth. I know more about more than anyone on the entire planet. You can imagine then how I do not appreciate being questioned," he warned.

Chace and I recoiled but he motioned towards the small empty space on the floor without hostility.

"I don't have any pillows or mattresses but this is where you can sleep," he said.

"I suggest you do so immediately, because if you are not adequately prepared to run from Martin's Shifthunters in the next two or three days, you will both soon be dead."

His voice was finalizing, and with that he nodded and left the room. The soft-sole boots he wore underneath his brown robes made no sound as he disappeared across the hallway, leaving Chace and I alone.

Chace abruptly sat down in the middle of our allotted space, taking up a good portion of it with his long legs. He looked around at the myriad of rarities scattered around the room and then closed his eyes and hung his head. He sighed heavily, and I could feel the shock and despair emanating from him. An enormous mountain of guilt settled on my shoulders as I watched him, but I had no idea what to say. I just stood awkwardly a few feet away, fighting against the self-hatred that I felt at getting him into this situation.

"I know we've got a lot to talk about but I'm pretty tired. Let's game-plan tomorrow," Chace said after a few minutes, his voice barely a whisper.

He was still sitting upright in the middle of the floor with his eyes closed, but I felt so awkward that I nodded anyway before realizing that he couldn't see me with his eyes closed.

"OK," I said back.

I eased down to the floor in the little bit of space opposite him and reclined uncomfortably against the hard edge of a wooden table. I closed my eyes too, but as tired as I was I found it hard to sleep. The sharp edge of the table cutting into the back of my head was an all-too-effective reminder of how long it might be before I saw my own bed again; playing against the backdrop of my eyelids were nightmarish visions of Chen Lake and his ominous threats.

I felt like in the span of a few hours my life had been turned inside out. The fact that my parents had no idea where I was ate at me, but it seemed insignificant compared to my need to figure out a way to keep Chace and I alive. *This* was a different kind of stress, and I wasn't prepared for it in the slightest. In spite of my powers, for the first time ever I prayed that I would wake up as normal, boring, Zade Davidson.

————

"Zade!"

"Zade!"

Apparently I'd finally managed to fall asleep, because the unwelcomed hiss of a voice sliced through my slumber. Someone was shaking my shoulder, trying to wake me up.

"Zade!" the voice hissed again.

How could it be morning already?

I didn't even remember falling asleep. There was a stabbing pain in the back of my head, and even as I hoped against hope that I had missed my alarm and the voice would be my mom waking me up for school, I opened my eyes to a chilly room that was far from my own.

"I'm awake," I groaned.

I peeled myself off of the hardwood wearily and saw Chace squatting next to me, his eyes bright despite the early hour.

"What time is it?" I muttered sleepily.

"7:45," he whispered.

There was a sense of urgency in his voice that I didn't understand.

"What's the problem?" I asked, rubbing the sleep out of the corners of my eyes.

"Look where we are," he hissed, motioning around the room.

Memories from yesterday began to filter in as I looked to my left and saw a row of human skulls.

"Mr. Stevens' house," I replied groggily, not yet seeing the point.

"Right," Chace answered.

"We have no idea where this is, and that puts us at a great disadvantage. If we were forced to run from here, we'd be totally lost. I woke up about 20 minutes ago and tried to do some thinking now that I'm rested. If anything Mr. Stevens said is true, Chen Lake could be here any minute with an army of shapeshifters, and we don't even know which way to run."

I nodded, but there seemed to be no immediate solution to that issue. I rubbed the sleep out of my eyes and yawned. I hadn't slept nearly enough yet.

"Well, what can we do?" I asked, seeking the root of this early wakeup.

"I don't know yet," Chace said, thoroughly disappointing me.

"But I do know that Mr. Stevens is not likely to save us from the Chen-grizzly again. We can't just count on him. We've got to come up with something of our own."

I rubbed my head, slightly perturbed that he'd woken me up early just to brainstorm. I didn't doubt Mr. Stevens in the slightest when he said that today was going to be a long day.

"I guess you're right," I said, sighing and then trying to shake myself awake.

"Do you have an idea?" I asked.

"If Mr. Stevens can teach you to use your shift, then yes I have an idea," Chace said.

There was a surprising seriousness in his tone.

"You still believe I can shapeshift?" I asked doubtfully.

Chace gave me a hard look.

"It would surely help," he said.

"GOOODDD MORNING!"

Just then Mr. Stevens suddenly appeared in the doorway behind Chace and greeted us vivaciously, startling us both half to death. He was wearing another one of those odd brown robes he'd worn when I saw him in the woods, and I could only tell the difference because the one yesterday had had a slight tear in the front.

"You can't just walk up on people like that!" Chace barked, whirling around.

His back had been to the doorway and he was caught totally unaware, and he gave Mr. Stevens an apprehending look. He looked genuinely offended.

"Always watch your back. Shifthunters will greet you much ruder," Mr. Stevens said.

He looked and sounded wide awake, and his voice was full of that casual dominance that made it impossible to challenge him.

"It's time to eat. I've made us breakfast," he added, drill-sergeant style.

There was no time to thank him, before either of us could open our mouths to do so he was heading back towards the kitchen. With a deep sigh apiece, Chace and I peeled ourselves off of the hardwood floor and followed him. The breakfast set out on the table was an unsurprisingly bland and meager meal of toast and apples... one apiece to be exact. It did little to appease my ravenous appetite, but I wolfed it down without complaining.

Chace and I were still fully dressed from the day before, and immediately after we had finished our skimp breakfasts Mr. Stevens ordered us out the front door, around the side of his house, and into the woods that served as his backyard. It was still torturously early in the morning, and Chace was accordingly skeptical and resistant, but I urged him to cooperate as we followed Mr. Stevens through a makeshift path behind his house and into a small clearing in the woods. The grass there was soft and plentiful, but with it being so early in the morning my shoes became instantly soaked by the hundreds of drops of dew that leapt from the grass. By the time Mr. Stevens stopped us in the middle of the clearing, my actual feet were damp.

"First things first," Mr. Stevens said, turning to face us.

He immediately shifted his attention distinctly towards me.

"What do you remember about your first shift?" he asked bluntly.

I thought back to the terrifying memory of running from Chen Lake's dogs, and then being gripped with the sudden and uncontrollable explosion of my organs. I thought about the vicious feeling of deadliness that followed, and the euphoria of tearing Chen's dogs to shreds. There was nothing I could compare to running through the woods in control of the most powerful body I could imagine.

"I remember running from Chen's dogs, and then all of a sudden I exploded. I obviously didn't expect it, and I truly had no control over it at all," I answered honestly.

"Once I shifted, the body took over. It was like watching a movie almost, because the tiger was like its own being. It wanted to protect itself, and I was pretty helpless to stop it even if I'd wanted to."

Mr. Stevens nodded, but he was still looking somewhat amazed.

"I know I've already talked about this, but the fact that your first shift happened just in time to save your life may be the most lucky, miraculous event I have ever heard of or witnessed in my entire 300 years of life. Even though the first shift is usually triggered by adrenaline, the fact that it also came when you were 17 years old makes the odds like one in five hundred billion or something. I've never heard of anything like it. The first shift is probably the most perilous moment of a shifters' life, and it certainly spells nothing but death afterwards. It is singularly amazing that your first shift actually *saved* your life."

Mr. Stevens couldn't suppress a little smirk this time, and I could tell that something about my random, uncontrolled shift appalled him. I felt a pang of pride on the inside, but I also knew that nearly all of it had nothing to do with me. Apparently this experience was still the end of my life.

"It's a good thing that Chen Lake didn't know you were a shapeshifter when you were inside of his lair," Chace pointed out then, looking at me.

"His grizzly bear form is the scariest thing I've ever seen in real life. Knowing that he actually hunts shapeshifters makes your escape pretty amazing," he said.

Mr. Stevens agreed, adding to Chace's observation.

"That is very true as well; fortunately for you the shifter hormone is undetectable until a shifter activates it during his first shift. Otherwise Chen or one of his men would have detected your scent immediately, and he probably would have likely killed all four of you before you even got to his building on Fordham Street."

Mr. Stevens' voice was as stoic as ever, and it started to dawn on me that his gloomy forecasts might really be an earnest effort to prepare me for what to expect in the future.

"From now on out you'll need a lot of scent-masking agents to stay out of the range of Shifthunters," he cautioned, and I suddenly remembered the thick cologne Mr. Stevens had always worn to school.

The same had been true of Chen Lake, and I now understood why it had been necessary.

"Normal humans can't detect the smell though, can they?" Chace asked.

His question was posed to Mr. Stevens, but he was looking at me with a tiny smirk and an expression that told me he already knew the answer to his question.

"No, normal humans can't smell the Shifter's Scent at all. The shifter hormone is merely an enzyme, but when it activates it also gives shapeshifters the ability to detect it. It's still not even a powerful scent, because as a human a shifter would have to be in the same room as the person to smell the Shifter's Scent on them," he said.

Chace nodded, and I could see that his analytical mind was soaking Mr. Stevens' knowledge up like a sponge. I wondered if it was just as hard for him to believe that this was real as it was for me. I rubbed a hand across my forehead and tried to process it all while Mr. Stevens turned towards Chace and pointed back towards the narrow gap in the trees where we had entered the clearing.

"In the trunk of my car is my silver briefcase. Bring that to me," he ordered.

Mr. Stevens produced a set of keys from his pants pocket and extended them towards Chace, who's naturally dominant nature caused him to hesitate before he took them. I could tell that he was rubbed the wrong way by Mr. Stevens' dismissive attitude, but with only a quick, bitter glance in my direction, Chace took the keys and obediently headed into the woods. As he walked away Mr. Stevens turned back towards me.

"Now, back to you," he said, commanding my full attention.

"How many times have you shifted since Friday?" he asked.

Although I was hesitant to admit that I'd tried to shift and failed in Chace's backyard, Mr. Stevens' face was hard to lie to.

"None... I couldn't do it," I admitted bleakly.

Mr. Stevens narrowed his eyes and looked surprisingly unsurprised.

"Why not?" he asked, staring at me intently.

I thought back to my embarrassing attempt and shrugged dejectedly.

"I don't know. I tried to imagine myself as a tiger, I guess. When I shifted the first time it felt like my whole body was exploding from the inside out so I just tried to think that into existence," I explained.

Mr. Stevens considered my answer for a second and then nodded knowingly.

"A common mistake," he assured me, clasping his hands in front of him.

"To put it briefly, you're focusing on the wrong thing. Shapeshifting isn't about becoming something else, it's about becoming another part of who you are. You can't just 'try' to become a Siberian tiger and all of a sudden do it. No one can do that. You *are* a Siberian tiger. The shapeshifter hormone has been lying dormant inside of your body since you were born, and as much as you had no control over being born, you had no control over eventually shapeshifting into a tiger. Although your first shift has occurred at a later age than I've ever seen before, a part of you that has always existed has now come to life. Once you understand that you are not just Zade Davidson the human, the actual act of shapeshifting will be as easy as flexing a muscle."

Although Mr. Stevens spoke with confidence, I still struggled to absorb his words. My memories from Friday notwithstanding, it was hard to imagine myself as more than the human Zade Davidson when I looked down and saw the same hands I'd always possessed. Chace appeared again through the trees then also, and I could see the protest in his body language as he walked over and handed Mr. Stevens his briefcase. Mr. Stevens accepted it without thanks and set it down at his feet.

"Now, we don't have all day to get this right," he said, continuing to ignore Chace and focus on me.

"You may have been taught by human scientists that shapeshifting is impossible, but in order for us to proceed you are going to have to throw those conventions out of the window. All you've got to do is *believe* you are a tiger, and you'll become one."

Like always, Mr. Stevens looked me straight in the eyes, and I took a moment to conceptualize the idea of my human body truly being able to transform into the body of a tiger. Even though I had supposedly experienced it once already it was still too awesome to really accept. A lump of nervousness quickly settled in my throat; I usually crumbled under pressure faster than a Styrofoam cup, and I felt the pressure building under Mr. Stevens' expectant stare.

"OK," I said lamely, and I swallowed thickly while Mr. Stevens continued his instruction.

"Concentrate on controlling yourself," he said, finally seeming to register my rising anxiety.

"The number one reason shifters die is because they cannot control their shift," he advised.

He tried to keep his tone encouraging, but there wasn't much he could do to sugarcoat that.

"Do most shifters never learn to control their shift then?" I asked uneasily, taking a deep breath.

"Well, remember, most shifters only shift once in their lives," Mr. Stevens answered darkly.

"The euphoria of a new body usually causes them to run off into the wilderness and forget that they were ever even human. The ones who do manage to downshift usually do so at tragic times, and they unwittingly return to human form when they are either underground, in midair, in the middle of the desert..."

I shuddered as he dismally trailed off, horrified by the idea of coming to my senses either trapped in a tunnel or plunging towards the ground. Mr. Stevens however started to back away towards the tree-line, pulling Chace with him.

"Once you do it once or twice you'll see that there's not much to the actual shifting part of things," he said as he backed away.

When Chace didn't move at first, Mr. Stevens gave him a stern recommendation.

"You'll want to stand by the edge. Even though he's your best friend, when Zade is a Siberian you'll look more like a meal than a friend," he warned.

I couldn't imagine attacking Chace no matter what body I was in, but at the same time I knew that my first shifting experience was more like a psychopathic hallucination than anything else. Even though Chace looked unafraid, I truly had no idea what I was capable of if I did manage to shift.

"*You* stand in the center," Mr. Stevens called out to me when he had positioned Chace and himself by the trees.

He pointed slightly behind where I was currently standing, and I took a couple steps back into the exact middle of the meadow, where the glimpses of cold morning sun were the brightest. The clearing wasn't a very big space, but I guessed there was now at least twenty yards between myself and my two companions standing at the edge.

As I stood there I watched Mr. Stevens drop his briefcase gently to the ground, and when he straightened I saw that he had taken out a small pistol. Clenched between his teeth he held a small dart as well, and he deftly took the dart from between his teeth and loaded the gun before looking up at me.

"This is Shifter Serum, which is the same invaluable fluid that I used on you last Friday," he said.

"It doesn't normally have sedative effects, but on Friday I'd mixed it with tranquilizer to make sure you wouldn't attack me once you downshifted. If I have to use it today, the inhibitors in the serum will just force you to downshift after a few seconds," he avouched.

As he tapped the side of the gun to ensure the fluidity of the serum, I eyed the weapon warily nonetheless.

"I won't shoot you unless it's absolutely necessary," Mr. Stevens assured me, stepping a few yards towards me and away from the edge of the trees.

"You can shift whenever you're ready," he said.

With his tranquilizer gun held readily I was even more anxious than before, but I closed my eyes in an attempt to calm my nerves. Despite the cold I felt my palms sweating profusely as I tried to block out all thoughts but one.

Focus Zade, you are a Siberian tiger.

I repeated the phrase over and over in my mind, trying to drill it into my brain. I forced myself to believe that the tiger body I had assumed on Friday was just as much a part of me as my own human one, and I could feel my hands clenching into fists as I concentrated and willed myself to transform.

"Breathe slowly, relax!" I heard Mr. Stevens' voice call.

Relax, I repeated to myself.

I pictured the elegant, striped face of a tiger in my mind and focused on it, mentally envisioning every detail from the deep, feline eyes to the vibrant fur and sharp whiskers.

Relax, I repeated again.

I consciously relaxed myself, taking long, deep breaths until I could feel my heart rate slowing and my hands unclenching.

I am a Siberian tiger, I thought with renewed clarity and certainty.

I am a Siberian tiger!

I accepted that as fact as plainly and simply as I could, and at that moment I felt every single bone in my body suddenly explode. In a bizarre flash of semi-consciousness I was only briefly aware of the painless-yet-grotesque sensation of my entire body expanding and restructuring, and then in a timeless instant I was hurtled back into a drastically altered reality.

An awesome rush of senses came crashing over me like a tidal wave, and every sensation suddenly erupted into high-definition detail. The forest instantly came alive with sights and sounds I'd never even dreamt of perceiving, and all at once I could hear a squirrel scampering up a tree to my left at the same time that I heard another rodent dart away behind me. As a startled flock of birds rose into the sky to my right, I was able to pick out each individual bird as it flapped across the break in the trees above me.

When I looked forward again I saw that Chace and Mr. Stevens had also transformed into unique blends of smell, taste, and visual detail, and even from where I stood I could now clearly read the Tommy Hilfiger insignia on Chace's belt and the time on Mr. Stevens' generic wristwatch. From my new vantage point my two companions suddenly looked small... like two supple lumps of human flesh.

Chapter 14

ZADE DAVIDSON

Castille, New York – October 15, 2013

With a deep, fearsome rumble, I let loose a growl that would give even the toughest man a chilling shiver. For me, there was no stopping the savage desires of the Siberian tiger; the human part of my mind that still recognized Chace and Mr. Stevens was absolutely powerless. The only dilemma I could hope to influence was which of the two humans I would attack first.

Oddly enough, the first thing that my tiger instincts and my human ones ever agreed upon was just that. To the interests of my ravenous tiger body, Mr. Stevens was the rounder and slower-looking target, and to my human side he was far more expendable than Chace. Although I truly didn't want to attack either of them, I felt my lips peel back over my teeth and a low growl come out of my throat.

"Stop!" Mr. Stevens shouted, leveling his tranquilizer at me.

He gave off that distinct, pungent smell that I now knew was the scent of a shapeshifter, and through the haze of my bloodlust I saw that his amber eyes were cold and ready to shoot behind the barrel of his gun.

I willed my body to stop but instead I coiled and crept menacingly towards him; in the presence of humans my natural solitary tiger instincts felt threatened. Before I could even hope to stop myself I ferociously leapt the last ten yards towards him in one effortless pounce, claws extended, and with similarly impressive speed Mr. Stevens and Chace dove out of the way.

I landed where Mr. Stevens had been a moment before – empty-handed – and then I whirled around to find him moving away from me and back into the open area of the clearing. His evasion enraged me even more, and I growled viciously and sped towards him again.

"Control yourself Zade!" Mr. Stevens roared, but his words meant nothing to me.

In less than one second I closed the distance between us and launched myself at him a second time, and although Mr. Stevens ducked away once more this time I was faster. A few of the nails of my massive paw nicked his arm, sending him spinning to the ground and the tranquilizer gun flying across the clearing into the grass.

I heard him groan loudly and spin away, but I was already turning and readying for another pounce. Somehow he was already getting to his feet by the time I was able to ready myself, but now I was between him and his only weapon. When he met my eyes I saw that his eyes had become fiery with anger at my display, and through his ripped robe I could see three fresh lacerations glowing on his right forearm.

"You will surely die if this is as good as you can do," he spat.

I heard him, but I couldn't stop myself from taking a threatening step towards him. My rage was sapping my human intellect and using it as fuel, and not even my thoughts were my own.

He insults you… yet without the Shifter serum he is helpless against you, I thought unwillingly.

I growled again in a low, murderous rumble.

"Your mind is weak," Mr. Stevens responded viciously, but he was backing away.

His voice was laden with disappointment, yet his scathing words continued to deflect off of me like water droplets against duck feathers. Somehow the tiger's instincts seemed even more powerful and dominating than they had been during my first shift. I was behind the controls of a giant, powerful machine, but none of the buttons would respond. It was *my* body, but it was possessed with an irresistible desire to kill.

Relax, I told myself.

I focused on Mr. Stevens' instructions despite the fact that I felt myself take another step towards him. With great difficulty, I tried to stop fighting the tiger's urges and instead embrace them as my own. Although the raw urge to kill was overwhelming and unnatural, I forced my mind to accept that I was now beset by the needs of a completely new being, and that just like human emotions, these desires needed to be massaged into control.

These men are not threats, I repeated to my own self, continuing to relax.

I could feel my breaths getting deeper, and as I relaxed some of the controls on my body came to life. Only a few yards from pinning Mr. Stevens against the far side of the trees I stopped advancing on him, and cautiously at first, I stretched my brain out into my heavily muscled limbs. I made a conscious effort to remain calm despite the giddy feeling that was building up within me, because I knew that both mine and Mr. Stevens' life likely depended on my self-control now.

Nonetheless, as I felt out every muscle, fiber, and tuft of fur, I was overwhelmed by the awesomeness of it. It was nearly euphoric when I was merely able to gently control my tail and drop it into a low and passive position. I imagined that it felt like being slowly cured from paralysis, and I stood there and tuned in to the thousands of sounds my ears could discern and let the myriad of new smells waft through my nostrils. It was an outrageously wonderful sensation, but I forced myself not to slip into nirvana.

Even though I could sense a bird in the trees thirty yards to the left, see a tempting groundhog only fifteen yards ahead in the woods, *and* smell Chace's Axe deodorant on the other side of the clearing behind me, I *had* to control myself. My brain was being fed a whole new uber-stream of data, and I had to make a concerted, conscious effort to streamline the information and not act impulsively. I was a human being inside of a Siberian Tiger body, and it was truly the most intense experience imaginable.

I was in control – finally – and I suddenly found it as easy as if I were in my human body to close my lips around my bared teeth and relax from my tensed crouch. With the same ease I reduced my killer glare into a passive gaze, and Mr. Stevens' eyes lit up in approval.

"Well done," he said, not attempting to hide his surprise.

He stepped towards me, patting me on the head.

"I was afraid I would have to use *this*," he said, producing a long, curved knife from a fold of his robe.

It was small and thin, but I could see a dark substance on the tip. Mr. Stevens let out a relieved breath and re-sheathed the blade. He walked around me in an inspecting circle then, patting my hips and sides like I was a lab specimen. He felt so small next to me now, and with all of this power coursing through my veins I suddenly felt intensely proud. Mr. Stevens seemed to be in awe of each dimension he inspected, and judging by my size relative to him, I was huge.

"You can downshift now," Mr. Stevens said when he appeared in front of me again.

His eyes looked bright and *almost* even approving, and with my shift firmly under my control my confidence was almost boundless. With a flex of my brain I fixated my mind on Zade Davidson, and I downshifted as easily as I moved muscles. After a flashing semi-consciousness and the twisting and reshaping of my organs, one second later I stood a few feet away from Mr. Stevens in my human body, completely naked.

From there, it took about five seconds for my euphoria to dissipate into the fog, and with a sudden return to reality I covered myself embarrassedly as the icy air fell over me. Behind me, I heard the sound of shoes squishing through the wet grass, and I turned to see Chace trying to hide an obviously uncontainable grin as he jogged over to us. When he stopped next to us he tried to give me a serious look, but a mocking smirk pushed its way through.

"I thought you were going to kill him," he said.

His eyes glowed with a three-way mixture of awe, disbelief, and elation.

"I thought so too," I admitted, covering my exposed areas with one hand and rubbing my frozen body with the other.

Chace and Mr. Stevens both laughed as I moved my legs incessantly, trying to conserve body warmth.

"Shut up - I'm the one who's out here naked!" I barked.

I was literally freezing my butt off... literally. Castille cold was a force to be reckoned with in these months, and somehow Mr. Stevens still walked away and left me to freeze until he returned a few seconds later with a few scraps of cloth and his tranquilizer gun.

"Here are your clothes," he said, showing me a piece of cloth.

The scrap he showed us was too small to even cover a poodle. All three of us laughed this time.

"I should have had you strip down first, because unfortunately that's not all you destroyed," he chided a few seconds after we recovered from our laughter.

He held out his ruined tranquilizer gun so that I could see it; the gun lay brokenly in his hands with the dart hopelessly lodged in the chamber and the barrel bent. I apologized sincerely, but Mr. Stevens gave a mild shrug.

"At least you've learned a lesson in controlling your shift. I have more tranquilizer guns," he said, and then he shook his head and dropped the broken weapon back into the front pocket of his hooded robe.

"In the meantime we'll get you into some clothes," he said, and after picking up his briefcase he led us back towards the house.

I was glad my control of my shift had put Mr. Stevens in a somewhat pleasant mood, because an hour later I was fully clothed and sitting with Chace in Mr. Stevens' kitchen, waiting for the latter to return with food. He had left us to check on the status of Chen Lake's search team and teach Biology class at Castille High, and we had implored him to bring us McDonalds following those activities. We were both starved, and after a great deal of necessary begging he had actually finally agreed.

Now that he was gone however, Chace and I finally had time to sit and think, and the full impact of the last 24 hours was becoming brutally clear. Besides our struggle to survive, our hearts were heavy with the knowledge that our parents were undoubtedly in some state of hyper-panic, and that we had no way of contacting them to let them know we were at least presently still alive.

We had discussed Mr. Stevens' prognostications for our survival, and neither of us wanted to admit that there was he could be right. I couldn't deny the truth though, and Mr/ Stevens had limited motivation to scare me unnecessarily. My life was most definitely in danger, and anxiety threatened to ruin any sense of my rational thinking. Contrarily of course, Chace's stubborn, analytical brain refused to rest in a state of defeat.

"How can they find us? They've got nothing to go on," he was saying meditatively, mostly to himself.

"My car is all the way in Montgomery Hills. I'm sure our parents have reported us missing, but I don't see what evidence the police could have found in the vicinity of my car besides Chen's shredded suit," he added, now talking to me.

"We're a long way from there," I said, nodding and shrugging.

"Do you think we should run?" I asked after a few minutes of thoughtful silence.

I figured it was the idea that Chace was considering, but he shook his head at my suggestion.

"I want to," he admitted, looking around at the small space of Mr. Stevens' kitchen warily.

"But I don't think we will last long if we do. Even if the shapeshifters don't get us I have no idea where we are and I have no cell service. It seems like there is a good chance we could just get lost in the woods and die anyway, especially because the way Mr. Stevens describes it we're in the middle of nowhere."

"So…." I trailed off, but Chace shrugged too.

"We trust Mr. Stevens," he said unconvincingly.

I said nothing, knowing that we had no choice. I felt sickeningly guilty that my parents didn't even know if we were alive, and I tried not to think about the agonized state of panic that was undoubtedly permeating my house right now.

"We've got to tell our parents *something*," I said eventually.

I had been trying to figure out how to contact them but had coming up with nothing, and to no surprise Chace gave me an exhausted look.

"Yeah, duh, but how would you propose we contact them?" he posed.

His tone was matter-of-fact rather than antagonizing, and he was right. For all intents and purposes we were completely cut off from the rest of the world.

"At least we're still alive," he said, looking introspective.

His somber look brought back the memory of how close he had come to dying yesterday, and it was closely followed by another thunder clap of guilt on my heavy conscience.

"You shouldn't even be here," I reminded him regretfully.

He narrowed his eyebrows, and in his eternal loyalty he gave me a doubtful look.

"We're best friends. You would be here for me," he contended flatly.

His trademark stubbornness was painted in his eyes. Chace was as loyal a friend as it seemed possible to be, and truly I could do nothing to change the fact that he *was* indeed here.

"Thanks, but its tough knowing that you're risking your life because Chen Lake wants to kill *me*," I said defeatedly.

Chace snorted.

"If it wasn't for Mr. Stevens swooping in at the last instant Chen Lake would've already killed me," he countered again.

"You're not going to survive without me, and I'm not leaving you here whether you want me to or not," he said, ending it.

I sighed and gave up, because as much as I didn't want him risking his life for me, a selfish part of me needed his company and was grateful that he was here.

After a few hours Mr. Stevens returned with the McDonalds, and to our pleasure he had followed our requests perfectly. Like vultures, Chace and I descended upon the red and white paper bags, ravenously consuming multiple value meals apiece. I washed down a final cheeseburger with the remnants of a tall glass of water and looked over at Chace, who was patting his freshly full stomach. He burped loudly.

"Thanks," he said, smiling appreciatively at Mr. Stevens.

"Yeah... thanks," I agreed.

Mr. Stevens gave a little nod.

"I'm glad you're full because there is no time to rest," he said, his eyes glowing readily.

It amazed me how his energy defied his age... and not just because he should have been in a coffin a century ago. Chace and I both sighed.

"I return with unfortunate news," he began solemnly, motioning for us to stay seated.

"As expected, Chen Lake knows that I've helped you. His Fordham Street stronghold had mobilized accordingly, and although his men haven't yet figured out that I'm employed at Castille High, they will figure that out in a matter of days. Once that happens we must run," he said.

Mr. Stevens' voice belied a controlled urgency as he switched his attention specifically towards Chace.

"I know you're athleticism has served you well thus far in life, but I don't know how much it will help against experienced shapeshifters like the ones we'll be running from," he cautioned.

"Before you decide to continue with us, you have the right to know that you are even less likely to survive than Zade. If it comes in the way of hunting shifters, Martin Evers' men don't regard normal human life very highly."

"I agree, it's not worth -" before I could finish piggybacking Chace shot me one of the most vicious looks he'd ever given me and I stopped short. He was rigid with resolution and looked sincerely offended.

"I'm staying," he said simply.

He looked Mr. Stevens straight in the eye, and our teacher answered him with a mildly surprised downturn of his lips. I wondered if Chace would ever know how grateful I was for his friendship at that moment.

"Fair enough," Mr. Stevens acquiesced.

"At the very least you can serve as Zade's brain," he said, shooting me a look of disdain.

Mr. Stevens looked ready to launch into another lecture, but Chace interrupted him with a question.

"So now that Zade has controlled his shift, what else can we do to survive?" he asked.

Mr. Stevens looked thoughtful for a minute then smirked.

"The best strategy would be to dodge the endless barrage of bullets, blades, and claws that are about to come your way," he advised sarcastically.

"You'll also want to hold on to any firearms you can get your hands on, and stay especially far away from shapeshifters of all kinds," he added a little more seriously.

Chace snorted and smirked now.

"Well at least that shouldn't be too hard. I've avoided them my whole life until yesterday," he said.

"Right, and if people don't even know that they exist there can't be that many of them, right?" I agreed.

Mr. Stevens pursed his lips and shook his head.

"Well no, statistically speaking there are not that many shapeshifters currently living," he began slowly.

"But if Martin Evers had never existed there's no telling how many there'd be. Because of his worldwide genocide however, there are only 350 or so shifters alive at any one time, and essentially all of them are Shifthunters. The extreme rarity of being a shapeshifter keeps us from being common no matter, but naturally we can live for half a millennium. Most of the Shifthunters alive are very old and very experienced by human standards, and as Rogues you will find it much more difficult to avoid them now that they are actively searching for you."

Chace and I both sighed at the end of Mr. Stevens' lengthy answer, and then ironically asked the same question at the same time.

"What are Rogues?" we asked concurrently.

"Well you're not technically a 'Rogue,' Chace, but a Rogue Shifter is any shapeshifter who is somehow eluding Martin Evers. Including us, there are less than six of them in the world," he said.

Chace and I both soundlessly mouthed the word:

"Oh."

"Well, how does shapeshifting *actually* even occur?" Chace asked then, changing topics.

"You're a biology teacher and even after watching it live – twice now actually – it seems physically and biologically impossible."

At first I was surprised when Mr. Stevens' eyes brightened at the question, but then I quickly remembered he and Chace's like affinity for the sciences. I cringed when he subsequently expounded into a brief exposition about the biological processes behind shapeshifting.

"Since it happens in the blink of an eye, it's been difficult to absolutely confirm my theories, but based on a few slow-motion recordings I've made it seems that shapeshifting is basically an instantaneous breakdown and reconstruction of your body. The hormone that causes shapeshifting causes your body to spontaneously multiply, shrink, or alter all of its physical parts until it has taken on an entirely different form. Basically it's exactly what you see when it happens: it takes the organs, bones, and tissues of a human being and reassembles them into the body of whatever other creature you 'shift' into," he explained.

Mr. Stevens looked pensive and intrigued, and I suddenly wondered how Mr. Stevens was ever able to coordinate a recording of shapeshifters transforming if he had always avoided them. However, he had been buoyed by Chace's attentiveness and continued on before I could interrupt.

"Interestingly enough, the human brain itself never reconstructs and instead just grows or shrinks to fit the natural skull size of a person's shift. This phenomenon seems to have no effect on cognition except that the human mind seems to be infused with the natural instincts of the other creature. The intensity of certain instincts in certain creatures is what can make the new body very difficult to control. Perfect examples are the territorial killing urges of the African Lion or Zade's shift, which are extremely hard to suppress."

I perked up at the mention of my shift, and Chace nodded in comprehensive amazement.

"What about creatures without brains?" he pressed.

"Have there been shifters who become jellyfish or worms?"

"No," Mr. Stevens replied, shaking his head.

"The only creatures I've ever seen shifters become are vertebrates, arthropods, or cephalopods. Which, if you've been paying attention in class, all have brains," he answered.

Mr. Stevens looked specifically at me then, and I had to admit that I had no idea what any of those three classes of animals were. Nonetheless, Chace naturally knew exactly what they were and was still bursting with curiousity about this shapeshifter world.

"I don't get it… the shapeshifting power is so awesome. How is Martin Evers able to get so many shapeshifters to willingly kill their own kind?" Chace continued.

"Survival," Mr. Stevens said plainly, this time without hesitation.

"Martin Evers is the most powerful shifter ever to walk planet Earth. In order to globalize his pursuit of exterminating the entire shapeshifter mutation, he hunts down the rarest and most powerful of our kind and gives them an ultimatum: join him or die. If they choose to join him, they are pledging every moment of their waking lives to killing the rest of the shapeshifters in the world. If they choose death, they are choosing the worst death imaginable."

Mr. Stevens' tone was frank and dark, and he sighed solemnly. From all appearances Mr. Stevens was extremely intelligent and resourceful, yet it was clear he viewed Martin Evers like an undefeatable Grim Reaper.

What an ultimatum, I thought to myself as I pondered it.

Not only was Martin killing *all* of the shapeshifters in the world, but he was also collecting the strongest possible couriers to assist him. No matter what Mr. Stevens meant by 'the worst death imaginable,' the idea sent a shiver up my spine.

"What about the police?" Chace countered then, unwilling to accept Mr. Stevens' defeatist assessment.

"What about the FBI? What about the CIA? None of them know shapeshifters exist? I don't understand how this genocide could be going on without *anyone* knowing. Has Martin Evers circumvented the entire U.S. government?"

Chace couldn't hide the incredulity in his voice, but Mr. Stevens merely snorted and then to both of our surprise, burst into a real bout of laughter. Chace looked appalled that his logical counterpoints were being laughed at, but Mr. Stevens' humor was short-lived enough for Chace to remain peaceable.

"I believe the President himself knows that shapeshifters exist, but he is one of less than two dozen normal humans that are privy to that knowledge," Mr. Stevens explained when he gathered himself.

"Almost all of those men are amongst the most powerful and influential on Earth, and although I don't know the details of the treaty between them and Martin, I can assure you that there is no man or government who would willingly stand against Martin's wishes. Martin has decreed that the existence of shapeshifters will remain a secret until they are long extinct, and that will be so. Any normal human who knows that shapeshifters exist is also aware of the death warrant that they would be signing if they were to spread that knowledge."

Mr. Stevens' voice had become increasingly serious as he spoke, and he presently paused, dire gravity painted in his eyes.

"The proper application of fear will drive any man to coercion, and Martin Evers' shift is a beast called the Wendigo. It is the vilest, most terrifying, and ever to grace the face of the planet. There is nothing in the world worth having to face him as the Wendigo."

The certification behind Mr. Stevens' words was hope-sapping, and the grave stare that he gave us eliminated all hope that this was some elaborate fantasy. Martin Evers, and the likelihood of our deaths, was very, very real.

"If he's one of *us*," I began despondently, cringing at the word,

"Why does he hate us? Why would a shapeshifter dedicate his life to killing other shapeshifters?"

Mr. Stevens looked unsure of how to answer for a moment.

"All I can tell you for sure is that Martin Evers' childhood was extremely rough… even by shapeshifter standards. By rough I mean that as a young boy Martin shapeshifted into the Wendigo and massacred his entire village… including his own family," he said.

We all fell silent as the horrific image of coming to your senses to see that you had killed everyone you knew permeated through us. There was no doubt that that *was* a rough way to start your life.

"What is the Wendigo?" I asked, curious but unsure if I wanted to hear the answer.

Mr. Stevens thought for a second and then seemed to flinch involuntarily.

"I cannot describe it except to say that the Wendigo is a being so terrible that I would compare it to your nightmares of a demon from the deepest pits of Hell," he said seriously.

As he apparently thought back on the vision of the Wendigo his face contorted into a look of utter distaste, and I almost shuddered trying to imagine what kind of demon the Wendigo resembled. I looked over at Chace and could tell that he was also imagining something infinitely nightmarish.

"Even considering that, I still don't understand why Martin is so determined to exterminate shapeshifters," Chace complained, still fighting.

"If the Wendigo is so terrible why doesn't Martin Evers just stop shifting into it instead of using it to kill people?" he debated.

"It's not that simple," Mr. Stevens answered, still looking solemn.

I appreciated his patience with our overflow of questions, but I could also tell that he had answered all of these questions many times before. I doubted there was anything we could think to ask him that he hadn't already considered.

"In short, a shapeshifters' shift isn't just an alternate body that is there for their pleasure," Mr. Stevens said.

"It's just as much a part of them as their human body. It would be just as difficult for a shifter to never return to their human body as it would be for them to stop shifting into their other form, and once you shift for the first time if you starve yourself from one form or the other you'll start to crave the other one. If you hold out too long, your subconscious will eventually literally force you to shift. Essentially, Martin Evers has no choice but to shift into the Wendigo."

I hung my head and rubbed my hair in further resignation. My heart was starting to thump faster and harder, and I could feel myself getting a little dizzy. When I realized that my hands were sweating I understood that this sickly feeling was the feeling of terror. Everything I'd heard tonight was fascinating, but it all meant one thing. I was going to die violently and soon.

I wanted to curl up into the fetal position, yet at that moment Mr. Stevens stood up abruptly and patted his kitchen table with a sudden burst of energy.

"Follow me," he commanded.

He moved towards the hallway sprightly and without a backwards glance, and Chace and I exchanged looks of confusion before following him into his small hallway, which was tinted a dim blue by the final remains of daylight. Mr. Stevens led us into his room across the hall this time, which Chace and I had yet to enter, and as we walked in I realized for the first time that there were no doors inside Mr. Stevens' house at all; the three rooms I had noticed were separated by walls only. It gave the small space a curiously open feeling that I hadn't paid any attention to until now.

Unsurprisingly, the room Mr. Stevens led us into was just as odd as the one Chace and I had slept in, and although at first glance it appeared to be Mr. Stevens' bedroom, it was unlike any other bedroom I'd ever seen. Piled onto the two desks at the edges of the room were stacks of neatly folded clothes, and they were arranged into two distinct groups: dress shirts like the type he wore to school, and more of those rugged, hooded robes like he'd worn earlier this morning.

On one desk there were a few more exotic-looking artifacts, and on the other desk there was a significantly high-tech laptop, but it was the object in the direct center of the room that was truly shocking. Literally growing out of the middle of the floor and through the ceiling was the trunk of an enormous tree.

"What in the world is that?" I asked as I gaped at the mammoth tree trunk.

The house itself seemed to be built around the tree. The top of the trees' roots snaked underneath the hardwood floor, and the back side of the slanted ceiling had a hole cut into it to allow the bushy top of the tree to branch out above the house. It was unlike anything I had ever seen.

"How could we not see this from the driveway?" I asked in awe when Mr. Stevens didn't answer my first question.

"You *can*," he answered smartly, moving towards it.

"But, since it's cut into the backside of the roof, from the front of the house it's hard to tell. With all of the other trees behind and around my house, depth perception makes it difficult to see that my house is actually built around one of them."

Mr. Stevens ran his hand along the trunk of the tree with distinct fondness and started to head around behind it. As he got halfway around it he motioned for us to follow him, and when we all got around behind the massive tree we saw a hidden set of wooden stairs diving down into the ground. It was essentially a secret basement cut directly into the floor, and after forcing ourselves to accept the extreme strangeness of this room we followed him down the stairs.

When I got to the earthen basement floor, Mr. Stevens was clicking on a string of bare light bulbs that illuminated what looked like a laboratory. Four stainless steel lab tables were arranged in rows in the middle of the room, all of them burdened by either vials, scientific books, or other experimental objects. Although the air felt cold and sterile, the earthy smell of the underground hit my nostrils instantly.

"This is pretty extensive even for a biology teacher," Chace commented as he came down behind me.

Mr. Stevens didn't respond as he continued to the back wall, and as we moved past one of the long lab tables I noticed a thin film of dust collecting over everything.

"I don't do much research anymore," Mr. Stevens said eventually.

His tone was regretful, and I ran my finger through the dust on one of the tabletops and was surprised by how much dust it collected.

"Why not?" I asked.

Mr. Stevens stopped at a large, brown wooden trunk at the far end of the lab, and he bent down to open it.

"There's not much left to discover. I've done more research than anyone who's ever lived," he answered matter-of-factly.

His voice had that conclusive yet ambiguous tone, and he changed subjects immediately.

"I brought you down here to show you our emergency kit. If Chen Lake discovers us here and we're forced to run prematurely, this is all the firepower we've got," he said.

He undid the black metal clasps on the front of the trunk and opened it, revealing an unexpected arrangement of things. Inside and to the left there were seven or eight handguns, a couple of which looked like the tranquilizer pistol he had brought out earlier. Judging by the stacks of ammunition heaped beneath the guns though, most of them shot real bullets.

On the right side of the trunk there was a white test tube rack full of different colored tranquilizer darts, and beneath that I could see the shape of a brown robe and a folded map. Mr. Stevens pointed to the test tube rack.

"The red feathered darts contain elephant tranquilizer. The green feathered darts are the opposite, containing purely Shifter Serum, which forces you to downshift. The black darts are a mixture, which is what I hit you with last week. I doubt they will be of much use to you though, because both of those toxins lose effectiveness against shifters who've been exposed to them often. Many Shifthunters are immune to both the Serum and the active agents in the tranquilizer."

Mr. Stevens paused to make sure both Chace and I nodded in understanding, and then pointed to the real guns, which I now recognized as silver, standard issue .45 caliber pistols... just like the one I'd seen him with at school. I remembered we'd never discussed that incident, but I decided to hold my curiosity for a more appropriate time... if one ever came. I already knew why he carried it now.

"Feel free to take and use any of these at your own risk, but you'll find it extremely difficult to successfully shoot Shifthunters without a lot of practice," Mr. Stevens advised.

Chace straightened up at the challenge, and I could tell that he took Mr. Stevens' advice as a slight.

"I don't know about that. I've spent my fair share of time at the firing range and I'm a pretty accurate shot," Chace said defensively.

Mr. Stevens looked up from the kit to give Chace a doubtful look, but Chace glared back at him. Mr. Stevens looked ready to take Chace's challenge, but I quickly knifed through the tension with a question for him.

"So I see we that have an emergency kit, but do we have an emergency *plan*?" I asked.

Mr. Stevens diverted his attention towards me, but his reply was dismal.

"Yes, the emergency plan is to grab whatever you can and run for your life," he answered.

His tone was humorous but most definitely serious. Chace and I both snorted and looked at each other hopelessly.

"Come on. I've got more to do today," Mr. Stevens urged us, closing the trunk.

Considering that Mr. Stevens had already basically assured us that we were going to die, neither of us saw the rush and Chace rolled his eyes before standing up straight. I gave him an agreeing look and then we followed Mr. Stevens back upstairs. Once we reached the main floor Mr. Stevens ushered us into our room across the hall and dismissed himself, and then a few minutes later he disappeared out of the front door in a brown robe. It was still early evening, and as the sound of his door shutting behind him rang in our ears, Chace and I now found ourselves confronted with more unwanted free time. Considering that free time at Mr. Stevens' house was just fodder for grim reflection, we sat down in our little room and were duly beset by our own personal whirlwinds of emotion.

The idea that I was going to die wrenched at my stomach like a vice-grip, and the more I dwelled on it or thought of flawed escape plans the more restless and distraught I felt. Eventually I made an effort to numb my mind by rubbing the dust off of an ancient-looking book and opening it, but the crinkly brown pages were full of unintelligible symbols and someone's scratch-notes.

The rage part of despair was kicking in and I wanted to throw the book across the room, but with a sigh of frustration I just closed it and pushed it aside. Chace, having looked over to see what I was reading, immediately reached for it and opened it back up. He pored over a few pages and then smiled at me.

"These are legitimate transcriptions of Aztec symbols," he muttered in amazement.

His eyes were alight with interest when they darted back down to the pages of the large tome, and I peered down at the ancient pages, which were filled with mostly symbols and only a few handwritten notes. It had to have been foreign to 90% of the population, but within seconds Chace was lost in the book, and as I watched him I found myself suddenly wishing that I could have found a passion for reading.

I looked around the room, which was overflowing with all kinds of texts, and knew before I even picked one up that I didn't have the attention span to get lost in a book like Chace did. I swallowed thickly, and with another sigh I sat there with nothing to do but ponder our dire circumstances and hold back the tears.

Chapter 15

ROSLYN VALEZ

Castille, New York — October 16, 2013

$\mathcal{A}$s I stood in a small clearing in the Castille woods, a light gust of wind disturbed the leaves around my ankles and swirled past my cheeks. Although the light from Seraphin's hand lamp illuminated the space well, the cold was making me slightly impatient. I looked at Chen and then back at the three kids he had tied to a tree in front of us; they were a raggedy bunch to say the least.

"Well?" I asked, eager to get out of the cold.

"I think they're lying. What do you think?" Chen returned.

I looked them over again and shrugged, unsure what to make of their story. I could understand why Chen Lake thought that they were lying, because he had been employing these three boys to make routine deliveries around the New York area for the last year or so. Until yesterday he had found them to be reliable, but from the combined accounts of Chen, Seraphin, and Roman, the boys had tried to steal some of Chen's more expensive jewels last Friday by switching the diamond pouches and bringing along a fourth member to run away with the diamonds.

Although the plan had technically failed when the fourth kid dropped the diamonds and escaped into the woods, that kid had shapeshifted into a tiger to do so and had successfully escaped Chen a second time in the Castille woods on Monday. Apparently the infamous *Gordon Stevens* had come to his rescue, yet his three cohorts tied to the tree claimed to have no idea about his powers, who Gordon Stevens was, or where he was hiding.

"I'm not sure why they would keep lying about it now," I admitted after my long moment of thought.

"They all say that they barely know him, yet they also know that we'll kill them if they don't give him up. Unless they are just willing to die for this guy they would have no reason not to tell us where he's hiding," I reasoned.

Chen tilted his hand back and forth, unconvinced, but Seraphin agreed.

"I think Roslyn may be right. When I chased them out into the street these three stuck together and ran to the same place. The other one ran off by himself," Seraphin said.

Seraphin was an able-bodied, middle-aged black man, and he truly was one of my favorite Shifthunters. Although I had no illusions of friendship in this world, Seraphin had been a Shifthunter long before I was born, and he was one of the founding members of Allard's infamous pack of canine shifters. He was a relentless hunter and an expert tracker as a dog, but as a human he was surprisingly passive and always reasonable.

"Should we uncork them and let them speak for themselves one last time then?" I suggested.

Chen nodded grumpily and Seraphin moved over to the boys, pulling the cloth gags from each of their mouths before returning to his place next to me. All three of the boys looked at us with eyes full of desperation as they coughed and gasped for breath.

"So, Seth… *this* is how you repay me for employing you?" Chen questioned, directing his gaze to the kid in the middle.

The boy was average height, pudgy, and wore a plain white T-shirt over his baggy camouflage pants. His eyes bulged with the fear of trapped prey.

"I'm sorry. We were just curious about the big diamonds, that's all. We never intended to steal them –"

"Save it," I said, cutting him off sharply.

His lies seeped through his skin like a vapor and we had gone through a similar routine 30 minutes ago.

Maybe they ARE going to lie their way to death, I thought.

If they can't even tell the truth about the diamonds there's no way they're going to admit any connection with this Rogue shifter.

I looked at the two others to perhaps seek truer answers from them, but the one in the middle was clearly the leader of the incompetent trio. The shorter, fatter one to his left looked ready to pass out from the tightness of his bonds, while the gangly pale one to his right looked too scared to speak.

"I already have my diamonds back," Chen said slowly, clearly seething and pausing after every word.

His voice was scalding.

"I want to know where to find Zade Davidson, and this is your last chance to tell me where he is."

Chen stared Seth down, but Seth only let out a whimper-sob of dismay.

"I don't know, Mr. Lake, I swear! We only brought him along and gave him the diamonds so he could be the scapegoat if things went wrong. We haven't seen him since school on Monday and we had no idea he could morph into a tiger. I don't even know what you're talking about," he wailed.

Tears streamed down his face, and the tall ginger to his right even eeked out a few lachrymose supporting statements of his own.

"Seth is telling you the truth, Mr. Lake. We didn't know the kid until Friday," he said.

Chen said nothing and looked over at the fat kid for a final confirmation, but he couldn't even speak. The rotund high-schooler was already sobbing, and his attempt to respond came out as an indecipherable streak of blubbers. Chen shook his head and turned towards us.

"If you ask me, the kid who shifted even seemed surprised when he turned into a tiger," Seraphin acquiesced, reiterating a sentiment he had made earlier.

Based on his description of the event, he and Roman had chased after the fourth kid until he dropped the backpack and ran into the woods, whereat Roman had stayed behind to check for the diamonds. Seraphin had then shifted and joined with Chen's hunting dogs to chase the kid down, and according to him the boy didn't show signs of the Shifters' Scent until after he'd shifted into a giant Siberian. At that point it had been too late for Chen's dogs, but Seraphin had escaped into the forest and returned to Chen with the report.

Regardless, the three kids in front of us had run the other way and apparently knew nothing of the ordeal, and now it seemed they had nothing useful to tell us. I was eager to cut to the chase.

"Well anyway," I said, holding one hand out towards them, "What are we going to do with *them*?"

Chen looked pensive, but unforgiving.

"Let us go, please," Seth whimpered.

"Well, regardless of whether they are lying about the shifter, they *did* try to steal my diamonds. Would shooting them be unfair?" Chen asked.

The trio let out a wail as I shrugged – I personally figured it was the fairest way to kill them if that was indeed the conclusion.

"For what it's worth, I personally don't think they're lying about the other kid. Are we really going to kill them? They're just human kids," Seraphin said.

I had been wondering the same thing, even though I was still unsure of these kids' intent. Killing humans was not part of our MO as Shifthunters, and if Chen killed them it would undoubtedly have to be cleaned up. Chen apparently agreed.

"Let them go," he said finally with a sigh.

It was a rare moment of mercy from the experienced SE, and the kids breathed a collective and relieved exhale. Still tied to the tree, they began thanking Chen profusely, and it wasn't until after a slightly surprised pause that Seraphin walked over to them and untied them. When they were released they hugged each other with the vigor of new life, almost falling to the ground as they cried and embraced.

"You now have three seconds to run for your lives," Chen added suddenly, tightening his lips.

"Huh?" Seth asked, looking up, but as the kids broke apart in a moment of confusion they wasted all three seconds of opportunity they had.

They were interrupted by the sudden explosion of Chen's body as he shapeshifted upwards into his giant grizzly bear shift, which in one instant took up almost all of the space of the small woodland clearing. Seraphin and I both rolled nimbly out of the way, but Seth and his two cohorts also wasted their final opportunity to run staring at Chen in awe.

"I was surprised when he let them go, but this was not what I expected," Seraphin whispered to me as he recovered and held up the halogen lamp that illuminated us.

He shook his head and chuckled in disbelief as ahead of us the massive Chen-grizzly swiped Seth's two friends to the side – which sent each of them flying into tree trunks – and then pounced on Seth before he could even get out of the clearing. With paws the size of potholes he pinned Seth to the same tree that Seraphin had just loosed him from, and with an earth-shaking roar Chen reared back and viciously chomped down on Seth's head.

Chapter 16

ZADE DAVIDSON

Castille, New York – October 18, 2013

*I*f the word 'boring' could accurately describe how monotonous the second half of Tuesday was, then I could only describe the days between Wednesday and Friday as lifeless. After the wildest four days of my life, the three following mornings were marked by early, groggy breakfasts, and each of them were routinely followed by afternoons that dragged on in dull slowness. The only times of interest were when Mr. Stevens would finally return in the evenings, because he would bring food and expound upon the ever-growing dangers of being a shapeshifter.

'Always be ready to run,' was a phrase and a mantra that Mr. Stevens instilled nightly, and it was one that Chace and I both knew we should take to heart. Mr. Stevens had made it clear that things could come crashing down any day, and accordingly every day once the sun started setting, Chace and I would pray that it would be Mr. Stevens coming through his front door and not Chen Lake.

Wednesday had been totally uneventful, and yesterday had only been interesting when Mr. Stevens had given us an influx of information about the chaos that our absences had caused. The reports were nothing short of what I had expected, and our little town was in a general state of disarray at our disappearance. There were now search teams and regional coverage probing the streets daily.

Even *my* name was in the newspaper, yet as Mr. Stevens had predicted, they were nowhere near finding us in this remote cabin in the woods. The sweeping part of the search was apparently still limited to the general town and woods near Castille, and Mr. Stevens had duly informed us that his house was over thirty miles from the nearest search team.

Unfortunately, he had brought other news that day that was much more disconcerting. In addition to Chace and I's disappearance, Seth, Slippy, and Ace were all dead. On Wednesday night they were found *mauled* to death in the woods near Historic Castille, and while the police had no leads, Mr. Stevens confirmed that it was the work of Chen Lake and that it was in an effort to find me.

As much as I hated the three of them, I had been totally numb for over an hour at the idea that they had died because of me, and it still was gut-wrenching to think about it. It pained me to imagine how Chen must've hunted them down, and how they must have felt when they realized that they were not just dying because of their plot to steal Chen's diamonds, but because *I* was some sort of mutant.

When I had finally been able to form words I was stricken with fear that my parents were in similar danger, but Mr. Stevens had claimed that danger to them was probably not immediate. He had explained that since my parents had been the ones to report me missing to the police, Chen Lake was likely to ignore them during his search. Apparently my parents would pass all background checks and appear very unlikely to know about my shifting abilities, which typically meant that Chen would find them more useful alive as bait than dead.

Of course that news did little to appease my fears, and he had subsequently ensured me that my house was under permanent surveillance by Chen and his men. He had explicitly stated that nothing would likely endanger my parents more than an effort to go home.

For the life of me I couldn't understand how shapeshifters like Chen could be so dedicated to killing their own kind, but with most of my time spent trying to think of a survival plan there wasn't much time to dwell on that. By now Chace and I had run through a full gamut of impractical or otherwise faulty escape ideas, and we'd considered everything from hiding out and building a makeshift underground shelter to trying to follow the blueprint for some primitive vehicle in one of Mr. Stevens' books. None of the ideas seemed more likely to save us than get us killed.

'The Art of Shapeshifting,' as Mr. Stevens called it, was so wild that it sounded like a predicament out of a horror movie. Everywhere I turned, more perils and imminent death awaited me. The man named Martin Evers seemed to have an unbreakable hold on the lives of all shapeshifters, and with the variety and power of his shapeshifter army there was little that could be done to stop him.

The Art of Shapeshifting was essentially running for your life in as resourceful a way as possible, because by the looks of it Martin Evers was more or less an invincible overlord. And, although Mr. Stevens refused to describe it, he was imperviously adamant about the lethal wickedness of the Wendigo.

Over the period of hours-long lectures, Mr. Stevens had tried to give us an arrangement of coaching tips on how to stay out of the grasp of Shifthunters, but much of it seemed beyond our abilities... both physically, mentally, and financially. The hideouts we could create would either need to be manually constructed or bought with large sums of money, and all the weaponry he suggested we procure would have to be stolen... or of course, bought with large sums of money.

At any point of any day we were susceptible to attack or discovery by any manner of creature that could be employed by Martin, from snakes to birds to people passing by on the street, and the scent of my active shapeshifter hormone was now permanently detectable by my kin unless it was heavily masked with cologne.

It was Chace and I against the world the moment that we left Mr. Stevens' care, and it would be mostly a trial by fire no matter how much he taught us. There were endless ways to get killed and not many ways to remain out of sight, and we were well aware that help was not on the away.

Even as Chace and I sat now on a quiet Friday night I picked at the dirt caked onto an old hourglass nervously and wondered how long I had to live. It was the second day in a row that we hadn't said very much in our afternoon free time, because truly there wasn't much to say when you were preparing to die.

"It's 9:30."

When Chace finally spoke his voice was hoarse and it caught me by surprise, and when I looked at him he pointed at the grandfather clock at the other end of the room. When his cell phone battery had died on Wednesday it had been one of his endeavors to repair the old clock to functionality, and now that he had it was our primary timepiece. It took me a second to focus on the hands of the clock now, but after a second I saw that it was indeed 9:30$_{PM}$.

"He's usually back by now," I said, trying not to sound ominous.

"I know," Chace replied, and his voice was concerned.

"He's not just late," he added.

"He's four and a half hours late. This is the first time he's even been a minute later than five o'clock."

I didn't like the anxious look that was creeping across Chace's face, and I felt it, too. There was something amiss if Mr. Stevens was four hours late.

"Come on," Chace said then, standing up.

In one motion he closed his book and put his arms into his jacket, and then he quickly scanned our room. With a few deliberate plucks, he proceeded to pick out a few expensive-looking artifacts and shamelessly stuff them into his jacket pockets.

"You're going to steal those?" I asked incredulously, still sitting down.

Chace gave me a vicious look.

"Yes, of course I am. We're going to need the money if Mr. Stevens doesn't come back," he said.

"Come on," he added impatiently, and without waiting for me to get up he headed out of our room and towards Mr. Stevens' kitchen. I finally got up and followed him, and when I reached the kitchen behind him he was grabbing his cell phone off of the tall kitchen table.

"Wait, are we just leaving now?" I asked as Chace started back towards the front door.

Things had escalated from concern to drastic action in the span of two minutes, but Chace finally paused for a second and then looked indecisive.

"Well, I don't know. I definitely don't like the idea of just waiting in Mr. Stevens' house, though. If we get caught in here we're trapped," he said.

I thought it over briefly, and considering that there was only one way in and out of this little cottage, Chace was right. We would have nowhere to go if someone besides Mr. Stevens found us here.

"OK," I agreed tentatively, but we only made it two steps down Mr. Stevens' short hallway before we were interrupted by an eruption of sound ahead of us.

The sound of speeding tires screeching over the gravel outside stopped us in our tracks, and then a second later Mr. Stevens came surging through the front door straight towards us, his eyes ablaze.

"Get into the basement!" he bellowed as he slammed and locked the door behind him.

"Get whatever you can out of the emergency kit and run for your lives!"

Chace and I stood frozen in the hallway for an instant as Mr. Stevens ran past us into the kitchen and grabbed something from a drawer. Then we were galvanized into action by the sound of gunshots.

BLAM! BLAM! BLAM!

As three bullets whizzed past us, all three of us dropped to the ground and involuntarily released a variety of curse words. The shots had come straight through the front door and into the back wall of the kitchen, barely missing us.

"To the basement! Now!" Mr. Stevens ordered.

With Mr. Stevens leading, all three of us crawled rapidly towards the door, our heads low.

BLAM! BLAM!

Two more bullets came slicing down the hallway as we slipped and stumbled into Mr. Stevens' bedroom, sending chips of wood flying everywhere. Chace and I exchanged a brief look of mortal fear as we followed Mr. Stevens behind the giant tree in the center of his room.

"Hurry up!" he ordered from ahead of us.

He had already made his way down into his basement laboratory, but Chace and I were still close behind him, almost falling over each other in our haste to get out of harm's way. By the time we reached the clay floor of the lab though, Mr. Stevens was already at the wooden trunk at the far end. When we got over to him he had already opened it up.

"Here," he said, jamming something into my hands.

Without thinking I took the shiny black object he handed me. When it touched my hands I instantly realized that this was the first time I had ever held a real gun, and I looked down at the black gleam of a Colt .45 pistol.

BLAM! BLAM! BLAM!

I cringed and ducked instinctively at the sound of yet more bullets crashing in overhead, but Mr. Stevens relatively calmly handed Chace another pistol and looked up from the trunk. It was only now that I noticed a streak of blood across his right arm and the tattered hole in his robe.

Chen must have chased him all the way here, I thought.

Mr. Stevens looked up from the kit and closed it.

"My normal escape plan is to shift and escape through the roof, but with you two here I'll try to distract them first. This is the last time I'll help you, so run at the first chance you get," he said with a grave, parting look.

He pointed to the guns he'd given each of us.

"You've both got six rounds; you'll want to use them wisely. Otherwise, you're on your own from here. It will never be safe for us to meet again," he said with a final nod.

He withdrew a final pistol of his own from the folds of his robe, this one much larger than ours and shining bright silver. I instantly recognized it as the same one I had seen him with in class that fateful day. Then, with his pistol brandished, Mr. Stevens disappeared back upstairs, leaving Chace and I to chase after him once again. By the time we clambered back up into the darkened room above a few seconds behind him, he was already gone.

I briefly wondered if the brown flash of his robe and the fleeting gleam of his silver pistol was the last vision I would ever have of Mr. Stevens, but then the urgency of our predicament took full attention when a bullet shattered the front window of the bedroom and set us sprawling.

"I'm running for the other side. We'll both watch the door," Chace schemed immediately, and then he leapt up and dashed across the room.

With clear athleticism he literally dove into the room on the other side, and I was suddenly alone in the dark. I looked ahead and saw that although the front door was still closed it was full of holes, and the dim illumination of moonlight and the eerie pause in gunfire sent my heartbeat even faster.

I strained to see across the hall but I couldn't see Chace, so I gripped my gun tightly and nestled against the trunk of Mr. Stevens' ingrown tree. As my eyes adjusted to the semi-darkness I crouched even lower, but then the front door came bursting down, sending splinters of wood everywhere. In response, a volley of gunshots rang out from both the kitchen and outside simultaneously, and I ducked behind the tree just as a squat, slithering shape materialized in the doorway.

What the- ?

As I peeked my head around the tree I saw that the creature moved with extraordinary quickness, and although a gunshot rang out from somewhere in the house the bullet flew above the creature's head as it flattened its body to the ground. In dodging another bullet the animal then scuttled into the same room that I was in, and it was then that I realized it was a very large crocodile.

It moved so fast that I didn't even have time to fire at it, and instead I ducked behind the tree in total terror as the croc struggled to grip the wood floor with its claws. From behind the tree I could hear its nails sliding across the floor, and then a second later it slammed into the other side of the tree with a reverberating thud.

Could it smell me?

I held my breath and tried to remain as still as possible, but when I heard the ferocious sound of the beast snapping its jaws together, an involuntary shiver went up my spine. The air was thick with a tense silence, but then the ominous click of the crocodiles nails against the floor told me it was moving again.

Still holding the same breath I listened intently to the slow, predatory cadence, knowing that I could be discovered and devoured any second. It wasn't until I could barely hear the clicking of its nails that I realized the croc had gone back towards the hallway, and then I finally let the air out of my lungs.

I wiped one hand across my sweat-beaded face, and then gathering my courage I peered tentatively around the tree.

In the doorway I saw the brutish outline of the crocodile craning its neck around the wall, looking deeper into Mr. Stevens' house, and then out of nowhere Chen Lake and another man raced through the splintered front door past it, guns firing.

The crocodile raced down the hallway after them, and suddenly a caterwauling of yells, bangs, and gunshots instantly erupted from the direction of the kitchen. My only thought was to run for it, and I headed towards the open hole of the front doorway with that singular focus until a tiny gleam caught my eye just before I reached the hallway.

I turned and looked closer instinctively, and when I did I saw that the eye-catching twinkle of moonlight reflecting off of metal was actually a tiny ray of hope. Mr. Stevens' keys, readily sitting on top of one of his brown robes, stared me in the face for a moment before I recognized the golden nature of the silver opportunity.

In an electric spur of action I went back and grabbed the keys, and then I literally dove across the hallway into Chace and I's room on the opposite side.

"Chace! Don't shoot, it's me!" I whispered as I skidded painfully into the base of the grandfather clock.

A crouched, dark shape started towards me.

"Holy – I almost blasted your head off!"

Chace's whisper was both relieved and full of consternation, but I was on the offensive for once.

"Look!" I responded, hurriedly holding our one chance at escaping up in the light so that he could see.

"I've got the car keys! Let's go!" I insisted.

Without waiting for Chace's answer I barreled out of the room, turning away from the kitchen and running straight outside through the broken front doorway as fast as I could. I could hear Chace behind me as I ducked low and raced across the gravel driveway towards Mr. Stevens' jalopy, and when I reached it the sound of avian shrieks joined the gunshots and curse words behind us.

Panic threatened to overwhelm me as I fumbled with the keys and unlocked the car doors, and then we dove in as soon as I succeeded. As fast as humanly possible I jammed the key into the ignition and started the car, and it thankfully rumbled right to life. Just as I looked up out of the front windshield however, Mr. Stevens' brown owl shift arced out of his open doorway.

BLAM! BLAM!

Two final gunshots rang out from down the hallway behind him, and after the second one Mr. Stevens' owl shift careened suddenly to the left, flapped once feebly, and pitched to the ground in front of us. For a moment I stared open-mouthed at the brown feathered body as it crash-landed on the driveway, but then I felt a painful thud as Chace punched me in the arm.

"Go! Go!" he bellowed.

I ripped the transmission into reverse, but just before I stepped on the gas Mr. Stevens showed signs of life. Splotches of blood formed on the gravel as he began to pitifully flap and inch against the ground towards the trees.

"Gooooooo!" Chace roared again, but instead of hitting me this time he merely pointed ahead.

I followed his finger to the open doorway, where I could now see Chen Lake, dressed in another regal business suit, coming towards us from down the hallway. I looked down to Mr. Stevens once more, and another one of his teachings popped into my head. It was supremely ironic for me to think of it now, because Mr. Stevens had seemed almost offended when I'd asked the question.

"How can we fight back against Martin Evers, then?" I'd asked after Mr. Stevens had given us another grim round of survival statistics.

"This is not a movie. There is no *chosen* one," he had answered sarcastically.

"Worrying about the fate of your shapeshifter brethren will only get you killed. Your heroics will be defined only by how long *you* survive."

BLAM! BLAM!

At the same time that I slammed on the gas pedal two bullets meant for our windshield penetrated the hood of our car, and in front of us Chen Lake and another suited man ran murderously towards us, guns drawn and aimed. They came crashing out of the doorway to Mr. Stevens' house as we accelerated backwards, and I turned around in my seat to navigate us in reverse past Chen's black Mercedes.

Chace, still facing forward, fired a round out of his window back at our pursuers, and he desperately informed me that the crocodile was now bearing down on us as well. In the chaos I heard more bullets whiz by us, but I was fully concentrated on avoiding impaling us on the trees.

My foot was pushing the old Toyota as fast as it would go, and an instant after we left Chen and his cohorts behind we came crashing down Mr. Stevens' long driveway and onto the street. We were totally out of control, and I whipped the steering wheel hard in an effort to straighten us out – but it merely sent us spinning towards a ditch on the opposite side of the road. The tires gave a chilling shriek as I slammed the stick shift into drive and stomped on the gas pedal, and my heart froze as the worn tire treads gripped the dirt precipice. They churned for a crucial second in the mud and I thought for sure we were going to go down, but then by some miracle they found traction at the last second. With a life-saving lurch we leapt back onto the road.

"Go, go!" Chace continued to urge, but this time there was a hint of exhilaration in his voice.

I had no intentions of letting the pedal leave the floor, and we peeled around the next turn only a few inches from the edge of the ditch on the other side.

"We've almost made it. Don't kill us now," Chace advised, peeling himself off of the passenger door.

"I'm not trying to," I agreed, breathing deep breaths.

We skidded around another turn and Chace strapped on his seatbelt. Even though I had gotten my license last year, with no car I hadn't driven much since then. I let my foot off of the gas a little and strapped in as well, realizing that my adrenaline was causing me to go way faster than was probably necessary.

I knew Chen Lake would undoubtedly be on our tail, but our poor car also seemed more ready to collapse after every turn. A dissonance of unidentified sounds from the engine continued to grow louder, and I was sure we were better off driving slower than conking out entirely.

As I drove, my stomach twisted into knots of nervousness and my mind fixated on the images of Mr. Stevens' final moments... the vision of him dragging himself across the gravel driveway replayed over and over in my conscience.

I did my best to convince myself that there was nothing I could have done to help him, but it was no use. Despite his bleak, sometimes heartless attitude, he *had* saved my life at least twice now, and at my first opportunity to repay him I had fled selfishly. Now he was dead, and it was at least partially my fault.

He was now the fourth person I had gotten killed in three days, and I languished in guilt for every minute of the next half hour. The woods were seemingly eternal, and when I looked down at the gas meter and saw that it hadn't moved a millimeter I knew it was obviously broken. I had no idea when the car might run out of gas, and it wasn't until I finally saw a road sign that a tiny spark of hope ignited.

Highway 45 – 1.5 miles

Highway 45 meant Castille, New York, and when at last I pulled onto the dark highway from whatever obscure exit we were coming, I realized how quickly I had forgotten what it was like to be normal. It had been five days since I'd been a member of society, and the sound of another car speeding past us was actually odd before it was comforting. Once I sped up to 60mph though, new problems arose. As soon as the red arrow touched the number 60 a loud pop came from the engine and the car pitched violently and dropped down to 40mph.

"This thing is about to break down, but my house is the next exit. Let's go there," Chace suggested when the car righted itself.

"We'll be lucky if this piece of junk even makes it there. Plus, Mr. Stevens warned us that it was dangerous to go back to our houses," I reminded him.

"I think it's mainly *your* house that we can't go back to, and I'm not going to talk to my parents, if that's what you're thinking. If we're going on the run we're going to need some money though, and we've got an emergency key hidden outside of my house. I'm just going to run in, get what I can, and get out."

I thought it over for a second, but the exit for Chace's house was fast approaching. Although the plan sounded dangerous we weren't going to make it very far without any gas or money, so I pulled into the far right lane and took the exit.

When we arrived at Chace's street all of the houses on Palace Rd were dark and silent, including Chace's. Even in the indistinct light of streetlamps, they all looked groomed and serene. We parked at the top of his hill and looked straight down at his house, which was a weird view in our current state. Ahead of us was a street we had spent many innocent days on, and the lonely basketball hoop in Chace's driveway brought back poignant memories of losing to him in every form of the game imaginable. Now that I was running for my life and wondering if I would ever be back here again, that all seemed very far away.

"It'll all come down to the alarm," Chace said after a minute or two, turning towards me.

"The security system will set the alarm off approximately two seconds after I open the door, which of course will wake up my parents. I've got to disable it before that happens."

I looked at Chace's darkened house and then down at the old-style digital clock in the dashboard. It read 11:58pm in dim, barely legible numbers. It was late enough that everyone in the area should be sleeping, but this was still a dangerous game.

"Don't you think the beeps on your alarm system will wake up your parents?" I asked skeptically.

"No, I've done this once or twice before. But if it does wake them up we're booking it out of here," Chace answered.

He leaned forward then and clicked open the glove compartment. He started pulling out papers and throwing them to the car floor, eventually producing a blank scrap of paper and a pen. He put the paper in his lap and hastily began writing on it.

"What are you doing?" I asked.

"Writing a note to my parents," Chace answered without looking up.

He scribbled for a few moments more and then looked up apologetically.

"It doesn't say much – I'm just telling them I'm alive but not to let anyone know. I doubt they'll obey it but we have to tell them *something*. I know it's too dangerous to go back to your house and I know you won't be able to give a note to *your* parents, but if you want to sign this one you can. They'll at least know you've made it this far."

I thought for a second and then nodded, fighting back the knot in my throat. It was hard to believe that this was real – that I was really leaving Castille indefinitely. I signed the note and handed it back to Chace without reading it, knowing that reading the note would only make things more painful. Chace folded the note in half and opened the car door then, and he moved with his head hung and a depressed heaviness.

"Be ready just in case something goes wrong," he said.

I nodded again, and then watched Chace make his way down to his front door and reach into one of the tall black plant urns next to it. There was a tense pause as he readied the key at the door, and then he opened it and slipped into the darkness beyond. I held my breath as the door closed behind him, straining to hear the sound of the alarm, but it was silent. Chace, like always, had succeeded.

For the first few moments I stared at the door to Chace's house and listened to the quietness of the night, but that tactic only made me feel more alone. When I leaned back in my seat though, I couldn't help but dwell on the fact that my parents would never know what really happened to me. It was as if the stars were aligned against me, and although I had been blessed with the powers of a universal dream – the ability to transform into a creature as awesome as a Siberian tiger – that same power was now turning me into a penniless fugitive on the run for my life.

My hands balled into fists as I dwelt on how unfair and frustrating my predicament was, but thankfully it wasn't long before the door to Chace's house reopened and he slid back outside. I pushed my introspection to the rear as he came running back up the hill.

"I grabbed a few things while I was in there too," he breathed as he climbed back into the car.

He opened a dark blue sling bag that displayed 'Castille High' in big white letters and I looked down into it.

"I've got my cell phone charger, as much money as I could find, and some of the valuables I took from Mr. Stevens. Everything else we'll have to get later," Chace said.

He pulled the drawstrings on the bag closed and I started the car up, suddenly supremely thankful for his company. Despite the guilt I felt at dragging him into this, I wasn't sure if I could have survived any of this without him.

After about 20 minutes we had sputtered to a gas station just outside of Castille, and then we quickly put $40 in the gas tank and hit the highway. Chace decided to take the first driving shift, and so with no destination I just sat in the passenger seat and watched the highway go by as we left Castille behind. Random flashes from my childhood raced uninvited through my thoughts

– raking leaves, walking home from school, my old room. There was a dull innocence to it all that I had once hated, and now I would give anything to have it back.

I swallowed hard and set my jaw when I thought about how just two weeks ago I had wished for a spark of excitement in my life more than anything. The irony bit harder than a great white shark, and it forced unstoppable tears down my face.

Chapter 17

ZADE DAVIDSON

Charles County, Maryland – October 19, 2013

*I*n order to keep Chace from seeing me cry I closed my eyes and tried to sleep, but for the first four hours of the car ride I tossed fitfully. By 5AM when I still hadn't gotten to sleep however, it became clear that sleep was not going to come. There was too much on my mind, and since we had no real destination the stretches of highway were endless.

I tried to focus on the fact that Chace and I had no choice but to run, but it didn't make me feel much better. Even though Castille was probably crawling with shapeshifters by now, I couldn't help but think that my parents' lives were in severe danger and I had done nothing to warn them.

Even Mr. Stevens – who had been our only ally thus far – was gone. Despite his insistence that he was out for himself, he had fought for us and had suffered the fate meant for me. I was sick with guilt, and as Chace and I headed south I saw that next to me Chace's normally cheery face was chiseled into a tight-lipped, statuesque stare.

Instead of his normal, relaxed driving pose, his hands gripped the steering wheel now with determination, and as his best friend I knew that there was a whirlwind of emotions behind that expression. Even when he saw me stirring from my sleep he stayed focused on the road, and it wasn't until a few hours later when the first blue light of sunrise crept over the horizon that he finally changed position.

"I'm hungry," were the words he said.

We had just blazed past a sign for a rest stop, and I croaked out a reply with a voice that was gravelly from the dryness of my throat.

"How far away did that sign say the rest stop is?" I asked.

"20 miles," Chace groaned.

I grumbled as well, as the mention of food had reminded me how long it had been since I had eaten. It also made me wonder how long we had been driving past these never-ending corn fields.

"How much money do we have?" I asked.

Chace looked grim.

"160 dollars. It's not much, I know, and we've got to make that last for gas and food until we figure out what we're going to do. Hopefully by then I can pawn some of these artifacts," he answered.

I nodded.

"Don't forget that the gas gauge is broken too," I reminded him.

"I know... we'll fuel up there too," he said.

However, when we pulled into the empty parking lot of the historic-style rest area it was devoid of a gas station. The short, brick building sat alone with the highway still in view behind it, and there were only food, restroom, and phone accommodations signs posted on the front door.

Despite the empty parking lot Chace parked the car in the back row, and then we stepped out of the relative warmth of the interior and into the cold of outside. Even though the bottom of the early morning sun had already risen above the tree line, it was freezing. With only the thin long-sleeved shirt Mr. Stevens had given me between my body and the air, I hustled inside as quickly as possible.

Inside, the rest area was clean but small. We hit the bathrooms near the door first, and then we looked for some sort of hot food. There was only one venue choice – a generic deli – but fortunately generic also meant cheap. Driven by our voracious hunger, we raided the menu for 99 cent egg muffins and orange juice cartons until the dent in our wallet became too large to justify for just one meal.

It was a filling and enjoyable endeavor, but literally as soon as I sucked down the last bit of my third orange juice, reality returned. We were on the run, and even though it hadn't even been a full day yet, I was already infused with the instincts of a fugitive.

"Staying in one place makes me nervous. Let's get out of here," Chace suggested.

I stood up from the table assertively, surprised at my own paranoia.

"It's your turn to drive," he said, handing me the keys.

I nodded and took them, not looking forward to driving now that I was full.

"Keep heading south?" I asked as we stepped outside.

Chace nodded and shrugged at the same time.

"Yeah, that's what I figured. It'll be warmer there at least. I'd planned on heading all the way down to Mexico or something," he said.

Chace's tone was serious, and as absurd as that idea would've sounded to a saner version of me it didn't sound so bad right now. If we were going to be homeless or anonymous we would need to avoid weather like this, and there were also a *lot* of people in Mexico. With a bunch of shapeshifters after us that didn't sound too bad either.

Even now as we walked out into the outside air of Maryland, it was still ice cold, and if we were going to be fugitives I had no desire to be cold at any point of the year. Unfortunately, the fear that gripped me when I looked up and saw a black Mercedes in the front row of the parking lot was even colder than the frosty air.

The ominous vehicle was parked directly to the right of the doors we came out of, and with its tinted black windows and glossy black rims, it was identical to Chen Lake's. For a second I couldn't help but stare at it in horror, wide-eyed and frozen by the fresh frost that shimmered off of its dark windows.

I was thankful that Chace grabbed my arm and pulled me away before I could gape at it too long, and I could tell by the strength of his grip that he had also seen and recognized the car. I wasn't sure what good it would do now, but I snapped my head down and tried to act normal as we sped towards our car.

"Keep walking," Chace muttered through gritted teeth.

I had no intention to do otherwise. It wasn't until we had tensely crossed the parking lot and hastily started the car that I chanced another look at the Mercedes. The passenger side door of the car had opened, and I waited for a terrible second for Chen Lake or one of his minions to accost us. Instead, the most beautiful girl I'd ever seen stepped out into the brisk morning, smoothing her jacket as she stood up.

Even Chace – whose female standard was astronomically high – let out a low whistle as we watched a ray of sunlight sweep against her silky light brown hair, and as she approached the entrance doors of the rest stop I caught a glimpse of tan skin beneath it. Just our glimpsing side profile of her face was angelic, and she moved with such divine female gracefulness that I didn't even bother moving the car until she had walked inside.

When the door closed behind her, Chace and I both laughed heartily.

"I thought you were going to pee yourself," Chace jabbed mercilessly, giving me a literal jab as well.

I elbowed him back instantly.

"At least I recognized that we could have been in danger," I retorted.

Chace merely laughed again.

"So did I, but *I* stayed composed! Next time you see Chen Lake make sure you don't just stare at him," Chace advised.

"Whatever," I said, shaking my head.

I was just glad that the Mercedes didn't belong to Chen Lake, and I felt more foolish for looking like an idiot in front of that girl than I did at Chace's taunting. In those five seconds her beauty had been spellbinding.

A few hours down the road though, the funny incident became nothing more than a memory and we were back on the run. It was ironic, because everything else I'd ever known seemed like a memory by then too. We were soon over 600 miles away from Castille in the fields of North Carolina, and nothing but our continuous driving seemed real anymore. When it was time for Chace to take over driving again late in the afternoon I was nearly falling asleep, and I was legitimately asleep when Chace tapped me on my shoulder and woke me up some time later.

"It's only halfway through your turn," I complained as I pulled open my eyes.

It had been a while since I'd been able to sleep as soundly as I just had been.

"I'm hungry again," Chace said guiltily as I sat up.

His face looked pained, and as if on cue, his stomach grumbled. I realized then that we were no longer moving, and when I looked around at where we were I saw that we were already in another rest area.

"I didn't stop until I saw a sign for McDonalds. I already got gas and we can both order off of the dollar menu," Chace said almost pleadingly.

I couldn't believe I had slept through a gas stop, and I was also skeptical of both our money situation and being in public for too long. When I looked around at the rest area that Chace had stopped at this time, I saw that it was exponentially more modernized, populated, and expensive-looking than the last one. Despite the fact that it was the only establishment in sight, lines of cars formed in the parking lot and at a big and brightly lit gas station next to it.

There was a steady flow of people coming and going, and amongst that flow I saw a father lead his wife and smiling daughter into the minivan next to us. As I contemplated our move I watched them strap her into her car-seat and smile at each other, and the genuineness of all three smiles sent a stabbing pang of longing into my side. I could almost see a bubble of innocent happiness around them, and I wondered why that bubble had never let *me* inside.

Nonetheless, when the car pulled out and another immediately replaced it, I started to get uneasy about the number of people here.

"Don't you think this place is too crowded?" I asked.

Chace looked around and then opened his door decidedly.

"No. No one knows us in Georgia. We'll be fine," he said.

"We've made it to Georgia?" I asked, surprised.

Chace nodded as I followed him out into the cool, but now warmer outside air.

"Yep, we just got here. I was thinking we would go a little further south and then head west from there. Hopefully we can go through Texas into Mexico," he postulated.

We pushed through a crowd of people at the entrance and surveyed the hubbub, trying to locate the McDonalds.

"Right, and *really* no one will recognize us in Mexico," I agreed.

We filed into line at the McDonalds, which was near the middle of the building, and watched a diverse array of people peruse the convenience store next to it. At the opposite end behind us more people sat in the white wire chairs of a food court, and almost all of them were either buried in their meals or watching the small TV's hanging near the ceiling. I half-expected to see myself on one of the telecasts, and was thankful when I didn't.

A few minutes later when Chace and I joined the group of people buried in their meals and sank our teeth glumly into McDonalds, I wondered how many more times I would be financially bound to the dollar menu. As thankful as I was to have food, I was currently fighting the smells of Teriyaki chicken and loaded nachos around me. My once-spoiled stomach already longed for variety, and sure enough, shortly after my last McChicken sandwich my stomach gurgled in protest.

"I'll be back," I said, excusing myself.

I made a quick move towards the bathroom, but halfway there my stomach settled itself. I breathed a sigh of relief – I hated using public restrooms for extended stays. But, since I was already on the way, I decided to go in anyway.

I headed straight for the sink, splashed my face with some refreshingly cool water, and looked into the mirror. It was the first time I had done so in days, so I wasn't actually too surprised by my tired-red eyes and dirty, uncombed hair. But there was something else about me that was different now – in my eyes I saw a new roughness that had never been there before.

The creases in my eyes and lips looked naturally less friendly and more defensive than I remembered them being, and my mouth seemed more ready to scowl than to smile. It wasn't anything that I was doing on purpose either, yet it reflected the way I felt. Happiness was a thing of the past it seemed.

After a moment I splashed some more cold water onto my face, and then feeling slightly revived I walked out of the bathroom and back into the rest stop. Across from the bathrooms a few people perused a smaller convenience store, and I watched them as I walked past. A middle-aged woman swiveled a rack of clothes, a toddler played a handheld video game as he sat cross-legged on the floor, a brown haired girl in a leather jacket looked up from a magazine and in my direction.

I met her brown eyes and stopped cold. I immediately recognized her as the beautiful girl from the other rest stop, and to my utter surprise, she smiled slightly when our eyes met. The perfection in her smile set loose a flurry of emotions so strong that I almost forgot to smile back, and as soon as I finally did remember to smile I quickly turned away, embarrassed beyond belief. She seemed to have recognized me from before, yet she was so far out of my league that I wasn't even sure we played the same sport. My pupils must have turned into heart shapes, because as soon as I sat back down at the table across from Chace, he gave me a funny look.

"What's the matter?" he asked warily.

He looked ready to run for it before I explained myself.

"The hot girl from that other rest stop is in the convenience store down there," I said, trying to sound nonchalant, but Chace immediately guffawed.

My face flushed red as a few people turned towards us.

"Shut up! You're attracting attention," I said sharply.

Chace brought his laugh volume down a little, but it was a minute before he finally gathered himself.

"I thought you'd seen Chen Lake himself. She wasn't *that* fine," he ribbed me.

I snorted in disagreement.

"She definitely *is*," I said vehemently and slightly jealously.

It was crazy to think about how much different my life would be if I were a guy like Chace, who could actually have a chance with a girl like her. It only made me feel minutely better when I remembered that I was a shapeshifter and therefore could probably never have a girl at all. Chace in the meantime laughed and patted me on the shoulder.

"Why didn't you get her number?" he asked half-sarcastically.

I snorted again and shook my head.

"We *both* know I had no chance. Thanks for rubbing it in," I said hollowly.

Chace chuckled encouragingly.

"Well neither do I," he said and he actually sounded sincere.

He stood up to throw out his trash, and I followed suit. Despite my inability to attract girls of her quality, if there were more gems like her in the southern world there would at least be a little more substance to this fugitive idea than I had thought.

Even though it wasn't my turn to drive yet I felt rested now, and I took over driving straight from the rest stop. By midnight I had taken the couple of obscure southbound exits Chace suggested that we use, and as soon as he was sure that we were on the right track he passed out.

Around us the road was empty and dark, and with Chace snoring away to my right and the car rhythmically clunking beneath us, I faded into a semi-conscious autopilot. My only conscious efforts were to stay on the road and not look at the clock, and it wasn't until I had been hearing the sound for ten minutes or more that I became aware of the humming of another car next to us.

Lazily, I looked across Chace's sleeping body and out of the passenger side window, and coasting almost casually alongside us was the one car I didn't want to see – a black Mercedes-Benz. I blinked to confirm that it wasn't a mirage and then wished against everything that it was just a coincidence, but it occurred to me then that even though the road was wide, there was only one lane in each direction on this road. This Mercedes was driving in the shoulder, and after the half-second it took to process the implications I snapped awake like I'd been struck by lightning and punched Chace feverishly.

"Wake up!" I roared.

Chace groaned and sat up, and when he followed my finger out of his window he turned towards me with his eyes wider than ever.

"How in the...?"

I pushed the pedal hopelessly to the floor, but before I could really launch ahead we were greeted by a jolting smash. My body whiplashed forward as the Mercedes rammed the back corner of our car and forced me to swerve into the middle of the road just to keep from swerving off of it.

BANG!

Before we could even settle for a second in the center of the road the Mercedes rammed us again on the other rear corner, and this time my attempt to keep our car from flying off of the road was futile. Chace and I both yelled for our lives as I cranked the steering wheel hard and slammed on the brakes, but we were sliding out of control. We spun at full speed across the opposite lane into the thick grass next to the road, doing two full spinning rotations before finally skidding to a stop a few dozen yards in.

For an instant our car rumbled doggedly, but then it died facing the road as smoke and dust billowed up around us. Inside the car, we were shocked but so far unharmed. The 'so far' portion was critical though, because although it was quiet for the little moment that the dust was settling, when it cleared the Mercedes almost immediately appeared on the edge of the road with its headlights aimed at us.

"Drive! Go! " Chace urged at the sight of the headlights.

I cranked the key in the ignition, but the car only made a few feeble sputtering sounds and gave out.

"I'm trying!" I said, cranking the key again.

The car sputtered even less this time, and I looked out of our front windshield at the motionless and terrifying black Mercedes. Next to me Chace quickly pulled his pistol out of the glove compartment and handed me mine, but as he did so I heard the distinctive thuds of car doors slamming shut. We both looked up at two figures advancing on us; one of them was slender and feminine, the other was large and brutish. Even though neither of the figures were Chen Lake, they both had their weapons drawn and aimed at our car.

"I've only got one bullet left," Chace informed me feverishly.

"If we stay in this car they'll turn us into pincushions, so on the count of the three we're running for it," he said.

I nodded, my jaw set. I was scared out of my mind and surely not ready to die in a shootout.

"One…"

As Chace began to count I slid my hand silently onto the door handle.

"… Two …Three!" Chace hissed.

At the sound of the word 'three' I shouldered my door open, took one leaping step, and then dove headfirst into the grass. The sound of gunfire rang out behind me, but I landed hard on my stomach and face without being hit. The impact of the ground knocked the wind out of me though, and as my chin hit the dust my pistol flew out of my hand. The grass was thick in every direction; I couldn't risk searching for it.

All I could do was roll over and try to breathe, but I couldn't. I thought I was going to suffocate from the pain in my stomach even though I knew I couldn't afford to. Desperately, I sucked in painful gasps of air and then pushing myself backwards on the grass, trying only to get as far away from the headlights and shouting behind me as possible.

"Don't move!"

A loud, commanding female voice suddenly pierced through the other sounds, and I froze instinctively and sunk down into the grass.

"Keep your hands where I can see them," the female voice barked.

My breath caught in my throat and I remained frozen for a second as I realized what was happening. I was caught.

"Any bullet wounds on him?" another rough voice asked, and then I realized that it wasn't me they had caught.

Chace, I thought suddenly.

The voices were coming from back near the car, and after a few more seconds of trying to catch my breath I turned around and started to inch back towards the sound of the voices.

"I don't see any holes in him but this isn't the shifter, is it?" the female voice asked.

I noticed that her voice carried an air of superiority, but I was busy wishing I hadn't dropped that gun.

"Yeah, the one we're lookin' for is a lot scrawnier than this one," the gruff voice confirmed.

The male voice sounded almost familiar, but I flattened myself even further to the ground and prayed that I was somewhere in the cover of darkness. When no one said anything for a second I shifted and then poked my head just above the top of the grass. In the little bit of light coming from the Mercedes – which was thankfully aimed a little to the left of me – I could see the shadow of a gargantuan man.

He was sitting sideways on the hood of Mr. Stevens' car, shotgun in hand, and even from this distance in the darkness there was no mistaking his ponytailed hair and muscular frame. He was the same man who'd tended Chen Lake's basement and chased me into the woods on Fordham Street.

In front of him guy and with her back to me, I saw the shapely outline of a girl. She had a handgun pointed at Chace, who was lying face down on the ground with his hands behind his head, cop-style.

"Well, Roman, unless you plan on actually shifting yourself you're going to have to hurry up and find that shifter," she said impatiently.

Roman groaned loudly and peeled himself off of the hood of the car as I ducked down.

"He couldn't have gotten far. I'll shine our high-beams out onto the field and we'll find him," I heard Roman say confidently.

A second later I heard the sound of the Mercedes door opening.

"Hurry up," the girl said impatiently.

"If the shifter is smart he's already left this guy for dead and is headed for the trees," she said.

Yeah right, I thought to myself.

I'm as good as dead without Chace.

I heard the door to the Mercedes shut and knew that the high-beams were coming on, which meant that there was now nowhere to run and nowhere to hide. My gun was gone and Chace was helpless and prone. There was only one thing left to do.

You are a Siberian tiger.

I focused my mind on that once-impossible thought and forced myself to know it just as I had done in the woods behind Mr. Stevens' house, and with surprising ease I felt my mind slide into that half-conscious state of shapeshifting. My normal human shoulders erupted into the muscular front legs of a Siberian tiger while my hips and thighs simultaneously stretched and reshaped into hind legs and a tail, and then in less than a second I had torn through my clothes and exploded out of the grass.

When my normal vision sharpened into the natural night vision of the tiger, the rush of senses flooded my consciousness at the same time that I saw a flash of light. The high beams from the Mercedes whipped in my direction, and instinctively I pressed my body flat to the ground and perked my ears ahead. It was amazing how nimble my behemoth shift was, because I heard Roman call to the girl from the car.

"I don't see any movement, how about you, Roslyn?" I heard him say.

His voice was loud and clear now.

"Not yet," the girl answered.

I could tell that her eyes were scanning the area intensely, and I could hear her take a few steps walk out into the grass towards me.

"Keep your eye on the other kid!" she barked back to Roman.

Her voice was close now, and with my current hearing abilities I could pinpoint her at 10 yards away. Even as lithely crouched as I was however, I felt exposed. It was now or never, and at the next crunch of her footstep I attacked. With unbelievable, instinctive speed, I sprang out of the grass and at the girl named Roslyn with enormous paws extended. With equally remarkable speed she attempted to move her gun up to shoot me, but I was an instant quicker and I smacked it away, sending her flying.

"Bastard!" I heard from near the car.

I whirled to see Roman charging me with his double-barreled shotgun extended, and I caught a glimpse of a Viking-like bush beard and multicolored tattoos before I was forced to leap out of the way of shotgun pellets and an explosive blast. To my feline ears, the sound was deafening, but I was too quick and I hurdled away in time to dodge another blast from Roman's shotgun. More pellets sprayed into the air but I landed without pain.

Knowing that his shotgun was double-barreled I also knew that it was out of shells now, and my human mind guided my catlike instincts into the offensive. As Roman backed away I vaguely noticed that he emitted the Shifters Scent, but as a human his bulk was no match for me. I was sure I had him dead to rights when he caught me by complete surprise by throwing his shotgun straight at me, and the bulky weapon smacked me directly in the face.

Slightly stunned, I stumbled backwards at the sharp pain that shot out from my nose, and when I blinked back my clouded vision I saw that all that remained of Roman were the tattered leftovers of a t-shirt and jeans.

Before I could process what that meant a dark shape materialized to my left, and then before I could react to the shape it slammed into me like a missile, tackling me to the ground. I kicked away and rolled back to my feet, but as I did so I briefly saw that I was under assault by a giant, full-grown crocodile... presumably the same one that had ambushed us at Mr. Stevens' house.

There was no time to avoid its monstrous, reptilian jaws, and this time they clamped down onto my hind leg with the force of a vice-grip. With vicious technique the Roman-croc twisted its body around my leg in the species' infamous death roll, and I roared in pain as he flipped my entire body over with my left leg as the axis.

It was the most intense, panic-inducing pain I had ever experienced, and I pulled at my trapped leg with desperate ferocity. As my flesh slid against the jagged crocodile teeth I roared in pain, and clawed at the crocs' snout with murderous intent. In the position I was in his eyes were just out of reach – and as I clawed at him his bite only tightened.

I was almost sure that my femur was getting ready to snap when the pain reached an excruciating climax, and in a final effort I twisted my already torn leg in a new direction and pulled with all of my might. The teeth dug gashing scores into my flesh but my leg ripped free, and in one heavenly instant I scrambled to my feet, taking up a defensive position that almost caused my tattered leg to give out.

I roared out again in another bellow of pain and backed up a step, but I was unable to see the croc. I knew it was going to come hurtling towards me at any instant, but it was short enough to be invisible in the tall grass. My leg was also pulsating with the worst pain I had ever experienced, and it was only out of natural instinct that I leapt into the air when the crocodile burst through the grass again.

Another jolt of pain tore through my leg, but even with three legs I got enough height to catch a glimpse of my surprised opponent beneath me before I landed on top of him. I felt the air whoosh out of the crocodile's lungs as soon as my immense weight dropped down on him, and fueled with the unstoppable energy of animalistic survival I simultaneously buried my own vicious jaws into the crocodile's scaly flesh and pinned him to the ground with my claws.

Roman thrashed wildly and attempted to throw me off with all of his strength, but I was heavier and stronger, and the force of my bite was murderous. Without any air flow he was weakened, and although crocodile blood filled my mouth it only fed the natural bloodlust that had risen within me. The world was only Roman's desperate hisses and gasps and my own primal grunts of effort, and I bit deeper when his tail whipped around in the desperation of his death throes.

"No!" I heard Roslyn bellow, but no help for Roman came.

I was overcome with blood rage, and it wasn't until minutes after Roman stopped moving that I finally released his limp body.

"I told you!"

When I finally stood upright to my full, commanding height and moved away from the Roman-croc, I heard the sound of Chace's boasting voice from somewhere near the car.

"I told you!" I heard him gloat again.

Confused, I turned around and saw that instead of lying face down on the ground he was now back on his feet near Mr. Stevens' car, triumphantly pointing a gun at Roslyn. She faced him with her hands in the air, and even from here I could see hatred in the set of her jaw.

"*You* are nothing but a fool," she quipped back at Chace.

She looked him in the eyes as she said it, and as I padded towards them she turned towards me. Her mesmerizing brown eyes met mine, and for the third time today the sight of her made me swoon. Roslyn was the same beautiful girl I'd seen at both of the rest stops, and as the puzzle started to fit together I realized that she had been following me all along. With an expression seemingly impossible for a girl as attractive as her, she ran her eyes coldly over my Siberian tiger shift and then turned back towards Chace.

"He may have gotten lucky today, but your friend has a long way to go before he becomes a shapeshifter of any worth," she said disdainfully.

Chace snorted and answered her sharply.

"Tell that to your dead partner," he said.

He jammed the gun at her threateningly but Roslyn didn't blink. I noticed that she was holding one of her arms tenderly, but she stared back at Chace.

"Death doesn't scare me," she said aggressively.

Her brown eyes had hardened into wrathful slits, and Chace's strong jawbone was clenched in an opposing frown. The rage that pulsated between them was raw and unforgiving as they stared each other down, and I could tell that violence was coming quickly.

I focused my mind on my human form and managed to downshift before Chace decided to shoot her, but when I came back to my senses I collapsed; the pain from the crocodile bite that bled down my left leg was amplified in my Zade Davidson body. The taste of crocodile blood to my human palette was also revolting, and all at once I coughed, puked, and fell into the grass.

At that same moment the triumph of victory evaporated; it was instantly annihilated by the sound of Roslyn's velvet laughter. As I collapsed to the rough ground with my naked human body I went from being thankful to be alive to being thoroughly humiliated and bleeding. I couldn't help but bellow in writhe in pain for a few seconds, and even after I reduced my cries to a whisper I was barely able to stand through the pain in leg

"It's a shame that such a marvelous shift is wasted on the likes of you," Roslyn said when I finally stood.

Chace looked at me gratefully, but Roslyn eyed me ill-sculpted human body dismissively.

"What are you trying to say?" I came back, insulted.

"I'm not *trying* to say anything," she snipped harshly.

"What I *am* saying is that no matter what you do, we are going to find you. When we do, Martin Evers is more than likely going to kill you. Once he sees how –"

"Shut up. *You* won't live long enough to see what happens to us," Chace interrupted her.

He took a threatening step towards her and recalculated his pistol at her head. Roslyn didn't flinch.

"*You* won't kill *me* either," she countered boldly.

"I can tell by the weight of that pistol in your hand that it's empty," she said.

I looked from her to Chace, suddenly unsure, while Chace gritted his teeth and looked ready to test her. Roslyn merely cocked her head to the side, taunting him.

"If you're so sure that there are bullets in that gun, fire one," she mocked.

She smiled encouragingly, and Chace didn't hesitate.

Chapter 18

ZADE DAVIDSON

Manning, South Carolina - October 19, 2013

*B*LAM!

There was a thunderous clap as Chace fired the gun, but at the last second he snapped his hand to the left and the shell whizzed a few inches from Roslyn's head. She finally showed some humanity and cringed slightly at the suddenness of it, but with impressive immediacy she snapped her head back into position, chin up.

Still not totally used to the sound of guns, I jumped a little at the sound too.

"Careful man," I warned Chace quickly, but he gave me a flitting, incredulous look.

"I'm not just aiming this gun at her for fun," he said tersely.

Roslyn snorted.

"You mean the gun with no bullets in it?" she revised smartly.

She smiled again, and Chace allowed a rare look of uncertainty to cross his face. Despite the fact that she had nearly gotten her head blown off a minute ago her voice was sure, and her dazzling eyes held Chace's fiercely. I wondered if Roslyn had goaded Chace into letting off his last bullet or if she had just been testing his mettle. Regardless, Chace's return look said if she was wrong she was dead.

"I think we should question her first," I said, trying to intercede, but before I could continue Chace squeezed again.

At the same time as the metallic click of an empty chamber rang out, Roslyn dodge-rolled away from Chace,, and with a lightning-quick dash she was in the drivers' seat of the Mercedes. Her movements were the insanely nimble movements of someone who was well-trained, and she had the Mercedes' engine fired up by the time Chace and I started to move.

"She's taking the car!" I yelled, but I could only take two steps towards her before a crippling ripple of pain in my leg froze me in tracks.

Chace continued after her while I doubled over and grabbed my leg, falling to the ground again as the Mercedes screeched backwards into the street. As Chace continued chasing after it, he aimed his gun and squeezed the trigger with futile repetition.

Having already reversed out into the highway, Roslyn deftly whipped the car into drive and sped off, and in seconds the lights of the Mercedes became mere specks in the distance. I groaned loudly and rolled over, and tears squeezed out of my eyes beyond my control. It felt like my leg had been severed from my body entirely, and it took Chace a long time to pull me up off of the ground. When darkness and silence quickly engulfed us, we stood on the side of the highway with Chace supporting me for a long, defeated moment.

Then I swayed and almost fell, and Chace had to pull me back upright. Now that my eyes were adjusted to the darkness I finally took a look down at my leg, and at the grisly sight I dry-heaved onto the pavement.

"You're losing a lot of blood," Chace grunted as he helped me towards Mr. Stevens' car.

"Yeah, duh," I said woozily.

I felt loopy and lightheaded.

"Well you're going to need stitches obviously, but in the meantime I'm going to make you a tourniquet to stem the bleeding," Chace said.

I nodded weakly. The sight of my own blood was starting to sap my consciousness, and Chace's voice seemed far away. I felt him walk me a little ways and then prop me against the side of the car, and then he disappeared for a second before reappearing with some sort of ripped cloth.

"Grit your teeth," he advised.

I barely had time to comply before he tied the cloth tightly around my bleeding leg, presumably somewhere above the wounds. I couldn't tell nor care; I bellowed as loud as my voice would allow as the pulsing pain doubled.

"I know it hurts man, but it'll slow the bleeding," Chace said, trying to sound reassuring.

With a patience only he exhibited, he dressed me into a foul-smelling pair of sweatpants and an old t-shirt that he pulled from the car, and then patted me on the back. No matter how long these clothes had been festering and gathering moisture in Mr. Stevens' trunk, I was thankful for them and for Chace's assistance. I thanked him aloud as he put my feet into decrepit boots whose soles were nearly as hard as the ground.

I was delirious, and all I had the strength to do was lean against Mr. Stevens' car and fight the urge to pass out. For a while time passed without me being very much aware of it, and then when I did lift my head it was at the sound of metal scraping across the ground. I tried to focus and saw that Chace had kicked Mr. Stevens' infamous briefcase across the ground in rage, and I heard him follow the action with more than a few choice words.

"Can you walk?" he asked a minute or so later after he'd picked up the briefcase.

I shrugged and then shook my head; I was dizzy from just holding my head up and the pain in my leg hadn't subsided much at all. Somehow Chace still interpreted this answer as an affirmative though, because he gave me an encouraging pat and put my arm over his shoulder.

"Good, because we don't have much of a choice," he said apologetically.

I moaned aloud in protest, but Chace ignored me and dragged me away from the car. I looked over at him and saw that he had tucked his empty pistol into his belt, shouldered his sling bag, and picked up Mr. Stevens' briefcase with his other arm. Even though we were moving very slowly and painfully, he had at least gotten us moving.

"Don't give up yet," he said when I paused only a few dozen yards the road.

I was walking as unconsciously as possible but my leg was killing me. I could barely suppress another excruciated whimper.

"It hurts," I said through a dry throat.

Chace took more of the weight off of my leg and helped me get moving again.

"You're still alive though man, and that's what counts. We've got enough money for a motel. I don't know if we can make it that far but if we do then who knows? We might still get away somehow," he said.

His voice was weary but somehow still heartening... optimistic even. I couldn't let him down yet. I gritted my teeth and picked up the pace a little, forcing myself to deal with the pain in my leg. It was hard to think about anything besides the pain, but I kept putting one foot in front of the other. Unfornately, even after hours of walking I didn't feel any closer to a haven, and harsh nighttime winds swirled randomly and ceaselessly.

They added a suffocating, biting harassment to our ailments, and time, pain, and the scenery all became a blur. I only became aware of the world around me when Chace would point out exit signs once every few hours – and none of them looked promising. Each exit ramp seemed to head farther away from civilization, and if I was going to live I needed legitimate shelter ASAP.

When the light of morning began to creep up later on, more and more cars started to pass us. At the sound of the first few, shockwaves of nervousness jolted me to attention, but after that there were too many of them to worry about. It gave me a new-found respect for refugees and escapees – the constant fear of capture was mind-numbing. In my little dark world, I wondered what people thought when they drove past two battered souls like Chace and I on the side of the highway.

By then I was practically dragging my right leg, and any moment I didn't spend willing myself another step I spent trying to quell the fear that an army of shapeshifters would show up at any minute. I was in far more pain than I had ever been in, and I knew I couldn't take it much longer. Even my good leg was sore beyond belief from the extra effort it was taking to keep my body moving forward on its own, and there was no doubt that in our current state Chace and I were nothing more than easy prey to Martin's Shifthunters. To be honest, I was relatively sure we had no hope.

The only thing that kept me going was the fact that we weren't *yet* dead, and giving up before complete bodily exhaustion seemed too cowardly for me to accept. I was near that point, but before that moment arrived Chace's voice finally brought good news.

"We made it."

His voice was hoarse and cracked from five or six hours of silence, but I'd been waiting to hear those words for every minute of those hours. Laboriously, I bent my stiff neck upwards and saw a lighted red sign reading Misty's Motel less than one hundred yards away. It was an island in a sea of fields and hills, but despite the fact that most of the lights on the lighted sign for Misty's Motel were blown, it shined like a beacon in the openness. My surprise was only trumped by the relief I felt.

"I finally saw an exit for a motel," Chace said exhaustedly.

The words were the sweetest I'd ever heard, but all I could do was nod a few thankful times. I hoped my gratitude showed. Chace then helped me up the last stretch of road to the motel, but when we got up to it we couldn't find a lobby. There was also only one car in the parking lot. For a second I feared that it was closed, but then Chace half-dragged me around to the side and found a glass partition and a cashier.

I tried to keep my balance while Chace talked to the dark, grungy-looking desk-person, and after counting out and paying the 60 dollar nightly rate, we received a key through a slot in the glass. The garbled sounds of a foreign language came from a radio near the cashier's hand the whole time, and for some reason the mangled sound of the broadcast was sickening to my stomach.

I held myself together until we were on our way up the stairs to the second floor, and then I doubled over in a fit of painful dry heaves. I had already puked everything out of my stomach back on the side road, but with only one leg to stand on I had to hold onto the railing to keep from falling down the steps as my body attempted to hurl up my stomach lining now. When the dry heaves eventually subsided I couldn't possibly have been more ready to collapse.

In a zombie-like trance I took in the two single beds that made up our motel room, and I died on the first one as soon as we walked in. I lifted my head only long enough to look around at the brown walls of the cheapest room I'd ever slept in, and then fell asleep.

When I woke up, the old digital alarm clock on our shared night stand read 4:30$_{PM}$. On the other side of the nightstand Chace was still soundly asleep; a tightly wrapped lump of comforter and pillows. Behind me, slivers of afternoon light snuck through our blinds, illuminating a dingy sink and pockmarked bathroom door. In between those was a small, dark brown dresser, on top of which sat Mr. Stevens' silver briefcase and Chace's navy blue sling bag.

I took it all in for a moment, and then felt a desperate homesick lurching. Everything about this place made me miss my parents' house, and the relative comfort and safety I'd once felt being there. At the time it *had* absolutely sucked, but it was sweet apple pie compared to this. With the added detriment of hellish memories and a throbbing gash from my battle with the Roman-croc, I couldn't think of being in a worse possible place in my life.

I only wanted to lie in place and sulk for a while, and I did just that for a long time. It wasn't until my bladder forced me to move that I stopped thinking about the injury to my leg or my old life in Castille. However, with the need to relieve myself imminent, I very gingerly made my way into the bathroom, hobbling with as little pressure as possible on my right leg. The bathroom was tiny and smelled like cheap chemicals, and after having trouble holding myself up while aiming at the low-sitting toilet, it flushed with an obnoxiously loud force. When I got back to my bed Chace was waking up, probably from the sounds of me moving around, and his raspy voice emerged from the ball of pillows and comforters on his bed when I laid back on mine.

"I'm pretty sure the only food we're going to find will be in a vending machine," he said both solemnly and sleepily.

I chuckled, amazed that those were his first waking words. His appetite was endless.

"How much money do we have left?" I asked.

"$23," Chace answered.

He sounded unconcerned, but his answer was disheartening.

"Geez, gas is expensive! How long can we make that last?"

Chace poked his upper body out of the covers.

"Not long," he said, shaking his head.

"I was going to suggest that we look for a pawn shop once we got down to a half tank, but obviously those shapeshifters showed up before we could do that," he added.

I rubbed my eyes and looked down at my injured leg, which I held carefully stretched out in front of me on the bed. It already felt better than it had before I went to sleep, but it still hurt like hell. I cautiously rolled down my pants and unwrapped my leg from the torn t-shirt Chace had used as a tourniquet, and saw that the jagged bite marks on my leg, which had been bloody gashes yesterday, were already starting to heal. There was still a row of toothy row of wounds down my entire thigh, but as I flexed my leg a little, I couldn't help but admire the fact that I'd already begun healing.

I touched one of the scabbed wounds delicately and felt strangely empowered. Watching the powers Mr. Stevens had told me about become real gave me a newfound sense of resilience. I lifted my head at the sound of Chace yawning and saw him stretch and cross over to the window. He groaned and cracked his bones as he pulled back the curtains and looked outside.

"Three new cars out there. No Mercedes' though," he reported after a minute.

I was glad to hear that.

"Good. Any vending machines?"

Once again Chace's mention of food had made me hungry too.

"It looks like they've got two of them. I see a Coke machine and a snack machine, but considering our funds we should probably just drink sink water," he answered.

The idea didn't sound appetizing to either of us, but it was one of many sacrifices we would have to keep making if we were going to survive. With an air of resignation Chace came away from the window and pulled our remaining cash stash out of his sling bag, separated out three dollars, and then put on his shoes.

"I'm ready to eat now if you are – what do you want from the machine?"

I shrugged.

"Zebra cakes… or whatever is most filling," I requested passionlessly.

Chace nodded and then headed out, but when he returned he was holding two granola bars and a few coins and looking further disheartened. He registered my look of starved disappointment and explained.

"These were all they had," he said as he tossed me one.

"On the bright side, we didn't miss out on sodas. The coke machine wasn't even on."

I looked down at the granola bar almost repulsively, failing to see the bright side at the moment. My stomach craved a burger, or at least something filling. Granola at the moment seemed supremely unappetizing.

I watched Chace take a dissatisfying bite out of his own granola bar before I did, and then 30 seconds later I had eaten the whole thing and was still as hungry as before. I sighed wearily as Chace flicked his empty wrapper towards a plastic trashcan on the other side of the room.

"We've got to check out of here by 10$_{AM}$ tomorrow morning," he said as the balled up wrapper crunched successfully into the trashcan.

"Ok," I said, looking around the room for the one hundredth time.

Even though that left us on the street tomorrow, we'd at least be sheltered for the night.

"I guess we need a plan then," I proposed.

"We need a *car*," Chace corrected.

"Our plan is to run to Mexico, but I doubt we'll make it walking and I haven't seen any signs of public transportation," he said.

"Yeah I doubt they have a cab service out here," I agreed.

"I guess we do need a car. It shouldn't be too hard to get one – we've got a whole 20 dollars to work with," I added sarcastically.

Chace snorted and laughed.

"We're not going to buy one. We're going to steal one."

The serious look in his eyes made me pause.

"You know how to hotwire a car?" I asked, my eyes widening.

"I know the *process*," he answered ambiguously.

I'd known him too long for him to beguile me *that* easily.

"So you've never done it. What are your chances of success?" I interrogated.

Chace tilted his hand back and forth in front of him, estimating.

"I'd say 75 percent. Even though I've never done it, I'm almost positive I can make it work on any older car," he said.

I frowned, hoping 75 percent was a legitimate estimate. It sounded rather high for a person who'd never actually hotwired a car before.

"What happens if you fail?" I asked.

Chace's answer was simple, and his face was as serious as ever when he said it.

"We run," he said.

I gave him a highly suspicious look, but he returned it with a smug one that dared me to think of a better plan. Unfortunately, we both knew I didn't have one.

"Fine," I said eventually.

Chace immediately clapped his hands together and smiled.

"We don't have any other choice. It's survival of the fittest out here," he started brightly.

"The one good thing about being in a fight for your life is anything goes. These shapeshifters chasing us are relentless, so we'll have to be relentless as well."

An unfamiliar look crossed his face as he finished his sentence.

"Thanks for saving our lives back there," he said abruptly but very sincerely.

"You technically saved my life. If it hadn't been for you that giant shapeshifter crocodile would've eaten me... as a matter of fact he probably would've shot me before even having to shapeshift. Watching you win that battle was the most awesome thing I've ever seen."

I thought back to my nightmarish battle with Roman. I'd *barely* won. Most of my memory was of pain and primal rage.

"I didn't have *that* much control over it," I admitted, but I still felt a little tingle of pride.

"Well, just know if you'd lost we would be dead," Chace reminded me.

Knowing that he was right made me think about the fact that amidst all of the trouble it'd caused me, I'd hardly thought about how awesome of an ability I'd been blessed with.

"I just realized I've never seen it myself. How big is my shift compared to other tigers?" I asked, now excitedly curious.

It was a question I'd been wondering about since the time I was sure that shapeshifting wasn't all a dream. Chace smirked.

"I don't know exactly, but it has to be twice as big as the Siberians in the zoo," Chace said.

His expression turned into a smile as my eyes widened in disbelief.

"Legitimately. It's awesome. If I'd known you could transform into that thing I would've expected you to fight the Chen-grizzly," he said with true seriousness.

I was surprised by the unchecked admiration in his voice, and an uninvited smile made its way onto my face now. His expression displayed the lone bright spot in all of this – my actual shift was incredible. There was an inexplicable elation at knowing that such a power was at my disposal.

"I can't believe it's real," I confessed as I tried to soak it in.

Chace snorted.

"Don't give yourself too much credit. These other shapeshifters aren't just figments of your imagination. There are more, real live shapeshifters out there, and they all apparently want to kill you."

Chace was excellent at sounding relaxed when he was saying something completely unrelaxing, and even now the seriousness of his words was offset by his natural lightheartedness.

"As soon as it gets dark I'm going to try the car," he said then, lying back down on his bed.

He let out a sigh as pulled his covers back up around him. Even though we were fugitives, he seemed so comfortable that despite my nervousness about stealing a car, I reclined onto my bed as well. The clock read 5:40$_{PM}$ now, but it had been a long eight days or so. I closed my eyes, thankful to at least be able to lie on a bed.

"I can't believe you're actually going to do it," I said.

Chace laughed.

"Tonight we'll find out what we're made of," he responded.

"Aren't you nervous?" I asked.

Even with my deep breaths and eyes closed, anxious butterflies stirred themselves up in my stomach. Ironically, *I* wasn't even going to do the hard work.

"Only a little," Chace answered honestly.

"I'd feel better if I'd tried this before, but I figure there's no real benefit in worrying about it. Either I'll succeed or I won't."

I shook my head in awe of his composure and silently prayed for even the smallest dose of it. I felt like just a droplet would be enough to keep me from going insane between now and whenever it was time to affect our plan. The problems that could arise if he failed – namely jail – were nearly as daunting as being caught by shifters.

While I pondered that, I eventually became aware of the background music of Chace's heavy, slumbering breath. Very soon I fell asleep too. Sometime later I awoke to the sound of Chace moving around again, and when he saw me sit up, he slid Mr. Stevens' battered briefcase towards my feet while he packed up the few things we had in our room.

"You'll have to carry that," he said.

"Yeah right," I answered as I picked it up.

I tried a few random combinations on the lock and then gave up.

"You can't open it," Chace advised, watching me.

"Why are we keeping it then?" I asked, but even as I asked the question the answer began to dawn on me.

"You think there's money in there?" I added before Chace could answer.

"He hardly let that thing out of his sight," Chace reasoned, his voice hopeful.

"He always talked about being ready to run. If this was all he was going to take with him on some harrowing flight, you'd figure there's got to be something valuable in there. If it's not money, it could at least be more of those ancient relics. Trust me Zade, if we get those in front of the right people those things are like money."

Chace put on his jacket and reached into the pocket. He pulled out the Mayan Black Jade Celt from Mr. Stevens' house and smiled. I shook my head in mock disdain s he tucked it back into his pocket, but I had to admit that I liked his thinking.

"I mean, I don't know the names of everything we've got, but I'm sure we'd be very OK money-wise if we could sell them. If we can escape those shifters for any length of time we could probably support ourselves for years," he said.

The sound of possibility in his voice made me hopeful. I looked back down at the briefcase in a new light, but as I examined the bruised but tough stainless steel shell and secure lock, it was clear we didn't have anything nearly powerful enough to break it open. Nonetheless, considering all of the wealth Mr. Stevens had lying around his home, I now felt there was a high chance it would be worth the effort to bring it along.

"Maybe one day it'll suddenly open and we'll find a fortune," I said wishfully.

Chace snorted.

"I don't think it'll *suddenly* open, but with the right tools I'm sure it *can* be opened," Chace assured me.

"What else do we even have left?" I asked.

"An empty gun, a cell phone charger, a cell phone –"

Chace cut me off at the word cell phone, shaking his head.

"No cell phone. It got crushed during the madness back on the highway."

Chace brought over his bag and pulled out his crushed iPhone. It was clearly useless, but Chace dropped it back into the bag and stood up.

"We won't be getting separated anytime soon so we don't need it anyway," he said assuredly.

He moved towards the window and looked outside.

"There's a little Volvo in the corner," he relayed after a few minutes.

"It's pretty much as far away from the motel attendant as possible. I feel like I should be able to do it."

I moved over to the window, nudging Chace aside so that I could see what he was describing. Underneath us to our right the attendants' cubicle jutted outwards. To my left in the far corner of the parking lot, I saw the red Volvo hatchback.

"I'm thinking you can keep watch behind the vending machines," Chace said, pointing to the two machines in between the car and the attendant.

Damn, I thought, gulping.

"How long will it take?"

"I have no idea," Chace admitted.

It wasn't an answer that calmed my nerves, but I knew I didn't really have much of a choice on this one. We couldn't afford to stay here another night, and we were shapeshifter bait if we tried walking anywhere. With the gashes in my leg, I doubted I could've walked far anyhow.

"Are we doing it now?" I pressed, not sure whether I wanted to procrastinate or get it over with.

"Now or never," Chace nodded.

He still sounded calm and self-assured, and by the time we got downstairs that made me feel slightly better. I loitered as nonchalantly as I could by the vending machines, but to be honest I couldn't help watching Chace. He had created some sort of lock pick out of a hanger from our motel room, but he had otherwise said he planned to use his bare hands. With his bent hanger tucked into the sleeve of his shirt, he strode boldly over towards the Volvo and set to work.

For a few uneasy minutes my head snapped rapidly back and forth between Chace, who was working the hanger in the lock as discreetly as possible, and the rest of the sparsely populated parking lot, which thankfully remained devoid of people. Finally I heard a little pop coming from Chace's direction, and I turned to see him sliding into the drivers' seat of the Volvo.

I breathed a sigh of relief as he closed the door softly behind him, thankful that at least the sketchiest part of it was over. Unfortunately, we were still only halfway there. If it was anybody but Chace doing the job I would've said it was Mission Impossible, but somehow now that he'd gotten this far, I had a feeling he could succeed.

I stretched and leaned against one of the vending machines then, looking around at the barren landscape. There was nothing to see but rolling fields. I took a few steps out onto the sidewalk and tried to see around the front of the little attendant's cubicle, but the glass partition was facing away from me, which meant that I would have to walk in front of it to see inside. I didn't think he could see us either, but I could only hope that the motel attendant was occupied with his radio and not paying attention to some video feed of the lot.

Minutes ticked by. I strained my ears for the sound of anyone coming in or out of their room. I listened for the sound of the attendant coming out of the brown metal door, but that sound never came either. Instead the sound of an engine rumble shook me to attention, and I nearly jumped into the air when I heard it.

I had been looking out down the long, empty road we'd come in on, but I whipped my head around in true disbelief as the lights to the Volvo clicked on. I couldn't have been happier, but I forced myself to contain my excitement. As was the plan, I calmly walked over to the passenger side of the car, opened the door, and sat down. Inside in the drivers' seat, Chace was smirking proudly with a detached steering column cover in front of him.

"Success," he said.

"I can't believe we're doing this," I said back.

My heart was pounding furiously, from both excitement and fear. Meanwhile Chace put the car into reverse with more of his trademark calmness.

"We've got to make this look innocent," he said, both to himself and me.

We crunched slowly down the L-shaped length of the motel parking lot and towards the exit at a normal pace. I looked out of the window to our right, trying to seem normal as well, and then the unthinkable happened. The door of a first floor motel room opened, and the figure of a middle-aged businessman appeared. In a frozen moment he looked up from texting on his cell phone, saw his own car driving away, and then with surprising swiftness looked back down and started dialing.

For an instant he looked right into my eyes through the passenger window, but I instinctively turned away. It felt cowardly but I couldn't let him see my face – *survival of the fittest*. In the grand scheme of things it didn't matter whether he saw my face or not though, and Chace and I both exchanged loud expletives as he simultaneously stepped on the gas. We peeled out onto the main highway and away from Misty's Motel, but in the rearview I could see the man yelling into his cell phone as he ran out into the parking lot after us.

"We're so screwed," I said, breaking the tense hum of the Volvo engine.

Chace nodded very slightly but didn't respond. We were flying down the road like old-school bandits, but the aura of stolen glory defiled our escape. Even after we hummed uneventfully down the road for a few minutes we didn't say anything; the truth was too brutal this time. There was nowhere to go and we were easy to spot on this open road... it was an inevitable fact that we were going to jail now.

And, as if jail itself wasn't bad enough, Mr. Stevens had warned us time and again against the dangers of going to jail as a shapeshifter. Somehow we had managed to find that fate anyhow, and now there was nothing left to do but drive and wait for the moment to arrive. As I took a deep breath to gather myself I wondered how long it would be before we saw helicopter searchlights in the sky.

Chapter 19

ZADE DAVIDSON

Atwater, South Carolina - October 20, 2013

Even though our new Volvo was significantly more capable than Mr. Stevens' jalopy, we still topped out just before the 100 mph mark. Chace and I both knew that a top speed of that caliber was not fast enough – and we both fought against the reality of incarceration over the maximized hum of the engine. The image of the shocked and enraged face of the Volvo's owner was seared into my mind like a talisman of our impending capture.

"We're going to jail," I said dejectedly, finally breaking ten minutes of defeated silence.

Chace's eyes belied his agreement, but his lips tightened in defiance.

"They haven't caught us yet," he answered, deliberately optimistic.

"*Yet* is the key word," I said despairingly.

I was already overcome with anxiety, and I couldn't help checking the rearview mirror every few seconds for the police lights I knew would soon appear. There was literally nowhere to hide in the open fields that stretched in every direction.

"When the police *do* show up, there's no sense in running. We're going to have to let them arrest us," Chace said decidedly, his voice stoic and cognitive.

He took his eyes off of the road for the first time and met mine with a critical look for a second.

"Don't try to shift and fight them. They're going to bring large numbers for a grand theft auto. We're both bullet-padding if we do anything aggressive," he said sternly.

"We're screwed," I lamented, fighting back a combination of exasperation and dread.

My mind was already filling with nightmares of a lonely cell, but Chace looked over at me again, this time his expression condescending.

"If we let them arrest us peaceably at least we won't be dead. I remember Mr. Stevens' warnings about how easily the shifters will find us in jail as well as you do, but they've found us everywhere else we've hidden anyway. Whatever method they use to hunt down shapeshifter inmates can't possibly be instantaneous, and we'll have a better chance of escaping from the police when they don't already have helicopters out looking for us."

I could tell that Chace was trying to sound like he had a plan, but I also knew that the truth was the opposite.

"If they bring less than three police cars I'm going down fighting," I rebuffed fierily.

Chace managed a scoff through the heavy tension.

"There'll be more than three police cars," he said confidently.

Less than two more minutes down the road, his projection was confirmed.

"Here they come," he announced, and in the glass of the passenger side mirror I saw a pair of police lights flashing in the far distance.

A second later at least five more sets of flashing lights materialized behind the first, and they were all racing towards us.

"Step on it," I advised.

Chace shook his head, his expression tight.

"Look ahead," he said darkly.

I whipped back forward and saw another smattering of police lights cresting a hill almost the same distance ahead of us. We were trapped.

"This is it," Chace said, taking a deep breath.

I felt us start to decelerate as he gradually let his foot off of the gas pedal. Knowing that we were truly done for sent me into a minor panic, but I knew that unless I wanted to shapeshift and go kamikaze, surrender was the only choice. Growing louder as the two groups of policemen closed in on us was the sound of police sirens, and it didn't take long for the sound to grow into a loud wail.

"Don't tell them your real name," Chace instructed, giving me a meaningful look as we drifted to a stop.

"Until they identify us they'll keep us in the holding cells. Neither of us have ID's or criminal records, so it might take a while for them to figure out who we really are. Hopefully we'll have an escape plan by then," he said.

"OK," I agreed shakily.

Every part of my body, including my lips, was as jittery as a 1960's washing machine. I was so nervous my body bordered on complete dysfunction, and the closest police cruiser was already screeching to a halt a short distance behind us. It was accompanied by the altered sound of a voice coming through a megaphone.

"Step out of your vehicle with your hands in the air!" the voice commanded.

It was tinged with a southern accent and sounded very unfriendly. Police cars had pulled up in front of us now too, and the officers inside of them were piling out with their guns drawn. Some of the weapons looked like the AR's I'd seen in Call of Duty. Chace killed the engine and we exchanged a last look.

"I repeat, step OUT of the vehicle!"

The megaphone voice blasted us again, and with a final nod between us Chace and I stepped out into the chaos of lights and noise.

"Keep your hands in the air!"

"Get on the ground, now!"

I raised my hands in surrender and squinted into the blinding lights as an instant mob of armed officers advanced on us, shouting instructions.

"ON THE GROUND!" a myriad of human police voices ordered again and again.

I gingerly laid myself cheek-down on the tarmac and closed my eyes, biting back the pain that seared through my injured leg at the movement.

"Spread your hands and keep them where I can see them!" a voice near my head directed gruffly.

I did as I was told.

"Like this," the voice corrected.

I felt the rough kick of a boot against my wrist. My arm slid painfully across the ground to the 10 o'clock position, and I moved my right arm into the same position on the other side before the officer could kick that one too.

"It's a little late to be cooperating," the same voice said almost amusedly.

I felt a set of hands pat me down extensively, but I had literally nothing on me. Once finished, I remained silent while someone proceeded to tell me my rights in a clipped, uninterested fashion. When they finished I felt someone's knee drive into the small of my back, pinning me to the ground, and I grunted in discomfort. Through my effort to breathe with the added weight, I tried what the other officers were saying, but it was hard to discern anything in the long minutes of scurrying bodies and brusque, business-like voices. I only picked up snippets of various conversations as officers passed by me.

"...probably just stupid teenagers," I heard an alto female voice say.

"...nothing in the car except this briefcase," another voice said.

"Well this one doesn't have any weapons on him," said the voice who'd read me my rights.

It came from right behind me, so which told me he was the one with his knee crushing my lungs. With his weight on top of me my diaphragm was too compressed for me to even speak, but I continued to try and catch parts of the various police conversations.

"Pretty decent hotwiring job for a kid," the female voice remarked some time later.

I couldn't help but smirk internally at Chace's seemingly limitless skill.

"You got any ID on you, kid?"

After a few more minutes of being smashed into the tarmac, the voice of the man on top of me addressed me again.

"No," I forced out.

I kept my face against the pavement and my eyes closed.

"Well, get him in the car then, Colin," an older, commanding voice ordered.

A hand grabbed me by the elbow and yanked me to my feet, but at that moment a minor commotion broke out on the other side of the car.

"This one's got a gun, Chief!"

I tried to see what was happening through a sudden uproar of gruff shouts and scuffling, but I was dragged forcefully in the other direction and made to walk away from the tumult. For a minute I was bewildered as to why Chace's gun wasn't in his bag, but then I remembered that he had tucked it into his sock in case he needed to flash it during an emergency in our car theft operation.

No matter, the pair of hands that was dragging me away from the sound pushed me up against a police car then, and with no regard for the pain it caused they twisted my arms roughly behind my back. The hands slapped cold metal handcuffs onto my wrists and cranked them until they bit into my flesh, and then before I could even grimace in pain I was thrown into the backseat of a police car.

When the officer slammed the door shut behind me the sounds of outside were instantly muted, but after a minute of fidgeting I was able to turn around and look out of the back window. The car I had been thrown in was a little ways down the road from the row of police Suburban's now blocking off the highway, and moving amongst them were a dozen or more officers. A similar number of Crown Victoria's were parked amongst the Suburban's. As Chace had predicted, the police had appeared in droves.

By the time I had a chance to take it all in, a younger officer opened the drivers' side door of my Crown Vic and poked his head in.

"Your buddy had a gun on him so he won't be going anywhere for a while," he said curtly through the partition, and then he slammed the door shut again.

His voice matched that of the officer who had initially pinned me to the ground, and I looked to the left out of my window and watched the inaudible conversation between him and a taller, graying officer. There was a distinct sense of authority and deference in the older and younger officers' stances, respectively. I remembered someone referring to the younger officer as Colin, who was short and brown-haired. He had the pompous, authoritative air of most cops, but he seemed very grunt-like compared to the elder officer, and considering the pain he'd caused me while he'd sat on top of me, that realization brought a tiny twinge of satisfaction.

From inside the police car I couldn't hear a single word of the officers' conversation, but after thirty minutes or more they exchanged words with another set of officers and then climbed into the front seats of my car. The older officer took the drivers' seat; neither officer acknowledged me. We sat there for a another few minutes while the older officer pushed buttons on his police computer, and then he clicked on the police lights and slowly pulled off into the middle position of a three vehicle procession of police cars.

It was a weird feeling being the criminal sitting in the backseat of a flashing police car, and it wasn't one I liked. Even though it was kind of empowering knowing that this whole police convoy was for me, I felt totally alone, totally defeated, and incalculably nervous. On the other side of the criss-crossed partition the two officers sat in smug silence; either staring blankly through the windshield or fiddling with the police equipment.

As I'd somewhat expected, the uncomfortable ride lasted for an eternity. It was impossible to tell where we were going in this unknown place in the darkness of night, but eventually we pulled up to Atwater County House of Corrections. It stuck out in the middle of barrenness just like Misty's Motel, but it was eight times as big and foreboding and was surrounded by a couple of layers of barbed wire fence. Judging by the sparsely populated, open lands of Atwater County, I couldn't imagine that there were enough criminals to fill up the oversized cubes rising up out of nowhere to my left.

"There's the big house at last," Colin pointed out.

I ignored his obvious observation. The daunting view of the dark and foreboding jail did not put me in a talkative mood.

"Pride of Atwater, Mississippi if you ask me," he continued anyway.

"Lucky for you, it'll be a little while before we move you from the holding cells to general population," he said.

Colin pointed to the farthest brick square to the right. I wondered why he was so talkative, but I took a mental note of where the holding cells were in relation to everything else.

"Stop talking to him Pickett," the older officer snapped at him as we passed through the security gate behind the first cruiser.

His voice was dry and commanding, and Colin looked like a scolded child as he deliberately shut his mouth. The older officer pulled our cruiser up to the brightened middle section of the jail and parked then, and it was all business from there. After two burly, unfamiliar officers yanked me out of the car and took me inside, I was run through the booking process.

Lights that were far too bright and probing followed me into every room as I was moved from rolling my fingers across fingerprinting ink to facing off against the mugshot camera. Handcuffs and shackles came and went from my wrists and ankles, and when I was finally left with my hands free I was put in a repulsively sterile interrogation room. From there, a tall, birdlike detective subjected me to an endless number of accusatory questions, ranging from my family and background to my motivation for stealing the Volvo. I ignored all of his tactics and was generally uncooperative, responding exclusively with the most succinct lies possible.

Another shorter, bald detective joined the first one after a while, but his presence did nothing to change my MO. In actuality the fact that they had brought in another needling detective pushed me over the edge, and with no freedoms and my frustration beyond the boiling point, I eventually stopped answering all questions and demanded a lawyer. Unsurprisingly my request was ignored and met with unrelenting glowers, and the accusatory detectives weren't sufficiently irked until the clock on the wall was significantly into the hours of the next morning.

When they eventually realized that they had extracted absolutely no useful information from me they finally gave up, and I was left sitting there alone for another few hours until I was reunited with Colin, who chattily moved me into a holding cell and locked me in. My mind had been mush for a long time by then, and I didn't ingest a single word he said on the long walk from the interrogation rooms to the holding cells. When he deposited me inside of one of the cells he left me shackled, and I accordingly shuffled over to the edge of the bottom bunk and sat down once he'd disappeared, mindlessly overcome by the throbbing pain in my leg and the hours of questioning.

This must be the end. My leg hurts impossibly bad. Where is Chace?

The same thoughts swam through my head in endless circles. Whenever I finally lifted my head up and looked around, I saw that across from my bunk bed sat a dirty white toilet flecked with irremovable brown waste and a similarly marred silver metal sink. Thick jail bars separated me from the dimly lit concrete hallway, and a smaller set of iron bars slashed through the daylight coming through a tiny window at the top of the back wall.

The little bit of happy yellow sunlight that danced on the diminutive concrete window ledge was more of a taunt than anything, and as I soaked it all in I slowly understood how physically trapped I was in this empty room. A gut-wrenching wave of desire for the simplest freedoms washed over me as I realized that no matter how bad I wanted to leave or what I would be willing to do to escape, my ability to leave this tiny room was totally revoked.

When I tried to take my mind elsewhere, my most recent memories were just a kaleidoscope of horrors – my thoughts danced from the terror and disrespect of being arrested to the accusatory, threatening interrogation of detectives.

For a minute I thought I would fall over the edge of insanity right then and there, but somehow I managed to hold it together by systematically taking each of the detestable events that had led me here and accepting that there was nothing I could about them now.

I focused on convincing myself that as long as I was alive there was hope for improvement, and when I looked eventually looked down and remembered that I still had the stack of papers listing my charges in my hand, I flipped them to the ground spitefully.

Nothing that had happened, from my first shift in the woods behind Historic Castille to our incarceration for grand theft auto, seemed to be my fault or something I could have controlled. I felt like a loose leaf in a whirlwind, and whatever my charges were my gut told me that they were inconsequential in my ultimate destiny. Despite the agony that these policemen and this jail cell was causing me, I could almost *feel* my shapeshifting affairs inexorably finding their way here, and as much as sitting in this cell tormented me, I knew that Chen Lake and his men were still out there, making their way here with a far worse fate for me in their hands.

Now that Chace and I were separated as well, I was probably worse off than Chen could even hope for. Without Chace's brainpower to complement the physical power of my Siberian tiger shift, I felt like gunpowder with no flame. If Chen or any other shapeshifters got here soon enough, it would seem to them that I had played right into their hands yet again.

———

The sun was even brighter when I woke up from a forced, broken sleep a while later, and it was the cacophonous clatter of sliding jail bars that rattled me awake. Probably more tired than before I'd slept, I snapped my eyes open, hoping they were at least showing the decency to feed me. Through the thin stream of afternoon daylight however, I saw a fully uniformed officer bringing even better news.

Looking battered but alive, the guard roughly shoved the bent head of Chace Redman through the shaft of sunlight and into our cell, slamming the gate shut behind him. The officer then stalked off wordlessly, but Chace managed a crooked smile as he scuffed his way in. It was probably the only sight that could have given me the small sense of relief I felt.

"Man, am I glad to see you," I noted with sincere appreciation.

Chace's smile grew a centimeter wider.

"Same to you," he replied.

He turned his head to the side so that I could see his other cheek, which was swollen and purple.

"These jerks are as racist as humanly possible," he muttered, shaking his head in disbelief as he made his way onto the floor against the back wall.

He showed me his arms and hands, which were bruised and raw. I also noticed that he was holding his left arm favorably. It stayed tucked in awkwardly by his side during all of his movements and I could tell that it was injured more than just the usual battering that came with being slammed against the ground. With us being from such a diverse town as Castille, the differential treatment was stunning.

"Are you sure it wasn't just because you had a gun?" I asked, both incredulous and outraged.

Chace shook his head knowingly, and I could tell that from that simple answer that his treatment was not because of his gun.

"They took my *unloaded* gun the second they found it. It was afterwards that I got all of these injuries," he explained.

His emphasis on the word *unloaded* was heavy and angry, and having never seen Chace really injured before, I looked him over more closely. From his injured arm to his purplish cheek, the sight was alarming, especially considering I had always imagined him as possessing a generous dose of invincibility.

"What happened to your arm?" I asked as he readjusted himself and grimaced.

He made a pained face and took a deep breath before he could answer.

"My shoulder's dislocated. As soon as they found the pistol in my sock they acted like I had tried to run, and some fat police officer pounced on me. He had to weigh 300lbs, because the way he put his knees into my back it popped my shoulder right out of the socket. It hurt so bad I cried. They didn't even have to put cuffs on me after that – they just kept dragging me around by my hurt arm and telling me to suck it up."

I had never dislocated any limbs, but if it was painful enough to draw tears out of Chace than I knew it must've been agonizing. At seeing my involuntary cringe however, Chace gave me a fearful smirk.

"I was actually hoping you could snap it back into place for me," he said.

"Yeah right," I deferred instantly.

Chace motioned around at our empty cell.

"Who else then? You don't need medical skills and it hurts like hell," he appealed.

He gave me a pleading look, and there was genuine pain in his voice.

"Please," he begged.

"Fine," I said after a moment.

Besides my lack of skill in any forms of medical practice, I was also highly creeped out by the idea of popping his bone back into place. He had to know he was signing himself up for torture, but nonetheless Chace spent the next five minutes trying to explain to me how to 'reduce his shoulder.' For my part I tried to ingest as much of the five minute verbal walkthrough as possible, but when I tried to physically apply his instructions, the process was anything but smooth. For twenty minutes we had to literally *press* through a plethora of errors by myself – each of which were met with bellows of pain from Chace – before we were finally rewarded with the pop of his shoulder sliding back into place.

"I hate you."

Chace slumped onto the ground the moment it happened, looking both exhausted and relieved.

"I told you it wasn't going to be pretty," I reminded him defensively.

He sighed again, panting heavily.

"It's ok. It's back in place now. Thanks," he breathed.

He sat up from the floor when his panting reduced into normal breathing, and he already looked more like the old, active Chace I knew.

"On the bright side it looks like Atwater County Jail is pretty undermanned and full of dimwits," he said, changing the subject.

"That guy who threw me in here was one of the cops who arrested us at the beginning, and I overheard him telling someone that he picks up extra hours doing guard duty. From what I saw, I think they've only got one guy at a time watching this whole holding wing."

I saw a familiar twinkle flash in his eye, but that bit of information didn't help me see any possible way out. I looked longingly at the hallway beyond the jail bars.

"I guess that's the advantage of getting locked up in the middle of nowhere," I said sarcastically.

"Only one man to beat," Chace said, ignoring my sarcasm.

"Plus, I think we're the only prisoners on this floor. I think I saw a couple other inmates on the lower floors, but I guess there's not a lot of criminals in Atwater County," he remarked.

"Or people in general," I added.

Chace chuckled and looked around our sparse cell, eventually turning towards the window near the ceiling. He examined the thick glass behind the bars for a moment and then sighed. It was clear that even if we could break the glass window somehow, not even a dwarf could fit through those bars or the concrete square it was fitted into.

"It'll take me a while to come up with any kind of plan," Chace conceded.

I gave him a 'told you so' look. I was highly doubtful that even with a few days to think on it there was any way for us to break out of here.

"I could use a shower," I said randomly as I examined the dirt buried beneath my fingernails.

I wondered when that would be an option as Chace chuckled and examined his own grunge. I couldn't even remember the last time I *had* showered. A while later Chace climbed onto the top bunk and fell asleep, but since I had just been sleeping I merely laid on the bottom bunk in endless boredom.

At long last I heard the sound of metal wheels rolling down the hallway, and as I'd hoped, the sound was followed by a smudgy stainless steel dolly. It was being pushed by none other than Officer Colin Pickett, who was still dressed in his full field uniform as he stopped the cart in front of our cell and pulled out two trays of food.

"Here's dinner," he said, looking us over comically.

I made my way over to the jail bars and took the two trays through the food slot as Chace started to wake up behind me.

"Trying to get a real identity out of you two has caused quite a little stir," the officer said as he handed me the trays.

"Neither of your fingerprints show up in the system, and we know the names you gave us are bogus. Chief says we can't proceed with anything until you admit that you're name isn't Stanley Pitts and your friend's name isn't LaHeisman James."

Colin shook his head and turned the dolly around, retreating out of sight along with the squeak of the dolly wheels. Meanwhile I handed Chace one of the brown cafeteria trays and we examined the food. In one of the little indentations on the tray was a rock hard biscuit; in another was a thick metal bowl filled halfway up with a light brown liquid that looked like soup. A yellowish chicken breast dominated the biggest square.

"Jail food," Chace muttered, sighing.

Not a droplet of steam lifted itself off of our soup bowls, and it felt lukewarm at best when I stuck my finger in it to test. The *taste* of food however, was no longer important. Food was survival now, and with that in mind Chace and I both made quick work of the cold, bland dinner.

It felt very good to have something in my stomach, but the sink water was a poor way to rinse it all down. Also, once dinner was finished, the perennial nothingness of jail returned. For a while Chace and I mulled over ideas for escape, but we made little progress and quickly found flaws in the few ideas we came up with. The windows were too small, and the jail bars were too strong. Finding a way to exploit Colin somehow was the only idea we didn't immediately shut down, but even then neither of us had much faith in our ability to guile our way out of here.

We ultimately succumbed to sleep quite early in the night with both of our minds and bodies exhausted, and nothing but each other for comfort. Still, despite my exhaustion, my sleep was broken. My dreams were nightmares full of police officers, jail cells, and torture at the hands of shapeshifters. During the moments I would shake myself awake, those nightmares remained all too real.

All around me were the ensnaring walls of a jail cell, and it was a sight I'd never considered really seeing. The feeling of con-striction ate at me every time I thought about it. In all of my earthly power I could still only lie there and sulk.

I tossed and turned for what seemed like an eternity, but it was still pitch black outside when Chace and I were startled awake. It was the sound of running feet that woke us, and that sound was once again shortly followed by the appearance of Officer Pickett. This time he had no silver dolly, though.

Instead he had a key in his hand, and as Chace and I each looked towards the jail gate, we saw Officer Pickett already hur-riedly unlocking the heavy door. We quickly got to our feet, and through the light of the hallway we could see that he was intensely rattled.

"What's going on?" Chace asked before I could.

"We're under attack," Officer Pickett answered, his voice pan-icky and vague.

Chace and I exchanged glances as my heart hit the floor.

"What do you mean?" I demanded.

Officer Pickett shook his head.

"I don't know," he said confusedly.

"Chief Adams radioed in to warn me that we were under attack and that it was in my best interest to run. He said that all of the other officers were down."

Chace and I looked at each other.

"All of the other officers?" I repeated.

"That's what the Chief said. I didn't see what happened, I've been sitting at the end of this wing with you two," he said.

Chace and I looked at each other again. It was too obvious. Our greatest fears were already being realized... much, much sooner than expected. It hadn't occurred to me that Martin could possibly be *this* efficient and powerful. We hadn't even been in Atwater County Jail for 36 hours.

"Wait," Chace said then, raising his hand to interject.

"If your Chief suggested that you run, why are you letting *us* out?"

It was a question I hadn't thought to ask, mainly because I was just willing to accept any offer to help us survive. Unfortunately, Officer Pickett swallowed culpably in response.

"Chief Adams – before the transmission went out – he said that she was looking for the two of you."

Officer Pickett's eyes mirrored the fear and urgency that just took over mine.

"Roslyn," I cursed.

Chace nodded in agreement, his lips tight.

"You know this girl?" Officer Pickett flared.

He took a step back and put a hand on his sidearm. We both put our hands up in defense, but Chace's face showed much more exigency than fear.

"Yes," Chace answered impatiently.

"We don't exactly *know* her, but if she is coming this way then we don't have time to discuss logistics right now. She's clearly dangerous, and if we want to live we've got to get moving," he urged.

Officer Pickett looked from me to Chace, indecision muddling his expression.

"Besides the fact that one woman has managed to down all ten of the other officers on duty here, reinforcements from the nearest precinct are 40 minutes away. You two are my only hope. If I let you out – whoever you are – *I* want to live."

The seriousness in his voice was dire. Then I realized what he was implying.

"You want us to give ourselves up?" I asked.

"You're using us as a bargaining chip?"

My voice was incredulous, yet Officer Pickett looked so serious that I thought he might break down. It took him a good minute to finally answer me.

"To prevent prisoners from escaping this ward, there's only one way in and one way out. If I happen to cross paths with this woman you called Roslyn on the way out, I need to have what she wants."

There was no animosity in his voice, only hard truth. Chace and I both knew that giving ourselves up was suicide, but it was equally suicidal to remain in this cell and wait for Roslyn to come find us.

"I have a family – a daughter. They need me."

There was almost pleading in Officer Pickett's voice, but he pulled his gun out of the holster and aimed it at us. We both put our hands up again, but then he dropped his keys to the floor and slid them over to me. They jingled to a sharp stop against the front of my worn boot.

"Undo your cuffs… quickly," he commanded.

I felt Officer Pickett's gun trained on me as I racked my brain for a plan and slid myself out of my cuffs.

"She's not coming to rescue us. She's coming to kill us. We can't just give ourselves up," I appealed.

"She's coming to capture him and kill me to be exact," Chace added.

"I know that doesn't make a lot of sense, but you have to believe us. If you give us over to her, you're signing our death warrant."

After I slipped out of my shackles I handed Chace the keys and he unlocked his as well. Officer Pickett looked stoic and moved the gun in Chace's direction next, but I knew there was no time to argue the issue right now.

"Either way we have to hurry," I urged.

"The more time we deliberate, the closer she gets to killing us all," Chace agreed.

Officer Pickett nodded, finally looking like he understood that.

"Hurry up and follow my directions then," he said.

Without asking another question he ordered us out of our cell into a long ugly hallway. We were the only delinquents in the holding cells, which was odd because there were so many silver-barred jail cells lining the hallway. Chace and I's cell was only three or four cells down from the end, where there were two doors beneath a glowing red exit sign.

The door directly beneath it was heavy and painted brown, and the other one to the right was transparent and made of bul-letproof glass. I assumed the latter door led to the guard room, because through the glass I could see an arrangement of electronic equipment. As we approached them, Chace pulled open the guard room door.

"Backup is still 30 minutes away, don't waste your time," Officer Pickett reminded him, pausing and shaking his head.

Chace was leaning in through the half-open guard room door with the receiver of a police radio in his hand, but at remembering the arrival time for backup, he scoffed.

"Right," he said.

He hopped down out of the guard room. Officer Pickett moved forward to open the Exit door then, but as he reached for it, it burst open from the other side. Officer Pickett instinctively reached back for his sidearm, but his hand never made it there. Two muffled gunshots came blasting out from behind the door and directly into him. He gasped, stumbled backwards, and then crumpled to the ground before either Chace or I could even move.

Chace, who was far more athletic and not hobbled by a leg injury, moved first. It was a grave mistake. As he tried to dive for the side of the hallway a dark figure swept out from behind the door like a wraith and whirled towards Chace's movement. In one fluidly accurate motion it raised a weapon and fired again. Chace roared as the impact of the silenced gunshot carried him into the ground, and he collapsed against the wall, unmoving.

The dark figure then turned towards me with such lethal swiftness that it took me a second to bring my eyes away from Chace's slumped body and focus on the figure's face. When I did I saw Roslyn's familiar, exquisite features underneath the hood of a black hoodie jacket. We met eyes for a second, and then a sudden tide of anger coursed through me and I clenched my fists involuntarily. Roslyn matched my anger by leveling her pistol at my chest.

"Don't do it," she said.

For a second I paused – there was something disarming about her beauty even with her gun pointed at me – but it wasn't enough to stop me. I willed myself into my alternate tiger body – ready to shift and kill her – except just before I felt the gratifying haze of shifting came over me I was thrown backwards by a penetrating impact.

Simultaneously the sound of another silenced gunshot rang in the hallway, and along with it I hit the ground. An instant later pain like fire erupted over the right half of my body, and I bellowed in agony as I realized that I had just been shot. I clutched my shoulder as blood seeped through my t-shirt and onto my hand, slowly at first and then more rapidly. I realized we were all going to die here.

"I warned you."

Roslyn's voice came from somewhere above me. I grunted in response, still in far too much pain to speak. It was like the force of a Mack truck had been packed into a bullet and driven through my shoulder. I forced my eyes open a sliver, and behind Roslyn's slender figure I could see Chace. He had propped against the wall slightly, but his head was down and his grey shirt was covered in fresh red blood.

Roslyn followed my eyes over to Chace's body and inspected him herself. She took a quick glance down at a watch on her wrist, and to my disillusion, a miniscule look of sympathy flitted across her soft brown eyes when she looked back at me.

"I hit him just below the ribs I think. He's going to die. If he was going to live he'd need emergency medical attention in the next fifteen minutes, and the nearest hospital is thirty minutes away."

She pursed her lips contritely.

"Sorry," she said.

The sudden, impossibly devastating realization that Chace had a bullet in his stomach and was going to die was almost twice as painful as the bullet wound in my own shoulder.

"Can you save him?" I asked through gritted teeth, holding my arm.

Just the motion of talking sent shockwaves of pain through me, and I fought through them only to see Roslyn shake her head.

"No, there's nothing I can do for him. Martin is expecting me to bring *you* back alive though, so I promise that if you come with me now – peacefully – I'll let fate take your friend naturally."

I watched Chace take a few pitiful, shallow breaths and felt so overwhelmingly guilty that I wanted to die as well. I was watching my best friend die and it was all my fault. He whimpered a little then, and I almost thought it would be better to have Roslyn end it, but I knew I couldn't bear watching or ordering that. All I could do was blink back my own pain and stare at his crumpled, bleeding body for a moment, unable to accept reality.

"Otherwise I finish him now," Roslyn said suddenly, her voice as cold as ice.

In conjunction she snapped her arm up and aimed her muzzled gun back at Chace.

"Don't!" I blurted desperately.

Roslyn eyed me, considering.

"I'll come with you…. peacefully," I implored.

"Please," I begged.

Roslyn thought for a second before she lowered her pistol, and when she did her expression instantly morphed into one of impatience.

"Fine, but hurry up. I've shown enough mercy on you as it is."

Somehow still beautiful despite her heartlessness, she glared at me as I gathered my resolve and used my left arm to agonizingly pull myself up off of the ground. My right arm was completely limp and useless, and even thinking about it sent amplified waves of pain through it. I was helpless, but Roslyn pointed her pistol at me anyway.

"Where are you taking me?" I breathed when I managed to get to my feet.

The room was spinning a little and a copious amount of blood was running down my arm, but I fought to remain conscious. Roslyn's looked me over pitilessly and answered brusquely.

"I'm taking you to meet Martin Evers," she said.

Chapter 20

ZADE DAVIDSON

Atwater, South Carolina – October 22, 2013

*A*s Roslyn used her gun to prod me towards the door we passed by Officer Pickett, who was lying only a foot away from the door, and as I made to turn the handle per Roslyn's instructions he actually stirred a little. In my concern for Chace I realized I'd totally forgotten about him, but at seeing his movement Roslyn stopped and looked down at him for a few seconds. He was still. She turned away, but at that instant he groaned mercifully. In a flashing movement Roslyn's pistol was aimed at his head.

"Wait!"

The words burst out of my mouth just in time. Roslyn snapped her head towards me with her finger on the trigger and the pistol still aimed at Officer Pickett.

"What's the problem?! The *only* reason I'm not shooting your friend is so that I don't have to explain to Martin why I had to kill you. You didn't bargain for this guy's life."

Her tone was one of fury, and she turned her icy gaze back towards the wounded and motionless officer before I could respond. Then, in the most bone-chilling display I had ever witnessed, she calmly unloaded one gunshot into Officer Pickett's and another into his chest. As the sound of the second gunshot dissipated down the jail hallway, she reached into a pocket of her leather coat, changed the clip on her gun, and nodded for me to continue down the stairs.

I couldn't follow her orders, though. My eyes were glued to the freshly dead body of Officer Pickett, which was now leaking even more blood. His passage from life to death had been so swift and so immediate. It almost forced me to take one long, last look at Chace, who I didn't want to draw unnecessary attention towards. He was still semi-consciously slumped against the wall with his arm over his bleeding stomach, but he was also at least still breathing shallowly. I knew that the final images of him and Officer Pickett would be burned into my mind forever.

"Get moving or I'll put another bullet in you," Roslyn said then, her tone still plainly unforgiving.

Her gun was back on me, and there was a deadliness in her eyes that I didn't dare challenge. With the heaviest heart imaginable, I turned away from my best friend and only ally in the world, and at Roslyn's direction I pushed through the painted doors and headed into the cement stairwell on the other side. She jabbed me down it at a quick clip, and with total disregard for my pulsating shoulder and my still-injured leg, she pushed me through another heavy brown door at the bottom of the stairwell and directed me out into a gravel courtyard.

Outside, two dark buildings loomed ahead of me to the left; to the right I saw the harsh silver of multiple rows of tall, barbed wire fences. The only light came from the two lamp posts near the squat, closer building in the center, which I recognized as the central office of the jail. Parked directly in front of it was a pristine, black Mercedes-Benz.

In the recesses of my mind I remembered being jealous of my Uncle Spencer's Mercedes, and I looked at this one now with cheerless irony rather than the fear I was used to. There was no hope for me now. As Roslyn ushered me across the gravel towards it, a man got out of the drivers' side of the car, expecting us. While we were still about thirty yards away, she stepped up close behind me and leaned very subtly towards my ear.

"You would do well to cooperate from here on out – the lives of everyone you love depends on it," she hissed gravely.

Her spontaneous advice caught me off guard and I almost turned to look at her, but a discreet and painful pinch kept me looking neutral. I was totally confused by both her motives and her words, and the latter scared me. There wasn't enough time to think about it though, because very shortly we had reached the Mercedes. The man standing outside of the car was holding Mr. Stevens' briefcase somewhat triumphantly, and he gave Roslyn a small, approving nod as we greeted him.

In just the small motion of his nod however, the unmistakable aura of raw power that radiated from him hit me like a brick wall. He was dressed normally enough – he wore elegant business slacks and a suit jacket – but his white-gray hair sat on top of a perfectly formed, youthful face. He was tall, and he stood straight and arrogant, and out of his youthful face peered piercing blue eyes that saw through me as well as if I was invisible. His arrogance wasn't the type that seemed challengeable though, and it was truthfully immediately intimidating.

"Zade Davidson."

The man expelled a voice that was easy yet gravelly; both calm and dangerous.

"Yes," I answered, anticipating.

"Martin Evers," the man introduced, but I had already guessed who he was.

He made no movement to shake hands, but instead turned his attention towards Roslyn.

"I recovered this from the Main Office. It belonged to Gordon," he said.

He handed her the briefcase, and she gave it an interested appraisal as she took it.

"I remember this thing. It's the first time I've ever seen it unattached to him," she said.

"Indeed," Martin agreed.

Then he turned back towards me. His eyes held mine with the crippling stare of someone fully aware of the fear they imposed, and with one hand in his pocket he stepped towards me.

"You've done a rather remarkable job avoiding my men prior to today," he said.

There was no congratulation or impression in his voice, only observation.

"Thus, it *is* nice to finally meet you. Later, we will have much to discuss."

For some reason it was scary to even be close to this man – despite his relatively harmless appearance and size – and it was because of that that I didn't realize the meaning in his words until it was too late.

"No," I tried to say, but my words were muffled by the hand in his pocket flashing towards my face.

The cloth he produced was on me just as I opened my mouth, and a grip like a vice grabbed my injured arm and held me from running while another vice grip kept the rag pressed to my face. I tried to move away, but I was choked and blinded by the cloth and incapacitated by the intensified pain in my shoulder created by Martin's grasp. I couldn't breathe underneath the fabric, and I involuntarily inhaled a full gulp of the chemically sweet aroma that soaked it. The smell was so strong that it made me stagger backwards, but Martin mirrored my fall and kept the thing over my nose. I couldn't fight the need to take another breath, and as soon as I did everything went black.

———

I awoke in what at first appeared to be total darkness, and my head throbbed like it had been smashed between two cymbals. I blinked a couple of times to try and clear my head and restore some semblance of vision, and as my eyes adjusted I realized that I wasn't quite in *total* darkness. There was a tiny bit of light coming from above me. There were a few rows of thin black lines cutting across the light, and when my vision focused further I realized that the black lines were the bars of a cage.

I tried to shift positions but my limbs felt impossibly heavy – like four tree trunks really – and a groan of extreme discomfort escaped my lips. There was a soreness in my neck that made me think I had slept for 20 hours with my head in freefall, and when I noticed that it also took a concerted effort to even swallow, it became clear that I was not only caged, but also heavily drugged. Beneath me I could feel the faint murmurs of movement; tires rumbling across tarmac.

My body was propped upright against the side of whatever cage I was housed in, which was unfortunately only slightly larger than I was. My feet were only an inch from the other end of the cage, and my head was very close to the top of it. Hard black plastic covered the bottom, and as I looked through the barred cage top again I saw that it was slid in amongst stacks of brown cardboard boxes. The little bit of light and air that I received was coming from a rectangular hole where one of the boxes had been shifted off-center. Through the light-hole I could see only whiteness.

Through the fogginess in my brain I tried to piece together the memory of how I'd gotten here and remembered the shock-white hair of Martin Evers... and the sudden flash of chloroform towards my face. I didn't want to believe it, but my current predicament could've only meant one thing: Mr. Stevens' projection of my ultimate, inevitable fate had come to fruition.

Martin Evers had captured me.

So... this is what it feels like to be kidnapped, I thought.

I immediately and instinctively wanted to scream for help, but I was essentially paralyzed. I could barely even stretch my neck towards the light to try and suck in some of the fresher air. My body and mind were sickened and immobilized by the combined effects of the drugs and utter defeat. I was sure that if my stomach muscles had currently had the power to contract, I would have thrown up instantly.

The abyss of helplessness that consumed my emotions was even worse now than it had been in the Atwater County jail cell. This cage confined me in an even tighter space, and although I could feel little pain, the distress of claustrophobia was worse. It ate at my insides like an acid, and it was almost merciful when the power of the drugs took over again and lulled me back to sleep.

The next time I awoke though, the pain in my shoulder from the untended bullet wound returned in explosive fashion. Time was incalculable, but I must have passed out again for a while because now that the effects of the drugs had dissipated somewhat, even the most minimal movements resulted in violent shockwaves of pain. Turning my neck sent a crippling shiver through my shoulder, readjusting my back caused the pins-and-needles numbness in my legs to erupt.

Consciousness itself was a form of torture, but whatever vehicle I was housed in eased to a halt very soon after I awoke as if my sedation had been meticulously timed. A few moments later I heard the grating sound of the trailer door opening, and amongst a bit of shuffling the box centered closest to the light moved aside. In its place Roslyn's face appeared, and despite my predicament I had to admit that it was still angelic. Her brown eyes peered down at me over her sharp little nose with a tender look that was somehow mesmerizing through my pain.

"You're awake," she said, smiling just a little.

Her voice was as alluring as her face, but I fought the urge to swoon over her. The girl hovering over me had just killed my best friend.

"Where are you taking me?" I tried to ask, but it came out unintelligibly slurred, and without the hostility I intended.

"Wuhhh ahh thuu achey bee?" was what I actually said.

Roslyn gave me another sympathetic, tiny smile.

"Don't try to talk," she said softly.

She unlatched the top of the cage and lifted it open, and as she did so I caught a whiff of her sweet perfume. I couldn't help but notice the divine grace in the movements of her hands as well, and simultaneously wonder how they could create so much evil.

She stepped back then and allowed me to take in a few deep breaths of air with the top open, which I gratefully inhaled. I closed my eyes to let the soothing oxygen fill my lungs. When I opened them again, Roslyn had whipped out a lengthy syringe. She flicked it a couple times, testing.

"Your shoulder is already healing up nicely," she mentioned divertingly.

I didn't want to take my eyes away from the needle she held, but I instinctively looked down at my wound, and before I could even assess how much it had healed she pounced. The syringe flashed in and out of my leg so fast that I didn't even have time to react. To be honest, I didn't even have time to feel the pinch of the needle. In less than two seconds Roslyn had retreated out of the cage and locked it back.

"Easy and painless," she said.

She smiled for real this time, looking me dead in the eyes for an instant. Her look was still gentle, and totally devoid of the heartlessness that I remembered from Atwater County Jail, but it was impossible to tell if it was just more of the faux-softness she had used to trick me an instant ago.

"The next time you wake up we will have arrived at The Warehouse," she informed me unashamedly, and she turned away from the harsh look of betrayal I gave her in return.

My heart stung with self-castigation at how easily Chace's killer had beguiled me – less than 24 hours after his death even – but with Roslyn's trademark efficiency and grace she replaced the cardboard boxes around my cage and disappeared. The anger that subsequently flared up in my chest was hot, yet it was futile. I was already slipping back into the netherworld, anesthetized by whatever fast-acting sedative she had shot me with.

I passed out again less than a minute after Roslyn left me, and when I woke up a third time I was back to square one with the drugs. The pain in my shoulder was gone again, but so was my functionality. The second administering of anesthesia must've worked on top of the first, because this hangover was twice as deadening. Everything in my body felt so heavy that I felt like it was being subjected to triple gravity.

Through my paralysis I searched for the feeling of the motion of the truck beneath me, but from what I could tell we were stationary. Considering that the last time I had woken Roslyn had come for me immediately, I strained my ears for the sound of people, but I heard only silence. The shifters operated with such efficiency that I had no choice but to believe someone would be coming for me soon nonetheless, yet I waited anxiously for that moment in vain. At least an hour of uneventful silence passed, and it wasn't until the end of that hour that I was at least able to turn my head slightly. Another hour later, as I began to be able to move my upper body, the pain and discomfort that wracked my body returned as well.

In my current, pitiful state I wasn't able to think about much – through the hours of agony my brain remained muddy and slow. The world was just a nonsensical mash-up of the pain from my gunshot wound, nightmarish flashes of Chace's dying form, and fear of what awaited me next. Part of me wanted to give in and die now, part of me wanted to live only for revenge. But, trapped here in this dog cage, it didn't matter at all what I wanted.

If I could have had one thing it would have been to at least be able to think clearly, but far before my brain recovered to normal functionality the silence was broken. The sudden, rough sound of the truck gate sliding up was quickly followed by a patter of footsteps, and then the boxes around me shifted again and white light flooded in.

This time the face that appeared was not Roslyn's however, yet in a way it was just as distinct. It was a man's face this time – a young man with light brown skin only a shade lighter than Chace's – but he was strikingly hairless, and his face was adorned with an array of piercings. Two gold hoops clung tightly to each of his nostrils, and at least a dozen more piercings lined each of his ears. The only hair on him belonged to his eyebrows, and even one of those wore a final, studded gold ring.

"He's awake," the face called in a surprisingly deep voice.

It may have been the deepest voice I'd ever heard, and when he spoke he revealed sparkling white teeth. Those too seemed unnaturally perfect.

"I'll bring him out," he boomed.

From below him the man seemed impossibly tall, and as he tossed the rest of the boxes deeper into the truck and away from my cage, he exposed a view of a crowd of people standing in a semi-circle just beyond the loading ramp of the truck. Once he had cleared a path to that ramp, he grabbed the bars at the front of my cage and swiftly pulled me out.

With the unceremonious scrape of metal against metal, my cage clanked loudly down the ramp and onto the cement floor of a small garage in the midst of eight expectant faces, all of whom scrutinized me with a mixture of curiosity and resentment. Roslyn's familiarly beautiful face stood out first, naturally, and I saw less hatred in her expression than I saw in the rest of them, but unfortunately the level of loathing in the others' eyes was very high.

Standing directly next to her was a wolfish-looking man with vicious golden brown eyes, and as ours met, they glared at me from beneath bushy eyebrows with a look that I could only describe as hungry. His long blonde hair was a dirty, unkempt mess, and his sleeveless t-shirt exposed powerful, hairy arms and protruding trapezius muscles.

On the far end on the other side of Roslyn was an athletic-looking man with brown hair and contrastingly well-kept facial hair. He wore a Manchester United jersey, but it wasn't just because of his attire that he reminded me of a professional soccer player. His athletic shorts and running sneakers surrounded chiseled calves and an unmistakably athletic aura.

Next to the wolf-man was a guy who was clearly the eldest of the group, judging by the age lines in his cheeks and forehead and the gray streaks in his hair. He had a large bird-like nose and his eyes looked weary, but the rest of his facial features displayed a sharpness that belied his otherwise aged appearance. Now that I appraised him I felt like his gaze was tainted with blandness and disinterest more than disdain, but there was still no hint of friendliness to be found in it.

As I continued down the half-circle I saw that next to him was a model-like blonde girl, who was only slightly shorter than he was. She looked out of place dressed in a high fashion business suit and carrying her little black purse, and a look of confusion muddled her blue eyes as mine fell on her.

Next to her was another familiar face, but it wasn't one I had hoped to ever see again. The face belonged to Chen Lake – who looked as repulsed and disapproving as he always did. He was wearing his standard suit, earpiece, and sunglasses, but none of those accoutrements hid his permanent sneer. That sneer turned even further down when I looked at him.

The last two men on the right were both black, and were both even taller than the elderly looking man with the bird nose. The one on the inside was as dark as night, but his skin was so smoothly and perfectly uniform that it was hard not to admire the perfection of it. He had a slender build similar to the man next to him – the light brown one who had pulled me out of the truck – and standing together they looked like twin towers of danger. Although the lighter-skinned man on the end was a little taller and bigger, the darker one sported two razor sharp eyes that bled pure evil.

As my eyes passed over them all I couldn't help but feel like I was in the midst of one of the more international groups of people I could have ever imagined, but they all stood together with a current of deep familiarity flowing between them. When my eyes finally and inevitably returned to Roslyn's face, the model-like blonde girl spoke up.

"This is the one who escaped you?" she asked, revealing a surprisingly heavy southern accent.

Most of the faces turned towards Roslyn at the girls' question, and I made a mental note of the undercurrent of deference that ran through the group when she spoke.

"Yes," she answered, looking directly at me.

"His shift is very impressive, and his control of it was enough to kill Roman."

People muttered unintelligible things under their breath and exchanged looks of surprise. I was almost sure I heard multiple languages in the ripple of disbelieving comments.

"He looks pretty weak to me," one of the voices announced skeptically.

It belonged to the athletic-looking guy to Roslyn's right.

"Thank you for your opinion, Scott, but his shift is as reported," Roslyn quipped in return.

The man named Scott rolled his eyes.

"Either way, his human body looks like a twig," he contended spitefully.

Roslyn gave him a long, sharp glare, but it was another voice that defended her point.

"Did you not just hear Roslyn say that the boy killed Roman?"

This time the voice came from the graying man with the bird nose, who folded his arms over his chest. Although he was defending my abilities, his gray eyes looked down at me with no semblance of reception.

"You and I both know how little that means, Allard. Roman was more threatening as a human than powerful as a crocodile. I doubt Martin will spare him. A powerful shift is nothing without a strong mind to use it properly," Scott said.

The graying man turned his frown a little further south.

"What you say is true, Scott, but one of my pack members is stationed in Castille – he and a few natural hounds were the ones who actually chased the boy down the day it was discovered that he was a shapeshifter. His account of the boy's shift is consistent with what Roslyn says."

The older man turned towards Scott with both ruminating indifference and subtle challenge, but his words sent my brain shooting back to my very first shift. The whole day was still burned into my brain in vivid detail, and I suddenly understood that the one dog who had escaped had not been a real dog at all. The recognizant look in his eyes, the peculiar smell – the dog had been a shapeshifter, and had in a way been the catalyst for me ending up in the hands of Martin Evers now. If it wasn't already clear, that realization made me even more aware of how truly omnipresent Martin's Shifthunters were.

Scott was still clearly unconvinced of my worth however, because he snorted provocatively in response to Allard.

"I see," Scott said, his tone sarcastic and dismissive.

"Maybe you should loan *me* one of your shifter-mutts sometime then."

Before Allard could respond to Scott's antagonism, the gargantuan wolf-man joined in the discussion.

"No matter what Allard's dogs say, I agree with Scott."

His voice was deep, and every bit as intimidating as his appearance.

"If it wasn't for the Traitor's help, this boy would've never been able to kill Roman. Martin will see his weakness... and kill him."

Although the man had initially been arguing his point to the ring of people around me, he finished his sentence by turning towards me and giving me a sinister smile of assurance. The white teeth that he revealed were savagely and unnaturally sharp, and I cringed at both the sight of his teeth and his bloody forecast.

"It is not up to either of you what happens to him," Roslyn interjected then, her voice forceful.

I could've sworn she swept her eyes past mine in the minutest glance of reassurance, but without any real pause she turned towards the wolf-man specifically, giving him a smug, reproachful glower.

"His shift rivals *yours*, Sebastian. He may or may not be fit to be a Shifthunter, but Martin will not kill him arbitrarily. He may just need a century in the dungeons to toughen him up," she said.

A century in the dungeons?

I had only a brief moment to consider the terror of whatever that meant, because at hearing Roslyn's assertion the man she had called Sebastian gave an instant, hearty guffaw and gave me an even eviler grin.

With his jagged teeth exposed in a smile he looked both dangerous and maniacal, and he suddenly walked up to my cage, put his hands around the sides, and put his face right up to it. I did my best not to meet his newfound look of murderous challenge, but from such a close distance he emanated a gross smell similar to wet dog, and when it hit my nostrils I curled myself towards the back of the cage almost involuntarily. Of course, my defensive move only widened his grin.

"Well," he began, straightening.

"This boy is no Brian Sann."

He thankfully stepped back into his place in the circle with a look of determinant satisfaction.

"No wonder Martin chose *you* to chase him down. He might be twice as old as Brian, but he's not even half as tough."

There was a chafing edge to his tone that elicited a glare from Roslyn.

"Whatever, Sebastian. No one is suggesting that either of them could fight you anytime soon. *Me* on the other hand… well I'd have killed you a long time ago if Martin would have allowed," she purred.

Her eyes flashed with velvet lethality, but a couple of the others allowed little chuckles at Roslyn's mocking intonation. Sebastian seemed to revel in it as well.

"Hah! You've got that backwards m'lady, but I truly hope that one day you have your chance," he retorted, chuckling.

I wondered if he took pride in the crude nature of his smile, because it seemed to appear on his face every time he spoke. I could already tell that he was the type who enjoyed brutal death and killing.

"I hope as well," Scott chimed in, joining Sebastian in his chuckle.

"It would be one helluva fight."

A few heads nodded in agreement, but the circle of people fell into a brief silence after the light mirth subsided. There was an undercurrent of tension flowing through everyone that I didn't understand, and they all spent a few more seconds looking me over critically. I had always been an unimpressive specimen, and curled up in this cage under the gaze of these eight men and women, I had never felt more unacceptable. None of the eyes seemed to appraise me with any level of appreciation.

"Well, my fellow Shifthunter Elite, Roslyn ain't the only one who's been out doing important things," Sebastian announced after a moment.

The attention turned towards him.

"Scamp and I stumbled upon a lil tea party two nights ago, and we even managed to capture one of 'em. I'd wager that even the little finch we caught is tougher than this boy here," he said.

"Tea party?" nearly everyone asked in unison.

There was an immediate skepticism in the crowd that caused Sebastian to throw up his hands up in mock defense.

"Don't jump down my throat now, people. Martin's already been informulated. It's part of the reason we've all been called out to this swamp. I'm sure he'll be fillin' us all in on what the deal is. But for those of you would like to see her..."

Sebastian moved away from the rest of the group and around the side of the truck and subsequently out of my sight. I heard the sound of a trunk door opening and shutting, and then Sebastian reappeared with a gold birdcage about the size of a trashcan, which he unceremoniously dropped to the floor next to mine.

The cage landed with a metallic clang. As the cage settled the tiny yellow bird inside was jarred against the bars of the cage in a way that had to be painful, and it slumped pitifully against the cage bottom as the clanging sound faded. Only I cringed at the sight of the poor creature's tiny, beaten form however.

"Please explain to me what you mean by *tea party*, Sebastian," Roslyn seethed.

Her voice teemed with the effort of barely contained rage. Sebastian answered her with mocking casualty.

"Tea party, meeting, whatever. It was a little gatherin' of shapeshifter scum. Me and Scamp found 'em all having some kind of meeting in a sky rise hotel in Toronto around three o' clock in the morning. It was mostly luck, because I normally do my sweeps in downshift and let Scamp do the sniffing, but because I hadn't been in wolf for a while I decided to do some late-night roof-hopping. From there I smelled the whole group like an indoor barbecue. Four shifters in all," Sebastian explained.

Everyone's eyes went wide.

"What were they doing? Did you recognize any of them? Do you even know what this means? Why hasn't Martin told us about this?"

Roslyn attacked first, and her voice came in an exclamatory flurry. She looked around, but no one answered her. Mostly, the expressions on the surrounding faces were of similar inquisition.

"I told you – I *just* caught 'em," Sebastian answered her roughly, looking offended.

"Contrarian to what you believe, Roslyn, Martin doesn't tell *you* everything. And to answer your question, I never seen *any* of 'em before and they *all* scurried like ants when we attacked. No loyalty among 'em it didn't seem like. We managed to kill the one who shifted into a horse though," he said.

"You let the other two get away?" Roslyn grilled him, her voice still fiery.

"I did better than anyone else would have," Sebastian barked back, baring his teeth in a defensive way now.

"I couldn't tell it was going to be exactly four shifters inside with just my nose. I thought it was just two or one big one who'd fallen asleep without downshifting or somethin'. When I came down through the ceiling I was as almost surprised as they were. It was as much as I could do to catch the giant horse and rip his head off, and you can thank Scamp for catching the little birdie."

The little caged bird issued a sorrowful chirp of anguish when Sebastian mentioned killing the horse, while another discordant murmur spread through the group.

"I can't believe there was really a gathering of Rogue shifters," the blonde girl mused loudest, shaking her head.

"How could this happen? We *just* caught the Traitor. As far as I know there should've only been two Rogue shifters left in the entire world besides this kid Roslyn just caught."

There were murmurs of agreement from some of the others.

"I don't see how they could have survived so long when they were stupid enough to expose themselves together like that," the darkest black man agreed in his heavy African accent, shaking his head.

It came out as a striking contrast to the drawl of the southern girl across from him.

"We'll find out," Sebastian assured her, his now-familiar Southern accent matching hers.

He jerked his head towards the little bird cage next to mine.

"This one hasn't downshifted, no matter what I've threatened to do to her, and I'm not sure how to torture information out of such a little imp without killing it. Regardless, by the end of the week we will either get her to lead us to her friends or we will bleed her out drop by drop."

All of the attention turned towards the helpless bird in the cage now, accompanied by deliberate nods of agreement. The vicious, vengeful intent was clear in every set of eyes, reminding me how many heartless killers I was currently surrounded by.

"She'll squeal," Scott said confidently.

"Martin has the ultimate trump card."

Scott made a unique face, one of reassurance mixed with trepidation. His generally pompous air made me believe that the latter emotion was one he didn't often experience.

"Martin will also be the one to determine what will be done next," Roslyn countered, her tone sovereign.

She raised her hand in authoritative dismissal.

"Now that you've all seen our newest captures, this meeting is officially adjourned. Like our partner Sebastian said – I'm sure Martin will be briefing all of us on how we will go about eliminating these newfound Rogues sometime tonight. In the meantime everyone should all gather reports from their subordinates and continue to make sure no *other* shifters are walking around alive."

Roslyn still seemed jaded by her lack of prior knowledge regarding the "Rogues," but there was a chorus of acquiescent nods, and then the Shifthunters obediently filed out of the garage behind me, almost all of them instantly producing Smartphones and cigarettes. Only Sebastian, Roslyn, and the coffee-colored, hairless Shifthunter who had taken me out of the truck remained behind. As the others disappeared, Sebastian picked up the bird cage from next to mine and then bore down over top of me, his expression mocking.

"They tell me you shift into a Siberian tiger," he said.

I nodded stiffly.

"Well that's pretty impressive. Do you want to know what *my* shift is?" he asked.

There was an excited gleam in his eye that caused me to immediately shake my head in response. For a moment I was sure he would tell me anyway, but surprisingly he turned away.

"Good choice," he said, patting the top of my cage roughly.

With the bird cage tucked under his arm he then headed towards a gray metal door at the back of the garage and disappeared behind it a second later. It was clear that it was time for me to meet the next stage of this process now, but without meeting my anxious and fearful look, Roslyn addressed the giant, lanky young man who had stayed behind.

"Pharaoh, take Zade to his cell if you would. Martin has ordered that he be placed in the same room as the Traitor – as a special punishment for the both of them. A little time in the dungeons will serve Zade well, especially after he learns what happens to shifters who think they can defy Martin Evers."

With a nod of authority she headed towards the same door that Sebastian had gone through, but she stopped just before opening it.

"Once you put Zade in his cell, come upstairs. There'll be much to do now that Sebastian has stumbled upon this little gathering," she added, turning back towards the Shifthunter she had called Pharaoh.

He nodded his perfectly bald head in understanding, and then without the slightest look towards me Roslyn disappeared behind the door, leaving me scared, bewildered, and in the hands of this strange, intimidating Shifthunter.

"Can you walk yet?" he asked gruffly.

The depth of his bass voice caught me off guard again, but before I could answer him he unlocked the cage and stepped back expectantly.

"I'm not carrying you, so you'll either walk or crawl," he informed me pitilessly.

He watched me as I paused for a few long moments, gathering my strength, and then with a great deal of effort I forced my aching limbs into action and pulled myself out of the cage. The mere effort of prying myself upward sent pain radiating from my bullet-wounded shoulder and I bellowed in excruciation, but with the side of the cage as a support I got to my feet nonetheless. I couldn't take more than one step forward however before my lower body was attacked by such a sudden and excruciating bout of pins and needles that my knees buckled and I fell forward onto my face.

I yelled out in even more pain as the collapse sent fresh pangs of hurt through my still-healing leg. Everything in me wanted to lie there and whimper in my agony, and I indeed stayed down for a minute, but out of nothing but pride and some misplaced desire to survive I bit down hard on my lip – hard enough to draw blood even – and willed my persecuted body back to its feet.

Standing on my own after so much time confined in a cage brought dizziness in addition to pain, but I managed to stay upright with the support of a grudging arm bar from Pharaoh. Regretfully I used his thick, sinewy forearm as a crutch while I waited for the majority of the dizziness to pass, and when my vision cleared I was finally able to appreciate his true, massive height. I couldn't estimate it exactly, but I was sure he stood at least seven feet tall. He had to bend down significantly to allow me to hold myself up on his arm, and true to his distrustful, Shifthunter ways, his other arm aimed the barrel of a silenced pistol down at me.

"It's precautionary," he explained pitilessly as he watched my eyes.

His hairless face was creased into an emotionless, deadened expression, and a second later he shook his arm away so that I had to stand on my own. He motioned the gun towards the door at the back of the garage edgily.

"It's time to get going, Shifter."

Enslaved, I slowly and painfully began shuffling towards the door. Even though I knew I was walking towards my death – or something close to it – I still clung to the last remnants of my desire to live. It drove me to stay upright instead of collapsing and forcing Pharaoh to shoot or carry me, and as those primitive emotions coursed through me, I realized that I was experiencing a truth of life here in this forsaken garage. I knew then that no matter how beaten or bleak the outlook, a living being will cling to its life until the bitter end.

At Pharaoh's prodding I then wobbled my way through the metal door, and the pace he now made me keep forced me to siphon off my philosophies and focus all of my attention on not falling down. On the other side of the door was a dark hallway with an uneven dirt floor and walls of roughly hewn stone, which made it even more difficult to walk. To even make it to the end I had to use the crags in the stone walls to drag myself to the rickety, ancient-looking elevator there. Many times I wanted to pause for a breath, but the constant point of Pharaoh's gun urged me forward the whole way.

When we reached the elevator, Pharaoh pushed a button on a blocky bronze remote that was crudely adhered to the wall, and then a dirty carriage opened up behind the creaky, iron elevator doors. The space inside was surprisingly large, but it smelled foul and Pharoah was still so tall that he had to duck to enter in behind me. Once we were both inside, he pushed the bottommost of four unlabeled buttons on the inside wall of the elevator, and the doors closed behind us. An instant later the old contraption lurched downward.

Brown dirt erupted around us on all sides as we plunged a story or so underground, and then after a few seconds we jolted to an unceremonious halt facing a crude square cut straight out of the dirt. The doors parted again facing the opening, and Pharaoh pushed me out into a packed earth passage that could only be described as dungeon-like. It was devoid of all life and signs of the above, and the only signs of human presence were the medieval wooden doors and lighted torch fixtures that irregularly dotted the underground avenue. The torch fixtures created but a meager illumination, and despite the lack of air flow they painted eerie, flickering shadows on the floor. The wooden doors were windowless, and it was as if going a level into the earth had taken me back a century or two, because the only traces of the current century came from the strange laminate printouts plastered to the front of each door.

"The Warehouse dungeons," Pharaoh's deep voice rumbled in toneless introduction.

This isn't real, I thought in response. The poorly lit corridor was utterly foreboding and hopelessly bleak.

Pharaoh didn't seem to be happy to be here either, because as soon as the doors of the elevator were wide enough for us to pass through, he shoved me out into the hallway at an even faster pace than before. The increased speed of our walk sent concurrently worse stabbing pains through my leg and shoulder, but between grimaces of agony I tried futilely to decipher the laminate printouts on the wooden doors. At the pace Pharaoh was pushing me however, all I could tell was that there was only one line of writing per laminate. The words were a blur.

After a while I instead took note of the sameness of each silent, wooden door, and the random, varying distances between them. Some were directly across from one another; others were spaced more than twenty or thirty yards apart. The lighted torch fixtures were randomly dispersed along the walls too – leaving significant stretches of darkness – but they coincided with the spacing of the dungeon doors enough that I was able to notice when the laminated printouts on the cell doors went blank.

We continued past at least six of those unlabelled dungeon doors, and then suddenly there were no more doors at all. Besides the couple of torches that were still intermittently creating patches of light, the course had become merely a tunnel. Pharaoh didn't slow though, and he kept urging me deeper and deeper down the seemingly endless passage.

During one of the longer patches of darkness I tripped on an indentation in the ground, and I cried out in pain as I fell to my knees. A shockwave of subsequent pain powered through my left shoulder when I instinctively caught myself with both hands, but I was only on the ground for an instant before Pharaoh yanked me back to my feet and gave me another unforgiving shove forward.

"Go," he ordered mercilessly.

Every step felt as if someone was sawing off my arm while simultaneously twisting a knife into my thigh, but I did as I was told for fear of death. Despite the fact that my ability to fight through pain had increased exponentially these last few days, we had to have been at least a mile or two from the elevator by now. My legs couldn't take much more.

A feeling of doom began to overwhelm me as I considered the likelihood that I would collapse and die here in this tunnel, and the tears that flowed down my face for most of the trek were streaming and uncontrollable. It was a miracle that I somehow remained on my feet long enough to see two doors finally and unexpectedly appear.

They were lined up approximately across from one another, and were as thick and uninviting as all the others, but an infinitesimal sensation of relief fell over me when Pharaoh stopped me between them. Even though they were undoubtedly my confining place, the walking was over. When I looked at the door to my left I saw that these doors had laminate printouts pasted on them as well, and when my eyes focused further I saw that these two print-outs had writing on them also. With apprehensive curiosity I read the one on the left first:

Mackson Kutter – Silverback Gorilla – 99 Years

Duh, I realized.

The laminates on the doors were simply labels. I turned towards the other door, expecting to see my own name printed on it. However, I had to read the name that *was* printed on the label four times to be sure I'd read it correctly. Pharaoh caught my eye as he opened the door.

"I think Martin is housing you with the Traitor in hopes that you might wizen up a little," he said, snorting in disdain.

"The Traitor?" I repeated, bewildered.

Pharaoh looked confused by my question, but instead of answering me he shoved me into the cell with one of his long arms.

"Ask him yourself," he said in his sonorous bass voice.

He punctuated the end of his sentence by slamming the heavy wooden door behind me.

Chapter 21

ZADE DAVIDSON

Everglades, Florida - October 23, 2013

*T*he thud of the door slamming in my face rang in my ears, but it was where it left me that really stung. I was back in an empty cell, and although this one was at least larger than the one in Atwater County, it was worse in every other way. Somehow in spite of its largeness it felt more constricting than an ordinary jail cell – which I hadn't previously thought was possible. I attributed it to the fact that this dungeon cell had no windows or semblance of outside air flow, except for the miniscule space between the bottom of the wooden door and the compacted dirt floor. The only illumination came from a smaller version of the lighted torches outside, which was affixed to the back wall and contributed to the polluted taste of the stale air.

For two minutes I stood facing the door, too dumbfounded and defeated to move, and then I was overcome by the defeat of being trapped again and I collapsed to the floor. Now, finally, in addition to the large amount of physical pain that I was in, my will was utterly broken. In a heap on the floor I began to sob like a baby.

Just being in this room – so alone and far removed from human contact – was torture in and of itself. My best friend was dead, and my whole world was a smoldering ruin. I was powerless even over my own body, and all I could really do was sob and wish for the days before I was a shapeshifter. It was ironic – in a totally humorless way – how much I wanted to go back to being normal.

The only way to soften the misery was to pretend I didn't even care about it, but even that was a futile attempt. It was surprisingly soon when I heard the unexpected sound of footsteps approaching, and I had no choice but to pay them mind when they stopped in front of my door. Just as I looked up from my pitiful position on the floor our door burst open and two plain-looking men appeared on the other side. They gave me a pair of puzzled, contemptuous glares, and then they literally *tossed* a human body into my cell. It flew past me and landed with a sickening thud a few feet inside – face down. The two men then spat a few unrepeatable slurs in my direction and slammed the door shut again.

As soon as the door closed I whipped around and stared at the body on the floor, shocked. Its shallow breathing was the only sign it was alive. I moved towards it and gently turned it onto its side, and although it was hard to tell at first because of all the wounds and swelling, after a few seconds of scrutiny I was sure the body belonged to Mr. Stevens. The brown robe I had last seen him in was long gone, but it was indeed Mr. Stevens' beaten, thin body that stuck out beneath the torn cloth outfit he now wore.

"Mr. Stevens?" I whispered hoarsely.

I noticed that his right hand was heavily bandaged and wrapped in dirty white tape, and as I looked closer it seemed looked oddly blunt. I stared at it for a second, somehow perplexed, and then I realized that the bandage was covering the end of a forearm, not a hand.

"Mr. Stevens?" I called again, this time more earnestly.

I gently patted his arm at the same time, and he groaned a little and stirred slightly. The part of his face that I could currently see was bruised and bloodied, but I watched him take some difficult breaths, and then bat his swollen eyelids a few times before opening them.

His signature golden eyes appeared when they finally creased open, and I was surprised to see that in stark defiance of his beaten body, they were as lively and defiant as ever. As they focused and moved from the ceiling down to my face however, they immediately closed again. I could see that even moving his face pained him, but he still managed to scrunch his eyelids tight shut of pure disappointment and heartbreak.

"You're alive," I said, clinging to that last positive thread, but Mr. Stevens was unresponsive.

I knew as well as he did that it didn't really matter that we were alive. His expression told me that we were in a place hardly better than death. I recoiled back against the wall then and watched him hopelessly, unable to embrace the comfort I had first felt at realizing that he was still alive. It was almost impossible to think that just weeks ago he was nothing more than my strange biology teacher.

I leaned my head against the rough clay wall and closed my eyes then too, but it was shaped with the curve of a crude swipe and couldn't have been more raw and uncomfortable. I couldn't sleep really, but I dazed in and out for long enough to be surprised when I opened my eyes and saw that Mr. Stevens had crawled into a ball in the other corner of the room. I barely had time to check for the rise and fall of his chest to see that he was still alive and then I succumbed to the sudden excruciating pain in my shoulder that had now erupted.

The effects of whatever drugs they had given me earlier were now completely worn off, and with that I fully embraced the pain of an open bullet wound. There was no adrenaline now, just the unbridled pain combined with rage and restlessness. I also knew from the speedy healing of my much-less painful leg injury that I was going to heal and survive, which somehow made it worse. With full feeling now restored, I could tell that Roslyn's bullet had gone clear through my shoulder and out the other end, which left the bloodied bandage wrap that they had it wrapped in as an endless source of the twisting, knifing pain sensation. For however long it took me to be able to even move, my world became a swirling tempest of despair.

No matter where my thoughts went – from Chace to my family to my own plight – they only added fuel to my fire of torment. I was only able to sleep after an inconceivable number of hours... when my brain literally forced itself to shut down because of its need for dormancy. I didn't have memorable dreams for once, but whenever I woke again life became pain once more.

Was Chace alive?

It was the only thought on my mind, and the more I thought about it, it was the only thing I could cling to. I was trapped in this dungeon, destined for some death-like version of life or very possibly real death. If Chace could somehow be healed from his injuries… it would mean he could have a chance at a normal, shapeshifter-less life.

Nonetheless I knew the chances were slim, and whenever I thought about it I couldn't help but feel like the odds were so highly stacked against his survival that all I could do was pray.

Life became an endless repetition of wallowing in anguish and then passing back into sleep, while Mr. Stevens remained curled into the corner, having shown no signs of movement or recovery since the first few hours.

At some long hour, there was a slow shuffling outside of our door, but I was still in too much pain to move. The shuffling eventually transformed to a sound on the outside of our door, but the door never opened and then the shuffling receded in the direction it came.

More hours passed in the same manner as those first few – complete with the random shuffling every so often, and with the atmospheres of suffering and misery dominating them all. The pain in my body receded slowly at best, and no matter how many hours passed, Mr. Stevens seemed unwilling to move from the curled ball he had become. As time ticked by undiscernibly and endlessly, it became my worst enemy. I hated every minute of life, and my affliction continued on unabated.

I had never been so singularly motionless or hurt ever in my life, and almost fittingly, it was very sudden when some unknown number of days later our cell door suddenly opened and Roslyn appeared.

As beautiful as she was, at this point I wasn't sure whether I hated her or Chen Lake more. Although the seemingly genuine look of empathy that flushed onto her face when she saw me was truly hard to hate, with Chace essentially dead and the pain from the bullet wound she had inflicted pulsating through me, I found her wholly condemnable.

"How's your shoulder?" she asked.

From her concerned tone no one would've never guessed that *she'd* shot me.

"Throbbing," I answered roughly.

My voice was hoarse from non-usage. Roslyn leaned close to me and gently laid a hand on my falling-apart bandage, but it sent a shock of pain that made me wince and jump away. She stood back up.

"I'd imagine it'll only be a day or two more until the hole closes up… and you don't have to worry about infections, if you didn't know."

She paused.

"This wouldn't be an issue if you knew to back down when you are at gunpoint, though. Next time you'll probably get killed, and if it's me on the other end of that gun, then I'll be aiming to kill," she said.

She somehow said that without sounding threatening, but as she took a look over at Mr. Stevens curled body in the corner she frowned in repulsion.

"I hope you also see where betrayal gets you," she added.

Her voice was suddenly laced with an unexpected hatred.

"Betrayal?" I asked.

Roslyn jerked her head back in surprise.

"Gordon never told you?" she exclaimed.

Her voice was a mixture of disbelief and outrage, but I had no idea what she was talking about.

"I don't remember him telling me anything about a betrayal," I admitted honestly.

"Well since he apparently hasn't told you, Gordon Stevens *was* one of us," she said.

There was resentment in the way she emphasized the word 'was'.

"Gordon was Martin's first Shifthunter. He *helped* Martin start hunting shapeshifters down – he was head scientist! For about 175 years, Gordon was as dedicated to killing shapeshifters as any of us. It wasn't until 1942 that he decided to turncoat."

Roslyn glared at him. I almost could imagine her attacking him right then and there, but she didn't. At the same time I was hit with a shockwave of pure appall. It was hard to believe that Mr. Stevens had worked for Martin Evers, helping to hunt and kill innocent people – innocent *young* people. As head scientist, his involvement was probably even deeper than most.

"How did he betray you?" I pressed, letting my curiosity continue to distract me from my pain.

"He tried to kill us all," Roslyn answered.

"First he disappeared – he went on a solo mission tracking some shapeshifter but never came back. Even back then our operation was so highly effective that we were catching shifters as children, which meant that after seeing the true efficiency of our operation firsthand, no Shifthunter would ever think of running. He'd also been Martin's most trusted confidante, so for ten years we thought he'd died on the mission. We never found the shifter he had claimed to be looking for though, and no one had seen or heard from him, so no one knew what happened to him. We sent search teams of SE's for years but they came back empty-handed and –"

As enraptured as I was, I interrupted her before she could continue.

"Wait – not even Martin could find him?" I interjected.

Roslyn paused and gave me a strange look.

"Until a couple days ago – yes he'd escaped even Martin," she said.

There was a tone of admittance in her voice, and it was just what I had been looking for. In a minor victory of sorts, I now had concrete evidence that Martin was at least not omnipotent. I had to hide my proud expression inside though; I didn't want to exacerbate Roslyn just now.

"Wait, you thought he was dead all this time?" I asked, but Roslyn shook her head.

"No – we've known Gordon was alive since the early fifties. Ten years after he disappeared, he returned. He snuck into our old headquarters like the worthless mutation that he is, and freed the twenty-two shapeshifters that were captive in our dungeons. All hell broke loose to say the least, and many Shifthunters died. Gordon himself, of course, escaped during the frenzy."

I could feel the anger in her voice.

"From *then* until now, we hadn't seen him. The fact that you view him as some sort of mentor will surely intrigue Martin, but as for me, I find it despicable. He knows better than most of us that Martin is too powerful to defeat… regardless of whether he is right or wrong in his convictions."

Roslyn eyed me and her brown eyes showed a burning passion of emotion. I wanted to ask more questions, but it took me a second to put them together in my head. When I stuttered in my attempt to continue Roslyn raised her hand to cease me.

"Martin is expecting you," she said curtly.

Her eyes were sharp and intractable, and they ordered me to my feet, which was a very painful task to accomplish. I looked one last time at Mr. Stevens' crunched, slumbering body and then Roslyn jammed her infamous silenced pistol into my back and ordered me out of the cell.

Was this the same gun that had killed my best friend? I wondered.

Roslyn shut the latch on the door behind us, and then she silently and quickly pushed me back down the underground hallways of the dungeons, now apparently unconcerned with the pain and difficulty it was causing me. At some point we came near the same dip in the floor that had tripped me last time, but it was similarly dark and my foot caught in it again.

I very nearly fell onto my face again too, but in a final balancing effort I stretched out my bad arm, which sent a ripping sensation and exultation of pain through it. Though I kept myself from falling *all* the way down, I bellowed loudly from the sudden pain. The twinge was so bad I could only walk about half as fast as I had been, and I held my poor left arm gingerly with my healthy right one.

"You may as well take that bandage off when we get back," Roslyn advised from behind me as I continued to groan ahead of her.

"If you're going to survive, you're going to need to get used to healing and being wounded sooner rather than later."

I was too wrapped in my own anguish to think about her words, so I kept moving ahead and a good while later we came back upon the old rickety elevator that had brought me down here. We climbed aboard, but unlike Pharaoh, Roslyn pushed the top button and we jerked upwards.

The carriage moved past the earth again, and then past a grayish cement door, and then past some more earth. When it finally stopped, the other side of the iron doors met with modern steel ones, and when they parted, I saw why this place was called the Warehouse. We emerged from the elevator into a vast room, with grayish cement warehouse walls that rose from a dirty cement floor in some places, and rows and rows of full warehouse shelves that were too tall to see over collected in the middle. Giant windows at the tops of the cement walls let in the light of day, illuminating the brown boxes and multicolored bins stocking the shelves. It essentially arranged the building into a maze of aisles, and congruent with the bursting stores of labeled goods, there was a forklift parked near the elevator that looked like it got plenty of use.

Roslyn led me away from the forklift though, and we headed straight down the first aisle ahead of us. From there, Roslyn coldly rammed her weapon into my back as a turn signal, and we made our way through the network of shelves to the far end of the warehouse floor. I was completely lost, but when she confidently led me out of one of the rows we came upon a large open space of floor with a low, metal staircase on the other side. The staircase led up to a peculiarly large metal box, which looked to be made of four walls of reinforced steel. It had no windows, and the door appeared to be cut flush into one of the metal sides, and after staring at it for a moment, the structure seemed to look more like a titanium bomb shelter than an office.

It was obvious who was inside. The way the obstruction sat isolated in the corner was subliminally sinister, and at Roslyn's unforgiving prodding we crossed the clearing and clanked up the staircase leading to it. With my worn gait and depreciating shoes, I made a dull metallic sound with each step. Roslyn's feet on the other hand made no sound as she glided up behind me.

When I went up the dozen or so steps to the landing and came around to face the tightly sealed door in the side of the cube, a dire rivulet of anxiety slid up my spine. I was suddenly aware of how afraid I was of the man who lurked behind that door, but before leading me through it, Roslyn whirled me around. Caught by surprise, I looked her dead in the eyes, and I was subsequently caught by even greater surprise when I saw a look of compassion in her expression. Her eyes held mine with a tender look of concern, and as much as I despised her for shooting both Chace and myself, she had never looked more beautiful. Her look of utter sympathy told me that despite all that had happened to me – despite what *she* herself had done to me – I was now about to face something even more unimaginable.

As soon as Roslyn realized that she was showing true emotion however, she snatched her gaze away from mine and rapped lightly on Martin Evers' door. Still a little caught up by the enigma of her personality, I took a last look out at the warehouse floor that spread away just below us. From our mildly elevated position I noticed then that despite the earlier signs of frequent use, no one had moved among the stockpiles since we'd come up here. Combined with Roslyn's rare and undeniable look of unease, the desertion only added to my rising feeling of dread.

I didn't wait long to realize that dread fully however, because shortly after Roslyn's knock, the sound of a recently recognizable voice bode us to enter. At the sound of the voice I turned my attention back towards Roslyn and waited for her to open the door, but she didn't. Instead she merely nodded towards it and retreated towards the railing with her arms folded tensely across her chest.

Now even more fearful, I faced the door for a final moment of angst, and then I gritted my teeth and used my good arm to awkwardly heave open a crease large enough for me to fit through. The endeavor shot new waves of pain through my bad arm, but I managed to squeeze into the office just before the heavy door suctioned shut behind me.

I held my injured shoulder for a second until the worst of the pain subsided, and then I looked up into Martin Evers' arctic blue eyes, which shone out fierce and unforgiving against the backdrop of the steely silver walls of his office. He was fair skinned and graying, but he exuded that same aura of youthful liveliness that Mr. Stevens once had. Behind his large, dark brown desk, he sat comfortably in a kingly leather office chair, and propped against the side of a glass ashtray was a lit cigar, whose smoky entrails made their way to a vent in the ceiling directly above him. From the slight whirring sound coming from the vent I could tell that its orifices were responsible for the ice-cold air that pumped into the office.

The floor of the space was metallic as well, but it was offset by a grand rug made entirely from the most enormous bear skin I'd ever seen. It stretched across a more than half of the entire thirty-square-foot office, and I then noticed the equally enormous bear head jutting out from the wall behind Martin, its mouth agape in a vicious visage. I'd always hated things like that, and I turned away from it to take in the rest of the furnishings, which consisted of an expensive-looking globe next to his desk and a large armoire full of other collectors' items of undeniable value. On top of Martin's desk his hands were folded next to a bulky, damage-proof laptop.

"Sit down."

Martin's voice was so commanding that I found myself obeying the order robotically, even though it was somehow casual rather than biting. As I crossed towards him his eyes ate into mine like daggers however, and when I got close I saw that his clean-shaven, chiseled cheekbones were set in a permanent, heartless scowl. I was also instantly and powerfully struck by the radiance of his concealed deadliness. It was a feeling that was hard to describe, but it honestly felt like it was an imminently dangerous proposition to even be physically close to him. The closer we came, the more my bones seemed to scream for me to run in the other direction.

When I sat down in the armchair across from him I was nearly frozen with apprehension, and both the armchair and my own body were nearly frozen from the frigid temperature. While I tried to keep from shivering in my seat and showing how terrified and cold I was, Martin of course seemed to take care in noticing me shakily sit down, while he himself reveled in his cold seat of power.

He seemed supremely relaxed as he analyzed my every movement, and the small creases of age in the corners of his eyes did little to hide the youthful ability his aura belied.

"Can you open this?"

His first question came frankly and nearly 30 seconds after I'd sat down, but he didn't take his eyes off of me as he reached under his desk and pulled out Mr. Stevens' battered, silver briefcase. Seeing it still intact caught me by surprise, but I had no idea what Martin Evers wanted with it, and with the intensity in the way he was looking at me, I was scared to tell him the truth.

"No. I've tried some combinations –"

Martin raised his hand ceasingly, cutting me off mid-sentence.

"Trying and failing is the same to me as not trying at all. Your failures are irrelevant. From now on your life depends on *success*."

Martin blinked once.

"Now, I'll ask you again. Can you open this briefcase?"

"No," I answered, again truthful.

I tried to sound assertive, but I wasn't sure if I could have successfully lied to Martin anyhow. Nonetheless, Martin's face contorted into a fleeting look of true disappointment and distaste, and he stared at me for so long then that I was sure he was seeing my thoughts and it became literally unbearable.

"What's in that briefcase?" I ventured extremely cautiously.

Asking a question was the only way I could think to break Martin's soul-stare, but although it saved me from having my mind read, his expression grew even darker. He took a single, calming breath and grimaced unhappily before answering me.

"I don't know," he said, sounding uncannily honest himself.

His tone was purely matter-of-fact, and I could tell by his expression that there were very few things that he did not know. After answering me however, he slid the briefcase back under his desk conclusively and reached into one of his desk drawers.

"Relative to shapeshifters, I don't mind you so much," he said suddenly.

Again he sounded truthfully matter-of-fact rather than complimentary, and he pulled a manila folder out of the desk drawer and laid it on the table while he spoke.

"You're quiet. Most Rogues who I've met with in a setting such as this are either blabbering children who don't understand what is going on or blabbering adults who are begging for their lives. The defiant ones sometimes try to threaten me or even attack me, but *you* just sit."

Martin's words came in a flow that seemed absently perplexed, and most of his attention appeared to be on opening the manila folder and examining the top page. After a moment he slid the manila folder over to me – nimbly so that it spun and faced me perfectly. I looked down at the cover, which had no labeling on it.

"I assume – since you are a friend of the Traitor – that you know who I am and why you are here?" Martin inquired.

The contrast between his conversational tone and his aura of hostility was disconcerting.

"Well – not really," I said, looking up from the folder to meet Martin's piercing gaze again.

"You recognized me the first time you saw me. What do you know about me?" he asked.

I gulped, knowing that there was no use lying to this man. His confidence was infinite.

"I know that you're name is Martin. I know that you're a shapeshifter and that you kill them," I said, saying only as much as necessary.

Martin looked back at me curiously, but didn't say anything in response. Instead he let the words hang, his expression motionless and showing nothing.

"Open that folder," he said after a long silence.

I looked down at it and nervously opened it. There was a very thick stack of papers between the manila flaps, and on the first one I saw a mugshot of Pharaoh, the same man who had taken me to my cell here.

His hairless brown head and sharp features stared out at me from the page, and above his picture the name Pharaoh was printed in quotations. Filling the rest of the page around his picture was a myriad of organized biological data, from his height and weight to his biological name and the names of his family members. I looked closer at some of the more critical data.

Discovered: Egypt 1918

Birth: Congo, 1888 Unconfirmed

Shift: King Cobra.

Living Family: Egypt, Democratic Rep. of Congo

From my peripheral I saw Martin motion for me to continue, so I flipped to the next page. It was a picture of the tall, brown haired guy who I had seen in the garage. The name Scott Elms was written above the picture. Below it I looked for the same row of info and saw:

Discovered: Great Britain 1900

Birth: London, Confirmed 1882.

Shift: Polar Bear.

Living Family: London, Newcastle, Crawley, Southampton

Now, I was starting to understand the potential horror of what I was seeing, and I flipped to the next page with a mixture of awe and trepidation. This time, Chen Lake's face looked out from the mug shot, and upon seeing it, a familiar wrath boiled up within me. I couldn't help myself from narrowing my eyes in hatred as I looked into his black eyes and evilly drawn lips.

I drew up the memory of his face twisting into the vicious maw of that grizzly bear, and subsequently I also spent a millisecond reflecting on the sadness of Chace's death. We'd escaped so much together, and to me it was as much Chen's fault as Roslyn's that he wasn't here today. When I eventually did scan some of his biography, I was mainly looking for a sign of living family that I could wreak revenge upon. I was disappointed.

Discovered: Japan 1856

Birth: Unknown

Shift: Grizzly Bear.

Living Family: None Remaining

"Chen has no remaining family," I said aloud, half-asking.

There was no doubt in my mind that Martin was well aware of my encounters with Chen.

"No," he said, shaking his head.

"Surprisingly enough however, I was not the one who killed them. Like Chen, they were Samurai, and they were killed in the Boshin War."

I nodded my head in enlightenment, but I had never heard of the Boshin War. By Martin's tone I assumed it had happened a long time ago, and I wondered if Chen was as detestable then as he was now. Regardless, Martin motioned for me to keep going through the folder, so this time I flipped open to a random page in the middle of the docket. When Martin saw whose profile I'd opened to, he made a lightning-quick downturn of his lips in a surprised expression.

The picture was of a girl named Elizabeth Rhodes. She looked just like any ten-year old, with a round face, blondish hair, and brown eyes. She was smiling in her picture, which struck me as odd, but then I realized it wasn't a mugshot like the first two I'd seen. It looked like a picture taken from somewhere else – like a family photo album or something – and judging by her biography, I would imagine the time and place of that picture was a much happier one than the one she found later. I read:

Discovered: 1942

Birth: Virginia, 1938 Confirmed

Shift: Cardinal

Death: 1922 – Battle Royale

I looked up at Martin in confusion as he reached across the desk and pulled the folder back over to him.

"She was one of The Traitor's first pets," Martin said with disgust.

"Long before he took a liking to you Gordon was growing weaker, and he'd become pitifully merciful. In the case of Elizabeth, her shift was a pint-sized Cardinal. I would have killed her instantly had Gordon not taken her under his wing before I could do so. In the end she was given a fair opportunity to fight for her life, but she was unable to earn her place in my army."

Martin looked utterly remorseless as he continued.

"Regardless of Elizabeth, I hope *you* are seeing the writing on the wall. There are two more folders just like this one, and together they are an archive of every shapeshifter born in the last two hundred and fifty years, both Shifthunters and Rogues alike. Since I have begun hunting them, not a single shapeshifter has escaped me."

The dark conviction Martin radiated was all in his ice-blue eyes, and they searched me with soul-seeing intensity. Through his passive exterior, his blackhearted words pulsated outwards like an invisible, demonic force.

"I am offering you a choice," he said, refusing to let me look away from him.

"In exchange for a lifetime of servitude as a Shifthunter, I will spare both your life *and* the lives of your friends and family. Instead of having you immediately executed, I am giving you the chance to pledge your *ultimate* allegiance to me, and become trained into a masterful Shifthunter. Your choices are servitude or death."

Martin's eyes showed no negotiability as he laid his offer on the table, and by the way he said the word 'ultimate,' I knew that I would be selling him my soul if I agreed to his proposition. His features concurrently turned as steely as the walls of his office, and immediately expectant.

"I'll do anything to save my family, but I don't understand," I parlayed, desperately stalling.

"*Why* do you hunt shapeshifters? Mr. Stevens told me that you are a shapeshifter yourself. Why do you want to bring about the extinction of your own species?"

Martin considered me for a moment as he pondered the one question I had wanted to ask him from the moment I'd heard of him. After a minute pause, he answered with the same assuredness as ever.

"Shapeshifters are not a *species*," he said flatly.

"I'm surprised Gordon never told you the truth behind our wretched kind, but shapeshifters are the monstrous result of a hormone mutation... a hormone that is present in all human beings. The Shifter Hormone – for lack of a better scientific term – is normally a low-count, harmless neurochemical produced by the brain. Shapeshifters however, activate this chemical and cause it to multiply, and once the hormone count reaches a certain level, they spontaneously shift into the abominations that you and I represent. If it wasn't for me, supposedly mythical creatures like werewolves, goblins, and trolls would be running rampant through society, killing off our normal human kin. Compared to them we're god-like, not only because of our ability to take on another form, but because our bodies regenerate in days from anything but absolutely fatal injuries. And, due to our hyper-regenerative cells, our natural lives last four to five hundred years. After our first shift we age five times slower than normal humans, and if we were left to our own devices, we would eventually take over their world whether we wanted to or not. Under my watch, that will not happen. As the most powerful of our kind I will control us and ultimately end us."

Martin finished his dissertation with an aura of importance and truth that made his words undoubtable.

"You make it seem like you're the good guy," I said, pausing for a long time myself as I struggled to wrap my mind around what he was saying.

Out of fear and deference I tried not to sound accusatory, but Martin merely shrugged.

"I don't expect you to understand, Zade. My men are not loyal because they believe in my convictions. Beliefs are weak. *Fear* is powerful, and I have yet to encounter a living creature that does not fear the Wendigo. My Shifthunters fear me so much that I've never locked the door to my office. Not one of them would dare set foot in here without me bidding them to enter."

Martin's words came as if to confirm the basis of my fears, and his eyes, blue and passionate beneath his sharp, white-blonde eyebrows, kept their cold-blooded grip on mine. There was nothing I could do to hide the turmoil inside of me from his gaze.

"I can see you struggling with this decision," he observed, still reading my mind with his eyes.

"To clarify, you should know that you will be sentenced to a century in my dungeons if you refuse my offer. I personally doubt that you will even survive one year down there, but with the way I use those years to strategically execute your family members and whittle down your bloodline, you'll obey my commands infallibly if you survive until they are finally over. You'll be endangering your last kin by refusing me then, and if *that* isn't enough to motivate you, then I'll have no choice but to execute you personally.... in Wendigo form, of course."

Martin perked up ever so slightly at mentioning the potential of the Wendigo, but I could tell that he didn't plan to give me more time to think about my decision.

"I understand," I said, slowly gathering the resolve to sign away the rest of my mortal existence.

"Good," Martin nodded.

His voice was ever-calm, but it still held that same undertone of distaste that made me feel like I had committed some unforgivable wrong against him. I looked away from his persecuting eyes and down at my hands in a final moment of consideration.

In my mind I knew I had done everything in my power to avoid this moment, yet I raged against the self-preserving instincts that welled up inside of me and screamed for me to accept Martin's offer. A waterfall of shame and guilt poured in on me when I thought about what that acceptance would mean.

Did I have the heart to kill innocent people – children no less – for the rest of my life? Did I have the heart to turn my back on Mr. Stevens, who had given up his freedom to give me a chance?

I thought about poor Elizabeth Rhodes, and couldn't imagine slaying child after child, all of them naive and absolutely confused by the wonderment of their powers. I thought about Mr. Stevens too, who was rotting and dying below us in a hole, and couldn't imagine pledging my eternal support to our enemy. Beyond both of those though, I truly couldn't imagine choosing the dungeons and giving Martin the final incentive to kill my parents.

No matter how miserable I'd been when I lived at home, the image of Shifthunters running into my old house and killing my peaceful, unassuming parents was as unbearable as anything I'd yet experienced. I pictured my dad with his feet up and his head buried in a science magazine, my mom tirelessly bustling around in the kitchen, shapeshifters bursting through the doorway guns ablaze and teeth bared... I couldn't even let my mind consider anything further than that.

"I'll do whatever it takes to save my family," I answered at last.

I tried to swallow my uncertainty as I clenched my hands into fists and met Martin's eyes.

"I'll become a Shifthunter."

Chapter 22

ZADE DAVIDSON

Everglades, Florida - October 24, 2013

I'll become a Shifthunter.

The sound of my own voice uttering those fateful words hung in the air for a long time, largely because Martin replied to that announcement with an extended, contemplating silence. I could see that my decision to join him had actually caught him by surprise, despite the fact that he had been encouraging me to make that choice. From my standpoint however, I would've had to be a true coward to choose the dungeons and allow him to kill my parents, and that made me wonder just how weak Martin thought I was. His next words answered my curiosity with a dagger.

"Your bravery is surprising," he said, but at the same time Martin shook his head solemnly.

"However, I am revoking my offer, and sentencing you to one hundred years in the dungeons."

The total reversal came so suddenly that for a minute I struggled to put together words and was speechless.

"What? Why –"

I got half of a frantic challenge out of my throat, but Martin ceased me with a swift and supreme hand.

"This is not debatable, of course. Based on your shift alone you have great potential, but if you are to become a Shifthunter I require your *ultimate* allegiance, and total obedience. If I allowed you to become a Shifthunter today, would you be able to execute Mr. Stevens? What if I demanded that you tie up loose ends and kill Chace's parents?"

Martin stared through me, seeing the truth as easily as if I'd told it to him.

"You could not complete either of those necessary tasks," he said, answering for me.

"When you become a Shifthunter, your entire earthly essence belongs to me. Only your immediate family is spared in the agreement. Any hesitance, any failure, and the agreement is terminated. If you are unable to complete the essential objectives, then you have become one of the useless, vile mutations that we are out to exterminate. If I would have accepted your pledge today than I would have had to kill you tomorrow, when you would've failed to execute Mr. Stevens and then kill the Redman's as directed."

Martin's voice was so even and emotionless that it was almost inhuman at this point, but the sharp-featured face that focused on me was all too real. Even as I tried to imagine myself killing any of those three people, I knew in my heart of hearts that I could never hurt them. By now I also knew that Martin was not going to waver once he'd made a decision, and thus it was only raw, final anguish that propelled me to plead my case anyway.

"Why do Chace's parents have to die? I'll do anything to save them. I could kill anyone that wasn't so personal. *Anyone*," I defended.

Tense with the fervor of desperation, I leaned forward and clenched my hands against the wooden sides of the chair so hard that I thought my fingernails would bore holes into them. Martin laughed in response. It was the first time he had done so since his interview had started, and it came out in a slow but resonant chuckle that chilled me to my bones and doused my final push. Even once he stopped laughing it took a little while for the residual sound of his mirth to fade away.

"When I let you out of the cellars in one hundred years I have little doubt that you will prove yourself valuable," he said when he was serious once again.

"For now, you'll see why you've got to be willing to do *anything* if you want to be a Shifthunter."

The finality of Martin's decree caused tears of frustration to well up in my eyes, but I fought them back and gulped down the lump in my throat.

"Give me a chance," I begged.

Martin just shook his head.

"Losing loved ones makes you tougher," he said, almost reassuringly.

"And you *may* just die down there," he added.

"If you don't make it, at least you won't have to live with the agony of seeing the deaths of your innocent family members."

There was a subtle, deep bitterness to his consolation, and it gave it the opposite effect. There was still no sympathy in his eyes either, and he fixed me now with a final glare of contempt.

"Zade Davidson, your sentence starts now. October 31, 2013. For your sake, I hope there's something left to preserve in the Davidson family line when you come out of there in one hundred Halloweens."

Martin finished his verdict by nodding and then extending his open hand toward the door dismissively. His voice remained as remorseless as it had been, and judging by his heartlessness alone I knew that Mr. Stevens' brief introductions were only a tiny glimpse into the creation of this monster.

"Roslyn has already been called away to other duties; Sebastian is waiting on the landing. He will take you back to the dungeons," Martin said as I got to my feet.

The tears of dismay, defeat, and injustice were fighting back to the surface, especially as I wondered how long it would be before I felt even the comfort of a cushioned chair again. All I could do was nod in numb understanding as I turned towards the door, and then I stiffly crossed through Martin's office with his eyes boring into my back. Once I managed the heavy door once again and squeezed out, I saw the wolfish man named Sebastian anxiously waiting for me on the other side.

"The dungeons," Martin called casually as the door closed.

Sebastian nodded and he smiled down at me contemptuously. He was wearing a ripped, sleeveless t-shirt and cargo shorts, but he didn't bother pulling out the gun he had tucked into his shorts like my other escorts had done.

"I knew you were one of *them*," he spat.

"Exactly what I expected. You won't survive your first year in the dungeons, and I can't say that I'm not glad about it. I hope I get a chance to hurry that process along to be honest," he said.

Sebastian used one of his massive hairy arms to shove me towards the stairs. Pain erupted from my injured shoulder once again, but he ignored my bellow of agony.

"Stop cryin'. You're on hundred year slave duty now, boy. A sentence in the dungeons means you ain't tough. You'll get used to pain one way or another," he said mercilessly.

I put up no resistance, but when we got to the bottom of the stairs he barbarically grabbed me by the back of my shirt and marched me through the maze of the warehouse floor using a combination of jerks and shoves meant to cause me further pain. Every time I cried out though, Sebastian lasered me with a barrage of abusive language.

I was absolutely helpless, so I suffered through his torture methods until we eventually got back to the elevator. I was sure we had taken a longer route than Roslyn had used, and by the time we got there the wound in my shoulder was a torrent of fiery pain – more than I had been in since my first day here. The fact that 100 years of imprisonment was staring me in the face actually helped, because it siphoned away some of my focus from the physical pain I was in.

Nonetheless, I was bent over double and whimpering pitifully the entire time we waited for the carriage. Once the elevator came Sebastian pushed me inside, but he thankfully stopped excessively wrenching my arm. And, although his direction was forceful on the trip back through the tunnels, there was only so much he could do if he wanted me to make it. I stumbled and half-crawled most of the way, and even hit the same indentation I had fallen on every other time. When Sebastian gave me a final, hard shove into my cell however, I was so pitiful that I almost savored the moment, because I had no idea how long it would be before I would even see the outside of that wooden door.

When it was slammed behind me, I looked up from my floored position at the thick wooden slabs that imprisoned me here and let the jarring clang of the door shutting ring in my ears for a little while. It was a loud, disturbing sound, but when I turned to look over at Mr. Stevens he was still in the same crumpled position in the far corner of the room. I could see that he was at least still breathing. As I watched him I thought about how quickly the fate he had warned me of had come to pass... for both of us. It had all seemed so impossible, and now it couldn't be any realer.

An entire century of confinement in this space loomed ahead of me, and it was likely a violent death awaited Mr. Stevens. Time was truly irrelevant now, and that left me with nothing to do but sit and think. A million and one thoughts went through my head as I sat there, but after countless hours they all became one incongruous nightmare.

The lives of my entire family – meaning literally anyone related to me – were subject to immediate, murderous conclusion. My best friend was still dead. All of my hopes and dreams were crushed because my life was futureless, doomed to a century of incarceration. By the time I got out of here, the things that I knew would be washed away and the world outside would be unfathomably different.

Whenever I looked at Mr. Stevens' pitiful form, I knew in my mind that he was essentially dead, too, because Martin had described his execution as a 'necessary task.' Despite Mr. Stevens' dark past, he *had* sacrificed himself for me, and I would forever be indebted to him. The sadistic nature of his current situation made it all the worse, because even when he was alive, he was only conscious long enough to endure more torture.

On top of it all, even with one of the most awesome powers I could imagine at my disposal, I was helpless on all fronts. Martin Evers was even more powerful than I was, and with his army of Shifthunters combing the Earth, he was out there hunting down and killing children even younger than I was every day.

The culmination of my life drove me to the brink of insanity, and I eventually became as statuesque as Mr. Stevens. I sat in the corner against the wall with my head slumped, alternately passing in and out of nightmarish sleep and mind-churning consciousness.

Although it was impossible to tell, I knew that at some point the hours counted and the days changed, but it didn't matter at all to me because I knew I had hundreds of thousands more waiting for me.

One hundred years, I thought over and over.

Within a week, I had declined into the hopeless brooding of a human permanently incarcerated, so much so that I hardly noticed when the pain in my shoulder was gone. Although I hadn't moved to test it, there had been no pain in my leg for many hours either. The shapeshifter healing powers had me feeling physically one hundred percent, but being free of the crippling pain did nothing for my spirits. It was only at very long last when Mr. Stevens stirred from his hibernation that I stopped letting my mind eat itself.

I had to have endured over a week of torturous solitude by then, but when Mr. Stevens slowly sat up and eventually addressed me, I was reminded of the calming effects of human contact, no matter how cold. He had looked healed somewhat, but there was still a long, highly distinct scar-line across one side of his face.

I realized that for him, the regenerative powers of shapeshifting were now a curse. He could be tortured to near death endlessly and recover every single time. I couldn't help but wonder if I would be subjected to similar torture.

"You chose the dungeons," were Mr. Stevens' first solemn words.

His voice was much heavier and weary now, and hoarse with effort. His once blazing eyes flickered with less brightness too, but they still reminded me of his keen intuition. Although I was surprised he had even been conscious enough to realize that I was here, Mr. Stevens had always had a way of knowing things.

"You're alive," was my answer.

I tried to remain positive, because I could only imagine how terrible life had been since Chen had captured him.

"Barely," he replied.

He pointed to his leg with a pained expression. His shin, which was visible right below the cutoff of his tattered pants, protruded ever so slightly, and though the skin looked to have recently healed over it, the bone-lump was gruesome. He had been given no splint or medical attention, and from the look of his lower leg, it had broken cleanly.

"They didn't hit me in the face so much this time, but they broke my leg," Mr. Stevens explained.

His voice was far more resilient than pitiful, but then he absently looked down at his stump of a left hand, remembering. The dirty white bandages still covered the end of a forearm.

"Did they cut off your hand too? That'll grow back, right?" I asked.

"Yes – they cut off my hand – but no, it won't," Mr. Stevens answered, shaking his head.

"Our regenerative powers only allow us to heal injuries; they can't re-grow tissues that aren't there, unfortunately."

Mr. Stevens examined his stump, prodding it gently with a couple of fingers from his other hand until a particularly forceful prod brought a grimace to his face.

"What have they been doing to you? Do they just torture you every day?" I asked, unable to mask my horrification.

Mr. Stevens shrugged without looking up.

"Eh, more or less. I'd guess they actually torture me every week or so, depending on how quickly I recover from my injuries. I usually get one day like today – where I'm actually able to sit up on my own – before they come back. It's not much worse than I expected, though. I've known Martin too long to underestimate his taste for revenge."

Mr. Stevens paused to cough excessively and take a tiny sip from his water tin. He resumed after a few breaths.

"Between having my hand chopped off, being hit with a car, and then being dropped to the ground from 55 feet in the air, I have to admit that Martin *is* getting creative," he added in grudging credence.

While he looked almost humored by the types of torture Martin and his men were cooking up, I shuddered when I imagined having my hand sawed off or being hit with a car. The vengeful torture Mr. Stevens was being subjected to was as bad as any nightmare, and I was admittedly terrified.

"*You* won't suffer like this," Mr. Stevens assured me then, noticing my look.

"My punishments are only so harsh because of my history with Martin. I'm sure he's mentioned that."

Mr. Stevens' reassurance brought a slight wash of relief, but I could tell that he was now referencing his nickname as 'The Traitor.' However there was no guilt on his face or shame in his tone, only acknowledgement. I took that as a cue to speak plainly.

"They call you 'The Traitor,'" I said straightforwardly.

"Roslyn told me that you used to work for Martin."

Mr. Stevens' face gave away nothing, but he nodded in a tiny bit of acknowledgment.

"I was the first shapeshifter Martin ever met," he clarified.

"He wasn't always the head of the Shifthunters, but eventually we became partners and I helped him hunt and kill shifters for a century and a half as his head scientist. I developed Shifter Serum and various tranquilizers for our army, along with helping him recruit new Shifthunters. I encouraged and helped him to forge alliances with world governments, and I even conducted extensive genetic research on the shapeshifter species. It was actually during the later stages of that research that I came to the discovery that caused me to defect, because after extensive testing it became clear that shapeshifters are genetically human. After experimenting on thousands of subjects from all over the world, it became evident that there is a dormant version of the shapeshifter hormone present in every human being. The only difference between normal people and shapeshifters is that the normally dormant hormone activates during shifters' youth, and once it does, the person shifts for the first time and activates the stimulant, regenerative powers of the hormone. If the person ever manages to return to their normal state, they become people like you and me and Martin."

I nodded, soaking in Mr. Stevens' honest revelation for a moment. I had always been curious about the origins of Martin's sadistic genocide, but now I was equally curious about Mr. Stevens' role. I was also still confused by his condemning nickname.

"I still don't understand why they call you 'The Traitor,'" I admitted, looking at Mr. Stevens questioningly.

"The Shifthunters call me 'The Traitor' because I turned on them," he answered plainly.

"Martin operates under the guise that he only kills shifters in order to keep us from running 'normal' people out of existence. Truly however, he's just biding his time in hopes of finding a way to extinct us. He believes that the shifter hormone should be altogether removed from the genetic makeup of human beings, and he is fine with murdering children every day until he can find a way to do that. Since the early nineteen-hundreds his army has been catching shifters within *days* of their first shift… and always as children.

But, back then, finding some type of cure for the hormone seemed medically impossible. As Martin's second-in-command from the beginning, the innocent blood on my hands was already enough to fill up a lake and overflow it. In 1937 I decided that I couldn't keep adding to that bloodbath, and I disappeared on a false mission to Australia. More importantly though, I returned to Martin's old stronghold in England five years later and freed all 22 imprisoned shifters from our dungeons."

Mr. Stevens spoke in his uninflected tone throughout his recap, but by the time he finished I was looking at him with true admiration. Not only had the man sacrificed himself for me, but despite his insistence that Martin could not be stopped, he had been willing to risk his own life to save other innocent lives. And, although I wouldn't see the light of day for decades, piece by piece the world of shapeshifters was becoming clearer to me. Even though I still didn't know exactly what dark beginnings had sent Martin on this crusade, I now knew that he had started with the brilliance of Mr. Stevens at his side.

"Compared to what I have done *for* Martin, freeing those pitiful 22 souls was a drop in the bucket," Mr. Stevens said then, deflecting my appreciation and seemingly reading my mind.

It's no wonder he and Martin were once friends, I thought.

"The true tale of how Martin and I became partners is a story for another time, but neither of us had ever met another shapeshifter and therefore at first we were friends. With such powers on our side soon our endeavors became grandiose, and he became fixated on what had started out as a peaceful undertaking. He had always been ruthless and domineering, but it was ten years or more before he started to use his greater physical power to control me. For a while, I served under him to protect my wife. She lived long and died of natural causes. But, after that, Martin moved his threats to my sons and daughters. He destroyed my entire family when he realized that I was alive and I had freed those shifters."

I was struck like I had been hit with lightning when I realized the type of retaliation that Martin surely would have initiated after such a treacherous move. It almost made me sick to think of how Martin – shifted into whatever monstrosity he became – had systematically annihilated Mr. Stevens' children or grandchildren. As if that wasn't enough, Mr. Stevens also had to live with knowing that he had provoked Martin into killing them. Between the internal conflict and agony that must have caused him and the bravery it would take to carry out that move, I now understood why Mr. Stevens was always so detached.

"I'm sorry," I said, and I meant it sincerely.

Mr. Stevens merely shook his head again and sighed, having apparently long ago come to grips with his losses. After a minute he looked back up at me, when he met my eyes I saw that his expression had changed to one of disappointment.

"You should have chosen to become a Shifthunter," he said, sighing again.

"I tried," I defended, caught off guard by Mr. Steven's sudden change of focus.

I thought back to Martin's devastating denial, and that same well of injustice bubbled up inside of me.

"Martin wouldn't let me. After I chose to become a Shifthunter, he revoked his offer and said that I wasn't 'mentally ready' yet. I didn't *want* to let my family down and spend one hundred years in his hellhole, but Martin made the choice for me. Plus, I thought you said killing innocent children was wrong."

My words came out thick and hot, because I was truly burning up with the enormity of the sentence that faced me. Mr. Stevens took my outburst without the slightest change of expression, however.

"You will have blood on your hands either way. Better it be that of someone who means nothing to you," he responded rather softly.

For once he didn't look me in the eyes as he spoke, and he looked away from me and stared reminiscently down at his snub wrist for a few moments. I wondered if our conversation might have indeed stirred his long-dormant emotions.

"I couldn't kill you," I admitted finally.

"Martin's first mission was for me to personally execute *you*, but you're the only reason I'm still alive. After you saved my life, how could I kill you?"

I looked down the whole time as confessed, and it took me a second to look back up and meet Mr. Stevens' eyes again, because I was oddly ashamed of my weakness and inability to kill him. I knew that he would have gladly accepted a death by my hand if I had successfully pledged my soul to Martin.

However, when I did look him in the eye once more, his expression was pure and unguarded for the first time ever. Through everything we'd gone through it was unquestionably the most honest, uncut moment we'd shared. We locked eyes for only a few long seconds, but in that time frame his whole ethos was laid out in front of me. It was as if he had told me himself that he had dedicated his entire existence to maneuvering for the greater good, and I could plainly see that the impossibly tough decisions he had been forced to make while working for Martin haunted him eternally. I could see right through *him* for once, and I knew then that although Mr. Stevens wished I would have been able to accept Martin's offer and rip him to shreds, it touched him that I could not.

Before looking away, Mr. Stevens nodded one time, and even though I knew he was internally crushed by the fact that we were both captured and doomed, his nod symbolized acknowledgement. I hadn't even known him *that* long, but I knew him well enough to take it as a sign of respect.

After that, Mr. Stevens fell back asleep. I lied awake for a while thinking about all we'd talked about, especially the nightmarishly deep tendrils of Martin's power. He was everywhere it seemed, and controlled everything. Mr. Stevens was just caught up in the bloody vortex like we all were.

It made me think back to days in Castille, when Chace and I used to hang out every day like the innocent boys we were. I thought back to a day last summer when Chace beat be 11-0 in basketball, without missing or shooting from inside the three point line. I had actually deflated a basketball with a brick during that game when my shot went directly off of the lower corner of the backboard, and Chace had proclaimed it to be the greatest shot ever.

It was wild to think of us evolving from those recent days into kids who were forced to run and hide and kill. From my first shift, when I'd uncontrollably ripped those dogs to shreds, I had been dancing with death. Though he had been shifted into a crocodile, I'd even killed a man, and that was something I had never imagined doing in my wildest dreams less than six months ago.

My life is a tragedy.

I couldn't look at it any other way. Sitting there, watching Mr. Stevens sleep for the hundredth time already, I tried to accept that everything I'd ever loved was gone, and that now survival was the only thing that mattered.

That sadness did eventually drive me to sleep, but my first nap was interrupted by the increasingly thunderous gurgling in my empty stomach. I couldn't even remember the last time I'd eaten, but with everything on my mind I'd done a decent job deflecting it so far. I thought to ask Mr. Stevens if my shifter hormones had anything to do with that, but no matter, it was a different ailment that truly bothered me.

The urge to shift into a tiger was becoming vexating. Although I was able to sleep here and there, I had to wake up often to manually suppress the urge to just shift. Although I could control my tiger form much better than before, I didn't feel experienced enough to chance it as hungry as I was right now. I couldn't trust myself not to accidentally eat Mr. Stevens.

So, instead, the days and hours continued to tick by in agonizing, uneventful sameness, except for the one time our torch had burned down to a nub. On cue, an older shifter by the name of Ackley had come to replace it, and when he entered, I had to say that he looked much too old to be carrying an AK47. I knew better than to underestimate anyone at this point, but from his old button down shirt to his plain jeans, he had a gaunt, awkward look to him.

When he'd entered, Mr. Stevens had awoken for a minute, and when I'd questioned him about Ackley he had explained that Martin had told him during some of their recent conversations that he was an aging shifter who served as the keeper here. Apparently Ackley's actual birth date was unknown, but the gray-haired shifter shifted into a leopard and had never left these remote swamps of the Everglades prior to Martin building his fortress here. He'd actually escaped detection until then because of that, but that was 50 odd years ago, and when Martin discovered him here he had actually been alone in the wilderness so long that it took a couple of years for him to become comfortable with human contact again. He had been kept alive mainly because of his unrivaled knowledge of these Everglades, and his eventual usefulness as a guardsman was more of a bonus.

It was another reminder of the permanent deadliness of every single Shifthunter, because once I'd learned that the man could morph into a leopard at any second, it absolutely gave him a new undercurrent of dangerousness. However, that conversation about Ackley's origins was the only one that took place between Mr. Stevens and I for the next seven or eight days – and by the end of that period my physical needs had reached levels that were downright unbearable. Our combined bodily releases had accumulated in a reviling pile in the far corner of our cell, and my mind had reached a state of delirium such that my brain could focus on nothing but the fact that I was trapped, starving, and overwhelmed by the desire to shift into a tiger.

The latter ailment was literally like a fire in my bones, because it was a burning desire that erupted from the very core of my being. By now there was no question that I would eat Mr. Stevens if I let myself shift in here, but the urges were becoming stronger and I was just barely able to keep myself from giving in to it. It was almost like a drug to an addict, because both my mind and body uncontrollably craved the whole essence and euphoria of my Siberian tiger body.

When I was awake, my hands were balled into tight fists to keep myself from accidentally shifting, and when I slept, my dreams were full of fantasies of exhausting the limitless powers of my tiger shift. The dreams were so vibrant that I'd awoken often with a psychotic jump, thinking that I'd really accidentally shifted.

On the other side of the cell, Mr. Stevens was often awake now, but he was always horizontal and totally quiet. We were both secretly surprised that no one had come to torture him yet, which was probably why he never moved except to sip from his tin can of water that Ackley had deposited during the change of the torches. My own cup of water had lasted two days, and was long ago empty. However, after making an effort to sip from his cup today and finding it empty, Mr. Stevens finally broke two or three days of total silence.

"I expect I'll be going back to the UA soon," he said hoarsely, tossing the cup towards the middle of the floor.

I was sitting up against the wall, watching him, and his eyes listlessly followed the circular trail of the cup until it came to a rest. Then he turned towards me, and I saw that although his eyes had regained some of the liveliness they once had, they were still haunted by a sag of inevitable defeat.

"What's the UA?" I asked, sounding as hoarse as he did.

"The Underground Arena," Mr. Stevens answered.

"Evidently, when Martin excavated these underground passages to make his dungeon, he eventually ran into a cavern, and since Martin planned to kill many more shifters than he captured, he decided to stop building holding cells and turn the cavern into a training arena. It's most often used to train his Shifthunters – like the old field grounds Martin had in our old castle – but in my case it also duals as a torture room."

I winced, feeling both guilty and sorry for my poor teacher. Martin Evers was going to every length to make the last days of his existence as torturous as possible, and he was succeeding mightily. And, since we both knew that Martin would kill him outright before he stopped torturing him, there was nothing I could even say to comfort him.

At that moment a faint sound began to reach our ears however, and I was absolved of any remnants of that duty. We both listened for a minute, and as the sound grew louder the sound became discernible as the rhythm of unhurried footsteps.

"Ackley?" I asked, not quite sure why I whispered.

Mr. Stevens leaned forward, listening more intently. He frowned.

"No," he answered.

"Sebastian."

As I too concentrated on the sound, I could tell almost immediately that the footsteps were much heavier this time, and they lacked Ackley's distinctive shuffle. My heart sank, and while Mr. Stevens closed his eyes and took a deep, resigning breath, the footsteps reached our door.

As Mr. Stevens had predicted, Sebastian appeared then, and he did so by unlocking and bursting through our wooden cell door like a rampaging beast and shattering the sober tranquility we'd lived in. With his hairy arms bursting out of a sleeveless t-shirt, he glared down at us from beneath his shagged hair and rugged beard with natural rage.

"It's time, Traitor," he rumbled.

Sebastian moved right past me without a second look, powerful and swift. His oddly triangular teeth glinted as he spoke, and he headed straight for Mr. Stevens, who didn't move a muscle as Sebastian approached him.

"Are you going to walk or am I going to drag you again?" Sebastian demanded as he stood over Mr. Stevens.

Mr. Stevens groaned, but didn't acknowledge Sebastian with a verbal answer. Instead, he took as long as possible to slowly get to his feet.

"I'll walk," he spat when he was finally upright.

Sebastian looked down at him, his eyes full of contempt, and then responded by violently yanking Mr. Stevens towards the door. As he was thrown outside of our cell Mr. Stevens nearly fell to the ground without the use of his right hand, but Sebastian turned towards me, ignoring Mr. Stevens for a moment.

"This is what happens to traitors," he growled back at me, acknowledging me for the first and only time.

His eyes gleamed with satisfaction at my condition, and then he turned out of the cell and slammed the door behind him. The sound rang in my ears as their footsteps receded down the hallway, and I was hit with a sickening feeling when I thought about where they were going. I forced myself not to imagine what kind of torture methods would be employed this time.

I was alone again too, and very quickly I missed having Chace's company. The memory of his genius, hilarity, and optimism pained me intensely. I wondered whether or not some miracle had kept him alive, and I tried for a minute to really believe he had somehow survived. When I thought about him now it felt right to pray, and out loud, probably louder than I'd ever prayed in my life, I prayed then that Chace somehow survived.

It was a feeling I wasn't used to because I'd only been to church a couple of times in my life, but the fervency of that prayer helped me not to succumb to a mountain of guilt and despair that weighed down on me like an anvil. I actually prayed for so hard and long that eventually I even fell asleep, and it was the soundest I'd slept in weeks.

Unfortunately that sleep only lasted a few hours before it was rudely interrupted by our cell door bursting open again, and I opened my eyes just in time to see Mr. Stevens being hurled back into our cell. His purple-faced body skidded face first into the middle of the floor, and behind it, Sebastian's mass loomed in the doorway, smirking.

"So, Zade," he sneered, glaring at me.

"Did you just think we were going to let you starve to death or what?" he asked, taunting.

"No," I admitted.

Sebastian's smirk grew a little wider.

"Good, because you won't be getting off *that* easy! Martin said we will be feeding you tomorrow, actually."

His voice tingled with anticipation, and the twinkle in his eye was one of both satisfaction and hatred. I was mystified by that, but driven by the edginess of my hunger I glared back at him with equal malice, and we remained in that battle of wills until he backed out of our cell once again and slammed the door shut in my face.

The sound of the latch being thrown into place on the outside was a loud *Clang!* and it rang in my ears bitingly as I looked down to see what kind of condition Mr. Stevens was in. After apprehending him for only a second, I cringed uncontrollably.

His face was a burnt, charred mass. The skin had been torched a dark brownish-black, and his head and eyelids were both hairless and cooked. His lips were so maimed that they had become crisped slivers, and although nothing but the upper half of his neck also seemed harmed, the burnt area was so horrifically destroyed that I wasn't even sure he was still alive. I stepped forward thinking to help him, but I stopped short when I realized that with the current condition of his face, every movement would cause him excruciating pain. I couldn't help but wonder what manner of methods were used to bring this about, and Sebastian's words repeated ominously in my head.

This is what happens to traitors.

Even after many hours those words didn't lose their menace. They came rushing back every time my eyes crossed Mr. Stevens' body, and I even puked once, when his zombie-headed form sat up to spit out copious amounts of blood. He had fallen back on his back immediately afterward, and he'd returned struggling through his shallow, wheezy breathing.

There was no doubt that Mr. Stevens was hovering on the edges of death this time, but I could do nothing for him, because

I knew that since he hadn't yet died, his regenerative powers would be too strong to allow him to pass over. It was a truly horrible dilemma.

Was it better for him to recover or die?

I couldn't decide, but before I could think further into it, the barely discernible sound of a different set of footsteps reached my ears. They were very light, and by the time I even really heard them our cell door was suddenly opening, and then Roslyn's lithe figured appeared. When she looked at me I saw that hint of pity once again, but then I realized that without weeks of hygienic care or sustenance, I must've looked pitiful.

As the door closed behind her and she came into the cell, she came over to my place in the corner and looked me over, and she seemed genuinely concerned. Even after she shot a quick, analytical glance over at Mr. Stevens, her gaze instantly returned to me and she crouched down in front of me to meet my eyes at my level.

"How are the urges?" she asked.

The urges were terrible, but I was momentarily swooned by her natural beauty from this close up. Her tan skin was full of life, her brown hair was full and healthy, and her brown eyes were inquisitive and tender.

"They're pretty bad," I said, swallowing.

Roslyn chuckled, and not only did she flash her dazzling set of teeth, but her laughter was simultaneously the lightest and most vivacious sound I'd ever heard. It took all of my earthly power to remember that she had killed Chace, and that only Chen Lake was more directly responsible for my current predicament.

"It'll be ok. You'll get to satisfy both your urges and your hunger soon," Roslyn responded.

She jerked her head bitterly towards Mr. Stevens.

"Martin's schedule calls for you to be fed at five tonight, otherwise I'd tell you to eat *him*," she said.

Her face contorted into a scowl for a second, but then she reached forward and pulled the loose collar of my torn t-shirt to the side. She inspected my shoulder, and where there had once been a bloody hole, there was now nothing but clean skin. No scars. Since I had been afraid to look at it all this time, even I was taken aback by how perfectly I'd healed, and it had probably been healed this clean for days by now. Roslyn looked up and met my eyes with an approving smirk.

"Your shoulder has healed nicely. It was only a flesh wound," she said.

She stood up satisfactorily, stretching a little. I forced myself not to be mesmerized.

"I actually came with news for Gordon," she said, returning to a business-like tone.

"Martin has some messages for him… whether he is able to receive them or not."

As quickly as if she had flipped some internal switch, the tenderness of her brown eyes hardened like cement as she moved over to Mr. Stevens. She looked down at him for an instant before prodding him with one boot like he was a dead animal. Mr. Stevens groaned in agonized response as her boot pushed against bruised flesh and broken bones.

"Can you hear me, Gordon?" she asked.

Mr. Stevens was motionless beneath her foot. Roslyn seemed not to notice, and stood over him like a gloating predator. She leaned in closer and spoke loudly, making sure that Mr. Stevens could hear.

"Martin has sent me to inform you of your impending execution. He has decided to have you publicly executed as an example of the death that awaits any shapeshifter that refuses him. He's scheduled the ceremony for next Sunday, one week from tomorrow. Over a third of our hunters will be present, because Martin plans to do this personally. He feels that the shapeshifter species needs a reminder of his power."

Roslyn huffed smugly and then pulled away from him, her face once again scowling.

"Wait, no!" I interjected.

The objection came out of my mouth vehement and unabated, but Roslyn purposely ignored me and continued as if I'd said nothing at all.

"There is more news," she said, leaning back down to address Mr. Stevens again.

"As you know, in recent months we killed yet another one of the shifters you freed – Percival Smalling. However, even more recently we have captured his equally vermin daughter, Angel.

She's a strong girl, but her shift is weak. Martin has been torturing her for information, and is holding out on killing her because he's been trying to pick her brain about the extreme rarity of having a shapeshifting father, especially one who creates little shapeshifter clans with other unknown shifters. He's going to keep torturing her until he finds out where the rest of her little shifter clan is hiding, but the bigger issue is the fact that there are unknown shapeshifters in the world who have survived past the age of thirteen."

Roslyn stared down at Mr. Stevens both angrily and pitilessly, and she seemed to revel in letting his scarred body absorb the news. As I watched her I couldn't help but wonder how Martin had implanted such a deep hatred for her own kind in her, and for all her beauty at moments like this it seemed impossible to believe that beneath her cruelty laid a core of good.

"Things like this stink of your hands, Gordon. Out of the eleven shifters who actually made it out alive on that day of treason, we've now killed eight and re-captured one. With you here in the dungeons there are only two more of those wretched lot left on Earth and your whole backstabbing plan will have finally been put to rest. No matter what you do, Martin always wins in our world. You of all people should have known better."

I was surprised at the subtle hint of resignation in her voice, yet as Roslyn gave me a parting look I saw that she was consumed by her duty as a Shifthunter, and the softness I'd seen when she first entered was nowhere to be found. She was more enigmatic than all of the girls I'd ever met before combined, and without a single look backwards, she opened our cell door and shut it soundly behind her, locking us in once again.

Chapter 23

ZADE DAVIDSON

Everglades, Florida - November 22, 2013

$\mathcal{F}$or the next few hours the urge to shift was like a tidal wave coming from the inside. And, besides that infinite desire to stand up and explode into a Siberian tiger, I was overcome by angst at the fate that awaited Mr. Stevens. He was going to be executed before my very eyes by Martin Evers, and there was nothing anyone in the world could do about it. The agony was so much that I had taken to grinding my head against the side of our hard clay walls in an effort to divert my attention from real life, because physical pain had become the only sensation strong enough to keep me sane.

I truthfully felt like I was on the brink of insanity when I was at last interrupted by the sound of heavy footsteps and our door banging open. Sebastian greeted me with a rough flashing of his jagged teeth.

"It's time to eat," he said loathingly.

In a flash he was in front of me, yanking me up by the arm. In Sebastian's grasp my once full arms felt thin and incapable, and with the dizzying sensation that accompanied standing up, I realized that I was truly deteriorating. I was still struggling to focus when Sebastian forcefully shoved me out of our cell and shut the door behind him, before once again vice-gripping my arm and continuing to drag me down the hallway. We were heading in the opposite direction Pharaoh had brought us in – the direction that Mr. Stevens had said the UA was – and we didn't walk that way for long before we came to a halt at a single, wooden door. It looked just like the doors to the cells – minus the laminates.

Well this is it, I thought in the brief moment I had in front of the door.

Then Sebastian unceremoniously pushed me through it one into a gigantic, stadium-sized cavern. When I caught my balance after stumbling through the door, I saw that the arena stretched away from our position in a giant, smooth dome, and it was lined to the ceiling by a different, morbidly gray clay.

As I took it in, my heart skipped a beat when I saw the three figures standing atop a grayish cleft on the back wall. From almost one hundred yards away on the cavern floor I met the observing eyes of Roslyn, Chen Lake, and an unrecognized brown-skinned boy who stood about half their height. As they looked back at me, it was instantly clear why this place was called the Underground Arena, because the sloping ridge at the back of it provided a perfect, raised viewing point of the spacious floor below.

On that floor was a monstrous set of stadium lights set up to the far left of the cave, whose stark glow and low hum of operation illuminated the place. Electrical wires ran from their base into a generator into which they were plugged. These lights illuminated the entire space of the cavern to easy visibility, but in their main spotlight was another unexpected and gut-wrenching sight…. a live, snow-white tiger.

It paced anxiously a couple stories below the three people on the ridge, tied to a thick metal pole by a collar around its neck. I stared at it as Sebastian pushed me further into the cavern, while the beast licked its lips and apprehended me as well.

"Don't be shy *now*," he chided tauntingly, looking across at the spectators on the ridge.

"Hey! Came here to watch the new one feed?" he called to them.

"We've been showing Brian some of the proceedings," Chen called back smartly from the cleft.

"Well, either way we'll find out if your boy is even worth his own meal ticket today!" Sebastian called again, changing his focus towards Roslyn.

Roslyn laughed down at him.

"You forget that I watched him kill Roman. He'll have no trouble at least *killing* his meal," she answered.

The sounds of the voices echoed off of the walls slightly eerily... almost as eerily as the way Roslyn had just mentioned 'killing my meal.'

I looked back down at the tiger, and I suddenly wondered what kind of sick plan was being set into motion. The blue-eyed cat watched us as Sebastian turned towards me.

"We don't respect dungeon-dwellers," he said repugnantly.

"If you want to eat, you'll eat one of your own kind. Martin special-ordered this here Bengal off of some Russian poachers, and I thought it was nice of them to leave her 20 days hungry before the delivery."

His Southern drawl glistened with excitement. I wanted to vomit. Even through my desperate hunger the thought of eating the exquisitely formed tiger across the room repulsed me. He pushed me towards the tiger, but I tried to resist and ended up unwillingly moving a couple of yards towards her. Her eyes never left me, and she stopped pacing as I came within ten yards of the end of her leash.

"Zade looks a little scared," Sebastian called across the cave.

There was unrestrained delight in his voice.

"He's always looked weak to me," Chen Lake responded snidely.

From my position just outside of the tiger's range, he and the others were approximately 25 feet above me up on the cleft. He glared down at me without his glasses on for once, and the black slits that were his eyes emanated with the same detest he had always radiated.

"I may be the one credited with discovering him, but I've actually never seen him shift," he said, chortling slightly.

"I'll bet forty thousand dollars that one of us has to save him," he offered.

"I'll call you on that," Roslyn accepted quickly.

I heard Sebastian immediately scoff behind me, while Chen's face contorted into a look of pleasant surprise. To be honest, the confidence in Roslyn's voice had surprised me as well, yet she met Chen's look with an unfazed challenge of her own.

"Deal," Chen accepted, satisfied.

From behind I felt Sebastian step up next to me, but ahead, besides a slight flicker of the eyes and a distasteful curl of its lips, the tiger seemed dead-set on me.

"Look—she feels your inner feline nature... Are you ready, boy?" Sebastian asked.

As I watched him walk past the tiger towards the pole connected to its leash, his expression told me that he very much expected the tiger to get the best of me. The cat only bristled as Sebastian passed her, and as her and I stared each other down, I couldn't help but once again think that this animal in front of me was one of the most exquisite creatures I'd ever seen. Her deep blue eyes were crisp and alert, and her ears were perked forward attentively. The stripes of black in her fur were placed with distinct femininity, and I wondered if my easy recognition of that was because I shifted into the same species of cat. I felt paralyzed against her, but not only was I now part of a forty-thousand dollar bet to kill her, unless I wanted to starve to death, I was expected to eat her remains afterwards.

No matter how horrific that was however, Sebastian unlocked the chain connecting her to the pole without hesitating. As the tiger livened with the slacking of her restraints, Sebastian walked back past us towards the door we'd entered through.

"Have at it," he said with faux-encouragement as he passed me.

I took one final look across at the three faces on the cleft and at the loosed tiger in front of me, and as I did, I knew that a terrible moment was upon me. If I had had any other choice I would have ran the other way, but with my choice made for me I took a single, tentative step towards the tiger, which hunched down menacingly and narrowed its eyes in warning.

Not the friendliest girl, I thought, and with that, I finally let the pent-up swell of the Shifters urge flow over me.

In a liberating instant, I willed my limbs into my Siberian tiger form, and as my mind slipped into the momentary haze of semi-awareness, my bones and tendons simultaneously twisted and exploded. After such a long hiatus, the uncomfortable, grotesque feeling of morphing was truly a welcome sensation, but in the same instant that it began the eruptive rendering of my

body was complete. Within one timed second my full consciousness returned, and when it did, the world came blazing back
through a lens that was a thousand times more vibrant.

I still stood in the same place, but now I occupied ten times
more ground, and for a second I could only revel in the glory of
flexing my mind through this thousand-pound body. It felt so
good to be finally unburdened by the shifters' urge that the sheer
size and power of my shift was both freeing and gleeful. The pinpoint vision, acute hearing, and ultra-perceptive sense of smell
combined to make my first moment back in tiger form so intense
that I had to use all of my physical restraint to control myself from
reacting to the other tiger.

Her smell was distinguishable and right in front of me, and it
awakened urges similar to those of seeing an attractive human being
of the opposite gender. She was now only half my size however, and
now that I was a giant male tiger instead of a puny human, her tiger-
blue eyes exuded much more fear than aggression.

Although I could also smell the additional scent of the
shapeshifters above and behind us, I forcefully ignored those stim-
uli and made my first move by taking a trial step towards the tiger,
who danced backwards with a discordant scraping of the dangling
chain tied to her neck. As she watched me warily from a few yards
further away, I felt absolutely no inclination to attack and eat her
despite my hunger.

She is food and necessary energy. Kill her.

I deliberately manipulated my thoughts, locking out all traces
of human compassion as I took more calculated steps towards my
prey, trying to corner her underneath the cleft.

Survival, I repeated over and over again.

As the female continued to back away from my stalking
advance, I felt my tail wagging behind me in natural preparation
for the attacking lunge. As I felt the limitless power within my
limbs humming at the ready, I bared my fangs in deliberate aggression and snarled. My cornered quarry watched my every move
with her eyes full of mortal defense.

You are a Siberian tiger, I told myself one final time.

A natural born killer.

In a flashing movement, I released the coiled springs of my
muscles and launched myself towards the tigress across from me. I

descended on her with indefensible speed, and with a swipe my gigantic right paw violently cuffed the side of her face before she could even react. The incredible impact sent her sprawling, and with an injured yelp, the snow-white cat hit the ground hard and skidded a few yards across the earthen floor.

When she scrambled back to her feet, half of her white fur was tainted with grayish-brown dirt, and her deep blue eyes were aglow with the fire of combat. She addressed me with a rumbling, feline growl, and while I internally fought against the guilt of desecrating the beauty of this natural creature, I challenged her with an exponentially deeper and more menacing roar of my own.

The sound shook through the whole UA cavern with a hostility that would make the bravest of men stiffen, and then I charged the tigress again, this time launching and hitting her square-on like a blitzing linebacker. Channeling a move I had watched Chace execute hundreds of times on the football field, I tackled her in one swift maneuver, and leveraging my greater weight and strength against her, I crushed the poor female to the floor beneath me and swatted away her parrying paws with ease.

At the same time, I rammed the crown of my massive head underneath her chin and drove her skull backwards into the ground with a crunch. Just like Roman before her, she was powerless to my size and muscle once I was on top of her. My own full strength was so immense that she was finished by just that single move, and it only took a few seconds for my leviathan mass to squish the air and life out of her lungs.

As soon as she went slack I leapt away from the motionless Bengal in swift victory, but I was filled with instant regret rather than elation. The sight of her crushed, innocent body was deeply saddening, and it made eating her now seem more impossible than ever. In direct spite of that though, Sebastian was flinging a flurry of curses at me from behind.

"Eat her or I'll rip one of your arms off, cake-puff!!" he bellowed.

When I turned to face him, I felt a little empowered by the fact that he was so much smaller than me now, but he looked unfazed by my display of power. He was still outrageously large for a human, and while I eyed him as the larger being for once, I could see anger boiling in his eyes.

"I'm not kidding. We'll rip your limbs off one by one before we'll let you starve to death! You've got one minute!" he barked commandingly.

He looked so infuriated that I thought he would burst, and I reluctantly turned back towards the crumpled tiger. I dreaded every step as I padded around to the front of her, and even through my hunger I had no desire to eat her. Nonetheless, I was a Siberian tiger, and I would do anything to survive.

I pulled my lips behind my vicious canine teeth and prepared to sink them into the neck of the dead female then, but at that moment, the seemingly dead tiger sprang to life and engulfed my head with *her* teeth instead.

She attacked with a ferocity and quickness that I would not have thought possible, and my world was suddenly a raging fire of teeth and claws. My strength advantage over my attacker was neutralized by her jaws being attached to my face, and even as I tried to use brute force to wrestle her away, I wasn't just lucky that her teeth had missed my eyes, I was barely able to keep her from slashing them out. She was on top of me, and every time I swatted her claws away, they returned with twice the furor.

The pity for this animal that I had felt just moments ago was now gone entirely – there was no holding back if I wanted to survive.

Kill or be killed, my instincts whispered fervently.

With a burst of pivotal, mortal desire, I wrestled her feet away with my lower legs and finally managed to wedge them underneath her, and at last I detached the tigress from my face with one explosive kick that sent her flying across the room. She landed on her feet, but they crumpled beneath her from the sheer height of the toss, and although my face was still burning from the pain of her attack, I was on top of her again before she could fully recover.

Now I'm going to kill you, I thought, and with my razor-sharp claws fully extended, my paws descended on her with the speed and force of unbridled assault.

I was many times more powerful than her, and her weaker bones and attempts to block me were truly futile. Once again it wasn't long before she lay motionless, but this time I was sure she was dead. I knew because she wasn't much more than a mass of broken bones and fur by the time I stopped assaulting her, and when I looked down knowing that I had just mutilated that once beautiful tiger into what I now saw, more fuel was added to my fire of rage.

The taste of blood was on my lips and the stain of it coated my fur, and with the fresh blood of that innocent Bengal now on my hands, I whirled towards Sebastian next, unable and unwilling to stop channeling my fury.

I stared him down and took a threatening step towards him, blinded by bloodlust and the true glory of being at the helm of this body. Sebastian met my glare with a grin and without the slightest inkling of fear, but even that admonition was lost on me in my current mania.

With two quick bounds I closed the 20 yard gap between us and leapt into the air to finish him, but when I landed with a murderous swipe of my right paw, I came up empty-handed. Thwarted, I spun around again, but this time I was greeted by the pungent smell of wet dog and the sight of an enormous werewolf in Sebastian's place.

It was only possible to describe the monster that faced me as a werewolf, because it was a genuine reincarnation of my childhood nightmares. The beast had a wolfish face, and with Sebastian's mouth open and arms raised in a roar, I saw that it was equipped with viciously long canines, hairy, muscular arms, and claws that were long and curved like reaper scythes. It stood on its hind legs like a person, and I guessed it to be about twelve feet tall and about the same weight as I was before it charged me on all fours and smacked into me straight on.

Not only was I caught off guard, but the initial blow was the most powerful hit I had ever taken, and all I could do was dig my claws into Sebastian's shoulders and hold on as our giant bodies rolled over each other. When we separated I could barely breathe, and I heard shouts coming from the ridge urging me to stop while I had a chance to live. I ignored them and bared my teeth in challenge, catching my breath as I intentionally refused to acknowledge the wolf's staggering strength and superior proficiency in battle.

As the Sebastian-wolf and I circled each other another time, I struggled with how deftly he alternated between walking on two legs and four, feigning attacks in a way that put me totally on the defensive. Every time he would half-charge me I would jump away, but even with my lightning-quick cat reflexes at work, a couple of times I was just inches away from his swiping claws.

Sebastian and I were two supernatural juggernauts, and after another dancing rotation, Sebastian charged me again. This time I launched back at him, and when we collided, I bit at his neck and arms with the pure intent to kill. With identical murderousness he bit at the same areas on me, and I felt my blood running down my sides when his claws ripped into them.

We fell to the floor and kept going at it, but in close quarters like this, his greater battle prowess was truly utilized. Only because of my intensity and desire to survive was I able to withstand the fact that for every successful slash or bite I managed, I received three times as many. Soon I was bleeding from everywhere, but my mind was not my own, and I kept attacking until Sebastian slipped under one of my out-of-control swipes and came up from underneath me with his shoulder, lifting and throwing me into the air.

I landed on my back, and the air whooshed out of my lungs when my spine connected with the earth. Combined with my loss of blood, I was hit with a blanket of dizziness, and with my vision getting blurry too, I was very slow getting back to my feet. Fortunately I could still see enough to see Sebastian's mass charging at me a final time, but he suddenly stopped short a few yards before he reached me. For a second I thought he was just backing off, but then I saw that a tiny black shape had appeared between us.

As my vision focused the black shape became a shiny black house cat, which now stood regally facing Sebastian, balanced delicately on the tips of its paws. Its stance looked decidedly aggressive, and while at first I was completely baffled by his wariness of an ordinary cat, I then saw that the cat was poising its tail upwards and forward like a weapon. When I looked even closer, I saw that emerging delicately from the tip of its tail was a long, barbed needle, and judging by the way the Sebastian-wolf backed away from it, that needle was lethal.

Sebastian, despite slowly backing away, growled viciously at the cat, and his shaggy, lumbering form looked vividly menacing now that I finally got a chance to look at him. Standing on two legs in his retreat he was humongous, but I saw that he could have been even taller except that his shoulders hunched forward noticeably to allow a seamless transition into a four-legged lope. His head was essentially the head of a wolf, except with a shorter snout and murderously extended canines, and his two upper arms were humanoid. Hanging on the ends of those arms were his dangerously clawed hands, which had caused the burning pain that erupted from my left side.

Though Sebastian still snarled aggressively he continued to retreat as the cat advanced on him with a series of nimble, offensive steps. As she moved, her shiny black tail danced with her, swaying and hovering, always at the ready. It was as if her tail had a mind of its own, with that mind's only purpose being to search for an opportunity to strike.

At the sight of the giant werewolf suspending its bloodthirsty rage in deference to such a tiny animal, I relaxed as well. Sebastian was unable to attack me without first getting past the cat between us, and with a steady mirroring of the wolf's movements, the little cat refused to let him past. After letting loose a furious bellow, Sebastian then stood upright, and with the bizarre look of transforming body parts, the Sebastian-wolf downshifted into a naked an infuriated human.

"I'll kill you!" he shouted, jabbing his finger at me.

"How dare you intervene in this?" he roared down at the cat.

He made a half-step towards me, but with the cat still in between us, he didn't dare do more. It wasn't until he stood calm that the cat stopped bearing down on him and turned towards me, and when it did, it did so with an elegance that I suddenly placed as familiar. She moved towards me with a fluid femininity that I easily recognized, and when I met the cat's also-familiar brown eyes, everything clicked. Roslyn's face – shifted now into the face of this little cat – eyed me with clear, livid purpose.

Downshift or die.

Her look left no doubt that following her orders was my only option, and it also made it immediately clear why Roslyn was so highly respected among the Shifthunters. As I took a couple of steps back and willed myself into my human body, my rage transformed into wonderment and understanding.

Unfortunately, when I arrived in my human body, I was barely able to stand. Lacerations covered my arms, neck, torso, and legs – meaning that I was essentially bleeding from my entire body. I sank to one knee instantly, and I groaned loudly as the pain that accompanied my wounds took the place of the adrenaline that had kept me going.

Ahead, Roslyn downshifted as well, and when her naked body erupted upwards out of the little cat in front of me, I forgot about her deadliness for a moment and was entirely enraptured by her perfection. As my eyes uncontrollably ran over her body, I knew that words could never do justice to the placement of her curves, the way her silky brown hair fell over her shoulders, or even the way her furious eyes bore down into mine.

"What were you thinking!?" she exclaimed, shaking me out of my gawk.

I stumbled for words.

"I don't know… I guess I *wasn't* thinking… I –"

"You would have *died* if I hadn't stepped in," Roslyn said, cutting me off curtly.

"Sebastian would have killed you, and I truly should have let him. Neither of us will enjoy the repercussions Martin sends down for this."

Roslyn's voice bristled with willfully contained anger, and from behind her, I saw Sebastian's beastly human form still glaring down at me murderously. As I tried to ignore the slicing pain and the blood that dripped into a pool on the floor, he stood upright on the other side of Roslyn looking only mildly injured and severely infuriated. Compared to his massive, chiseled frame and Roslyn's accentuated figure, I couldn't help but feel frustratingly inferior.

"Foolish or not, if you hadn't stepped in I'd still be trying to bite Sebastian's head off," I responded through gritted teeth.

I looked at my two captors defiantly.

"If it wasn't for this wench stepping in between us you'd already be dead," Sebastian retorted.

I watched his hands clench into fists, but Roslyn stayed him with a sharp look.

"You would both be dead if you hadn't deferred to me," she reminded us.

Her tone was authoritative and confident, and as I watched her angelic human figure eye Sebastian and I in warning, I was once again reminded of the deadliness behind her beauty. Her intrigue pulled at me like a vortex, but the three-way tension between us was interrupted by Chen Lake and the unfamiliar boy joining us from off of the cliff.

Although his glasses were missing, Chen was wearing another unmistakably expensive business suit, and he slung a black backpack down as he arrived. As Roslyn took a t-shirt and sweatpants out of the backpack and slipped lithely into them, Chen turned towards me with the most contemptuous frown imaginable.

"Well, Zade, I yet again find myself appalled to see you alive," he said.

His voice dripped with condemnation, and now that he was without his usual glasses, his expression of hostility was even rawer. Unlike that day he had confronted me in front of Castille High however, I was aware of my powers now, and my return look was equally hostile.

"I actually plan to outlive *you*," I countered insolently.

As I tried to stem the bleeding from a particularly bloody gash across my ribcage, I kept my eyes on Chen Lake.

"I'll kill you myself if I ever get the chance," I added, infusing my words with the hatred I felt for him.

Chen laughed loudly.

"I hope you get that chance, because I knew you were weak from the moment I met you. Even after finally seeing your shift for myself I would welcome the chance to fight you. Your battle technique is horrendous, and your strength of mind is even worse. The fact that such a powerful is wasted on the likes of you is truly a shame."

Chen shook his head and looked down at the boy next to him.

"Brian Sann, meet Zade Davidson. After all of the other pathetic shapeshifters you saw today, know that this one is the worst."

The young boy to Chen's right, who looked to be about eight, nodded in my direction expressionlessly. Despite his youth there was a darkness about him, and when I nodded back at him he refused to meet my eyes. When they did flicker briefly towards Chen, I saw that his eyes were a bright green that stood out strikingly against his brown skin and jet-black hair.

"Brian is everything you will never be," Chen said to me, patting the boy on the shoulder.

"He is powerful as a shapeshifter, but he will one day be even more dangerous as a man. He understands that the true power of a shapeshifter lies in the cunningness of his mind, and he will outlive you because of that."

Chen gave me a final look of smugness and disgust and then turned towards Roslyn.

"Brian and I are catching a flight back to Castille for more training. We'll catch up with you three later," he said.

As Chen steered Brian headed towards the door, Roslyn waved for Sebastian to follow them.

"I'll take Zade back to his cell," she said.

"Call Ackley and tell him to bring Zade's meal back for him."

Roslyn met Sebastian's narrowed, resentful eyes with a look of command. Outranked, Sebastian hocked loudly and conjured a thick wad of snot, which he then spit at me with as much disrespect as he could muster. Although he was twenty feet away, it flew past Roslyn and landed only an inch in front of me with a sickening plop.

"Enjoy your carcass," Sebastian snarled, and then he followed Chen and Brian out of the UA.

Chapter 24

ZADE DAVIDSON

Everglades, Florida – November 22, 2013

*L*ess than an hour after Roslyn escorted me back into my cell, Ackley arrived with the dead body of the Bengal tiger female. With the help of a burly, unidentified guard, he'd slid the tiger in on a large utility mat and left it in the center of the floor, and for the next few hours I'd sat in my usual corner, watching it.

Besides the awkward, broken angle of the animal's neck, it didn't look any less magnificent now, even in death. Although her snow-white coat was dirty and battered, her elegant stripes and lithe construction were still striking and wholly unappetizing. As I repeatedly traced her alluring pattern with my eyes, I could only think about the guilt I felt at having slaughtered such a rare beast like a farm animal.

Remorse and compassion will only get you killed. Your survival is dependent on ruthlessness and selfishness, I kept telling myself.

It was a painfully slow process, but as I literally forced myself to embrace those sentiments, they gradually began to replace my feelings of sadness and regret. When I thought about how even the dead Bengal in front of me had used my own compassion against me, the ideals of strength and self-preservation began to fill my consciousness even faster than my empathy vacated it. The more I dwelled on the stolen majesty of the dead tiger and the necessity of a survival-only attitude, the more the old Zade Davidson faded into the recesses.

By the time I stood up to shift, I felt like a totally different person. After tossing the tattered shirt and ragged shorts Roslyn had given me into a corner, I shifted with the ease and determination of making a fist. After I felt myself seamlessly morph and expand into the shape of a giant Siberian tiger, I knew then that at least the act of shapeshifting had finally become second nature.

When I returned from the semi-haze of shifting to my Siberian tiger form, the extreme claustrophobia that washed over me provoked me more than it pained me. Now that I was twelve feet long I could barely even turn around, but I doggedly ignored the sensation of bodily constriction and focused on filling my stomach to stay alive.

With a final burst of courage, I sunk my saber teeth deep into the tissue of the dead tiger and ripped off a large chunk of flesh. The sound of my teeth tearing the gristle from the bone was a grotesque crunch, but to my current palette the Bengal flesh tasted like meat, and I swallowed the first mouthful with a heavy gulp. It was a defining moment, because as bloody and raw as the meat was, the sensation of that first morsel of food settling in my stomach was liberating.

I cannibalized the rest of the once-gorgeous cat with a ravenous appetite, and I felt like each bite that I swallowed hardened my resolve a little more. When I was finally full there was nothing but an ugly mess of bones left on the mat, and I licked the blood from my stained lips and nudged the carcass towards the door in satiation.

The feeling of fullness that came over me then was heavier and more drowsing than any I'd ever felt, and without bothering to downshift, I curled up into a massive ball. In my current form I had about as much space as a human sleeping in a closet, but the softness of my own orange fur was like a natural pillow, and it felt like many hours before I awoke once again.

When I did, it was to the sound of footsteps way down the hallway. As a tiger I could hear the sound way in advance, but eventually it led to our cell door opening. As I lifted my head to see who was entering this time, my eyes focused on Ackley and the same guard that had brought in my meal, and they both had AK-47's pointed threateningly at my face.

Ackley was apparently the most taken aback by my size as a Siberian, because he pointed at me furiously with his free hand and yelled clear words of warning in some unknown, guttural language.

"Make one move and you get fifty rounds in the skull," the other man translated.

He was bald-headed and dressed in standard riot gear, and even minus his helmet he looked very much like a soldier. His head was a perfect rectangle, and he paired it with a chiseled jaw and a frank, unapologetic voice.

Both he and Ackley kept their guns anxiously aimed at me as they dragged the carcass out of our cell, but while they did so I sat there with motionless uninterest. Once the mat was in the hallway, they swiftly shut and bolted the door, and as the sound of the mat sliding down the hallway slowly faded from my pinpoint hearing, I put my head back down and went back to sleep.

When I awoke the next time some hours later, I finally down-shifted back into Zade Davidson. The first thing I became aware of when I returned to my human body was the returning pain that surged over me, and before I got dressed I tenderly inspected the fresh lacerations that still covered my whole body. Long red welts patterned my arms and legs, and a giant open gash ran from the underside of my armpit to my hipbone. The blood had congealed only enough to stop the blood from flowing freely, and just looking at it made me wince. With caution so as not to reopen my wound, I slowly got dressed again and gently resumed my position in the corner.

I remained there for essentially all of the next 50 hours or more, and during that whole time Mr. Stevens and his pitifully charred head remained curled away from me facing the wall. Many times I passed in and out of sleep, but even when I awoke it was only to suffer through periods of utter silence and minimum brain activity. There was nothing good to think about or even hope for, and thus I continued in my cycle of semi-consciousness until I eventually awoke one time and saw Mr. Stevens sitting upright against the opposite wall.

After shaking off the grogginess of perpetual stagnation, my eyes focused in on the progress of Mr. Stevens' facial healing, and unfortunately the results were still pretty gruesome. Although his skin was showing *some* signs of recovery, for the most part it was still destroyed. His eyelids and lips were starting to flesh up a little after having been burnt to a crisp, but the top of his now-hairless head was still scarred blackish. The rest of his skin was a burnt reddish-brown, and his ears remained crisped and shriveled.

When we made eye contact, his golden irises shown out even brighter against such a ruined countenance, but they had no remnants of the liveliness and fire they once had. When I sat up, he looked me over dully, and when his eyes inspected my filleted arms and legs, his eyes silently asked what had happened to me. I related the tale of my UA feeding in response, and to my surprise, Mr. Stevens was able to respond as well.

"I don't understand why Roslyn didn't let Sebastian kill you," he said.

His voice was raspy and strained, and it also came with a lisp because of the state of his tongue and lips, but I could understand him.

"Sebastian wouldn't have killed me," I contended, but Mr. Stevens only shook his head.

"Sebastian would most definitely have killed you, and Roslyn knows that," he said.

It was hard to judge his expression with his face so immobile, but to me he seemed to look thoughtful for a second.

"Maybe she likes you," he mused.

I shook my head this time.

"No, she doesn't," I negated confidently. "She killed Chace."

Mr. Stevens' eyes widened in tragic disappointment and for a second he was speechless. Considering that he'd spent the last month or two getting shot, captured, and tortured, I realized he'd probably forgotten all about Chace, and the sadness that crept into his eyes told me that this was the first he'd heard about his fate.

"I'm sorry to hear that," he wheezed out eventually.

I looked down at my hands and forced down the tightening in my chest as I remembered my best friend.

Vengeance, I thought to myself.

"I'm getting used to death," I said aloud thoughtfully.

Mr. Stevens nodded knowingly.

"Your own life is all you have now," he reminded me.

Mr. Stevens had been warning me of that reality since we'd been hiding out in his home in the Castille woods, and now I had finally come to accept that.

"I know," I sighed, looking down sadly.

After a brief silence however, I remembered a slightly off-topic question that I had recently been hoping to ask him.

"Hey," I said, regaining his attention.

"About Roslyn, her shift is only a regular black house cat, except for that barbed tail. I'm guessing that's what makes her so dangerous?"

After sitting up a little straighter, Mr. Stevens nodded slowly.

"Yes. The reason that Sebastian was afraid of her was because her tail carries a unique, fast-acting neurotoxin. She can kill a man in ten seconds with a single sting, and with a few of them she could bring down a werewolf just as easily," he explained in his weak voice.

The effort it took him to talk sent him into a brief coughing fit, but I was captured by the implications of having that type of lethality at your disposal. It immediately made me think of only one other question.

"Why doesn't she just kill Martin, then?" I protested.

After recovering from his coughing spell, Mr. Stevens shook his head in rejection, confirming my suspicion that a solution as simple as that was too good to be true.

"Well, the longer a shapeshifter lives, the closer their two forms grow. By the time Roslyn was even born, Martin's human body and the Wendigo were highly synergized. His human body had already evolved to adapt the Wendigo's immunity to poisons."

Mr. Stevens coughed some more and then reached for his water tin. After turning it upside down and sipping the last drop, he coughed again. With a groan, I grabbed my own nearly-empty tin and brought it over to him. As I made my way back to my seat, he appreciatively drank the last of my water and tossed the two empty tins to the side.

As silence fell between us for a few moments, I thought about Martin's seeming invincibility, especially considering that he was apparently immune to poison. Mr. Stevens *had* warned me all along that there was nothing that could be done against him, but it didn't take the sting out of learning more about the depths of his power.

The longer our silence continued though, the thicker I could feel an unspoken tension permeating the room. Although our sense of time was vague and estimated at best, we both knew that the moment of Mr. Stevens' execution was very near, and it was impossibly hard to think about anything else when we were just sitting there.

"Chace and I kept your briefcase you know," I said then, trying to keep us talking.

I had hoped that idle conversation would at least help divert our attention from the heavy gloom, but upon hearing news of his briefcase, Mr. Stevens' eyes brightened with more interest than I expected.

"You know where it is?" he asked.

His voice sounded a slice away from hopeful, which made it harder to tell him the disappointing truth.

"Well, yes," I answered.

"Chace and I kept it until we got arrested. Unfortunately now it's in Martin's office," I reported solemnly.

Mr. Stevens sighed, but he didn't look particularly disappointed.

"It's OK. Martin will never be able to open it," he said, somewhat to his himself.

His voice had an air of smug satisfaction.

"What was in there?" I pried, unable to contain my curiosity.

Mr. Stevens stared at me for a minute before he answered me.

"The key to killing Martin Evers," he finally said.

His words were succinct, but my breast burst when I heard them.

"What do you mean? I thought you said there was no hope against Martin Evers," I challenged him, not hiding the accusation in my voice.

Mr. Stevens let my words hang for a second before letting out a single chuckle. The sound caused him to cough in a fit and he laid over on his side to recover from it.

"I didn't say there was *hope*," he managed to breathe out.

He propped himself up on one elbow for a final explanation.

"There is still no hope. The briefcase is best used a tool for survival, which is why I haven't used it to make a stand of my own.

Even if I had though, challenging Martin would have upset the balance of the world, because as of now, the world lives in ignorance of shapeshifters. The few lives that it costs to keep things that way are a small price to pay compared to the thousands it would cost if I were to utilize the weapons inside of that briefcase."

Mr. Stevens managed the whole sentence without coughing, and he only let out an uncomfortable-looking hiccup before sagging back towards the floor. As he started to turn towards the wall I could tell that he was getting ready to fall back asleep, but now my desire to know what was in that briefcase were burning brighter than the flames of the fresh torch on the wall.

"Tell me what's in there. If I ever get the chance to get out of here I'm going to fight back," I pressed him.

From his position facing the wall, Mr. Stevens let out one more chuckle. I waited a minute for an answer to follow that, but after a while I took his long silence for a no.

"Tell me how to open it then," I pleaded one final time.

Mr. Stevens didn't answer and remained motionless, his breathing heavy. After a minute, I slumped against the wall and closed my eyes in rejection, wondering what I had done to drive God's will so heavily against me. It was obvious that my existence had been destined for thwart and failure, and as I sat there my imagination craved to know what type of weapon Mr. Stevens possessed against Martin Evers.

I wasn't sure what he meant by the 'thousands of lives' that it would cost to use that weapon, but every ounce of tribulation that I had endured up until this point welled up into one goliath ball of desire to open that briefcase. By the grace of God, it was then that Mr. Stevens' voice suddenly began reciting numbers.

"Nine-Zero-Seven-Three-Five-One-Zero-Seven."

He said the numbers only that one time, and it was all I could do to snap upright and capture them, desperately scrawling them into the dirt of the cell floor as I went.

"Thank you," I said sincerely.

As I expected, Mr. Stevens showed no sign of acknowledgement, but after ten minutes or so I could tell that he had fallen fully asleep. From the moment he'd spoken the numbers however, I'd been staring at the combination I'd written into the floor. Like a maniac, I stared at it until the point that I'd never forget it, and for hours I engraved the image into my mind, vowing all the while that if I ever got to that briefcase I would use whatever I found to kill Martin Evers. After all he had taken from me, he owed me his life for taking mine.

That spirit drove me even when the vigor and intensity of my memorization elapsed into true mania many hours later, and yet I still fought against tiredness and still continued to repeat the phrase to myself. It wasn't until my eyes were blurry beyond use that I finally scrubbed the code back into the dirt and fell asleep.

I slept for a long time that episode, and when I awoke I was surprised to see that once again Mr. Stevens was already awake. Like usual, he was propped against his side of the cell wall statuesquely, and his eyes were fixated on some invisible point on the floor between his legs. I could tell that his mind was far away.

I stretched a little and sat up as I woke, but I didn't dare interrupt Mr. Stevens' last bit of time to himself. He was facing an execution that was inevitable and terrifying, and everything he had fought for was defeated. There was nothing for me to say, and with silence once again carrying the room and his execution even more imminent, my mind was fixated on the moment when we would hear the sounds we both dreaded.

Almost as if to confirm the feeling that I had in my gut, it couldn't have been more than two or three hours before the distant jingle of keys reached our ears, and after I perked up to listen more intently, they became accompanied by the sound of boots.

I remembered from my long jaunts through the dungeon passages that the closest occupied cell was a good distance away from ours, but as the sounds made their way closer to us, the murmur of agitated voices and the thud of slamming doors joined the dissonance.

Across from me, Mr. Stevens remained in the same position, as if he hadn't noticed the increasing noise at all. With his head down, his hands folded, and his breathing forcedly even, his eyes never left the floor.

Within a few minutes the sounds of the boots reached our door, but they were directed across the hallway at first. I heard hostile threats precede the sound of bodies barging through a door, and then after a period of indiscernible commotion our own cell door suddenly came bursting down.

I jumped back as six heavily armed men poured in an unceremonious rush, squeezing past each other to arraign us. They were outfitted in bulletproof vests and moved like trained militia, and their heads and faces were uncovered, revealing hard expressions on the other end of their automatic weapons. Mr. Stevens finally looked up as they entered, now greeted by gun barrels and the heartless, hate-filled eyes of Shifthunters.

"Hands behind your backs," the Shifthunter in front ordered gruffly.

I had never seen him before, but he was tall and brown-skinned, and he was noticeably older than the others. His light green eyes flashed recognition when they landed on Mr. Stevens.

"That's the Traitor," he said, pointing at him accusingly.

"Bartolo and I will bring him upstairs, flanked by Dyson and Kyle. You two get the other one."

Before I could move, two of the men behind the Shifthunter in charge came forward and grabbed me, twisting my arms behind my back and handcuffing me without the slightest inkling of humanity. The leader and the short Spanish man named Bartolo did the same to Mr. Stevens, with all six keeping their guns permanently aimed at us.

"Like Martin said, the Traitor is the only one who's immune to the Shifter Serum, so give the kid one of these," the leader commanded.

He grabbed a syringe out of a pocket of his pants and tossed it to one of his grunts. The man drew the needle and plunged it into my arm without hesitation. I roared in protest, but he yanked the needle free and tossed it to the side.

"Get him in line with the rest of the slime," the commanding officer said, producing two black cloths from behind his vest.

He passed one of them to the same man who'd injected me, and a second later he threw the bag over top of my head, smothering me in linen blackness.

"Get this thing off me! Get this thing off me!" I lashed out, but there was no answer.

Instead rough hands forced me blindly ahead, and I was moved out of our cell by the vice-grip of the two men in custody of me and the solid jabs of their guns in my back. As I was ushered down the hallway, it gradually became alive with sounds, and through the din of voices and shuffling bodies ahead I heard a girl's voice holler a particularly loud torrent of obscenities before her rant was halted abruptly by the sound of a dull thud. I tightened my own lips underneath the cloth, following the direction of the guns in my back for a long way before the surface beneath me changed from dirt to metal.

After a little shuffling I heard the creak of elevator doors closing, and then we jolted raucously upwards. When the doors scraped open again I was ushered out of the elevator, and I could feel the sudden expansiveness of the main floor even through the cloth bag over my head. I could feel lots of other bodies around me too, and combined with the many voices and footsteps that joined them, I felt like I had entered into some kind of convention.

With each of my arms in the clench of one of the guards however, I was directed through the traffic aggressively and precisely, and we stopped, started, and turned left and right endless times. We had to pause for a few extended periods because of what sounded like scuffles ahead, but after a dark, jarring journey the guards eventually slammed me to a final stop.

My heart pounded in anticipation as I stood in place, still blinded and in the grip of the guards. I had no idea what to expect, but I could do nothing but stand there and wait, which I did for quite a few minutes. Naturally, there was no warning when the black cloth was ultimately ripped off of my head, and at the same time as a bright light flooded into my eyes, another pair of hands shoved a gag into my mouth. Before my eyes even adjusted to the light another set of hands quickly layered a few strips of masking tape over my lips, and then I was left standing there, gagged and handcuffed.

At first I couldn't do anything but choke and try to breathe, but after a few frantic seconds I managed to pull my tongue underneath the gag and push most of the cloth forward onto the roof of my mouth. That maneuver cleared my airways just enough, and I blinked back tears and inhaled reviving air through my nose as the Warehouse floor around me took focus.

What I saw when my vision cleared was a bizarre picture. A large square of the Warehouse floor had been cleared, and a rectangle of handcuffed shifters filled the area. I was the very last person to file in line, and a couple dozen men and women of all shapes and sizes fanned out away from me in a shackled group until they reached the base of an empty, raised stage.

Around us, Shifthunters were perched on the tall shelves that had been pushed away to clear the floor, dressed in the same black vests as the ones who had pulled me out of my cell. They surrounded us on all sides, and they carried a range of shotguns and rifles in their hands. They each watched us with trained acumen, while more Shifthunters on the ground patrolled among us, all of them eyeing us with a mixture of apprehension and loathing, ready to shoot.

When I turned around I saw more Shifthunters fanned out in an even larger square behind us, lined up like we were but without the shackles or gags. In the brief glance I took, I saw that many of them looked older and more veteran, and they outnumbered the shackled shifters three-to-one at least.

Amongst the bound, I saw that the man next to me was a regular looking guy. He looked just like any other middle aged man – his hair was just beginning to gray and he had a rough, stubbly beard – but his head was hung and his eyes were closed and he was rocking back and forth on his heels like an insanity patient. I wondered how long *he'd* been in Martin's dungeons.

I looked directly in front of me then and was shocked to see that the person standing there was nothing more than a girl. She had curly blond hair and couldn't have been more than eleven years old, but she stood rigidly in line, facing forward with stark defiance.

At the same time that I was awed by her courage, I also doubted that she could see what was happening ahead of her, because looming in front of her was a giant Olympian of a man, every bit as big as Sebastian or Roman. He was chiseled like a Greek sculpture, and to be honest he looked completely capable of bursting out of the handcuffs that chained him. His clean military buzzcut suggested a level of upkeep that seemed impossible with the state of life in the dungeons, but with all the guns trained on him and an injection of Shifter Serum, I knew he was currently as powerless as the rest of us.

As my eyes wafted over the rest of the masses I saw no one else of particular interest, until my eyes were attracted to some shuffling ahead on the raised stage. Martin abruptly appeared on it, and as he crossed towards the center, he captured the attention of every being in the room with an intangible charisma. Considering his rank as overlord of the Shifthunters –and the fact that his protesters were bound and gagged – he had no need to ask for silence.

Martin's footsteps as he advanced to the front of the stage were the only sound, and even from the back row I could only compare his eyes to roving lasers, which inevitably pierced any object whose path they crossed. They searched out souls ravenously as they scanned us, and despite being just one person amongst a large crowd, I made a conscious effort not to make eye contact with him. Nonetheless, the contrast between the youth of his face and the stark white of his hair was evilly magnetic, and of course his eyes found mine for a powerful second. I felt ready to crumble to my knees when they remained on me as he started to address us.

"I am not one to waste much time with ceremonies," he began, before finally releasing me from his gaze.

His voice rang out clearly for everyone to hear without the aid of a microphone, cutting through the silence as cold and unnerving as ever. The 150 people crowded around the space of his stage were all eyes.

""I will not waste time with introductions either, because you all know who I am," he continued.

"You all know that your lives are in my hands, and that you live only because you are an able, selflessly loyal Shifthunter. If you are bound and gagged, you know that you only live because I see the potential for you to be useful in this purpose, and now that you're gathered here, you can see how many other people are like you, and how many of them pledge their undying allegiance to my cause."

He motioned around at his Shifthunters, and as I took another look around at the large militia behind me and the scouts surrounding us, his army indeed looked fearsome. Knowing that any of these people could spontaneously morph into some other creature however, made it very, very scary.

"There are only 26 of you, yet this is only a sampling of my entire force," Martin continued once again.

"The choice I've given you is an ultimatum, and you will either serve me or die. You can live on the outside like the

Shifthunters around you or you will be killed like this Traitor in front of you. His death will be a demonstration for those of you who think that you can run away, or challenge me, or hide, or even defy me in any way. There is no forgiveness," he concluded.

He turned around then, and as he waved behind him ten figures appeared on the stage. As they came forward I recognized the first three as Sebastian, Pharaoh, and Mr. Stevens. Pharaoh and Sebastian were hauling Mr. Stevens forward by his armpits, and he hung limply between them with his feet dangling a few inches from the ground. When they got to the middle of the stage, Pharaoh and Sebastian stood him up on his feet and backed away into the semi-circle of the others.

The other people on stage were Martin's Shifthunter Elite, and amongst them were Roslyn, Chen Lake, and the little boy I'd seen with them in the UA. I also recognized some of them as the other people who had greeted me in the garage, but all nine of them stood on the far left... a spectator's distance only.

Mr. Stevens was alone at the front across from Martin, and there was a gut-wrenching suspense in the air as the two men eyed each other. Mr. Stevens was battered and handcuffed; Martin Evers stood tall and intimidating. I wasn't even there, but I realized that my heart was pounding in my chest like a drum. I was as scared for Mr. Stevens as if I were in his place.

"Are you ready to die, Gordon?" Martin challenged, loud enough for all of us to hear.

He paused for a second to let Mr. Stevens answer, but he didn't. Mr. Stevens merely stood in place and stared Martin in the eyes. Martin gave what looked like a tiny smirk, and then his human body erupted upwards, twisting and expanding until it was replaced by the gargantuan form of a true demon... The infamous Wendigo.

It was a massive, hunched beast, and it was so terrifying to behold that it was almost impossible to describe, let alone look at. Although it was manlike in shape, it resembled nothing I'd ever seen. It was nearly twenty feet tall – considerably taller than the Sebastian-werewolf – and large tufts of white hair shot from the top of its head and covered its back. Opaque, bluish skin covered its distinct, sinewy muscles, and vicious hands with long, curved claws flexed like weapons. On top of its rippling shoulders sat a skeletal face with deep sunken eyes, pointed ears, and a jutted jaw that made its head look distinctly animalistic. Unlike the wide, dagger-like teeth of Sebastian's werewolf shift however, this monster revealed rows of thinner, razor-like teeth that were each probably as long as my forearm.

At the mere sight of it every single person in the Warehouse recoiled, including Martin's own Elite. When it emitted a bellow of dominance, the sound was shrill and demonic, rasping out in a guttural, stuttered cadence that shook me to my core. It sounded something like the velociraptor from Jurassic Park™, but deeper and more dog-like. The fear that it sent resonating through me was the kind I knew I would never forget. Whatever Martin had become was unforgettable in the worst way, and its mere appearance was a shocking insight into why Martin hated shapeshifters. After viewing it personally it was impossible to argue that the Wendigo was not a beast borne straight from the Underworld.

After finishing its roar, The Wendigo then looked down at Mr. Stevens in front of it, and an involuntary terror shook him, causing him to take a step back. The Wendigo was on him before he could take a second one. It moved like a blur, and its killing hands engulfed Mr. Stevens' body like a ragdoll, raising him up horizontally in front of its face.

Before Mr. Stevens could even fully let loose his final howl of death, The Wendigo then literally ripped him in half, in what I was sure was the most bloody and brutal vision I would ever see. There was utter silence as the Wendigo stood there holding the two halves of Mr. Stevens' body in the air, and life seemed to stand still. I saw the same fear that I felt in the eyes of everyone I saw, and we all watched the Wendigo throw down the lifeless lower half of Mr. Stevens before holding his upper body up in front of him.

We all knew what was coming next, and without hesitation The Wendigo ripped Mr. Stevens' head from his torso and dropped his lifeless upper half to the ground as well. When the beast finally flung Mr. Stevens' head directly out of one of the windows in the high rafters of the Warehouse ceiling, it flexed its claws victoriously and let loose another savage roar. I swayed from nausea and shock, sure that the event I had just witnessed had changed my life forever.

Chapter 25

ZADE DAVIDSON

Everglades, Florida - November 24, 2013

*A*fter a blindfolded trip back from the Warehouse floor, the first thing I did after the same four guards unbound me and locked me in was look over at Mr. Stevens' permanently empty side. When I thought about his sacrifices for me and then the manner of his death, my stomach turned from dismay and sadness and I puked in my favorite corner.

I sat a little to the side of it this time, and after that the first few hours back in my cell passed quickly, mainly due to the overall numbness I felt. I had that feeling that you get when you watch a really compelling movie – after it's over your legs feel like jelly and you can't stop thinking about it. Except Mr. Stevens' execution was not a movie – it was a real-life memory so horrific that it could not have been conceived or replicated by a human being. The image of the Wendigo, from its blue skin and undead-looking face to its white hair and clawed hands, was eternally branded into my mind.

The reel of Martin Evers brutally killing Mr. Stevens kept playing over and over in my head like a nightmare, and it was chilling to know that even the stoic bravery of Mr. Stevens had withered under Martin's blue-eyed stare, only then set in the deep, bony sockets of a demon's face.

At least 24 hours passed before I was finally able to shake the agonized churning in my stomach, but even after that the vision of the Wendigo haunted me. Time was boring, uneventful, and headed to eternity, and my last vision of the outside world was the worst one I'd ever seen.

I realized suddenly that until now, despite everything that had happened to me, I had held out hope. As naïve as it was, I had believed that somehow I was going to get back to my normal life, or at least some type of life on the outside of this cell. When I looked up at the brown cove around me now though, I saw how misplaced that hope was. There was no Chace Redman to come up with some brilliant scheme; there was not even a Mr. Stevens to break up the monotony of imprisonment. There was literally nothing in my cell; nothing more than specks of dirt that I could use to break through the wooden door keeping me in here. There was really no way out this time, and now – finally – I was truly hopeless.

With the time wearing so long I was also getting extremely thirsty, and as much as I wondered when Ackley would be coming back with the water tin, I almost hoped he never came. Perishing of thirst this week would be better than living out the next hundred years in this hell-hole, especially when I would only come out and start killing children in order to preserve the Davidson family line. Everyone I'd ever known would be long dead by then.

As I expected however, Ackley *did* eventually returned to replace my water tin, and with his gun aimed more purposefully at me now, he exchanged my empty one and locked me back in. When I looked at my replenished water tin however, I noticed that the word 'replenished' was a drastic exaggeration, because it was only filled about one inch from the bottom. I drank it all in one swig.

When another thirty or four hours passed after that, I was of course extremely thirsty once again, and as I laid in my cell my tormented soul cried out in total despair. My life had been reduced to pure agony. Time was unimportant and senseless, and I was totally alone in a medieval cell dozens of feet underground.

I had seen the light of day for the last time for 100 years… Or so I thought.

On approximately the fourth or fifth day after Mr. Stevens' execution, I heard what began as a similar, faint commotion in the hallway. At first I wondered if Martin had plans to execute someone else, but then I noticed that unlike the systematic sounds of the guards ushering us upstairs, these sounds quickly escalated into a faint raucous.

From this far down the tunnel I could only make out the shouting voices and slamming doors, but when an inhuman shriek and a distinct, animal roar pierced the ensemble, I knew this was definitely something different. I stood up and pressed my ear to the door, listening, when I heard the sound of gunshots. They assured me that there was now only one thing to do. I pounded on my door like a madman and screamed my lungs out, desperate to grasp this impossible glimpse of hope.

"HELP!" I bellowed over and over with all my might.

I knew I was close to 100 yards away from the rest of the cells, but the fear of being left out during my only chance of escape only drove my fists harder and my voice louder. Partially driven by the insanity of confinement, I beat against the door with such furor that I didn't hear the sound of feet dashing up to the outside of my door.

"Move back!" a man's voice barked.

I was caught off guard, but I jumped back with all haste and then heard the heavy deadbolt on the other side of the door slide free. Simultaneously a foot kicked the door open, but I only had time to glimpse a flash of dark skin and long hair on the man in front and the strikingly blond hair and childish face of the girl I'd seen at the execution behind him. Then they disappeared back down the hallway towards the elevator with urgent speed.

For a second I stared at my open door – dumbfounded – but then I heard the voice of the girl.

"Run!" she shouted.

Her instruction was all the impetus I needed, but when I took off down the hallway after them I only made it a couple of steps before I remembered the other occupied cell across from mine. Despite my vow to commit myself only to my *own* survival from now on, some spirit drove me to turn back, and after unlatching and kicking open the door I saw the Herculean captive from the execution sitting passively on the far wall of the cell.

His blond hair looked as kempt as it had the other day, but he just sat there cross-legged and tranquil, and when he looked up at me his clean-cut face was sculpted into an expression of uninterest. He didn't move an inch upon seeing his opportunity for freedom, and for an instant I just stood in his doorway, perplexed by his passivity.

"I don't know what's going on, but this is probably our only chance out of here," I told him with as much urgency as I could convey.

The man continued to stare at me without any sign of acknowledgement, but without waiting another second I turned away from his open door and started sprinting towards the exit again, running headlong through the dark and winding corridor.

After a minute or two I ran past the nearest dungeon chamber, but instead of being shut and locked it was now empty and thrown open. After another minute I had passed three or four more cells – each as empty and open as the first – and I began to wonder what extreme level of chaos was occurring aboveground.

I didn't wonder long though, because just then my foot caught on a large, solid object and I went careening forward in an unexpected and painful face-plant. Pain flared through my chin, elbows, and knees, and I blinked through a face full of dirt to turn back and look at what I had tripped over. In the semi-darkness I saw the outline of a dead body, and when I looked closer I recognized it as the guard who'd come with Ackley to take the tiger carcass away from my cell. Judging from his macabre wound, he had taken a bullet to the head.

With a mixture of wonderment and fear I eventually turned away from his lifeless body and climbed back to my feet, but now I ran through the winding dungeon corridor with the speed of singular opportunity. His death had reminded me of the slim chances I still faced, especially because there was only one way out of here. As I continued without incident for a few minutes though, my mind raced in time with my footsteps and I even began to hope that there was a chance I could escape this place. Naturally right then I heard a sudden barrage of gunfire right around the corner, followed by another and then another.

I tried with all my might to stop myself before I rounded the bend, but I was running too fast to stop that abruptly. Instead I skidded to a stop around the turn in the dungeon corridor just in time to see a short, rotund man fall against the wall and gurgle in agony. I was instantly glad that it wasn't the two people who'd freed me, but at the same time the unfortunate man sank to his death only ten yards in front of me, his shirt riddled with bullet holes.

About 50 yards behind him I saw the rusty framework of the elevator at the end of the hallway, but simultaneously I saw Chen Lake step out from inside the cell across from him, dressed as crisply as ever in a business suit. I recognized the MP5 submachine gun he held loosely in his hand with the speed of a seasoned video gamer, and I could see the murderous look in his facial expression.

Did the other two get past him alive? I wondered as I backed away. Chen advanced on me.

"Well, look who it is," he taunted with a hint of pleasant surprise.

I kept backing away from him, but even as we moved back around the corner there was nowhere to run. When Chen raised his arm I thought for sure he was going to shoot me dead, but he surprisingly tossed the weapon to the side.

"Now that I've finally caught you on a day where I'm allowed to kill you, I want to do it with my bare hands. I want to put the head of your tiger shift on my wall in my Castille office. *None* of you insurgent pigs are going to make it out of here alive, but especially not *you*," he snarled.

As he finished his sentence, the very essence of his voice and presence emitted a hatred for shapeshifters that seemed impossible. At the same time, his body began to explode upright, expanding and stretching into the menacing shape of his grizzly bear shift. With my very life on the line I took a final leap back from him and shapeshifted as well, and after a brief moment of semi-stasis we faced off in animal form, each of us taking up the entire space of the hallway with our massive bodies.

We were squared off inevitably now – like two enormous mice opposing each other in a tube – and I stared into his black, grizzly bear eyes with every ounce of hatred I had built up stewing in my cell. The sound of the roar that I let loose in response to Chen's grizzly bear bellow was so loud and deep that it was literally empowering, and we collided in a frenzy of slashing claws and biting teeth.

The initial collision was thunderous, so much so that as we rolled in a ball of blades we literally dislodged some of the hallway walls. When we separated I was already out of breath, having put every ounce of my energy into parrying the giant brown arms and vicious maw of a grizzly bear. We launched at each other again, and from then on for every attacking swipe from one of us there was a return blow from the other.

Chen's battle strategy was one of brutality and accuracy, and repeatedly he would ram the crown of his beastly bear head into my chest, knocking me back each time. The blows crushed against my ribs and under my jaw, and I was sure that at least two of my ribs were cracked by the third time his head rammed them. I compensated for this power with pure fury, so much so that I was literally engulfed in it. Although it was hard to breathe, the pain in my chest was nothing compared to the desperation with which my fangs and claws sought Chen's throat.

I had a little bit of practice fighting against massive killer beasts now, and through the bloodlust my own injuries were invisible, while Chen's fur was becoming increasingly matted and bloody, especially near his jugular, where my efforts were targeted. As the battle wore on his charges and swipes started to become slower and more predictable, and that realization only fueled my flame. Every time I would absorb a ram I would dig my fangs and claws into his neck with mounting fury and killer intent, and by his fifth or sixth attempt to plow through me I had determined a strategy.

As he came forward with his head down like a ram I rose up on my hind legs, and when the Chen-grizzly was within reach I punched downward into the back part of his head with both fists. The beasts' momentum carried him straight through me, but as I was tackled underneath him I felt only a dizzied, wild swing from one of his massive paws.

He was clearly stunned, and I rolled under his chin with explosive power. I got my giant fangs into his neck for the death-hold and held on with a rage that was so blindingly intense that I didn't notice the exact moment that he Chen-grizzly stopped fighting back. When I did eventually release him I was even more powered up than I had been during my battle with Sebastian, and I was elated when I saw that I had torn him to shreds. All of the pain I had endured up until this point had created an unquenchable vengeful spirit in me, and I had lost myself in unleashing that vengeance on Chen Lake.

Despite my continued need to run, I couldn't stop looking at him, and I realized then that I hated him with a special passion. As I looked at the giant dead body of his grizzly bear shift I knew that no matter what happened next, I had now eliminated one of Martin's Shifthunter Elite with my own hands.

After downshifting, I took a second to absorb the size of the Chen-grizzly from a human perspective, and then I turned back towards the elevator. Not even vaguely caring about my nakedness or the fresh blood that stained my hands and face, I also ignored the sharp pain in my ribs and made my way to the elevator.

Once inside I pushed the top button, and as the rickety elevator jolted upwards I spat copiously, trying to shake the foul taste of blood in my mouth. When the contraption snapped into place and the first sliver of light appeared between the doors, the uproar outside hit me like a sonic wave. By the time the doors were fully open, I was thrown into an environment somehow even more frenzied than I'd expected.

While streaks of sunlight filtered through the high windows of the Warehouse, the air inside was alive with the sounds of a full-scale war, complete with frequent cries of agony, automatic gunfire, and distinctively animal bellows. Directly outside of the door there was another dead, mangled body, and I crouched low while still inside the carriage, surveying the chaos ahead.

Although a giant wall of crates formed a wall across from me and blocked my vision of what was happening on the ground, I could see that in the rafters above only one gunman remained free, while at least two lied dead on the rails. The one who was still alive was shooting wildly while running towards the far end of the Warehouse, and at least six large birds flew through the air around him and around the Warehouse ceilings, all of them engaged in aerial combat with both the fleeing Shifthunter and each other.

The scene was an obvious free-for-all for those of us looking to escape, and I took a moment to gather myself and re-focus on the one and only goal. The Warehouse exit was now an all-important destination, and with my determination refueled I stepped over the dead body in front of the doors.

A soon as I did, a giant vulture appeared out of nowhere, screeching towards me like a feathery missile with its talons exposed. As fast as I possibly could I dove flat to the ground, and

I felt the giant bird rush past me with its talons only millimeters from raking gashes into my back. As I climbed back to my feet and watched it swoop away another bird suddenly appeared in the air, heading straight for it.

I watched in awe as the unaware vulture was abruptly intercepted on its upward flight by a smaller black falcon, which flew into it with incredible, targeted speed. The impact sent the two birds tumbling out of sight in a flurry of feathers, and by the time they would have hit the ground I was already running along the crate-wall, looking for the exit.

BLAM! BLAM! BLAM!

As soon as I rounded the first corner, bullets suddenly whizzed in front of me like killer bees. I looked ahead to see that an armed Shifthunter had appeared on the far end, and I turned back just as two more gunshots whizzed past.

Survive, I thought.

I bolted across the opening then, ducking behind more crate shelves and running wildly into the maze of shelves that made up most of the Warehouse floor. The Shifthunter shouted after me in some European language, but I ducked behind a few random aisles of shelves and quickly lost him.

The rows of shelves were organized in straight lines, but they criss-crossed and were placed perpendicular at seemingly random junctures. Sometimes the walls were made up of giant trailer cubes, sometimes they were made up of rubber bins, sometimes they were made up of wooden or cardboard boxes.

Endless storage, but apparently organized in a way that did nothing to help me find the Exit. As I ran in seeming circles I was totally lost, and I became more frustrated knowing that every second that passed decreased my chances of ever finding the Exit.

The only advantage of the maze-like setup was that it made it easier to lose my pursuers, and as I dodged through the aisles I often was forced to turn backwards and run the other way because of one raging brown bear, two Shifthunters in human form, and a wounded but dangerous ostrich.

Multiple times I had been tempted to shift, but I had determined from the number of dead animals that I saw that shifting would probably get me killed. It would surely draw much more attention to me, and I was quite sure that I could not just fight my way out of here with brute strength.

Instead I ran as fast as I could, switching aisles and combing the Warehouse floor with systematic desperation. I prayed for an Exit sign each time I switched lanes, but the whole time I was forced to duck away from death-trap aisles of armed Shifthunters or dangerous animals... while simultaneously ducking and dodging the myriad of birds that still screeched and dove overhead.

It seemed to me like the avian armies above were somehow multiplying as time went on, and at one particular point a Shifthunter in the rafters fought off an attacking snow owl and then jumped clear off of the rafters... only to shift into a hawk midair and arc out of sight. Less than a minute later I saw the same Shifthunter swoop in and dispatch a Rogue shapeshifter who had climbed on top of one of the Warehouse shelves right in front of me, and I took off the opposite way before the vicious bird could come after *me*.

I was as frustrated and terrified as I had ever been, but I knew that I couldn't afford to panic right now. I *had* to find the Exit, and a few seconds later I came out from the end of the aisle and finally saw something besides the maze of bins and crates. Ahead of me now was the cleared area where we'd watched Mr. Stevens' execution, and in the middle of this area I saw the breathtaking sight of a giant black wolf engaged in mortal combat with an even blacker and larger panther.

With a quick glance to the left I saw the empty execution stage looming eerily at one end, and as I looked across the clearing I saw Martin Evers' cold steel office tucked tidily into the opposite corner.

Not JUST Martin's office, I thought suddenly.

Mr. Stevens' briefcase is in there too.

For a quick second I sized up the long distance across the clearing, but just then the two battling beasts tumbled across my vision less than ten yards from my face, tight-locked in a ball of claws. From this close the sound of them tearing at each other was thunderous, and as they rolled away from me I took the nanosecond of opportunity I had and took off for the stairs.

I knew I was heading straight into the heart of the enemy, but I knew that even if I miraculously survived and escaped the

Warehouse today, my life would still be distinctly hellish. Without Mr. Stevens' briefcase it would also be distinctly purposeless, and with that thought in mind I decided that even though Martin or the Wendigo could pop up at any moment, this opportunity was worth dying for.

As naked as a bandit I pumped across the floor in a full-out sprint, and after breaking past the panther and the wolf I reached the stairs and vaulted up them two or three at a time. When I reached the top landing I paused in front of the door to look and see if anyone was watching me, but as I looked around I surveyed nothing but continued pandemonium. I quickly turned back around then, and with a jolt of resolution and vandalism I wrenched open the heavy door and stepped inside.

As the door hissed shut behind me, the tranquil, undisturbed air of Martin's office replaced the discord of battle outside. As I shivered in the frigid temperature of the room, Martin's proud and fateful words came back to my mind.

I've never locked the door to my office. No Shifthunter would ever enter here without my permission.

I couldn't help but mock him in my mind now.

Too bad I'm not a Shifthunter, I thought to myself as I crossed to his desk.

I felt a roiling pit of giddiness in my stomach as I moved into the heart of the enemy's lair, but I fought against the urge to literally trash the place. My survival conscience told me that knocking over Martin's gold encrusted globe or throwing down his large tapestry of London would only waste valuable time, and I instead plucked Mr. Stevens' briefcase from its place behind Martin's desk with expediency.

No sooner had I started heading back towards the entrance however, when the heavy door jolted inwards from the other side. When I saw who advanced into the room, my heart iced over. Roslyn's perfect features were lined into an infuriated and unforgiving scowl, and she glared at me from behind a shiny pistol.

"What do you think you're doing?" she demanded hotly.

The way that her gun was aimed stiffly at my forehead told me that she was prepared to kill me instantly, and I swallowed and put my hands up, holding the briefcase in one of them.

"I'm running for my life," I admitted.

My voice was thick with the shock of seeing my death in front of me, but I knew there was no sense in lying to her. We were enemies and she had me trapped. There was nothing I could do now but stare into the barrel of her weapon.

"What are you doing in *Martin's office?*" she asked, editing her question sharply.

Her eyes glittered with rage and remorselessness, and I was almost scared to answer her for fear that she would shoot me dead the instant my words displeased her.

"I came to get Mr. Stevens' briefcase," I answered cautiously, again truthful.

I was doing my best to die honestly, but Roslyn just stared at me with her finger itching on the trigger. Her eyes ate into my soul as if they couldn't wait to watch my spirit pass out of my body.

"Get out of here," she responded suddenly.

Despite her directive her pistol didn't waver a millimeter, nor did her eyes. My mouth hung slightly open; I was so stunned by her words that I didn't move either.

"Now or I kill you," she ordered bitingly.

As much as I knew that Roslyn was the queen of beguile, I spurred into action and moved towards the door, trying not to visibly show how nervous I was that she was going shoot me any second. When I reached the door alive I let out my first little breath, and then I pulled the door open and moved out onto the landing with my heart pounding in my chest like it wanted to break my ribs.

With the briefcase still in my hand I heard Roslyn's light footsteps on the metal landing as she stepped out of the office after me, and I could feel her gun still aimed at the back of my head. With my mind nearly mush from anxiety, I headed towards the steps as calmly as possible.

"What I have just done for you is unspeakable. The next time I see you I will kill you," Roslyn whispered in my ear as I reached the top step, and then she disappeared into thin air before I could even register her words.

When I whirled around there was nothing but a pile of clothes in her place, and I spun back forward to see her dodging down the stairs, already transformed into her elegantly lethal cat shift. After standing there for a second in pure shock I sprinted down the steps after her, and as I reached the bottom I watched her nimbly intervene in the ongoing battle between the giant wolf and the panther. With lightning-quick agility she ran between them and moved past the wolf, leaping onto the panther and latching onto its shoulders with her claws. In a flash of violence her scythe-like stinger stung the big cat in the neck repeatedly, and before the animal could claw at her Roslyn leapt away, dodging out of sight between the Warehouse stacks as fast as she'd come.

As the battle paused, the wolf stood across from its adversary in realization, watching as the panther failed in its attempt to take a step towards him. Its next attempt resulted in the beast collapsing to the floor, and then it abruptly twisted and changed shape until it became a brown-haired, middle age woman.

I tore my eyes away as she began to spasm on the floor, writhing in the agony of the poison that coursed through her. As I took off the opposite way I sprinted down yet more warehouse aisles, and as I ran I saw nothing but walls of storage once again, this time in the form of towering stacks of green rubber bins.

When I reached the end of the first aisle however, I finally saw something with potential. The row of green bins had finally led me to the wall at the far end of the Warehouse, and at the end of this wall I saw an unmarked brown door. Although I had no idea whether or not it was an exit, I headed straight for it with all due speed.

For once there was nothing in my way, and besides the added encumbrance of the briefcase slapping against my bare leg as I ran, I surprisingly made it to the inconspicuous brown door without encountering any new dangers. As I blasted through it and pulled it shut behind me, I felt the noise of the bloodbath on the Warehouse floor become instantly muffled, and at the same time I saw that I had come into a dark and narrow stairwell.

I had no time to wait for my eyes to adjust to the darkness though, and in near-blindness I immediately dashed down the spiraling staircase, almost falling head-over-heels in my haste to distance myself from the chaos of the Warehouse floor. I would've rather fallen all of the way down rather than be caught from behind, but even running at top speed I somehow managed to stay on my feet the whole way until I finally came to another door at the bottom. After taking a quick second to regain my balance and catch my breath, I then exploded out of that second door directly into the sunlight of late afternoon.

Through the sudden, unfamiliar glare of the real sun, I looked around and saw that I had burst out of a lonely side door of the enormous structure of the Warehouse, which loomed behind me with concrete walls that stretched fifty feet high or more. To my right the walls were incised with three giant garage doors, all of them currently closed. An unoccupied, unmarked moving truck sat in front of one of them, and moving away from the garage doors was a long, cleared driveway, which spanned about 40 yards wide near the Warehouse but tapered thinner until it became a single lane trail into the woods. Besides the cleared area of the driveway, large tropical trees pressed up against the Warehouse walls and windows on all sides, leaving the massive structure apparently nestled smack dab in the middle of the forest.

As I looked to my left I briefly hoped that I could disappear directly into those woods, but as I looked for an entrance it quickly became clear that there was no way to navigate the tight-knit overgrowth of trees. The clearing was my final obstacle.

Still naked, and with the briefcase still in my hand, I then summoned all of my remaining energy and booked it towards the end of the driveway, churning my legs with the urgency of seeing freedom within reach. Halfway there, I was rapidly beset by the drone of a helicopter. Like watching the glory of freedom turn to black in front of me, the sound was quickly accompanied by a looming shadow over top of me.

Run faster or die, I told myself.

I was already running faster than I'd ever ran in my life, but fueled by pure adrenaline I threw the briefcase high into the air then mid-sprint, willing myself into my tiger body at the same time. I shapeshifted and came to just in time to make an athletic leap forward, and I caught the briefcase with my tiger jaws just before it hit the ground. Invigorated and empowered, I made a break for the cover of the trees with the incredible speed of my tiger shift.

Over top of me the helicopter closed in like a buzzing predator however, and as I leapt the final bound into the safety of the trees I braced myself for a barrage of gunfire. It came just as I landed, but the barrage didn't come with the violent roll of a machine gun, but rather the soft muffle of tranquilizer fire.

I felt the sharp pinch of three or four needles hitting me in the back, and I knew that the worst was upon me. After all I had gone through, I was going back to the dungeons... a fate that I knew to be even worse than death.

Just kill me and end it, I silently pleaded.

I could only take a couple of steps into the cover of the trees before my powerful limbs felt loose and weak. I couldn't even keep my jaws closed, and Mr. Stevens' briefcase tumbled out of my mouth onto the dirt. No matter how hard I willed myself to keep going, my body wouldn't respond.

The sounds of the helicopter started to sound far away too – when in reality they were closer than ever – and I collapsed to the ground as the last of my strength dissipated. With the sedatives taking full effect it was hard to focus, and as I laid over on the hard ground beneath me it felt as feathery as a cloud. As my blurred vision finally faded to blackness then, I saw the shapes of two men jumping out of the chopper to get me.

Chapter 26

MARTIN EVERS

Atlantic Ocean, November 27, 2013

I took a deep breath and then leaned my head against the plush leather seatback of my private Cessna, closing my eyes for a second for a moment of thought. As the luxury plane soared comfortably through the sky towards London, I continued to revel in the relaxed sensation of victory, even though it had already been four days since I'd executed Gordon Stevens and finally satiated the bloodlust of the Wendigo.

The terrified look in his eyes when I'd killed him was a picturesque image permanently burned into my mind, and I savored it. In that moment I'd earned a victory that I had been waiting to claim for 70 years. During his lifetime Gordon had proven himself to be both my first Shifthunter and my only real adversary, and now he was finally my *slain* adversary.

I thought back on his final moments now and remembered how his golden brown eyes had maintained their signature flame until the end – until that last moment when the Wendigo was before him. For those few seconds I had been able to totally forget the nearly 200 years we'd spent hunting shapeshifters together, and I was able to see him for who he truly was… a despicable shapeshifter who was as terrified by the Wendigo as anyone else.

I then remembered the liberating power that surged through me as I tore Gordon into irreconcilable pieces, and a warm shiver came over me. Nearly a third of my army had been summoned to the Warehouse to witness the event, and I was equally pleased that they had all been reminded of the reason they served me. I was confident that even all of my Shifthunters combined couldn't stand against the wrath of the Wendigo, and if any of them had wondered if that were true, they now knew the truth.

When I'd looked out from stage and surveyed the faces of my army, I'd realized that every living being in that room was only alive because I allowed them to be. 250 wretched shapeshifters, and all of them at *my* immediate mercy. If I had attacked them they would have all died by my hand, no matter what weapons they deployed against me. The Wendigo was too fast and too strong, and I only spared them because I had discovered long ago that the most efficient way to hunt shapeshifters was with shifters themselves.

As that old remembrance passed through my mind, I opened one eye to look over at my newest Shifthunter Elite, and I took a brief second to admire the young, bronze prodigy. It had been less than two months since I'd plucked him from the edges of the Brazilian rainforest, and as I'd gotten to know him, I'd found him to be very different from most kids his age. Even besides his immensely powerful shapeshifting abilities he had an absolute understanding of good and evil and still had no qualms with merciless killing... at only nine years old.

Combined with the sheer size and power of his gigantic serpent shift, he had also quickly drawn the jealousy of Sebastian, which was funny to think of as I watched him sleeping soundly on one of the pearl leather seats. Sebastian had spent over 100 years killing, plundering, and hunting, and yet I still wasn't sure who would win in a fight between them.

I closed my open eye again then and as my mind drifted back to Gordon, I thought about the unfortunate fact that I would never open his briefcase. Curiosity was one of the few human weaknesses that I still harbored, but as I laid there and wondered what in the world that man kept in there, I decided it was time to get rid of his memory once and for all. With a quick instant of resolution I made a mental note to destroy the briefcase the next time I was back at the Warehouse.

"Six hours to London," an attractive female voice then said over the intercom.

Perfect, I thought.

My pilot was actually another of my Shifthunter Elite – Aurora Auclair, and between the three of us we would be ending the intolerable 'resistance' Sebastian had stumbled upon. The little girl Sebastian had captured – Angel Smalling – had remained stoic and uninformative despite our torture methods, but the one tidbit of information we did get of her turned out to be just enough.

When she had accidentally revealed that her father was Percival Smalling, it had given us a new clarity about both her history and his brazen race into the Arctic. We had initially been on to a strong shapeshifter presence in London when we'd stumbled upon Percival, but he had shown himself quickly and led us on a chase southward through Africa and all the way to Antartica before we could actually kill him. It was now clear that he had sacrificed himself as a diversion.

Angel's revelation had circumspectly revealed to us the hiding place of one of her friends, and we were on our way to their London outpost now. As soon as me and my SE's found and killed her cohorts, I would have her executed as well.

The fact that Angel was born to a shapeshifting parent was the only reason she yet lived, because it was a rarity among the shapeshifter community that I had never heard of before. For research purposes I intended to keep her alive until her DNA was completely analyzed, but once that was done, Percival and his motley crew of Rogue shapeshifters would all be as dead as Gordon Stevens.

With a swallow of satisfaction and my eyes still closed, I moved my hand to the side of the armrest and pushed the intercom button.

"Thank you, Aurora. Sounds good," I said.

Without opening my eyes I then blindly closed the shutter on the large oval window to my left, which darkened the cabin beneath my eyelids. As I laid there I pondered the great irony of my existence – which was the fact that through killing my fellow shapeshifters I found life. I had lived my entire life synergized with the Wendigo – the prototypical killing instrument – and it just so happened that the only way to save the world from my plight was to use my powers to wipe out my kind entirely.

It was a destiny that I embraced, and I had long ago grown to love The Wendigo like my own human body. Just the thought of spending time in that form caused my mind to float towards dreams and memories of its irresistible power, and I started to fall asleep. No sooner had I drifted off into a Wendigo dream however, when my phone buzzed on the end table next to me. I blinked my eyes open unhappily and looked down at my screen to see that I had an incoming call from Roslyn. I answered.

"Martin," she breathed as I picked up.

The distress in her voice came through the phone with a tone that caused me to sit up.

"It's me. What is it?" I asked.

"It's Angel! London is a diversion. Her friends are *here*, and they've freed all the shifters in the dungeons," she said in a panic.

"What!? They did what?!?" I roared into the phone.

The power of my voice sent Brian shooting upright across from me.

"It's chaos – they freed *all* of them. Shifthunters are dead everywhere. I was on a shipment run when Chen called me and said someone had gotten out of the dungeons, and by the time I drove the supply truck back to the Warehouse it was chaos. I can't even find Chen," Roslyn answered.

Her voice belied rare anxiety, and as I listened more intently I could hear the sounds of battle in the background, confirming her words. Rage surged through my bloodstream.

"Kill every Rogue shifter you can and line up their heads so we can see who's escaped. I will be there in four hours," I ordered her fiercely.

I slammed the phone shut and pushed the intercom again, bellowing at Aurora to change her coordinates and head back to Florida. I could barely believe what I'd just heard, and it had evaporated every last droplet of the satisfaction I had just felt. Now it was time to truly raise hell.

Chapter 27

ROSLYN VALEZ

Everglades, Florida — November 28, 2013

*T**his* was truly chaos. In all of my days as a Shifthunter – including the first time Martin's dungeons had been jailbroken – I had never witnessed such a state of wrath, hostility, and murderous intent. Of course there had been an innumerable number of tiny blips in the plan during the last 70 years I'd hunted shifters, but most of our trials involved issues of politics.

I could remember many times that Martin had gathered us Shifthunter Elite and berated us about killing people in public, shifting in public, or destroying important objects, but these issues always involved careful, coordinated damage control, and even then it was often enforced and manipulated by human governments. This was totally different.

For the first time our own true mission was threatened, and the brazen jailbreak that had happened here yesterday had caused more bloodshed in our ranks than ever before. *Fifteen* Shifthunters – including our groundskeeper Ackley and the highly dangerous Chen Lake – had been killed in the battle. Chen Lake was a Shifthunter Elite, and besides the fact that he was nearly 200 years old, the last Shifthunter Elite to die at all had been killed by Martin himself over 45 years ago.

The fact that there was a group of Rogue shifters alive and outmaneuvering our army was the ultimate disrespect to Martin's mission, and considering the technology and resources at his disposal, Martin was nearly immolating. Although I was almost certainly his most treasured Shifthunter, my mere presence at the time of the event had been enough cause for him to chew me out worse than he had in decades.

Martin had done everything but smack me across the face, and the verbal thrashing he had brought down on my head was beyond anything I could remember from him. Although I had destroyed the video evidence of it, I also knew I deserved the attack that Martin had rained down on me because of my inexplicable decision to let Zade walk. I had been left with no choice but to sheepishly endure his harsh criticism, and while I desperately wanted to consider why I had even done that, the hellstorm that was following prevented from me working it out yet.

Upon returning to the Warehouse, Martin had proceeded to shoot the three freed shifters who had given themselves up, which meant that out of the seventeen shifters we had previously chained in our dungeons there now only remained one. We had found Mackson Kutter still sitting in his open cell during our sweep of the underground, and surprisingly Martin had agreed to let him live.

It was a testament to Mackson's enigma, because not even Martin could understand Mackson's motives. Even though we had found his cell door standing wide open he hadn't tried to escape… yet he refused to serve Martin as a Shifthunter. He had done the same thing when Gordon had freed the Rogues many years ago, but now he was on the 99th year of his 100 year sentence. He was rumored to shift into a mammoth Silverback Gorilla, but as a human he was so deadly that at feeding time he was able to kill his gorilla brethren with his bare hands. He never spoke, and with no other reason to shift only a few of the elder SE's had ever seen him do it.

In terms of the other Shifthunters who had been present during the jailbreak, there was a similar genocide to that of the three prisoners. Any Shifthunters wounded with dire injuries – regardless of their shift or their ability to recover – had been killed on the spot like they were Rogues. Besides the two escapees and their rescuer, only two other Shifthunters and myself remained from the carnage. Martin had made it clear that no shapeshifter was safe after yesterday's events, no matter what your allegiance or rank was.

Now, as I looked around at the other seven people watching him, I couldn't help but be struck by how much power he had so quickly gathered. Relative to a world of constant killing, things had been relatively comfortable for quite a while before now, and seeing all of the Shifthunter Elite gathered here at once made me realize the real power Martin wielded and the drastic change ahead. As far as I could remember this was the was the first time all nine of us had ever been gathered in an emergency situation like this, yet with a series of phone calls Martin had gotten our whole remaining contingent into a clearing on the ransacked floor of the Warehouse in less than 24 hours.

Allard Clearwater, the leader of a pack of shapeshifting canines, sat to my right, and the rest of Martin's Shifthunter Elite sat in a row to my left: Sebastian Niles, Scott Elms, Aurora Auclair, Pharaoh Egypt, Brian Sann, Drerer Mark, and even the Invisible Hand, Raz Na. I focused on him at the far end particularly for an instant because of how rare it was to see his bronzed skin and straight-black hair in person.

With strong Middle-Eastern features and a short cropped beard he was almost as mysterious as Mackson Kutter, except that he *had* agreed to serve Martin. However, in what capacity he served Martin no one but Martin himself knew, and Raz himself spoke to no one else. All anyone besides Martin knew about him was that he lived alone in the Mountains and that when a target was tasked to Raz, they were dead. Rumors abounded amongst us about what his shift was, but Martin had assured us that none of us were close.

He was expressionless at all times, yet today even he sat facing Martin with his eyes fully aware of the magnitude of these days. Between all of us there was over a thousand years of life experience, and together we had probably killed ten times that many people. Not counting Raz, we shifted into a Werewolf, Polar Bear, Bald Eagle, Giant Scorpion, Giant Serpent, and King Cobra respectively, and between us there was no living creature on Earth that could survive if we wanted them dead.

Martin knew this to his core, and he was fully prepared to use this knowledge against us now because currently the one glaring flaw in his theory was the fact that there were now at least six shapeshifters alive in the world who he wanted dead. Three of them had just staged a breakout in our own headquarters, and no matter how they had survived to this point, Martin was now going to employ us to our full potential to bring them down. We would kill them all or we would all die trying.

"Target Number One!" Martin bellowed then, dragging a blackboard out in front of us.

After a short debriefing detailing the events of the escape and belaboring the failures of our forces, Martin was beginning to show us the exact reasons why he had really gathered us here. 'Angel Smalling' was the name written on the board.

"This young lady is the only one I want alive, and she is our number one priority. I want to kill *her* myself. For those of you who do not know, she shifts into a small yellow finch but she's as quick as a whip," he said.

He posted a picture of her bright eyed face and golden yellow hair underneath her name.

"She is the one who the others came here to rescue, and being that she is also the daughter of our deceased foe Percival Smalling, she is more than likely the leader of the group of Rogues who ambushed us yesterday. I do not want her to live to see one day in 2014. She *must* be arraigned," he said, eyeing us demandingly.

He took an extra moment to make sure we each registered mortal understanding before he turned back towards the board and erased Angel's name. He replaced it with the name 'Phoenix Bello,' and from a stack of papers in his left hand he put up a passport photo of a regular looking black man – except for the exceptionally neat dreads and bright earrings that he wore.

"Target Number Two!" he said, slapping the board for emphasis.

"Phoenix Bello. After we traced his picture from the cameras, we tapped our database and found him listed as a normal human. Whether or not he is a shapeshifter is still unknown, but he is the person who snuck in here and freed everyone. The video suggests that his knowledge of the layout of our Warehouse was intimate, which leads me to believe that we either have a rat on our hands or a highly advanced Rogue shifter. No matter, he must be killed."

Martin pulled down the picture of Phoenix Bello and erased his name, and then put up the words 'Unknown Third Shifter' and a grainy picture of a Blackhawk helicopter.

"The cameras on the outside of our walls captured *this* highly expensive chopper swooping away from our compound, and since it isn't registered to me, I'm assuming that this was the group's get-away vehicle."

Martin looked livid as he looked around at all of us again. I knew full well how powerful and unpredictable he was, and a shiver of true fear went down my spine.

"The days of spending money lavishly and living comfortably are over. There will be no more hunting shapeshifters when *you* see fit and deploying *my* lackeys to do your dirty work. Each of you will be working constantly, and every dollar you spend will be in an effort to make sure we kill all of these scum," he told us.

His voice was still controlled, but his eyes and facial expression seethed. His posture was unmistakably aggressive as he addressed us.

"I can assure you that they *will* all die," Allard said firmly from the other side of me.

His age and insight was something that even Martin often regarded, and Martin gave an infinitesimal nod in appreciation. After hundreds of years of service to Martin, Allard had many, many descendants spread around Europe by now, and his investment in Martin's cause ran deeper than most.

"Yes, you will kill them all," Martin answered him, looking around at us.

"Or else I'll kill each and every one of you."

Martin was a cold man, and when he locked eyes with each of us for a brief second we all felt his chill. Not a soul even remotely challenged him, and when he felt that we were all in understanding, he shook his head and sighed. That usually meant that more retribution was about to rain down on us.

"From now on, your outposts are also null and void. I will control my entire army myself, and you will all report directly to me from here. Each of you has been assigned a room in the living quarters, briefing packets will be disseminated and updated weekly via your mobiles, and we are installing upgraded camera systems and mobile posts throughout the forest and Warehouse. Your funds will be coming from me exclusively, which means that all of our business operations will now be run directly by me also. I will be withholding nothing in this effort, and we will be moving tactically and relentlessly over every inch of planet Earth until these shifters are dead. Are we clear?"

There was no groaning or looks of disappointment from any of us, despite the gut-wrench we all felt inside. This ultimatum was life or death, for both of us and our estranged families, and considering our decades and/or centuries of training, we each gave a strong 'Yes' to Martin's question.

"Good," he said when he was satisfied again.

He then turned back towards the board.

"Target Number Four!" he said, erasing the name 'Unknown Third Shifter'.

He replaced it with the name 'Zade Davidson' and put up an accompanying picture of the kid's high school photo. In the innocent-looking picture he looked about as average as I remembered him, but not totally unattractive. His tiger shift was still the most beautiful thing I'd ever seen, and although I hated to admit that, I especially couldn't afford to think about it when Martin turned back around and looked straight at me.

"Zade Davidson," he said, still staring at me.

"This will actually be *your* first target, Roslyn."

His voice was full of accusation and implication, and his accusatory stare turned me inside out.

Chapter 28

ZADE DAVIDSON

Amazon Rainforest — November 28, 2013

Even though my head felt like it was made of lead I woke up with a start, and at the same time that I opened my eyes the nightmarish memories of my capture flooded back to me. Martin had captured me despite my most desperate efforts, and fearing the worst I jolted upright, fully expecting to see myself once again trapped within the suffocating, earthen walls of a cell.

Instead I saw a dark-skinned man with dread-locked hair sitting across from me, and in place of the silence of the dungeons I realized that the air was filled with an obnoxiously loud whirring sound. Sitting next to him I recognized the curly blond hair and innocent face of the little girl who'd been standing in front of me at Mr. Stevens' execution, and both faces smiled at me when they saw that I was awake. I blinked back the heavy fogginess and the rapid onset of confusion and recoiled suspiciously.

"Where am I?" I questioned them jointly.

"In a helicopter," the girl answered simply.

Her voice was friendly, and I looked around to see that I was indeed sitting in one of two helicopter-seats on my side of the gray metallic walls. The seats were small and gray also, and they looked like they folded up into the wall if necessary. The distinct sensation of motion I then began to feel turned the girl's words to truth, and I narrowed my eyebrows with even more suspicion.

"Why am I in a helicopter? Where are you taking me?" I demanded next.

The man answered this time, seemingly taking no notice of my defensive attitude.

"Well, we've actually been discussing that," he said.

His voice was as friendly as the girl's, albeit much deeper.

"Your memory might be a little fuzzy from the tranquilizer, but we're the ones who freed you from the Warehouse. We had just escaped the complex ourselves when we saw you making a break for the woods, but we didn't know how to pick you up. We knew you would think we were part of Martin's army no matter what we said, so we had to make a split-second decision and we decided to tranquilize you. We only did it to help you," he said reassuringly.

The man extended his hand.

"Phoenix Bello," he introduced.

I hesitated, extremely cautious but slightly hopeful, and then shook his hand.

"Zade Davidson," I returned.

The girl next to him reached out her hand in introduction as well.

"Angel Smalling," she said, and I shook her much smaller hand next.

As she introduced herself I recognized her name from that day Roslyn had mentioned her to Mr. Stevens, and as I faced her now her bright green eyes looked me over curiously. They gleamed in remarkable contrast to her fair skin, curly blond hair, and youthful face, and looking her over in return it became instantly clear that only a monster as heartless as Martin could have tortured a child like her. However, after we shook hands she addressed me in a voice that sounded impossibly adult-like and well-versed for the way she looked.

"You don't have to be afraid of us," she said soothingly.

"We're just a band of Rogue shifters trying to stay alive. I understand how crazy that sounds – because we are the only band of Rogue shifters in the world – but we've decided that if you're with us we're going to drop you off in the Amazon while we wait for things to calm down," she explained.

Her face was dead serious, but I was bewildered by both my situation and the last part of her sentence.

"You're going to drop me in the *Amazon*?" I asked, slightly incredulous.

The man named Phoenix made an apologetic expression, but nodded nonetheless.

"Well, we're in the same business as you. Angel, Perry, and I are kind of an alliance, and our only goal is to stay alive and out of the hands of Martin Evers. Angel's father Percival used to be our leader of sorts – he found Perry, Tiago, and I when we were just children – and he raised us like his own, teaching us how to control our shifts and avoid getting killed by the Shifthunters. When he and his wife had Angel twenty or so years ago and we learned that she was also a shapeshifter, it became too dangerous for us to remain together. For the last fifteen years or so we've all been on the run, living in various apartments all over the world and rarely ever seeing each other. However during our yearly reunion last year in London a Shifthunter caught on our trail, and when it turned out to be one of Martin's SE's Percival sacrificed himself by leading the Shifthunters on a chase through Africa to save the rest of us. Since then we've been scrambling, and when Angel was captured two months ago we were only holding an emergency meeting to divvy up food and money. Somehow Martin's werewolf pet and his imp-friend stumbled on us and killed Tiago, and while Perry and I barely escaped with our lives, it was thanks to Perry's genius and the GPS chips grafted into our hands that we were even able to locate Angel. We waited to execute the breakout plan you saw today when we saw Martin's jet leave."

"I actually had no idea they were going to come for me," Angel said, looking deeply touched and deeply relieved.

She kept her focus on me though.

"We'd like you to join us," she said.

"But once Martin hears about our escape, things will be more dangerous than they've ever been. We'll all have to split up, and the reason we chose the Amazon is because exotic locations are by far the safest."

She looked at me earnestly, and I fought off the fog of the tranquilizer and tried to take it all in. There was no question that this was a much better proposition than rotting away underground, and as I looked at my two rescuers there wasn't a single hint of the subtle Shifthunter hatefulness I had become accustomed to.

"How do you know *I'm* not dangerous?" I questioned, determined not to let my guard down too easily.

The one named Phoenix smiled.

"Well, you were in the dungeons for one. We figured that if you were evil and dangerous you wouldn't turn down the benefits of being a Shifthunter," Angel replied simply.

I smirked in agreement.

"Fair enough," I acknowledged.

"If I join you and you drop me into the Amazon though, how will we meet up again?" I asked.

"Well, we *do* have some insurance of our own," Phoenix answered, smirking himself.

"We've already implanted a GPS chip into your right hand."

I immediately looked down at my right hand and saw a tiny mark on the back of my hand between the bones of my middle and index finger. As I examined the tiny spot I knew I couldn't react to the twang of outrage that I felt, because even though they had placed a tracker in my hand without my consent they hadn't tried to kill me and had probably actually saved my life. They'd even offered me to join their little fellowship of Rogue shapeshifters, which at the moment seemed like my only option for survival.

"It's surgically removable," Angel said, trying to sound reassuring.

I nodded and looked back up at them.

"It's OK, and I appreciate you all offering me to join you. I promised myself that if I ever got the chance for revenge against Martin I'd take it. This is my best chance," I said.

They both smiled and looked at each other, and they each reached out to shake my hand.

"We don't really get to make friends… ever. We really are glad that you'll join our little family," Angel replied, looking pleased as we shook hands.

"You were the only other shifter we saw make it out alive, and after we saw your shift we couldn't help but be in awe. It's magnificent," she added.

Phoenix nodded and beamed in agreement as I reached out to shake his hand, but as I did so I was hit with a sudden wave of nausea. Fortunately it must have shown in my face, because Phoenix managed to get a red bucket under me an instant before I puked into it. I came up after a minute out of breath and slightly embarrassed, but with the motion of the helicopter combined with the layover from the tranquilizer my stomach was in turmoil.

"Don't worry, that's why we've got the bucket. Go back to sleep," Angel urged me, standing up and patting me on the arm.

I nodded in appreciation, pushed the bucket away under my seat, and with a groan I laid over on my side. The room was spinning when I closed my eyes for a second, but when I opened them again I saw Angel looking down at me with a concerned expression. I felt a strange, warm feeling; it had been so long since I'd met people who didn't want to kill me. I gave her another appreciative smile and fell asleep on the cushion instantly.

After a long, dreamless sleep I awoke to someone gently shaking me, and I opened my eyes to see Angel's friendly, childish face a few feet from mine once again. When I sat up I felt rather refreshed and much better than before, and I rubbed the sleep from my eyes wondering how long I'd been asleep. It was impossible to tell time with the window shades shut in the cabin, but it felt like it had to have been a rest of quite a few hours.

"It's almost time for you to jump, did you get enough sleep?" Angel asked after I sat up.

I nodded and yawned.

"Best sleep I've had in months," I said honestly, and we both chuckled.

"I'm glad," she responded, and she sat down on the bench across from me.

She looked sorry that she had to wake me up, but she jumped right down to business anyway.

"I know it's a lot, but we've got some important information to give you before we drop you," she began, looking me in the eye.

"We've outfitted you with a survival pack, and the supplies in there should last you two months if you ration them well. We've also given you a few knives and a pistol for protection beyond your tiger shift, because unfortunately you're pretty much on your own until we return. We won't be able to contact you during the whole time we're separated, and Perry has the sole GPS locator for the chip implanted in your hand. It'll work no matter how many times you shift though, and with that we will be able to find you wherever in the world you end up. As long as one of us is alive, we *will* be back for you," she assured me.

The look in her eyes was full of promise... more than I could have ever asked for from a total stranger. I took a deep breath and nodded in understanding.

"Ok," I said, trying to prepare myself.

"I'm not sure how to survive in the Amazon though," I admitted, trying not to sound as anxious as I felt.

Angel gave me a knowing look.

"Well, it's definitely dangerous... but so are you. When all else fails remember your tiger shift. We chose the Amazon because your natural instincts are well-suited for the forest," she advised.

The confidence in her tone and expression actually made me feel slightly reassured, and I nodded again in an attempt to build up my own confidence. My tiger shift *was* powerful, and although I would be in the middle of the woods on my own, I would at least have a very, very good defense mechanism.

"Hold on," Angel said then abruptly, and she stood up and darted into the cockpit in a blond flash.

Confused, I sat alone for three or four minutes before the doors opened again and Angel came out leading Phoenix and another man, who was similarly tall but white-skinned, lanky, and tattooed. His dirty blond hair was spiked punk-rocker style, and he immediately came over to me and shook my hand with a smile.

"Perry Waters," he introduced himself.

"Zade Davidson," I replied.

Perry noticed my look of confusion as I surveyed all three of them standing around me, and answered my question before I could ask it.

"This is a very new helicopter. Auto-hover," he said, smirking.

I nodded in understanding as we all enjoyed a small laugh.

"We've got something for you," Phoenix said.

He suddenly held up Mr. Stevens' silver, steel briefcase, and after a second of silence I couldn't contain my smile. I hadn't had time to think about that scarred old briefcase, but the fact that I still had it sent a stream of satisfaction through me.

"You had this with you when we picked you up outside of the Warehouse," Phoenix said, handing it to me.

When I took the briefcase I held it in front of me for another second and looked at its battered surface with something like fondness.

"Thank you," I said, putting it down next to me.

The three friends looked satisfied, yet Angel was already getting down to business again, and she nudged Perry in the side.

"Perry and I are going to be staying at our hideout in Alaska," she said.

"If there's one benefit of being alone it's that you won't have to put up with this geek for four months straight."

Phoenix spurted loudly as Perry threw up his hands at being called a 'geek.'

"You say that now, but you two will be glad to have each other," Phoenix countered.

I nodded in agreement.

"Where are you going to be?" I asked him.

"The Gobi," he answered, looking highly unexcited about the idea.

Perry looked apologetic but resigned.

"Well, it truly won't be fun for any of us, but Angel and I will be the ones keeping an eye on Martin's activities. Even if things are worse than we expect, I'd say it'll be six months maximum before we will all be able to meet up again," he said.

Despite his tattoos and casual appearance, Perry spoke with a distinctly intelligent diction.

Six months, I thought to myself, trying to build up my resolve. With my tiger shift at my disposal, I felt some cinfidence that I could do it, but I was definitely nervous when Angel handed me a large, light green backpack and smiled.

"You ready?" she asked.

I looked at all of the gracious, expectant faces and stood up and fitted the backpack onto my shoulders. As I noticed that it had more buckles and straps than a usual backpack, I also noticed a parachute string hanging from one side. I slowly strapped in and took a deep breath.

"Don't worry, we aren't that high up. Just make sure you pull the red string before you hit the trees," Phoenix joked, grinning.

I let out a tight laugh and then tightened all of the straps across my chest even more. As I looked again at the red string dangling from one end of the backpack my throat and stomach tightened.

Sounds easy enough but I've never parachuted before, I thought to myself, yet as I picked up Mr. Stevens' briefcase I remembered the fact that I would discover its mysteries ahead of Martin, and the thought gave me a jolt of determination.

"Well, I guess I'm ready," I said, gripping the handle of the briefcase.

"Good luck," Perry answered, and then with a nod of encouragement he headed back into the cockpit.

At the same time, Phoenix moved towards a rectangular cutout in the side of the helicopter and then twisted its silver handle and pushed it open. The open hatch instantly allowed in a deafening rush of fresh air and amplified the thrum of the helicopter to a roar. Phoenix beckoned me towards him.

With a nod and a smile Angel gave me a thumbs-up and waved me towards the hatch also, and almost like a zombie I walked over towards it. I intentionally didn't look outside, and instead I closed my eyes for an instant.

Only six months, I thought to myself, trying to summon as much bravery as I could.

You can do this.

When I opened my eyes Phoenix gave me a parting nod, and when I then turned towards the hatch my mind fixated on Chace for a moment. I thought about how he'd sacrificed his bright future to save *my* miserable life, and the burning guilt I felt because of his sacrifice flared back up inside of me. I owed it to him to do everything in my power to stay alive and reward his dying efforts… no matter how impossibly foolish they were.

With a tight grip on both the briefcase and the parachute string I closed my eyes then… and with a final sigh I stepped out into the sky. Although I was instantly hit with the fluttery feeling of weightlessness, I imagined opening my eyes and seeing the front door of 1212 Unseen Road one last time.

I'd hated that place, yet I felt a pang of sadness knowing that I would never see that front door again. I was a shapeshifter now – a Rogue – and there was truly no going back to the normal, boring Zade Davidson. All I could do now was cling to the fact that despite Martin Evers' efforts, I was still alive and free.

Alive and free, I repeated again to myself.

I had taken those two words for granted before, but now a fragment of elation tingled my senses when I knew that they were true. The fact that life and freedom were mine gave me the last bit of determination I needed to open my eyes, and when I did I saw myself plummeting towards a dazzling green sea of treetops. The lush greenery stretched out in every direction below me, and the breathtaking view was both the scariest and most beautiful vision I'd ever seen.

Book 2 Excerpt (Sneak Preview)

ROSLYN VALEZ

*A*t the edge of our eyesight in the darkness, the two other helicopters blazed forward, cutting a path through the surprisingly harsh winds. Although it wasn't raining on the ground, brief jets of moisture splattered against the chopper's windshield as I followed them through the night sky, and I pushed the throttle down even further for more speed.

Phoenix Bello and Angel Smalling?!

After all this time we finally had them pinned, and there was no way they were going to get away from us now. I took a deep breath and took a quick look at Brian to make sure he was doing alright, and I saw him grip his seat tightly and nod.

Behind me in the rearview I saw our backup right on my tail, and they followed suit as we matched the hard left bank cut by our prey. Now that it had been almost six hours of this cat and mouse helicopter game I could feel the desperation and fatigue in their efforts, and they each skimmed low over the trees with less suddenness than before. They were both excellent pilots, but we were professionals as well, and each move they made we matched.

There was nowhere for them to land safely in the middle of the Amazon, and like her father before her, Angel had chosen an oddly remote location for her final desperation flight. I could only guess that they planned to meet the third member of their resistance somewhere out here, and even then they would never find a place to safely pick him up. The moment they slowed down enough for us to start shooting at them they were dead.

"Where do you think they're headed? They've gotta be running low on fuel by now," Cristian radioed in from the chopper behind us.

"I'm thinking a clearing of some sort, maybe a rendezvous with the third Rogue? They can't possibly fly too much further," I said back.

"Roger that," Cristian agreed.

I looked down at my fuel gauge and estimated that I didn't have more than 100 miles left, and we had almost that far to fly to get out of this forest. If these two were going to make a move they were going to have to make it soon, and less than five minutes later they did.

In an abrupt motion the two helicopters split apart and veered in totally opposite directions, one of them flying up and to the right and the other diving down to the left. I instantly called orders back to my support.

"We'll take the diver! Keep the flyer off of us!" I commanded, and at the same time I dove my helicopter down towards the trees after the first of the Rogues.

They weren't stopping yet it seemed, because they leveled out just above the treetops and whizzed along in a straight line, distancing us from the other two. I looked up through the top right corner of my windshield and saw Cristian and the other Rogue veering far away from us.

"Stay on that one!" I called through the radio.

"Roger!" Cristian called back.

With Cristian's piloting skills I had no doubt that he would catch whichever shifter he was after. With my own piloting skills I had no doubt that I would catch this shifter faster.

"Get ready," I told Brian, and he picked up his assault rifle from the floor in front of him and rolled down his window.

Even though he had taken to one of the smaller automatic rifles because of his size, the gun was still bigger than him, and he didn't have much shooting practice either. Brian was a natural at all things Shifthunter though, and his bright, innocent-looking green eyes shone with a look that I had come to know as readiness.

When I re-focused on the helicopter ahead I pushed the throttle all the way down, and keeping the chopper just inches away from the tops of the trees I started to gain on it. Even besides my superior flying skills our helicopter was also a faster model, and Brian saddled up in his seat as I closed the distance between us to 50 yards in the matter of a minute. I radioed our support one last time.

"I'm taking this one down!" I called, and then I pulled the headset around my neck and lifted the helicopter up into the sky, arcing up and then back down so that Brian could get a shot.

He rolled down his window with a quick button-push and then he let loose three rounds from his rifle at the perfect time.

TINKTINKTINKTINKTINKTINK!!!

Bullets laced into the side of the Rogues' helicopter as we swung around to the other side of it. Realizing they had been hit, the helicopter lifted upwards away from the trees.

TINKTINKTINKTINK!!

Although he wasn't perfect with the next round, Brian shot with the skill of someone far beyond his years. The next volley he let loose streaked across the top of the enemy chopper again, and this time the vehicle pitched and careened to the left as a billow of smoke rose out of it.

A surge of excitement came over me as I dove down after it, because as the damaged vehicle slowed there was still nothing but trees in every direction. I still couldn't understand the logic of the Rogues' plan, and thus it was to my utter surprise when the helicopter in front of us suddenly flipped around to face ours.

"What are they doing?" Brian asked in Spanish, but before I could answer I saw.

As soon as I slowed down in front of the hovering helicopter the door suddenly opened, and then Angel Smalling dove out of the open door and shifted, disappearing into a tiny yellow speck.

Other Thanks:

Greg Landrum

Tereza Landrum

Alex Ptaszynski

Eric Mondesir

Justin Darden

Mike Gordon

Vanessa Jones

Lauren Haney

Kyla Hammond

Tavis Smiley

Thomas Knox

Babu Baradwaj

Chili's Bar & Grill

Regina DeLeon

The Pino Family

Reginald Elliott

Michelle Radford

Hope and Joi Gaddy

Harold Massey Sr. & Jr.

Jesse Kim

Diontae Jones

Claudius Gray

Patricia Hickerson

Crestwood Estates

HCCLSM

Columbia Community Church

Russell Forte

Tyrell Fridie

Urijah Johnson

Alexis Santana

Tifani Moss

Robert Williams

Trinity Brown

Heather Brimer

Kalissa Moss

Cheston Harrington

Howard High School

Morehouse College

Dog Ear Publishing